One Thing Better

JESSICA SHERRY

Published by Jessica Sherry
Copyright © 2023 by Jessica Sherry
jessicasherry.com

ISBN (Print): 979-8-9887254-1-1
ISBN (eBook): 979-8-9887254-0-4

Book Cover Design by Ink & Laurel

Printed/Published in the United States of America

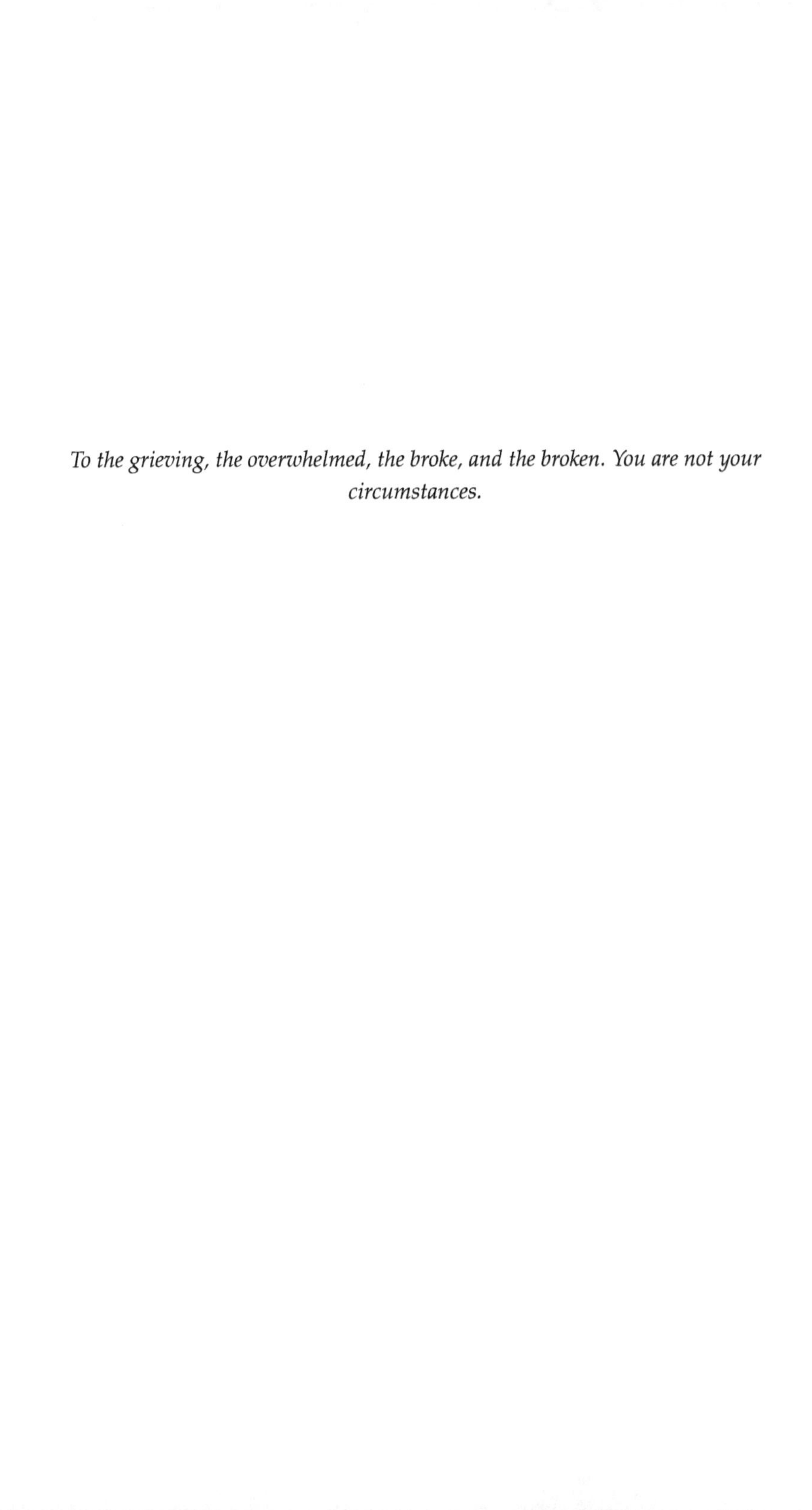

To the grieving, the overwhelmed, the broke, and the broken. You are not your circumstances.

Author's Note

Dear Reader,

You're about to read an emotional, feel-good romance set during the 2020 pandemic that features realistic, wounded characters and sensitive subject matter. Lena suffers from grief and anxiety and finds comfort in Ben, a stoic police officer who has been through his own struggles. Listed below are topics that may be upsetting to some readers. If you'd rather not know any spoilers, please skip to chapter one with my thanks for reading.

For those who prefer to know, this book deals with the following difficult topics: anxiety disorder, panic attacks, PTSD, loss of a parent, physical scars, and hearing impairment. It is set during the COVID-19 pandemic (no related deaths). Firearms are mentioned, and there is a scene involving the use of them non-violently. There is profanity and mild sexual content.

Please be assured that I have done my best to handle these topics with respect and sensitivity. Thank you for reading.

Jessica Sherry

1. How Do I Say Goodbye – Dean Lewis
2. My Mind & Me – Selena Gomez
3. Calm Down – Rema, Selena Gomez
4. Move Bitch – Ludacris, Mystikal, I-20
5. I'm A Mess – Bebe Rexha
6. Build A Bitch – Bella Poarch
7. Roxanne – Arizona Zervas
8. All My Friends Are Rich – UPSAHL
9. Don't Freak Out – Huddy, Iann Dior, Tyson Ritter, Travis Barker
10. Spirits – The Strumbellas
11. Enchanted – Taylor Swift
12. Fuck, I'm Lonely – Lauv, Anne-Marie
13. Voices – KSI, Oliver Tree
14. Billie Eilish – Armani White
15. Broken – Lifehouse
16. I Think I'm Okay – Machine Gun Kelly, Yungblud
17. Firework – Katy Perry
18. Hot Girl Bummer – Blackbear
19. Be Real – Kid Ink, DeJ Loaf
20. This Is How You Fall In Love – Jeremy Zucker, Chelsea Cutler
21. Brutal – Olivia Rodrigo
22. To Die For – Sam Smith

23. In Your Room – The Bangles
24. What A Time – Julia Michaels, Niall Horan
25. Good Things Fall Apart – ILLENIUM, Jon Bellion
26. I'm A Mess – Avril Lavigne, Yungblud
27. Follow You – Imagine Dragons
28. No Bad Days – Macklemore, Collett
29. Glorious – Macklemore, Skylar Grey

CHAPTER
One

IS it weird that a grocery store can feel more like home than the place I actually live? That's how I feel about Sunny's Beach Market. With its shimmering brightness and ultra-friendly employees, it feels like they've captured the sun and held it inside just for me. The *ah* feeling I long for at home only happens when the automatic doors slide open here, where everything is fresh, modern, friendly, well-stocked, and, most importantly, in proper working order.

Two years ago, I first pulled into this parking lot after a physically strenuous visit with Mom's rheumatologist left her in bed, aching more than usual, and me scrambling for cheering-up supplies. A muggy spring rain had made everything gray and annoying, but that didn't matter here. Traversing the wide, gleaming aisles, I didn't get in anyone's way, nor did they get into mine as my cart filled with baking supplies and Mom-comforts. In line, the cashier asked what I planned on making—I *love* to talk baking. The bagger insisted on carrying my single paper bag out for me and held an oversized umbrella for us as we walked to my car. There, she handed me a coupon for free ice cream on my next visit before wishing me an amazing day. *Free ice cream? Who does that?* Since my social interactions had been mostly limited to doctors and nurses and were rarely positive, being there felt like a spa day, especially for an exhausted caregiver with zero time for a real one. I've loved Sunny's Beach Market ever since.

Falling in love is all about the little things. Well, at least when it comes to grocery stores. And this one has an entire aisle dedicated to alcohol.

Today, I'm on another grocery supply run. My brother's plane has just left the airport, spiriting him back to California after a visit that began fourteen days ago when our mom died, and tonight's the first I'll spend alone in my crumbling family home. *Why do things always feel worse at night?* Supplies will help.

Well, not really "supplies," but wine. I need wine.

I ignore pricey bottles for something more budget-friendly. It's a classy move, anyway—buying wine in bulk. So what if it's boxed wine? It's practical, easy to open, and eco-conscious. And it's best to bypass a corkscrew search in *that* house—the place that holds everything you need if only you could find it... and it's not broken... and it's safe to use... and I'm tired just thinking about home.

Anxiety rising, I close my eyes and inhale the clean air. Then, I drop a merlot and a chardonnay into my shopping-for-one cart. That should do it. It doesn't scream desperation or loneliness. It says I'm having a party.

A *nice* party.

A *wine* party.

Not that anyone cares. Besides, after three years of a stalled life, I'm all about catching up on things I've missed—*I have a list.* Tasks take on more importance when they're on a list. And when it's a long one filled with overwhelming must-dos for restarting said stalled life, it's smart to begin with easy items first. *Get properly drunk.*

Another cleansing breath pushes me toward the dairy section. *Cheese goes with wine, right?* An extra-large can of Cheez-Whiz clangs into my cart. Again, practical and easy. That's another thing I haven't had in forever—junk food. For far too long, it's been a low-sodium, low-fat, and low-flavor rotation of chicken or fish with vegetables. My taste buds need stimulation to shock them alive again like Dr. Frankenstein reanimating dead cells with electricity. Cheez-Whiz coated Flaming Hot Cheetos should work... *must hit the chip aisle.* Junk food ranks high in my revised priorities.

So does personal care. The burning wood stove odor embedded in my hair provokes a bothered sigh. Since the wood stove is *that* house's only heat source, the campfire smell can't be helped. But maybe it could be masked with the right body spray. I hunch over the cart as I detour down the health and beauty aisle. *Posture, Lena!* My mother's voice skips through my thoughts. *No, not now. Don't be a sad sack.*

I'm not sad. I've barely cried in weeks. I pass by the Visine, wondering if eyes can get so clogged with dust and soot that they can't produce tears anymore. That's probably it—that and icy determination. I *hate* crying. Even more, I hate letting people see me cry. Who needs rubberneckers for their emotional trauma? Not me! *This is my mess. I'll deal with it. Nothing to see here.*

The body sprays pull me into a hypnotic stupor. *What mixes well with campfire? Cucumber Basil, Pineapple Mango, Strawberry Cheesecake. Do they have a marshmallow scent?* Grabbing the *Coconut Rum Cake*, I read the label, hoping it'll advertise a *100% Odor-Masking Guarantee.*

"Help you find anything, ma'am?"

"Shit!" I curse and perform a cat-like jump at the voice.

A *male* voice.

Talking to *me*.

"Sorry. I didn't mean to startle you." The dazzling smile of a neatly buttoned-up and well-groomed Sunny's employee meets my dumb-founded shock, which is doubled because he's delightfully good-look-ing, even if he's too young.

I return the *Coconut Rum Cake* to the shelf. A weak hand wave suffices for a response when words stick to my throat. *God, what's wrong with me?*

"Having a good day so far?" His raspy baritone sends a warm tingle along my spine, forcing me to straighten my back. *Posture, Lena!*

I manage a weak, "It's not bad, thanks." His eyes land on my bare ring finger before bouncing up again. *Is he checking me out?* The innate mechanisms in place to decipher such things grind with rust and malfunction. *No, he's just being nice.* Maybe he's a hologram, and I'm blind-testing a new customer service feature. Or perhaps the Sunny's gods zeroed in on the lonely woman in aisle eight and sent her what she *really* needs—a meet-cute. Or at least normal human interaction that doesn't involve anything medical, funeral, or family-related.

"Glad to hear it." His warm hazel eyes stay laser-focused on mine like it's part of their training—OSHA guidelines, cash register opera-tions, and making single thirty-somethings feel *seen* again. "Is there anything I can help you find today?"

Answers stream my thoughts, but none I can say. *A decent place to live. Days that are better than* not bad. *Someone to talk to.* Even worse, I gawk like he's asked me to solve for X in a complicated equation. Is this what happens to thirty-somethings after a long hiatus? X must be the last time I had sex. *God, how long has it been?*

Unable to math out the answer, I shake my head. "No. I'm fine. Thanks."

He points to his name tag. "I'm Ashe. I'll be at customer service should any needs arise."

"Ms. Lena Buckley," over the loudspeaker makes me jump. Again. "Please return to the pharmacy."

I whip my cart around, nearly losing the Cheez-Whiz and cutting off Mr. Sunny's McDreamy as I rush away. Norman, pharmacist and old high school friend, holds up the bag of unused pills I handed him twenty minutes ago and waves me toward the storefront.

"Giving me that refund after all?" I'm only teasing. Big Pharma doesn't do take-backs, even if something doesn't work or gets you addicted or, hell, kills you.

Norman smirks anyway. "These pill vials aren't all filled with pills, Lena." The bag rattles as he shakes it.

I extract a vial, opening it. Coins spill onto his tidy counter. "What the hell?"

"Clever recycling, I guess. I removed all the medications. It's good of you to return them properly, especially the pain pills."

"I lucked out that you're an official take-back site. Couldn't flush all these pills down the toilet. Not at *that* house."

The bright lights shimmer off his forehead as he nods. "There's a coin machine in the vestibule. You could exchange them for cash."

More wine! I scoop up the bag.

"Oh, Lena, wait." Norman flips through the plastic pouches on his shelves. "You have a prescription for once." He holds up the baggie and mouths *Xanax* before asking if I still want it.

"Gosh, no, Norman. A kind ER doc insisted on the prescription, but I'm fine now." My hands strangle the cart handle, recalling the ER visit for Mom—the third one that week—and how the doctor ended up treating us both when I had a panic attack.

Norman's pressed lips curve into a look of pity, making me sink. "Is your brother still in town? Sophie could bring over another casserole. Lucas loves her eggplant parm."

"Ah, tell her thanks, but it's just me now. I'd hate to waste Sophie's good food."

He eyes my stacked boxes like he might ask about my imaginary wine party, so I wave goodbye and head to the vestibule. Nothing against Sophie. But, with a dozen dishes still crammed in the fridge, I wouldn't know hers from anyone else's and don't want more to go to waste.

Besides, I'm into junk food now.

The machine clanks as coins slide into its mysterious underbelly. Last night floats back to me with every metallic clink. Lucas and I sat on the patio. Ever the Eagle Scout, he built a fire in the wobbly fire pit. In equally precarious lawn chairs, we bundled in blankets against the bitter wind—still better than being inside that terrible, memory-filled disaster I call home.

His words echo through my thoughts. "I want you to have it. All of it."

I said nothing.

"It should go to you," he went on. "You've been here. You've taken care of everything."

I wanted to say, *yes, I've taken care of everything, and now I'll have to take care of everything else.* But I didn't. A teacher married to a lawyer and living in Malibu with their amazing daughter, Lucas doesn't need coins in medicine vials. His broke and unemployed older sister, though, can't turn away his charity.

Pouring more coins, I muse over Mom's creative money-keeping. A strange paranoia prompted it like travelers separating their cash between pockets, bras, and suitcases so hypothetical robbers couldn't get away with everything. As if after being robbed, the victim might raise her fist in triumph. *"Ha! You didn't check my shoes, loser!"* Of course, thieves would prefer the pills to loose change these days—an irony Mom never would've understood.

Thirty bucks richer, I reenter the store near Norman's pharmacy perch, where he flashes another coy but sympathetic grin. "Oh, Lena, I almost forgot. Happy Valentine's Day."

"Um, thanks. You, too." *Shit! It's Valentine's Day?*

My pace quickens through the red and pink balloon monstrosities, gaudy flower displays, and awkward men perusing the Hallmark cards. *How'd I miss this?*

I grunt, imagining the sappy choices on TV tonight. *Where was I?* Oh, personal care. I beeline for my previous aisle, grateful that GQ-Sunny's Ashe isn't in it. Though I love Sunny's, they can't meet *all* my needs.

Resuming my deliberations over fresh-smelling beauty products, I take more deep breaths. The campfire smell takes me back to last night and Lucas's generosity.

He doesn't understand—*why should he?*

"I hate leaving you like this," he said. "I haven't done nearly as much as I wanted."

"It's okay. Drew and Luna miss you, and you miss them. You should be with your family," I said, hiding the defeat I felt.

In his defense, he's done a great deal in a short time, and I told him so. He stayed an extra week, meticulously sorting his old things and shipping boxes to California. He saved baby clothes—just in case—baseball cards, Boy Scout memorabilia, and the rainbow wine glasses Mom adored. He passed on the floral china, silver flatware, doilies, and tea sets. "Who bothers with that anymore?" he said, making me sad. What will happen to Mom's treasures now?

He stacked wood and mowed the high grass I'd let go last summer. He forced me to sort her closet, where we salvaged beautiful dresses and suits he dry-cleaned and donated to our old high school's theater department.

Oh, and he left me a list. Lucas *loves* lists—but not fun ones like mine. *#1 Take unused medications to a proper disposal site. #2 Clean out fridge. #3 Wash Casserole Dishes* … and so on, like I'm a child, even though I'm older and have survived far more difficult things than he has. But he means well. He *always* means well.

"You're in your head too much again, Lena. I can tell," he said, mid-listing, "Come with me. Leave this place and Nervous Nellie behind for a few days."

When he was eight, he thought himself so clever calling me that. He first stole the idea from our parents, who used the term affectionately, somehow. Then, when he found *Nervous Nellie* amongst his *Garbage Pail Kids* cards, it stuck. The card depicts a freaked-out girl sitting in a dark, cinderblock corner, biting her nails down to the bloody bones. Though exaggerated to delight middle schoolers and younger brothers everywhere, my fingers used to bleed from constant nail-biting, too—an unconscious anxiety habit kicked thanks to my ex—not a good Valentine's Day story.

Giving up on odor-enhancement, I grunt and refocus. Shaving cream. Razors. *God, how long has it been since I shaved my legs?* Cheap, disposable razors land in the cart. Suddenly, my "not bad" day feels worse, somehow.

Maybe I should've agreed to the getaway. I'd be on a plane with Lucas right now while he regales me with mixed drink recipes we'll try at his poolside bar—*Frosé Cocktails, Gin Fizzes, and Baileys espresso-tinis*—and books I must read, and tapas I must sample... *Ah, Malibu.*

My cheeks perk in a strange smile. He's only been gone an hour, and I miss him.

But I'll trade North Carolina for California soon enough. A pool house apartment, a job at a posh restaurant called Root & Bone, and living with my only remaining family—everything's set. It's better to move with nothing hanging over me and no reason to return. Besides, leaving *that* house empty isn't wise. It's an open invitation to whatever wants to come in—robbers, nosey neighbors, critters, poltergeists, *anything.*

Coins in medicine vials? Really, Mom? Lucas will say. "Aw, she left you a treasure hunt." And I'll roll my eyes and say, "No, she left me more work to do." *Haven't I done enough work?*

Inside, I wilt, feeling terribly selfish.

In line, the *Redbox* selections near the exit divert my attention. That's another thing I haven't done in a while... pick a movie just for me. I've seen enough TV crime shows and sappy Hallmark originals to last a lifetime. I need bad words. Gratuitous violence. And hot, shirtless, muscled men... ones I don't have to talk to.

"Looks like my kinda party," a voice interrupts my movie deliberations. A fifty-ish blonde gives me an approving grin, motioning to my cart like we could be besties based on its contents alone. *Friends—another thing to put on my list.*

"Yes, I'm having a party. A wine party. I thought, wine not?"

She leans in with a gracious laugh, bringing a whiff of gardenias and leather. "Don't look now, but a cutie in customer service has his eyes on you."

Of course, I look. Sunny's poster boy Ashe offers a flirty wave. I gnaw at my bottom lip, feeling a rush of heat—not the good, sexy kind but from nerves. "Um, he's just my Sunny's groupie. You can rent them at the service desk."

She laughs good-naturedly.

Feeling encouraged, I attempt more conversation. Her cart has three bags of birdseed, duct tape, and a frozen pizza. I don't know what to say about that, so I point to the logo on her hot pink, collared shirt. *Pines & Palmettos Equestrian Center.* "You're into horses?"

"I better be. I've got a hundred and seven of 'em."

"Mom says you can solve all of life's problems on the back of a horse."

"Sounds like a smart woman."

"She is." My breath hitches, squeezing my throat. "I mean..." My last words to Mom bully their way into my thoughts... *Please, don't leave. Stay with me. Fight through.*

It's like someone's smashed wine boxes on either side of my head, knocking my dust-clogged tear ducts free—I sob uncontrollably. My Sunny's meltdown has tarnished my bright home away from home and sends me scurrying to hide in the real one.

CHAPTER
Two

SOLO WINE PARTIES aren't a good idea, not in this house. The power goes out on my second glass. My brain works sluggishly to fix the problem, letting my overactive imagination play up. *What's that scratching noise? Is that a shadow moving outside? What if the power didn't go out but was cut? And someone's creeping closer?*

Tightroping between anxious and panicked, I regret the wine and the *Criminal Minds* binged while drinking it.

Deep breaths. Slow down. Everything's okay. Mom's voice ghosts in my head, mixing with other mental noise. *Blunt force trauma. Shallow grave. Bones breaking.*

I bang my feet twice on furniture on my way to the breaker box. The house is so damn dark. Darker than most homes, I suspect. The living room, kitchen, and dining area form a vaulted, open-concept cave with burnt red shag carpeting, wood-paneled walls, and heavily draped windows because, *God forbid,* a glare catches the TV.

On the cobweb-covered back porch, my fingers slide over switches in the breaker box until I find the one tripped. Flipping it restores the lights, but not my motivation to keep drinking.

Growing up, I loved this house. Sleepovers, Halloween parties, laser tag, and epic hide-and-seek games are bright spots in my memories. I fell in love with baking in *that* kitchen, and late-night blueberry pancakes became a tradition. It was everything a home should be.

But time wrecks things. Well, that and my parents' inclination to *keep everything* and *make do*. With never enough money to fix anything properly, my folks relied on patchwork home improvement, mostly done themselves or with the help of some "guy down the road." When Dad died, those fixes and favors vanished, too.

Now, it feels nothing like a home. Not when it's so dark, cold, and quiet. Not when I feel so alone here. So, my wine night ends with me sober and restless on the couch in my makeshift bedroom.

The next morning, sipping coffee at the kitchen table, I peruse Root & Bone's website, which features an entree of pork tenderloin with purple cauliflower puree and a red cabbage and apple salad. I lean closer to eye the scant portions. At least there will be room for dessert. I skim to the bottom to find the options—seasonal fruit, cheesecake, or vanilla sorbet. No wonder Lucas says the restaurant needs me.

Mom and I often made fun of Root & Bone. Never around Lucas, of course. He and his husband, Drew, believed in the bouchée restaurant enough to invest. But to us, the fanciness failed to satisfy. Mom used to say that her curves laughed at the portion sizes. As a curvy woman myself, I had to agree. But it wasn't just about leaving the table hungry. Cooking is an act of love—I never felt any love in that food. Or any emotion whatsoever. When I met Brian, the head chef and co-owner, I understood why. He's a human robot.

And soon, I'll be working there, and Brian will be my boss.

Curious, I turn to online job sites. Dishwashers, cooks, cleaning services, catering—having done all those before, a sudden unease stirs at considering them, like I'm picking second chance opportunities from hundreds of bad dates and saying, *"Is this really all there is?"* For someone with three-quarters of a business degree, a failed bakery, and three years of unemployment, it probably is. Root & Bone is probably the best I can do.

Feeling chilled despite my jeans, long-sleeve t-shirt, and thick cardigan, I glare angrily at the wood-burning stove. It'll demand my attention today—it's a pushy and controlling roommate. Sometimes, it's like I live in *The Little House on the Prairie*, only that house seemed easier to maintain and, well, less creepy at night, maybe because they had each other.

Chair legs scrape the dingy floor as I stand. I slide into my rubber boots but don't bother with gloves. Outside, the February wind pinches my exposed skin.

Holding a log in one arm and reaching for another sends a tooth-pick-sized splinter into my finger. "Motherfucker!"

A rattling truck up the driveway stops my loud cursing. My visitors look horrified, but I don't care if Jack and Alice Harvey disapprove. Being the foul-mouthed girl next door has its advantages—usually that they keep their distance.

Jack meets me at the woodpile, scratching his forehead under his tattered ball cap. Maybe it's the crime shows talking, but he looks like a serial killer. Dark overalls, dirty and stained. Well-worn work boots. A grimy towel bulges from one pocket, a tool handle from the other—a small hammer, maybe.

"Everything alright, Lena?"

The logs fall to the pile as I hold out my hand. Blood oozes from the wooden spear jutting from my index finger. Jack yanks it out, and a sad whimper escapes me.

"Should wear gloves, little lady."

Alice bustles over with authority. "Bless your heart, Lena. How 'bout we fetch you a bandage, and you make us some coffee, huh?" Her dainty arm circles my shoulder, escorting me to the patio. She smells strongly of lavender.

"I don't have your casserole dish yet, Alice… if that's why you're here."

"Oh, well, we're just here to chat."

One rule of country life is that people just stop by, expecting spontaneous hospitality. Before and after the funeral, this place resembled Grand Central Station for all the do-gooders toting casseroles. The visits have dwindled lately, except for the occasional person stopping by to ask for their casserole dish back. *#2 Clean out fridge* made Lucas's list for a reason.

Jack's heavy jowls push up as he smiles. "Is Lucas around? We wanna talk business."

"Lucas left. What business would you have with him, anyway?"

"He's the man of the house now," Jack says. Alice doesn't bat an eye at that remark—no surprise.

"*I'm* the man of the house. If you have business to discuss, it's with me," I say.

"Okay, then. We've got good news." He scoops up six logs in one arm and motions for the door.

Inside, he tends to the stove while I dab my wound with a paper towel.

A seasoned snoop, Alice tours the room, eyeballing family photos and peeking under china cups on Mom's hutch for their identifying stamps.

"Your momma has such beautiful things," she says.

Things you have no business touching. I ask how they want their coffee.

"One *Sweet and Low* and a splash of cream," Alice says.

"I'll take a cup exactly the way you make it. Ruth always said you make the best coffee."

I shrug lightly. With few other bragging rights, Mom often praised my coffee.

Jack settles into a chair, searching for conversation topics amid the scattered debris on the table. Unread mail, no. Wilting houseplants, no. The twelve-gauge shotgun leaning near the door, no. He eyes my laptop screen. "What's going on here? Job hunting?"

"Researching, for now."

"You're still headin' to California, right?"

It isn't a pushy question, but I feel shoved off a mountainside whenever asked, like Wile E. Coyote—hanging midair and waiting for gravity to catch up. "That's the plan."

I deliver their mugs, luring Alice to the table. Before sitting, she dusts off the cushion like a home plate umpire. *The house isn't that bad, is it?* Then, a light flips on—I see the dusty film atop the glass table, dirt and firewood bark trailing to the wood stove, and smudges on the sliding glass doors behind them. Mom would be mortified.

I'm not, though, as this supports my bad-girl-next-door image. "What's the good news?"

He tosses his hat on the table and rubs his shorn head with his free hand like it helps him think. "Me and Alice want to buy your property. We'll take it as is. It's been hard on you, keeping up with the place."

"It's not so bad." *Defensive about the same place that thwarted my wine night, really?*

They share a knowing grin.

"Come on, Lena. This place is one stiff wind away from falling over." He takes a long sip. "My, that is good. You should be, um, what're they called? Gals who make coffee?"

"A barista."

"That's it."

Alice takes the tiniest sip I've ever seen. "Yummy."

Her vibe matches her husband's. Her heavily made-up face, Sunday clothes, and tightly rolled hair give her a fifties throwback look, like she's stepped out of a minor role in *I Love Lucy*. Combined with her sly grin and dark, sinister eyes, I imagine her pulling a butcher's knife from her purse, chopping me to pieces, and baking me in a pie to serve to her friends, all while smiling and singing a hymn.

Okay, maybe the hymn's a bit much. And yes, too many crime shows.

Jack meets my eyes again. "I'm happy to call Lucas. Ruth said she was leavin' everything to you kids."

"She did, but Lucas turned it all over to me. His husband's a lawyer. He signed the papers before he left."

Jack's brow pinches together like two caterpillars banging heads. *Is he bothered by the mention of Lucas's husband or that this little lady would make the decisions?* "Well, he did right by you, then. You took good care of Ruth."

My shoulders slump. "What's the offer?"

"Two hundred thousand. Just pack what you want to keep, and we'll take care of the rest."

The rest. Like Wile. E. Coyote finally falling, the weight of *the rest* heaps on my shoulders. Sheds, outbuildings, an enormous barn with stables, a car graveyard, and the house—not quite a hoarder's den, but close.

My parents never turned anything or anyone away. In its heyday, it was a haven for foster kids, rescue pets, and even two cyclists who stopped in for water and shade because the house looked so friendly.

It's not friendly anymore.

Jack's offer should inspire a celebratory dance like Mom used to do over good report cards. But I can't move. Or speak.

"Sellin' to us'll save you from showing the place and dealing with agents," Jack says. "Why not just make it easy and get your hiney to California sooner?"

My throat tightens. *Why not, indeed?* One working toilet. One working shower. Each in a different bathroom. Faulty breakers. A forty-year-old oven and stovetop with only three semi-operating coil burners. A wood stove that barely heats a room, let alone the whole house. And—

"Shit!" A scurrying mouse forces my legs onto the chair. It stops, looks at us defiantly, and strolls under the piano. "Damn, mice!"

Alice shrugs, as if thinking, *of course, there're mice* here.

Jack belly-chuckles. "It's just a little country fella. It's cold outside. He's trying to get warm."

I scoff, pulling my sweater tighter. "Joke's on him."

Mice are another shit-rule of country life, showing up even in clean, fully-operational homes. Here, in this cold, dark, quiet house, they congregate like teenagers at a rave. A poolside Malibu vacay can't happen because the mice would erect a rodent kingdom, forcing me to play executioner when I returned. I can't deal with that.

Embarrassed and agitated, I desperately want to shake his hand and be done with it. "What, um, what would you do with it?"

"Turn it into farmland. We want to grow—"

Alice's stern throat-clearing stops Jack. He gives her a funny look before saying, "Grow stuff. We want to grow things."

Marijuana, I wonder. Not that it matters.

The Harveys own the farm next door. Mom's twenty-five acres mean expansion—an opportunity that rarely happens out here, where people hold on to their homesteads like precious relics.

He leans forward, the chair creaking. "I'll leave the tree. I promise you that."

The tree. I deflate like a punctured balloon. When it came to her death, Mom wanted two things: to die at home and to have her ashes strewn at her tree. I haven't done either. Her urn sits on the kitchen countertop, waiting.

"What do you say, Lena?" he pushes.

Nothing. I say nothing.

Alice taps her chest like this soothes her. "Oh, Jack, give her a minute to think. It's not like Lena can just pack up that tired Honda and make way for the bulldozers... She just lost her momma. She needs help, too."

Tired Honda? "I'm fine. I don't need any help."

She stands up, practically twirling in her dress. "First, you need a dumpster. Cousin Tommy runs Waste Management. For a few hundred, he'll park one in the yard and haul it away as many times as you need."

Arguments stream in my head, starting with the few hundred I don't have.

"Muscle, too. We'll send our boys over every day after school to help you lug the big stuff."

"Alice, that's unnecessary."

"Hogwash!" Her sappy voice turns eerily stern, shutting me up. "Football season's over, so Will and Max need somethin' to do."

"It'll keep 'em out of trouble," Jack says.

She returns to Mom's hutch, knocking the wood with her fist. "We'll get you a portable moving container. I gotta guy for that, too."

"Alice's contact list reads like a who's-who of Wilmington. Anything you need, she's got a number for it."

"With a pod container, you can pack as you go. Easy, peasy."

"Oh, since she's job huntin', what about Jason?" Jack perks up.

Alice's dark eyes become cat-like in pouncing intensity. "You're right, hon. I never thought you'd mesh well in California, Lena." She grabs a pen and an overdue bill from my mail stack, scribbling. "My nephew Jason Ford owns The Bean Machine in Asheville. His restaurant's been around for years now, so no chance of it tankin' like your bakery did. Email him your resumé. He's lookin' to hire a pastry chef."

Panic edges the corners of my plastered smile and automatic nod. Sitting on my trembling hands, I measure my breaths. *Slow down. In and out.* "Um, thanks. You've given me a lot to consider."

Their expectant faces prod me to say more, but nothing ekes out. I glance at their mugs to see the progress. Jack's drained his, but Alice's is barely touched.

She flashes her salesperson's smile. "Well, we're happy to help. That's what neighbors are for."

"I'll, um, think about it." My words tremble slightly.

Alice looks ready to convince me, but Jack puts his beefy hand on hers. "Lena, you sure we shouldn't call Lucas?"

We *do not* call Lucas. Streaming assurances and thanks, I stand, encouraging them to do the same. Jack complies first, complimenting my coffee again before lumbering to the sliding glass door. I yank it open, eager for them to exit so I can lock it and draw the curtains. Only Alice whips around. Too close to her, I stumble, knocking into the dusty shotgun leaning by the door.

The gun slips, falls, and fires.

An explosion of dust and paper billows from the bookshelf across the room. I blurt expletives while my guests seem relatively unaffected, like with the mouse. *Just another day in the country.*

Jack immediately moves to secure and disarm the weapon. "That could've hurt someone, little lady."

"I-I'm so sorry. I hate the damn things," I say, voice definitely shaking now. "I'm scared to touch them."

"Bless your heart, Lena. This house is nothin' but a big booby trap," Alice says. "You definitely shouldn't have them 'round if you're afraid of 'em."

"Mom liked keeping them close for protection—she has them stashed all over the house. Is it a country thing? Keeping weapons at hand like you're expecting a zombie invasion or Michael fucking Myers?" Unable to hide my trembling voice, I lock my fidgeting hands behind me.

Jack rests his hand on my shoulder. "It's safe now. Don't worry."

"All I do is worry in this house," I say weakly.

She reaches for the bill and pen again. "Here, I got a guy for guns, too. He'll disarm 'em and dispose of them safely and responsibly. We need you to feel safe, hon. Call 'em. TODAY."

"Anything you need, little lady, just holler," Jack says, heading to his truck.

Alice's bright red lips press into a tight smile like she's about to offer comfort. "My Corning Ware dish is white with blue flowers. I'll get it next time."

CHAPTER
Three

I DRIVE AWAY from *that* house, with its mice, guns, and overwhelming neighbors, taking country roads way too fast in my Honda Pilot—the *only* thing I own, well, that I earned myself. *Tired Honda? Damn it, Alice.* I crank up the volume on the radio, blasting hip-hop, and mentally kick myself for not telling them *yes* with a wide smile, a thank you, and a curtsey for good measure.

Two hundred grand would secure my new start in California. Or, hell, anywhere I could find a good job, ideally in a restaurant I like and where my brother isn't part-owner. In a more reasonable cost-of-living locale, I could buy a small house outright—a tempting alternative to Lucas's pool house since I'm thirty-five and I've *never* had my own place.

Seriously—how can I be this old and have nothing to show for it?

Needing to go faster than the country roads allow, I hop onto the interstate toward Wilmington. I pass grumbling tractor-trailers and overstuffed minivans, beach-bound for cheap, off-season vacations. DVD screens brighten the backseats, where kids and dogs cram between coolers and totes. My hands strangle the wheel as my right foot dips lower.

Eventually, traffic congestion inspires a detour. I fly across an intersection, heading cityward through thick-bellied oaks draped in Spanish Moss and bloated old houses with manicured everything.

Whipping around slower vehicles with racecar-driver acumen, a brief but much-appreciated *I-drive-better-than-you* feeling couples with *Ludacris* blasting over my speakers. *Move, bitch. Get out the way.* I flick surging energy from my trembling fingers. *Is this helping or making things worse?*

Flashing blue lights in my rearview answer my question.

A tree-lined street in a charming neighborhood offers a safe stopping place. I put the window down and turn off the engine. My head rests atop my hands on the steering wheel. *No, no, no.*

"Good morning, ma'am," the officer says, jolting me from my hair-covered pocket of shame. He tells me his name, but it doesn't stick.

Lifting my head, I plaster on the best smile I can manage. Only he fails to match it like most people do. His chiseled face seems permanently fixed on tough-guy-having-a-bad-day, and the jagged scar stretching from his left eyebrow to his ear suggests he's earned the demeanor. He's military-crisp with blond hair, cropped short, and highlighting his protruding ears. Meticulously tucked, ironed, and assembled, everything about him assures me I'm not getting out of this.

"I was speeding."

"Yes, ma'am."

"I have a good reason," I say, trying to come up with one.

He glances at the detachable handicapped decal on my passenger seat and the wheelchair behind me. "Are you in medical distress?"

"No. Those aren't mine. I mean, I didn't steal them, either. They're my mom's, and I haven't cleaned out the car yet. Thank God you can't ticket me for being messy, right?"

Though I believe my comment to be at least smirk-able, he responds with nothing but a monotone, "No, ma'am," as if I'm serious.

"How fast was I going?"

"Fifty-three in a thirty-five, ma'am."

"It's my rubber boots. They're heavy."

"You were driving erratically."

"It's Wilmington. I'm fitting in."

"And your tags expired in January."

"Shit. I'm—um—shit." My head gently thumps against the steering wheel. A call to Lucas looms in my future—begging for money until the house sells. And *worse*, sitting through a lecture from my *younger* brother about safe driving and fiscal responsibility.

"Sounds terribly expensive. Any sales going on this week? Three for the price of one? You should talk to your higher-ups about offering deals for people who drive cheap cars. Save the expensive tickets for the BMWs, Mercedes, and Range Rovers. You should pick on them first—not sad-sacks driving fifteen-year-old Hondas."

He locks eyes with me. "Are you under the influence of drugs or alcohol, ma'am?"

"I wish!" My stomach dips, and I regret my words immediately. His eyes narrow, but he says nothing. "No, I'm not on anything. And sorry. You're just doing your job—I know. But everything's personal when it happens to you, you know?"

He nods slightly. "Care to explain your hurry?"

"Honestly, officer, I have nowhere to be. No destination. Away. I just wanted to get *away*."

"From?"

My hands tighten on the wheel as possible answers stream into my head. "Um, everything. Things have been rough lately." The words choke out slowly, and I regret them like I'm spewing my private drama on someone who's wandered into my theater by mistake.

Through a weak, pinched smile, I scrutinize his slightly cocked brow. "I see your concern-meter rising. I promise—I'm in no danger, either from myself or others. My car's my escape pod. I was enjoying it a little too much."

"Recreational activities would serve you better, ma'am."

His robotic demeanor makes me laugh, but tears slip out, too, as if I can't have one without the other. I swipe my eyes quickly. "You're right, officer, um…"

"Wright. Ben Wright."

"See? You are right." The name pun makes me chuckle, but he remains stoic. "I'm Lena Buckley."

"Driver's license, registration, and proof of insurance, Ms. Buckley."

A frenzied search ends with me dumping the contents of my purse and the glove box into the passenger seat. *I can't afford this. Jokes aren't working. Tell him he has nice eyes. A kind smile… wait, he hasn't smiled. Play the grief card. Can't get much better than a dead-mother excuse.*

"I deserve the tickets." My fingers tremble as I hand him the items.

"Are you alright?"

"Yes. Just nerves." I stretch my fingers and smile assuredly. "Sorry, I'm such a mess."

"No apology necessary. It happens. Sit tight." He leaves me for the computer in his patrol car.

"Flirt with him, Lena." I imagine Mom beside me with her cane propped between her legs. She shakes her head while I argue how wrong that would be, though I absolutely would've tried—*and did*—in my younger days.

"What's the problem? He's handsome," I imagine her saying, *"in a rough and tumble way."*

Is he? Too worried about my financial ruin, I haven't noticed, but a quick glance in my rearview confirms it. There's *something* about him, like his refusal to smile just to match mine means he's not fake and wouldn't lie either, which I find very attractive—not that I'll give her the satisfaction. "You think all employed males are handsome."

It's bat-shit crazy—*I know*—but I hear her laugh at me. I wonder how long it'll be before I can't remember it anymore. Or even imagine what she'd say in such circumstances.

For now, Imaginary Mom suggests pick-up lines. *How about movie tickets, instead?... Want to serve and protect me over dinner tonight?... There're some recreational activities I'd like to do with you, officer....* Things she'd never want me to say, *really.* Though she never quite understood my anxiety, years of dealing with me made her an expert at using distraction to thwart my panic attacks. And she's still the only one ever to try.

But make-believing our conversation provides little comfort. This'll be at least five hundred, more with the insurance hike if I can still get it. I'll return the unopened wine boxes and pour buckets of loose change into the coin machine—anything to spare myself from asking Lucas. My anxiety bitches—what I call my debilitating inner voices—go for a full-on attack. They rarely miss an opportunity to make me feel horrible. *How could I do this? Broke, unemployed people have no business speeding, wasting gas, or forgetting to renew their license plates.*

I'm barely resisting a panic attack by his return.

He hands me my items while delivering his spiel. Some words stand out—*court, fines, whatever.* My inner monologue takes center stage. *The panic's bad enough. Please, don't cry. Or hyperventilate. Or cry.* I'm desperate for home and some light day drinking when the power outages can't deter me.

Finally, he hands me the folded paper, which I quickly toss on top of Mom's handicapped placard. "Thank you, officer. I'll think of you when I pay up."

A slight smirk pokes his clean-shaven cheek—the first hint that he's not *RoboCop* after all. *But did I say something funny?*

"I'll think of you next time I pull over a luxury vehicle. Good day, Ms. Buckley."

He doesn't give me a chance to commend his joke—at least, I think that's a joke. Said with such speed and awkwardness, it's hard to tell, especially since he turns and walks away as soon as he says it. Most joke-tellers wait for a reaction.

That the encounter is over, and knowing the damage is done, calms me immediately. Deep, tension-releasing breaths settle my panic.

I pull off the shoulder slowly, using my blinker and checking every mirror. He follows but U-turns at the next intersection. For more distance, I stay residential, ogling massive homes through frustrated tears, and lacing through the city until I reach desolate country roads again. I pick turns indiscriminately, wanting, almost needing, to be lost.

Dingy gray fields sweep my window before a farm comes into view. A bright red barn centers paddocks of grazing horses. A sign for Pines & Palmettos Equestrian Center marks a dirt lane, so I turn in and park by the barn. I take a deep breath. *What am I doing here?*

In the passenger seat, the ticket paperwork flaps open just enough to see large block lettering atop the page. *WARNING.* Scanning the terse *suggestion* to renew my tags, I gape, a little breathless. No court date. No fines. No trouble. A choking laugh rumbles from me. Then, I read what he's written at the bottom.

Things will get better

CHAPTER
Four

THE BUSY FARM draws me from my Honda with a mix of curiosity and excitement. Things are definitely better *here*. Riders kick up dust in an arena while trainers call instructions. Parents line the fence, taking pictures of their kids who seem too young and small to sit atop something so large. There are older equestrians, too—teenagers taking jumps and an adult lunging her horse in circles. Focused enjoyment is the prevailing mood in the arena.

As I pass the stable's entrance, two horses clop out, sandwiching the woman from Sunny's. She yanks them to a halt.

"Well, look what the cat dragged in. You found me!" Her buttery Southern accent and wide smile soften my awkwardness.

"I was driving by and saw your sign. I'm sorry about my spectacle yesterday."

She flings the leather straps. "No need to apologize. You doing okay? Did you chardonnay your troubles away?"

I laugh at her clever rhyme and wish I could say yes. "I'm fine, really. Just embarrassed."

The speckled gray horse groans as if bored. "Don't be. It was worth it to see those Sunny's employees jump to your rescue."

I laugh again as it replays in my head. My sudden tears set off a chain reaction, starting with being swarmed by employees as if their training includes a crying-woman-contingency. "I got about ten coupons out of it."

"There you go! Next time, I'm crying for coupons, too. And, it was a good test."

"Test?"

"For the Sunny's groupie givin' you the eye. I've never seen a man disappear so fast. If a grown man can't handle a woman's tears, what good is he?"

"Oh, right. I forgot about him," I say, brow creasing with the realization. "Assholes are my specialty. I'm very good at attracting and repelling them."

Her approving look mends my uncertainty as if we share a secret life code. "Well, the coupons'll serve you better."

The speckled horse grunts and nudges her with his head. "Okay, Shadow." She huffs. "My babies are all dressed up with nowhere to go. A couple booked a trail ride but canceled last minute." Her face lights up. "You interested?"

"Me?"

"You've ridden a horse before, right?"

"Ages ago. I'm not even sure I could do it now."

"It's like riding a bike. Shadow, here, doesn't know any speed but slow. Besides, I fancy a ride. Let's do it together."

"How much is it?"

"It's on the house. Stop overthinking and say yes."

"Okay, yes." I smile weakly and hope no one gets hurt. "I'm Lena Buckley."

"Gloria Oxendine. You hear that, boys?" She turns to each horse. "We're back in business!"

Gloria positions Shadow by a step stool and nods to me. I step up, eyeing the saddle like it's a bridge to hell. *Can I even do it? Will my thighs stretch that far?* My heart rate kicks into hyperdrive.

"Take your time. We all gotta go at our own pace. Right, Shadow?" She rubs Shadow's nose, and he whinnies.

My joints crack and pop like *Rice Krispies* in milk as I hoist into the saddle. Shadow shifts under me. My butt chunks press up against my thighs, feeling uncomfortably pronounced.

"Sorry, Shadow."

"Whatcha apologizin' to him for?" Gloria asks.

"My fat ass."

"Honey, his ass will always be bigger," she says. We eye his bulbous rump and laugh.

After a quick tutorial that brings back hazy memories, she hands me the reins.

"Go at your own pace. We aren't in *any* hurry." Gloria clicks her tongue. Side-by-side, the horses move. "See? Nothing to it."

Shadow farts, getting attention as we pass the fence line. Riders laugh and shake their heads as if he's known for this. *Great, she gave me the farty horse.*

We circle the property on a worn, rugged path. I'm nervous, scared I'll do something wrong. Yet small things chisel away at my anxieties. The brisk wind feels good, cleansing. Shadow's horse smell reminds me of riding with Mom and Lucas. High up, opening my chest, shoulders aligned, and back straight, breathing feels almost meditative, like this thing I've forgotten how to do correctly until now. And *things will get better* repeats on a loop.

The path narrows with encroaching trees and thickets. Gloria nods for us to go first, so I shift my hips forward and click my tongue. Ahead, a muddy ditch splits the trail. I steer Shadow toward the narrowest part and coax him onward. He hesitates before stepping back.

"Come on, Shadow. You can do it," I say with gentle heel kicks.

He putters his lips but clears the gap. I laugh at his blundering move as we ascend to the other side. I pat his neck. "Good boy."

"Well, color me impressed, Lena. Most first-timers balk at this part, but you took it like a pro. You make a great team."

Though swelling with pride at this rare compliment, I shrug it off. "Yeah, the crying girl and the farting horse. We belong together."

"Trust me. You can do worse than this handsome devil." The path widens again, so Gloria falls in beside me. "Speakin' of, are ya datin' anyone?"

"No. Not for years. Too busy taking care of Mom. Before that, I was married."

"Girl, you've come to the right place, then. Tell me what happened… the more detail, the better. Don't be shy."

She asks like my pathetic marriage story rivals celebrity gossip.

"Um, there's not much to tell. I loved him. He loved the idea of me— not the reality."

"Reality tends to do that to marriages, and I've had three."

"Three? Really?"

"The first one died, rest his lovely soul, the second one left, curses on his, and the third… well, I put him out of his misery… and mine. He's buried out here, somewhere." She glances around as if trying to remember where she put him.

I laugh. I don't know if she's joking, but somehow, I don't mind if she isn't.

With a playful wink, she urges me on. "Tell me about this guy."

"Well, Mark always knew what he wanted, and he got it." I scoff, puffing out warm air in the cold. "Have you ever known someone who made life look easy?"

"Oh, yeah. They're the worst!"

"Maybe, but I was enchanted. He wanted to be the perfect husband, and he was, mostly. He, um, still is, to someone else. I was the problem."

"Somehow, I doubt that." Gloria's eyes narrow like she's mentally picking me apart. "Sounds like a lot of pressure, anyway."

My forehead creases. "Maybe. He finished college. To be with him, I didn't. He never understood my anxiety disorder because he never struggled with anything. He had a good, stable career. I jumped around hourly jobs until I opened my bakery. When that tanked, I felt like a huge loser. He seemed to agree. He was loving when it suited him and an ass about whatever didn't. Anxiety, panic, and failure didn't. But that's not why I left."

"Why then?"

"He supported my business because *that's* what good husbands do. They mow the lawn and hold your hand and tolerate your fanciful endeavors. That used to be great—him ticking all the boxes—but it wasn't honest. I knew things weren't right whenever he ate my desserts. He'd take a bite and say, 'Delicious,' no matter how it tasted. I left out the sugar once on purpose—the cupcake was little more than flavored bread. Guess what he said?"

"Delicious," she sighs.

"Yep. His so-called support was a cruel joke. He didn't love me. He put up with me. He couldn't be bothered to cause a conflict or tell me the truth. That's not a marriage. It's a lie. It broke my heart that he'd lie about a damn cupcake."

"If he'd lie about that, then…"

"Exactly. That's not love—not the way I want it. And he hated me, in the end." Mark's last words to me rage in my head. *You're right. I don't love you. How could I? How could anyone?*

"Ah, honey. That sounds painful."

An uneasy chuckle manages to break through my angst. "Wanna know what's painful? Trying to explain to everyone in your life that you're ending your marriage over a cupcake."

She laughs. "It's not exactly as cut and dry as an affair or some other atrocity, but I get it. If you don't have honesty in a marriage, you don't have much of anything. Well, pretend I'm your fairy godmother. What kind of love do you want?" She waves her whip over my head, wand-like.

"Um, I don't want love."

"Sure, you do. No one *really* wants to be alone... not for long, anyway. You can't let one mistake ruin you forever. He hasn't. If you put it out there, maybe the universe'll bring it to you."

"I'd rather the universe bring me a steady paycheck and a decent place to live." My eyes roll at her obvious disappointment. "Fine. I'd settle for a decent kisser who makes me smile."

"No, I mean your ideal love. No settling."

"Fine, an excellent kisser who makes me laugh."

Gloria gives me a disgruntled side-eye. "Best be careful. The universe delivers on low expectations, too. That's how I landed husband number two."

To satisfy Gloria, I inhale the brisk, piney air and clear out my snarky, jaded mental trash. I've thought little of love since losing it, but it's a strange day already, and what I *really* want flashes unmistakably in my head—a bright neon sign in the cloudy windows.

"I want someone who needs *me* and doesn't make me feel bad for *whatever* that is. I don't want to be handled. I want to be held. And delighted. And... cared for and comforted. I want him to long for my company. To ache for me. To stand up to me when I need it, and get on his knees when I need that, too. I want someone who loves me too much to lie about anything. A guy who'll say my food sucks and will fucking devour whatever doesn't. I want a partner, not a damn pretender, someone who believes in me. In us. No holding back. Ravenous. Messy. Sexy. But above all, honest."

"Yes! Dang girl, that's good!" Gloria beams. "Real over perfect."

"Can't get more real than me. I'm jobless, practically homeless, and destined for my brother's pool house. I have absolutely nothing to offer, and I suck at relationships."

"Everyone sucks at 'em when they're in the wrong ones. In the right one, you'll do fine. Besides, Shadow likes you, and he hardly likes anyone. That speaks well in your favor."

I run my fingers on Shadow's sweaty neck. "That's good enough for me."

As we walk through the wooded trail, our silence prompts a flood of memories. Family horseback riding stopped after Mom's rheumatoid arthritis left her too hurt to try, and Lucas and I didn't bother without her. Regret fills the spaces between steps, remembering when the house was cozy, the garden teemed with vegetables, and horses ate carrots from my hands. *Why hadn't I loved it then? Why had I taken so much for granted?* It feels like I've spent my life making do instead of enjoying good things. My life feels like, well, a shadow. What I'm meant for is around the corner, if only I could attach myself to it.

We circle to our starting point, and I'm sad it's over. It's been so long since I've enjoyed myself that I've forgotten what it's like. Hell, even Shadow's farting and questions about my ex don't detract from the good vibes of a somewhat strenuous, outdoor activity and what it's done for my anxiety. I feel almost… normal.

"How much for lessons?"

"Forty-five a pop or five for two hundred. You interested?"

"I'm financially challenged right now."

"We're here if you change your mind."

She takes a picture of me hugging Shadow's neck while he gives Gloria an annoyed look like he's so over it. I share it on Instagram: *Made a new friend today. He's a little gassy, but I think I'm in love.*

After a fast food pitstop and a calmer drive home, I prop the warning ticket mid-kitchen counter against Mom's urn, folding it just right to see the message.

Things will get better

They have to, right? Mom scribbled something similar to me in her medication journal.

You deserve more than this.
Dream something better.

She said the same thing when I moved home with my tail between my legs—marriage and bakery over. *Those dreams failed, and that's okay. Dream something better.*

I find the note in Mom's medication journal, still on the counter. I tear it out and prop it next to the warning ticket message. Advertising good thoughts might push back some of the bad ones. It won't make anything worse, anyway.

I get the fire going, pour Pinot, and lament the single sauce packet they've given me for my fries. Opening a junk drawer for extras, I find one suspiciously old special sauce. A freebie kleptomaniac, Mom never left a restaurant empty-handed.

Scanning the rest of the drawer, I throw packets by the handful into the trash, bypassing batteries, flashlights, and coins. As the drawer empties, satisfaction sweeps over me.

When I first returned home and realized Mom needed me to stay, I dreamed of something better for us both. I planned to recreate the home I remembered—clean the house, get rid of junk, plant a garden, and repair things properly.

But caring for Mom overwhelmed and exhausted me. Instead of big transformations, I settled for a single daily hope: *make one thing better.*

An azalea in a bud vase on her dinner tray. Reading to her. Whipping up a small sugar-light dessert. Every day, I tried to make *one* thing better. On hard days, I couldn't even do that.

But this rekindles my mantra. It isn't much, but this drawer is a little better, and it feels good.

That's not all that feels good, I realize, eyeing an ibuprofen bottle's expiration date. *I rode a horse.* My inner thighs ache, but it's a good ache —soreness I'm proud of having—so I don't bother with the ibuprofen. It's expired, anyway.

I smirk at Mom's urn. "I rode a horse today, Mom. Can you believe it?"

"I always knew you'd love it if you gave yourself the chance. We'll make an equestrian of you yet," I can almost hear her say.

A small leather pouch shoved between D batteries and restaurant napkins catches my eye. I open it, expecting safety pins or toothpicks—a total Mom thing to store in a change purse since coins belong in pill vials.

But it's cash with a picture shoved inside—me around ten, feeding Mom's horse, Lady, an apple.

The picture isn't surprising. Mom kept them everywhere. She used them as bookmarks and carried them in her purse.

Counting out exactly two hundred dollars, though, makes me smile.

CHAPTER
Five

"NINE-ONE-ONE. WHAT'S YOUR EMERGENCY?" Her words sound muffled, like I'm underwater.

"It's my Mom. I can't wake her. She's unconscious."

"Is she breathing?"

"Breathing? I don't know. I'm having trouble reaching her."

"Tell me where you are, honey."

"Home." I spit out the address, kicking through loose blankets to the surface. I sit up, gasping. *Wait. Why am I out here and not in her room?*

"Help's on the way, hon. Wait, Carsley Road? Is that you, Lena? It's me, Miss Leslie."

Miss Leslie? From Sunday school, the Boy Scout troop, and Mom's funeral. I choke, stomach turning with nausea. *Please, don't leave. Stay with me. Fight through.* "Oh, shit."

"Lena, take a deep breath. Are you alright?"

"Miss Leslie, I had a nightmare, and I—please, cancel this call."

"Well, an officer's comin' by to check on ya. Stay on the line until he arrives. Are you in *any* medical distress?"

"No, I'm fine. I'm awake now. Please, do we have to make a big deal?" Shame brings tears. *What the fuck have I done?* The dream replays on a wicked loop—me peeling through bedding, looking for Mom, and finding her pale, eyes closed, unresponsive. *It may already be too late.* "I'm fine now, Miss Leslie. Truly."

"It's policy, honey. You call, and we respond—no matter what. Don't worry, though. These things happen."

Do they? I doubt it.

"It's like old friends payin' you a visit, huh?" A half-hearted chuckle merges into a sigh. "Maybe leave your phone in another room when you sleep? You don't need it beside you anymore, right?"

The circular drive becomes a flashing light parade—it feels like they sent everyone on shift from officers to firemen. I'm mortified—dragging these poor people out here for my overburdened psyche. In rubber boots, a long t-shirt, and using Dad's flannel button-down as a robe, I stand on the raised patio, gushing apologies.

"Yes, Mom's dead..."

"No, I'm not on anything..."

"Just a bad dream..."

"No, I shouldn't sleep with my phone..."

"Yes, sleeping in a real bed rather than a couch might help..."

Once satisfied that my alarm is an imagined one, the parade retreats.

In the bathroom, I cry on the toilet as my stomach rumbles and retaliates over the rush of anxiety. When it refuses to flush, I break down more.

But the fix requires focus—a needed distraction. It takes half an hour to safety-pin the broken chain back together. Sure, I could replace the toilet's inner workings with the help of *YouTube*.

But why replace a part when the whole thing needs replacing? It's an oblong, yellow toilet from the eighties that matches the yellow walls and the pale, flecked Formica countertop. The toilet bowl is so water-stained that it always looks gross, no matter how clean it is. The floors around the toilet bend underfoot, thanks to unchecked leaks, never fixed properly. The two other bathrooms suffer the same fate—making do has cost them their usefulness. Everything here is on the edge of brokenness.

Sleep now impossible, I turn to job hunting. I email restaurants, coffee shops, and bakeries. I loved working in a kitchen. Few jobs offer that fast-paced energy while creating something people enjoy. Of course, I'll have that at Root & Bone, making this job search superfluous. Only part of me wants to find a job on my own, closer to what I know, and in a restaurant I'd enjoy. What's wrong with having a backup plan?

Barbara Moore, my mother's best friend, shows up mid-morning chauffeured by her grandniece, Dot.

I don't love Dot.

"Dang, Lena." Dot leans against Mrs. Moore's MINI Cooper and lights a cigarette. "You look awful."

Meeting me on the back patio, Mrs. Moore gives me the same critical once-over she often delivered in her high school chemistry class when I failed a quiz or forgot my homework. "I heard you had a rough night."

It's no surprise that she knows. Bereaved Lena Buckley rousing emergency services over a bad dream surely proved irresistible chit-chat material for Miss Leslie.

"I'm fine. That was an accident. Nothing to worry about."

My most assuring smile leads her inside. With Mom, Mrs. Moore's visits were a godsend. She'd come over every other morning, push me out of the house, and when I'd return, she'd have Mom bathed, dressed, and laughing over some shared joke they'd kept over their sixty-plus years of friendship.

I first met Dot at Mom's funeral, where she asked if I needed a roommate since the house was empty—not for her, but a friend "having a hard time right now." I nearly lost it, but Mrs. Moore said, "Dot speaks first and thinks later. Let it go."

Easier said than done, and with my luck, it's no surprise that Mrs. Moore no longer goes anywhere without her.

I start coffee in a china cup, which seems to match Mrs. Moore's dainty frame, wispy gray hair, understated jewelry, and floral, well, everything.

Mrs. Moore sits at the clutter-covered table, pushing aside mail. "I hear you're still sleeping on the couch."

"Wow, Miss Leslie gave you a full report."

"Well, if you're going to gossip, you might as well do it right," she says, smirking. "Sleeping in a real bed might help."

"It's not the couch, and it's the only decent mattress in the house." The formal living room couch centers the house, where I could hear Mom at night and stay semi-warm. "I'm fine where I am... and that won't happen again."

Cigarette smoke follows Dot inside, clashing awkwardly with the wood stove smell. "Damn cold out there." She rubs her hands together. "I'll take one of those, Lena. But, no froufrou frills, okay? I like it black."

I reach for a chipped poop emoji mug that Dad brought back from

New York City. He was a truck driver and often picked up funny souvenirs from his travels. Smirking, I start Dot's coffee.

"We have business to discuss, Lena." Mrs. Moore's curt announcement comes with a tiny sigh. "You need to take care of things."

"What things?" I ask, though I don't want to know.

"Women are attached to their baking dishes."

I grab the cream from the fridge, groaning. Uneaten concoctions stack the shelves, crusted and moldy.

"Holding onto them is downright rude," she says.

"I never wanted them in the first place."

"These ladies did a nice thing for you and Lucas. They want their Pyrexes back. If you don't take care of it, I'll organize an intervention." A sly grin pushes up her pale cheeks. "There's a battalion of church ladies armed with rubber gloves and sponges ready to invade your kitchen."

"Okay, I'll get it done."

I deliver the coffee and change subjects. I tell her about the Harvey's offer, my adventures riding Shadow, and finding the money.

Mrs. Moore stares over the reading glasses she wears even when she isn't reading and speaks in her delicate but strangely authoritative voice. "Take the lessons."

"No way. That money will go to bills." I motion toward the mail beside us. "I won't be here long enough to commit to five lessons, anyway."

"Sure, you will. California can wait."

"Why should it? I can't wait to get out of here."

"But California?" Dot scoffs. "You won't last five minutes in Malibu."

My left eyebrow creeps up. "Why not?"

Dot shrugs her beefy shoulders, running a hand through her pitch-black hair. "You'll hate it. The traffic. The surfer dudes and Barbie dolls. Doesn't seem your style."

Dot wears baggy, black capris overalls with thick knee socks, Timberlands, a thermal shirt topped with a plaid flannel three sizes too big for her—she's no style guru and hardly qualified to judge me or my Malibu-ness.

"She means Malibu would be quite a change for anyone," Mrs. Moore says.

"Everything *has* changed. And I need a change from all this." I motion toward the wood stove and ancient couches. "My best opportunities'll be in Malibu."

"Then, what's this?" Dot points to my job search smugly. "Looks like you aren't thrilled about Malibu either." She laughs before singing the Arizona Zervas' song dominating the radio lately, *"Malibu, Malibu, spending Daddy's money with attitude. I'm going to call you Roxanne, Roxanne."*

Dot sloshes her mug on the table, splashing my mail, which she, of course, does nothing about. "I need a cigarette."

With Dot gone, I say, "I made some local inquiries in case California falls through. That's all."

"Did Lucas say it might fall through?"

"There's always a chance—a high one with me. The job hunt is extra insurance for getting out of here."

Mrs. Moore doesn't speak, as if digesting my words gives her heartburn.

"Things were tolerable with Mom around. Now, the place is colder and more broken than ever." I inhale sharply. Last night replays in my head. *That fiasco would never have happened in Lucas's pool house.* "I hate it, Mrs. Moore. I *hate* being here."

"You hate what's happened. We all do." She places her cup on its saucer. It's nice seeing Mom's antiques in use. "Lena, you're recovering from a traumatic time, grieving, and not sleeping well. You aren't yourself. What about making things better, huh?"

Once, Mrs. Moore asked me how I managed when things were tough. I shared what I'd been telling myself every morning. *Make one thing better.* If I could do that, it'd be a good day.

I rest my face in my hands and huff. "There are too many things, and I'm tired. With the Harvey's offer, I can move sooner. And the sooner, the better."

Dot slips back inside, bringing a second wave of smokiness and cold air with her.

Mrs. Moore pats my hand. "You shouldn't rush, Lena. This is your family's home. It's full of history and stories and, yes, junk, too, but it's your parents' legacy. You should go through it properly, or you'll regret it. It'll take time. Months, probably."

"No way. The plumbing or lights won't last months. The mice'll plan a coup."

Dot perks up as if my struggles amuse her. "Oh, what's up with your plumbing and lights?"

"Dot's a general contractor," Mrs. Moore says, almost beaming.

"Wait, *you're* a general contractor? You're employed, beyond driving Mrs. Moore around all day?"

"Well, I'm a *new* general contractor. An electrician, too. I was working with Dawson and Sons, but not being one of the *sons*, I only got boring jobs. Now, I'm my own boss, you know, when I'm not Aunt Barb's chauffeur." She hands me a crumpled business card, which she takes back as soon as I look at it. "I've also been a Coast Guard technician, a construction worker, and a truck driver. A jack of all trades."

I'm a jack of all trades but a master of none. Dad used to say that about his unprofessional fixes. I bite my tongue.

"She's cheap, enthusiastic, and looking for clients," Mrs. Moore says, not realizing how it sounds. Dot and I share an amused grin.

"Tempting, but I'll make do until I leave. And that'll be soon."

"Don't rush it, Lena. What's a few months? Don't you want to leave with the satisfaction that you've taken good care of your family home?"

Maybe I can't just walk away. But I hate that I can't. Living here indefinitely, when anything can and will go wrong while going through every drawer, the closets, the sheds, the barn—I cringe and my heart races with the sheer magnitude of the project. *Where would I even start?* Alice's voice coos in my head. *You need a dumpster, and a storage unit, and muscle...*

"Don't get overwhelmed. Make one thing better at a time." Her blue eyes twinkle as she leans closer. "Some relaxation would be good, though. How's your anxiety been lately?"

My eyes pinch, glancing at Dot. I couldn't control what Mom divulged to Mrs. Moore, but my anxiety disorder should fall under a best-friend-confidentiality clause. Luckily, Dot's distracted by the fireplace's stonework. "Fine. Everything's fine. Really, it's fine."

Unconvinced, she nods, anyway. "Take your time, Lena. Figure out what you truly want. In the meantime, take the lessons. It'll be good for you."

After last night, I can't argue. The hope of turning Shadow into my new escape pod offsets the weight of everything else. A little, anyway.

SHADOW WHINNIES when Gloria and I approach, swishing his tail like he's brushing off flies. He doesn't seem happy with what we're about to do, and I feel bad, like I'm roping him into the horse version of me washing casserole dishes or lugging firewood. Life is full of bullshit must-dos. I hate inflicting them on someone else.

"Come on, Shadow. Be a good boy, and I'll give you a peppermint," Gloria says, nearing him. "Shadow loves peppermints."

I sigh, grateful he's getting something out of it.

She unwraps a puffy peppermint, catching Shadow's attention. He whips around and takes the treat from her hand. Then he nudges her arm for more. She slips the halter over his face and hands me the lead rope.

Shadow doesn't move when I pull the rope. He nudges Gloria again, but she puts her hands up.

"Give 'em a good pull to let 'em know you mean it."

I tug the rope forcefully enough. Reluctantly, he ambles forward.

Gloria pats Shadow's side. "Next time, you'll fetch 'em yourself."

I nod with trepidation. *Must remember peppermints.*

To tack up, we maneuver Shadow into a stall. This takes time since it means turning him around, and he's reluctant to go where I lead him. I get it. I'm nervous, fumbling with everything. He's not taking me seriously yet. I'm not, either.

It's another beautifully busy day at the barn. Everyone looks equestrian-chic in their long-sleeved shirts under vests, form-fitting breeches, and paddock boots. Next to Shadow, a girl in pigtails saddles another horse. A child no older than seven trots in the arena atop a horse a hundred times her size. A white cat lounges casually on a picnic table. Everyone's comfortable. Everyone belongs.

Not me, though, especially not in my UNC sweatshirt, old Nikes, and jeans, like I've wandered in off the street. And it's almost painful, how out of place I feel.

But Gloria's friendly smile counters my negative thoughts. She hands me an oval brush with a strap for my hand. "First, we take care of his coat and hooves."

This, I can do. My tension eases. We aren't starting with complicated gear but with care. Care is in my wheelhouse.

Running the brush along Shadow's velvety gray and white body comforts me as much as him, I think. He's soft, and the brush kicks up tiny dust plumes. His horse smells—sweat, leather, oats, and hay—mix with the cold air, and everything feels warmer. Tugging out a briar in Shadow's half-tail launches memories of brushing Mom's long hair before braiding it. And, much longer ago, her brushing mine. It's easy, perhaps even natural, to get bogged down by chores, one to the next, without being present and appreciating the lovely specialness of being *the one* helping someone else, to be entrusted, to be a true comfort. I'm struck by how precious caring for someone is, in a weird and overwhelming way—even if you fail at the responsibility one day, the opportunity is a beautiful honor. Shadow's *letting* me do this for him. It's something I *can* do. It's a privilege—the caring.

Gloria shows me how to scrape muck from his hooves. With a tap against his leg, Shadow shifts his weight, allowing me to lift his hoof—a pleasant surprise given his attitude when we started.

Our intimate dance finishes. I relax. Shadow seems tolerant. Gloria shows me the tack room, where she pulls items off the racks and hooks. I carry everything to Shadow.

Saddle pad, *check*. Brown leather English saddle, *check*. Girth wrapped around his midsection to hold the saddle in place—tighter and tighter still—*check*. Bridle and reins. We adjust straps, lengthen the stirrups, and tighten the girth once more. Shadow's ready.

I mount him, slightly more confident this time. He huffs as we mosey toward the arena.

"Sit like you mean it. Put your shoulders back. Get some air into those lungs," Gloria tells me.

My back pops as I straighten. Everything I've done lately has felt hunched over. Watching TV. Carrying wood. Hovering over out-of-date magazines in waiting rooms. Leaning over a hospital bed.

Don't think about that. Think about the beauty of good posture.

Mom used to get on me about my posture. She'd tell me how Grandma made her prance around the living room, balancing three books on her head. I'd smirk and ask if that was while wearing a corset and trudging through knee-deep snow. She'd tell me how easy I had it, and I couldn't argue. I did have it easy. Then, I went out into the world and made everything hard.

"That's better," Gloria says. "You look good up there."

I *feel* good up here. It's invigorating doing something for me, away from *that* house, and getting out of my head, *mostly*. I wish I'd had that when caring for Mom—a place where I could breathe. However precious the caring is, it's much better when peppered with self-care. I lost that in the chaos.

Gloria instructs me on tightening my reins and turning. It's like driving a car, except for my lack of control and Shadow's incessant farting.

After two laps at a pleasant walk, Gloria teaches me a sitting trot. Heels down. Legs not squeezing the horse. Hands on reins. Butt moving with Shadow's trot-rhythm.

Her instructions done, I say, "It's my first day, Gloria. Can we *not* go zero to sixty in one lesson?"

"Girl, you're doin' better than you think. You got this."

Gloria clicks her tongue, and, as if in cahoots, Shadow obeys her, upping his pace into a bouncy trot without my say-so. It's a hard ride. I'm all over the place, barely keeping my balance. My body flops like I'm skin and meat only—no bones, no muscles. Funny how those absent muscles will hurt like hell later.

"Find the rhythm."

I breathe, straighten my back, and match his movements.

"There you go!" Gloria says. "Lovely!"

Yeah, right, I want to say, but don't. Only a well-meaning, perhaps delusional teacher would say that. *Is anyone watching?*

"Look where you want to go," Gloria says. "Focus on the path ahead, Lena, or you'll confuse him."

Confuse him? How would he know where I'm looking? Gloria later explains that horses are amazingly sensitive to their riders. Turning, even slightly in the saddle, means a turn to the horse, the same way tightening your legs against the horse's sides says go faster—an easy mistake I'm desperate not to make.

"Shadow's like a mood ring. Whatever you're feeling, he'll know it."

I rub Shadow's neck, and he gives me a side-eye. "Sorry for bringing you into my chaos, Shadow." Gloria snaps a picture and texts it to me.

Once in the car, I pull out my phone and look at the pic. Despite my Nikes and mud-splattered jeans, it doesn't make me cringe like most do. I'm smirking at Shadow, and strangely, it seems he's smirking at me.

I post it. *Second date as sassy and gassy as the first. A promising start.*

At home, I pull into the tree-lined drive and circle behind the house. Though it's barely after four, the winter sun creeps behind the barn, casting a deceivingly warm glow over the property. Sunlight cuts through the trees like a natural disco ball, making everything beautiful, even what's not. And I think, maybe, I can handle the tree.

With Mom's urn, I trek toward the barn. My parents' twenty-five acres start from the road with a driveway flanked by horse pastures, long empty. The wood fence has crumbled into knee-high weeds and thickets. The house centers the property—a large brick and cedar farmhouse with a wraparound porch that's no longer safe to walk on. Adjacent to the house and driveway, a weedy sandpit holds rusty swing sets and fallen slides. Mom once had her extensive vegetable garden near the playground, so she could tend it while watching us play. I smile, remembering digging up potatoes with my bare feet and tossing back cherry tomatoes from the vine.

I cross the circle where the driveway ends, eyeing the gambrel-style barn ahead. The second-floor loft door looks like a Cyclops' eye, watching me as I get closer. I remember running through the main floor's brick alleys, petting horses through the stall windows, and enjoying hide-and-seek with Lucas. After the horses died, the stalls became storage sheds for remnants of past lives, mine included. The second-floor loft overflows with junk well older than me. The barn, hell, the entire property, looks dissatisfied with its neglected existence.

I relate to that sentiment.

I trudge by sheds, a crumbling chicken coop, old cars, and one truckbed camper, all sitting crookedly in the tall grass. My parents paid cash for every vehicle they owned and, strangely, never parted with any, no matter what the state. The red Honda hatchback resembles a cardinal hiding in the grass. My grandfather's long, light green Lincoln that Lucas and I affectionately named the Pickle Mobile, sinks in with its flat tires. Dad's gray pickup truck and Mom's black Explorer cap off the unusual graveyard.

What will I do with all this? My anxiety stirs over the work ahead, *the rest* weighing against me—a burden meant to be shared with Lucas, if not for his generosity. With every step, I feel more inadequate for the task.

An acre-sized pond gleams in the sun's leftovers. Mom's tree borders the pond—a truly ethereal beauty amid the overgrown chaos. It's a spindly grand oak, thick-based and broadly spread. The Spanish moss is a fancy dress swaying in the breezes. A homemade swing hangs from a thick branch overhead, making me smile.

The tree's why Mom wanted this property. She called it her saddle-tree. A saddletree is an A-framed structure that holds a saddle—hardly a fitting moniker for a tree. But she said that it was the foundation, the thing that held up her dreams for this place. So, it stuck.

It *is* the loveliest tree. As a kid, I thought it magical—my own cloud-tickling beanstalk or otherworldly wardrobe. It's been a home base, a hiding place, our jungle gym, and our reading nook. I grew to love its peaceful beauty and the comfort I found there. Those feelings were a novelty then. Now that I'm older, peace and comfort are both more necessary and harder to find.

I move closer, holding tightly to Mom's urn. This was her favorite place. It's where we played while she fished, where she'd think, ride horses, sit a spell. It's "where you kids were conceived," she often kidded, to our infinite horror. When Dad died, she spread his ashes here.

I open the porcelain lid, hands shaking, palms sweating even in the cold. I freeze, unable to take the next step. I spent three years caring for her, doing things I never thought I'd do, and I can't do *this*? *This simple thing?*

"Lena, why do you make everything so hard? Try enjoying yourself, for once, please," I recall what Mom once said while fishing not ten feet from her saddletree. *"Worrying doesn't help anyone, least of all, you."*

But worrying is what I'm good at, and it doesn't feel right, leaving her here.

I plop onto the swing, making the tree branch creak from surprise. Warm tears dot my freezing cheeks. So much for *caring* being in my wheelhouse.

CHAPTER
Seven

THE LIGHTS FLICKER in the shower the next morning. I freeze, holding my breath, as if my stillness might satisfy the house gremlins wrecking their havoc on an already crumbling home. But the window-less bathroom goes black. Stumbling from the tub, I bang my shins on Mom's metal stool and the space heater, still hot. I wrap myself in a towel and head to the breaker box.

With shaking hands, I flip the switch, but nothing happens. Mom's bedroom and my only working shower no longer have electricity.

I get dressed. In loosely-bunned wet hair, I plop into a lawn chair on the patio. *What if the rest of the power goes out? Or the roof caves in? Or the last remaining toilet breaks for good?*

My financial needs stream like TV headlines: *Electrician… Dumpster… Storage unit… Bills… Food…* And I lament the two hundred I blew on horseback lessons.

A vintage Ford Bronco with a shiny Navy-blue paint job and chrome details rumbles up the drive and stops behind my tired Honda. A vaguely familiar man emerges. He's tall and lanky, and his light brown eyes glow behind his gold-rimmed glasses. A hazy memory swirls like a ghost.

"Joe Jones." He sticks out his hand.

"Lena Buckley. Did you help my dad with his pickup truck once?"

"Not once. Many times."

Ah, one of Dad's magical *guys down the road* called to fix things. He was also at their funerals. I don't know where to take the conversation, so it's a relief when he says, "You've got some old vehicles behind your property."

"Yes. My parents buried dead vehicles in the backyard like family pets. Why?"

"Mind if I look?"

"Okay. Let me get my coat."

I return, wearing a coat over my sweats and carrying what keys I could find quickly.

Joe's smile widens when he sees the graveyard up close. He goes to Dad's pickup first—a gray monstrosity with a bright red velvet interior. When Dad's truck starts on the first try, roaring lion-like with energy, we gawk in utter disbelief. After six dormant years, this thing still works while half the house's electricity doesn't—an ironic footnote to an already fucked-up day.

Joe delights in my grandfather's Pickle Mobile. I scream when a raccoon scurries from the camper, but Joe keeps his cool. He muses over the red Honda hatchback. Finally, he tries Mom's Explorer. It doesn't start. He pops the hood, fiddles with the engine, and checks the interior.

"The transmission," I say, remembering. "It broke down when I moved home. The thousands needed to fix it seemed wasteful—not that we had it—so we retired the Explorer and I became Mom's chauffeur."

He glances at the graveyard. "I'll buy all of 'em, if you're willin' to sell."

"I wouldn't feel right taking money for this junk. What would you do with them?"

"Either use 'em for parts or fix 'em up. With the right attitude, everything's got potential."

I don't see it—not with these rust heaps or anything here, really. Seems wasteful to try making miracles out of this junkyard, like he's a fairy godmother transforming pumpkins into carriages.

My hesitation encourages him to explain, "My wife's a social worker at a group home. Sometimes, they take field trips to my garage to learn about cars. When they age out of the home, they need wheels. So, if they help with the restoration, they get the keys."

My breath catches. Mom was an orphan, too, placed with a childless older couple. Both died before I knew them, but Mom loved them dearly, which was why she and Dad fostered, too. She wanted to give kids like her a chance, a safe place, a home, however temporary.

That also explained Mom's hoarding, as if losing the basic things every child should have—good, loving parents and a reliable home—she subconsciously held on to *everything*.

"Okay, Joe. If you haul them, you can have them."

"Deal." He adjusts the rearview mirror and fiddles with the center console. "Lena, check it out." He hands me a black sock with something shoved inside. "It was rammed beside the seat."

My mouth drops at the wad of cash. Money in a sock definitely fits Mom's M.O., but the discovery flusters me.

Joe's unfazed, though, as if weird shit is another country rule. "Are there fish in that pond?"

"Yes."

He exits the car and heads in that direction. I follow, stuffing the sock in my coat pocket. We stop along the water's edge, across from Mom's saddletree.

"Wow. You've got a beautiful place here. Mind if I bring my girls by for some fishin'?"

"Mom used to catch trout and catfish. You're welcome to fish anytime, until I sell the place. I'm moving to California with my brother, probably."

Joe leaves with a promise to return for the cars and fishing.

Five thousand fucking dollars. I return to my patio spot with wine this time. I'm bothered—the cash hidden inside the car could've paid for fixing it. *How'd I miss it when I cleaned it out? Why was it there in the first place?*

A memory stirs—a call from Mom before opening my bakery. I felt bothered then, too. My bank account drained like it had a gushing wound, straining my already weak-ass marriage. Sweet Dreams Bakery —*yes, I get the irony*—failed before it began, and everyone knew but me.

Still, Mom offered the usual Mom-encouragement. "Lena, I have some money to help you get started."

"That's sweet, Mom, but I don't need any help."

"No, I *want* to help. It's just that… Well, I can't find it. I withdrew it and put it down somewhere. It's driving me crazy, looking for it."

What should've sparked concern amused me at the time. The house swallows things, and Mom was always hunting for something. She never found the money—a good thing since it would've been wasted along with the thousands I put into it and never saw again.

"Why a sock, Mom?"

As the question clouds the cold air, I imagine Mom doing laundry—*ah, a rogue sock.* She searches for its mate but doesn't find it. *What to do… what to do…* Since throwing the lone sock away is clearly out of the question, she invents a job for it—sock wallet.

I laugh, tipping my wine glass toward the graying clouds. Mom's creativity yielded many interesting results over the years. Decorative door hangers from leftover felt. Pillows from old t-shirts. Toy storage from Maxwell House cans. Mom never met an object she couldn't find at least three uses for beyond its intended one. I tear up over yet another thing I took for granted.

"All these feelings over a damn sock."

Focus on the money. It solves my electricity problem. I could fix the toilet, too. Make things easier while I'm still here.

My phone announces Lucas on FaceTime. It's his preferred communication method because I'm a human emoji board—very Audrey Hepburn meets Reese Witherspoon, he explained once—making me super-easy to read.

After chit-chat, I tell him about Jack and Alice's offer.

"Well, that'll pay for your move and cushion your bank account. Maybe you could get a new car, one that's more environmentally friendly."

"I haven't said yes yet. This house is an enormous project, Lucas. There's so much to do." I tell him about the bakery-sock money and my plans for it.

"No, Lena. Don't do that. Don't sink any money into that house. Money spent on repairs will be wasted when you sell. Take Alice up on her offers. The dumpster and storage unit make sense. Repairs don't."

"Lucas, I *need* light in the shower."

"Use a lantern. You can make do."

I wince. *Make do?*

"Lena, the smarter you are with your money, the more you'll have for your awesome new life. That's what you want, right?"

"Yes." I force a weak smile at his sympathetic face.

"Don't treat the house like the bakery. It'll never give back what you put into it."

"Okay, okay." I move the phone against my leg to hide my exasperation. Maybe Lucas makes a good point, but did he need the bakery to do it? Now a fan of day drinking, I refill my glass while he over-explains his points.

Finally, he sighs when I don't say much. "Love the horse pics, Lena. I'm glad you're doing something *just for you*. There's an exceptional equestrian center here, and Luna's interested, too. You could do it together!"

I sigh, imagining myself as Luna's activity-chauffeur—probably in my new Prius—and horseback riding becoming a chore I do for my generous hosts. Then, I regret my bad attitude. *Of course*, I'd love riding with Luna.

"That'd be terrific, Lucas."

"All the ritzy parents send their kids to train there, so it must be top-notch. I'll look into it. I'm so freaking excited about you moving here."

"Me, too." A new car and top-of-the-line equestrian lessons—my expected windfall drains away in one measly conversation that began with him telling me to be smart with my money.

Off the phone and in the house, I stoke the fire and search the fridge for something to eat. The stacked casserole dishes fill the shelves. I line the dishes on the counter and dump, scrub, and rinse until they're pristine.

Then, I set up a table on the covered back porch and lay out the dishes. A thank you sign taped to the table completes the picture I post: *I have your casserole dishes.*

Though ransom-like, it works. Getting Mrs. Moore and her church-lady brigade off my back *definitely* makes one thing better for me.

Then, I take Lucas's advice. I swallow my diva-ness and call Alice, promising to consider their offer once I have a handle on the work ahead. After twenty minutes and dozens of *bless your hearts*, she promises to arrange the dumpster and storage container. She also commits her boys, starting tomorrow.

At the table, I eye her note. Alice's handwriting is a frenzied mess, not the orderly script I'd expect from someone so controlled. The numbers are discernible, but after ten minutes of puzzling it out, I only get an 'e' and a 'w' out of the name—not enough to call. I enter him into my phone as *Gun Guy*, and then resort to texting. I explain my situation, bookended with…

Hello, my name is Lena Buckley. Alice Harvey gave me your number…

Would you be willing to help?

Moments later, he responds.

Thursday. 5:00. Address?

I type it in with my thanks, grateful it's not a prolonged conversation.

I give up trying to read Alice's nephew's email, and Google The Bean Machine in Asheville. I don't expect much. Alice Harvey's spent the last twenty years ironing her husband's overalls and obsessing over casserole dishes, so maybe she's not the best resource for career advice.

But The Bean Machine is an eclectic-chic city café straight from my most optimistic restaurant dreams. Rustic gourmet dishes with Southern flair fill the menu, accompanied by a note from the chef: *The menu changes with the availability of fresh foods, the seasons, and Jason's often-eccentric whims.* His whims don't bother his customers, based on the glowing reviews. The Bean Machine is an Asheville favorite.

Jason Ford looks a smidge older than me, tattooed, bearded, with a dashing, playful smile. He holds his Hangover Cure—a towering Angus burger with a poached egg, Hollandaise sauce, thick-cut apple bacon, and an applewood and onion jam.

I beef up my resumé, describing my best bakes: Fruity Pebble cupcakes, hot fudge cake brownies, French toast donuts with a candied bacon crumble, my Cookie Monster mini-bundts. I include pictures— my funny shag cake for an eighties party and the *Starry Night* cake for the college's art show. Suddenly, I long for baking in a way that I haven't since closing the bakery. I want to be covered in flour, my arms sore from kneading, and my senses tingling from the gorgeous kitchen smells.

But *that* kitchen sours my excitement. With the wonky oven door and the unpredictable coil burners, I doubt I'd find any joy in attempting something delicious in *that* kitchen.

I hit send on my email to Jason Ford, and think of my KitchenAid mixer, Breville toaster oven, and supplies. *Where are my things? And what state are they in?* Like everything else, dust-clogged crevices and rusty mechanisms may be all that remain of my treasured tools.

Within hours, Jason emails back. *Aunt Alice told me to expect your email, but despite that, I'm excited to meet you.*

I laugh while a vaguely familiar rush invigorates me. Nervousness mixes with surprised relief that putting myself out there earns a positive result. *This could be something truly great for me.* Such promise hasn't tickled me since I first flicked on the neon OPEN sign at Sweet Dreams Bakery… before that, my wedding day.

Okay, those ended badly, but maybe this won't. I refocus on his email.

Since Asheville is over five hours away, he offers to pay my expenses for a working interview. *Baking in a real kitchen. An all-expense paid night away from mice and power outages.* Even my anxiety bitches struggle to find fault in that. Besides, it's smart to have a backup plan, I tell myself whenever Lucas pops to mind.

With plans set, there's no sense in worrying over it. But I will anyway—anxiety is notorious for ignoring reason. *Need a distraction.*

I stare at Mom's china hutch—a large but beautiful piece with an unfortunate mustard-cherry finish—and think of Joe's attitude about potential. What if I sanded it and stained it a different color? It'd be perfect for displaying Mom's china in my new home—wherever that might be.

Energized by my accomplishments, I go out.

At Lowe's, I buy a blue stain that reminds me of the ocean, sandpaper, and paintbrushes, a large Coleman lantern for the bathroom, and a pack of ultrasonic plug-ins that promise to repel mice. *Why didn't I know about these sooner?* I stock up on extra cleaning supplies and plastic bins.

At Sunny's, I hungrily tour the baking aisle, taking my sweet time, and splurge on baking essentials. My shriveled creativity rehydrates, plumping back to life with the nourishment of new ideas and this strange sensation. Hope. My cart fills with my excitement.

The evening passes with wine and making do in Mom's old kitchen.

CHAPTER
Eight

SHADOW DOESN'T ENJOY most people, but he's okay with me. He's like the neighborhood grump on his front porch, yelling at kids and dogs to keep off his lawn. But his bad attitude hides an inner charm. I don't hold it against him. We understand each other.

With my peppermint bribes, I wrangle Shadow—*all by myself*. Like the Asheville interview, it's acceptance I don't expect. I run my fingers along his velvety jowls, and he lets me nuzzle his long face with mine. The warm closeness invigorates me. *Things will get better.* Maybe that'll keep proving true.

But soon, he bucks his head and putters his lips, telling me that's enough.

"I'll take whatever love you give me, Shadow." I laugh, tickling his chin.

I lead him from the paddock. We shimmy passed a little girl standing with her mom. "That one's not pretty enough to ride. I want a pretty horse, Mom."

Shadow farts. The girl scoffs. And for that, Shadow earns an extra peppermint. A patchy-gray, heavy-set, half-tailed Appaloosa, maybe Shadow isn't traditionally good-looking, but who the hell decides those standards, anyway? Rich equestrians? *American Girl*? *Disney*? Shadow is Shadow—*that* makes him beautiful.

I don't freak out when Gloria orders the sitting trot or teaches me a posting trot. I listen, breathe, and focus on our movements. It's meditative riding without fear getting in the way. It's being in my head in a good way.

Still, there are distractions.

A teenager expertly trots a blonde horse called Diesel before attempting crossbar jumps. Diesel stops short each time, either startled by the obstruction or stubbornly refusing the extra work.

On the road nearby, cyclists stream by the fence line, riling up the field horses. They break into frenzied gallops as if joining the race. Their activity reflects in the other paddocks, as horses copy the excited behavior—a kind of mass hysteria, spreading from one horse to the next.

Mid-arena, Gloria takes it all in. "The horses are in full form today, ladies."

Uninterested, the teenager retries the cross rails, only for Diesel to jerk in refusal.

The activity steals my focus, pricking my nerves over what'll happen next. Anxiety has taught me that chaos is often contagious. I slow Shadow to a walk, rubbing his neck.

"Everything's okay, Shadow," I say for both our sakes.

The galloping field horses buck, neigh, and bolt toward the electric fence. The teen rounds the perimeter, passing us as she struggles with Diesel. Across the lane, the hyper horses converge on their fence as we near it. I hold my breath—*will they stop?*

Diesel bucks forward. The teenager sails over his head, flips mid-air, and lands on her backside.

Holy shit! Reins tugged to a stop, I swing my leg over and slide off. Everyone rushes to the fallen teen, but closest, I reach her first.

"Are you okay?" I glance her over for askew limbs, gushing blood, and protruding bones, but she's intact.

"I think so." She seems surprised, too.

Gloria grabs Diesel's reins as he stomps around the fence line. "Mya, what hurts?"

Her bottom lip quivers as she verges on tears. "I don't know… Nothing, really." She rubs her backside as another instructor checks her limbs and helmet.

"Take deep breaths," I say, like Mom used to tell me whenever my panic threatened. "Slow and steady." Mya grabs my arm to help her out of the dirt. I brace her as she tests for injuries. Her shoulders relax.

"You've had the wind knocked out of you, girl," Gloria says.

"Yeah, I'm okay."

A younger student laughs. "How many times have you been thrown off a horse now, Mya?"

"Eight. Such a scaredy-cat, Diesel." Diesel putters and nips at her hands.

Gloria laughs. "If I had a dollar for every time a horse freaked out 'round here, I'd be richer than Midas."

The small group launches into horse freak-out stories. Hearing about broken bones and airborne riders should dent my riding confidence, but it comforts me to learn that horses panic, too. Most of their stories start with a horse getting spooked. Anxiety isn't a human exclusive—it's universal, natural even. And another lovely thing connecting me to Shadow.

Stories exhausted, and Mya back to normal, Gloria hands her the reins. "You know what to do."

With the smiles, pats, and *you've-got-this* sentiments offered, Mya stands up straighter, beaming with confidence.

My list of things I've missed the last few years and need to catch up on expands again. Connecting with Shadow's one thing—bonding with other humans, well, that's another, and everyone needs a cheering section.

Moments after Mya's acrobatic fall from Diesel, she gets back on. No stewing in defeat. No worrying over it happening again. Just acceptance —eight falls and counting. She's even proud, like each one earned her a mental trophy. I wish all recoveries could be so beautiful and easygoing.

Gloria and I untack slowly. She amuses me with her most recent dating app adventures while I gawk and wonder why she even bothers.

"Bad dates are like falling off your horse," Gloria says, shrugging. "It happens, but you learn and try again. Plus, they give you good stories to tell."

"I'd rather stay comfortably atop my horse."

"Your high horse, you mean?" She laughs.

A loud whinny catches our attention. At a hitching post, two saddled horses wait. A cream-colored horse paws at the ground and nips at her tight tethers, frustrated that she can't reach the grass. The copper horse beside her bites a large clump and holds it out to her. She takes the grass, pressing her lips to his like kissing.

Gloria slaps my arm. "Ha! See, Lena? Romance ain't dead, after all!"

I scoff slightly, rolling my eyes at her, though I'm charmed by the sweet gesture. I record it. But bypassing romance talk, I post the clip with: *Sometimes we all need a little help.*

"Sometimes, we all need a little help, Lena." The words echo from my first appointment with my therapist. At fifteen, *this* Nervous Nellie'd finally raised concerns. My constant upset stomach, headaches, depression, and anger forced Mom to do something no Buckley had ever done —*get professional help.*

And it did help. I learned about triggers, self-talk, and how to keep my anxiety bitches in check through relaxation techniques like deep breathing and redirection. More importantly, my therapist showed me I was more than my anxiety, but an intelligent, able person, mature enough to accept help.

At home, I barely have time to trade my mud-covered Nikes for my rubber boots before company arrives.

Will and Max Harvey look nothing like serial killers. I'm strangely surprised to see two average-looking seventeen-year-olds drive up on ATVs wearing t-shirts, jeans, boots, work gloves, and easy smiles. They sweetly call me *Miss Lena* and don't seem bothered when I ask for their help clearing out the covered three-car carport—a space that's never, in my memory, held a car. With two ports free in no time, we move Mom's hutch there for refinishing.

Then, I take the boys to the barn. Cobwebs dangle from the beamed ceiling like ghostly party streamers. Bug carcasses and mouse droppings litter the floor, while dirt and dust hide the brick walkway underneath.

My apologies for the state of things are thwarted when Will or Max —I can't tell the twins apart yet—says, "Wow, this place is great." He points to a door tucked between stalls and blocked by a rusty feeding trough. "What's this?"

"Creepy bathroom. No one's been in there in years."

He climbs the stairs beside the closed door and points to another at the top. "Where does this go?"

"Um, a loft." I want to warn him about the bats I'd seen in the rafters as a kid, but he's already exploring.

His brother peers curiously into the horse stalls. "Are those old comic books?"

"There's a little of everything in here."

He side-smiles. "Do we get to go through all this stuff?"

I nod, wondering if Will and Max are on psychedelic drugs. My gut says no, while their exuberance over a junk-filled barn screams a definite maybe.

"Sweet," he mutters, sorting through comics.

His brother races downstairs. "Will, it's huge, full of stuff. I saw an old Nintendo and an Atari." I make a mental note, differentiating Will by his slightly fuller face.

"Awesome. Check these out." Will holds up comics.

As they dive into boxes, I realize I *need* them. I *need* their help. I *need* help in general, just like I did when I was that pissed-off teenager in a therapist's waiting room. Like with Mya's epic fall, help and encouragement make for a much quicker recovery.

Though relying on others is sandpaper against my independent tendencies, I'm relieved. Like when Mrs. Moore helped with Mom… or the day I drove my packed Pilot home expecting lectures and disappointment, only for Mom to hold out her arms and say, *"Get over here, girl."*

Will holds up comic books. "Can we borrow some?"

"Take whatever you'd like."

"Sweet." Will smiles. "Where do you want to start, Miss Lena?"

"With my kitchen supplies. They're here, somewhere."

They fan out into stalls, opening boxes. I do the same, moving things aside to dig deeper.

"Does your tractor work? We could hook this trailer up to move stuff easier," Will says.

I follow his voice to the rusty red wagon Dad used to hitch behind the lawnmower. He used it to tote wood, downed branches, and hay, but mostly he loved taking spins with Lucas and me as cargo. I remember giggling incessantly over the bumpy terrain.

"Yes, great idea."

Will races off to get the tractor while Max and I continue searching. He finds my light blue KitchenAid mixer and attachments. I see another box of mixing bowls, spatulas, sifters, rolling pins, and measuring spoons and cups. My Breville countertop oven and recipe files matriculate next.

Sifting through my old things, a familiar ache forms. Failing was such a damn surprise. When you put everything you are into something that means the world to you, you expect it to work. *How could it not?* Marriage. Business. Mom.

"Failure's always an option, Lena, no matter what people say. It's what you do with failure that matters," Mom said.

I didn't do anything with my failures. Instead, I retreated and crawled under this enormous, dust-filled, cluttered, dirty rock. *Nothing ever works out for you.* The words circle like ghosts. They highlight my failures, like important notes in schoolbooks I need to remember for my mental essay on how history repeats itself.

Maybe not this time.

Will arrives with the tractor. He attaches the rusty trailer, and we load the boxes.

"Check it out." Max holds up tools from a box. "There's a tarp, sander, paintbrushes, sandpaper—everything you need to refinish that hutch."

Bonus, I think, as we load the trailer. Max drives to the carport. We find folding tables and set up a workstation for my hutch project. After sodas and cupcakes from last night's baking, I send the boys home, careful not to work them too hard on the first day.

I stare at Mom's hutch in the carport before taking a picture. I post it: *Time for a makeover.*

The sander rattles and hums, and my mind drifts. I plan to stay up late, fine-tuning recipes and practicing for my Asheville trip. It's a good feeling to be excited about something.

And damn, it's time for me to get back on the horse.

Mid-daydreaming, a gentle but authoritative tap on my shoulder conjures a guttural scream. The sander drops, scuttling to a dead stop at my rubber boots before I look up. My breath catches, and I choke out an awkward, "Ah, it's you."

CHAPTER
Nine

"*YOU'RE* ALICE'S GUN GUY?"

If he recognizes me, Ben Wright doesn't show it. He's just as imposing out of uniform—tall, a solid 6'2", with broad, packhorse shoulders. He makes me think of football players, brick walls, mountains—he's a human *Iron Giant*.

A gentle giant, *I think*, remembering his note. *Things will get better.*

I stand up straighter. At a respectable 5'8", I'm no slouch, either. "Sorry, I, um, couldn't read Alice's handwriting enough to figure out your name. Not that I would've made the connection." I scoff, flushed with sudden nervousness. "I, um, wasn't myself that day… not sure I'm myself now, either. But it's a weird coincidence, right?"

His face reveals nothing.

My awkward laugh fills the silence. "Ah, you don't remember me—course not. You must pull over scores of people in Wilmington." Though the truth, it disappoints me. *Am I really so unmemorable? Are frazzled women driving like maniacs to nowhere in particular an everyday thing for him?* I dust my hand on my jeans and stick it out. "I'm Lena Buckley."

"I remember you, Ms. Buckley." Glancing at my rubber boots seems like confirmation, but he's not amused. Not with me or the coincidence. He shakes my hand and returns his to his hips before scrutinizing his surroundings.

I tuck my fidgeting hands behind my back. "Um, thanks for sparing me the tickets. That meant a lot to me… and the note."

"It's no trouble, ma'am."

"I updated my tags." I motion to the Pilot with its fresh stickers.

His stone-like disposition gives way, but only for a nod when he sees my license plate. "You need my assistance?"

My smile deflates slightly. "Um, yes, thanks—my parents' arsenal. I don't want them, but I can't throw them away or sell them to strangers. I don't want them ending up in the wrong hands. I assume you don't belong to a doomsday cult, live in a compound, or stockpile weapons for nefarious purposes?" A coy smirk travels my lips as I maintain eye contact, but he's stoic.

"No, ma'am."

"What would you do with my guns?"

"Disarm them. Destroy anything unusable. Sell or donate to the department or reputable citizens, according to your wishes, ma'am." He cocks his head. "Unless you'd prefer training."

"You'd teach me how to shoot? Guns make me uncomfortable. So, no, thanks."

"Proper training might alleviate your discomfort. Having a firearm and knowing how to use it might make you feel safer, living in the country alone."

My left eyebrow creeps up, weirdly offended that he thinks I need a gun to defend myself. I've outwitted the mice, no guns necessary, *thank you very much*. And wait, how does he *know* I'm alone?

"I'm moving soon, so no safety course needed. I just want them gone. But thanks for helping me out."

"At your service, ma'am."

Mom's winking face pops into my head as if she's hovering over his shoulder. *He's at your service, Lena. You should put that to the test.* An exasperated chuckle ekes out, but a quick wave moves us toward the house and covers my silly outburst. *I hope.*

Silently, he follows me to the sliding glass door, and we move inside the dark cave. I motion to the shotgun still lying open on the dining table from where Jack left it.

"Vintage model. No safety." He examines it, sniffing the air. "It's been fired recently."

"I knocked it over, and it went off." I motion to the empty shelf across the room and brace myself for a safety lecture.

Only, he says nothing.

He returns the gun to the table, still open. "Can this be the collection point?"

"Sure."

Turning toward me, his brow creases at something over my shoulder. *Please, not another mouse.* But it's his warning ticket note, propped on Mom's urn. *What's worse? Rodents or my weird shrine?*

"It's a nice reminder, that's all." I put on a cool-front and point to another shotgun leaning against the dark wood paneling.

He disarms it and lines it up with the other. I open the cabinet behind his head, where he retrieves Dad's revolver.

This silent process continues in the living room, where he disarms a .22 caliber pistol from a junk drawer and another shotgun by the exterior door in the kitchen. In the formal living room, he sees my makeshift bedroom. I'm embarrassed by the bra draped over the wingback chair and the dirty clothes on the floor—he's all tucked and tidy—but he says nothing, not even with his expressions.

In Mom's room, a small handgun sits by perfume on her vanity. He deals with that while I grab the ammunition boxes from her desk. We systematically transport the items to the kitchen table, laying them out neatly in rows like we're creating a display.

I pass him a curious glance. "You don't talk much, do you?"

"No, ma'am." His eyes crimp slightly. "Should I?"

"You be you, Ben."

But me being me, the silence becomes too much back in Mom's room. I wonder what he's thinking—all these weapons decorating the house like we're a family of paranoid doomsdayers. Moving Mom's wheelchair and walker aside, I say, "Growing up, Mom and Dad *never* kept them like this. They were safely out of reach. But when they didn't have kids at home anymore, they kept them close at hand for protection, I guess. Please, don't think us strange."

His eyebrows scrunch. "No, ma'am."

"They taught my brother and me early on about gun safety. We even learned to shoot, but Lucas and I didn't like it—not like they did. It's different for us, you know? Growing up with news of mass shootings. Anyway, it's been so long since I've even held one that I feel skittish about it now. My parents weren't hunters… just protectors, if that makes sense. I only ever saw them shoot snakes and a fox at the henhouse once. And they always missed."

I slide Mom's case out from under her bed.

Ben opens it. "A pearl-handled Beretta nine-millimeter." He sounds slightly impressed.

"A Christmas present from Dad. Mom enjoyed shooting... and collecting things. I never understood the fascination, but she'd take guns over diamonds any day. For her, it was strangely romantic."

He nods like he understands.

I run my finger along the smooth, cold handle, missing Mom and feeling sentimental about her things. "Maybe I should keep this one."

"If you do..." he says softly, "please allow me to teach you how to use it properly. It will make you more comfortable. I promise your safety."

I don't doubt it. He seems like a check-everything-twice type. Still, I hesitate. Hearing *distant* gunshots makes me cringe, let alone allowing it in my backyard. But he's a kind stranger doing me a great favor, and he's right. If I have a gun, I should know how to use it and feel comfortable with it. "Okay."

We detour to his blue Jeep that looks like a shiny, new toy fresh from the packaging—something you want to play with—and my Pilot seems especially tired sitting beside it.

He unlocks a metal trunk in the back, digging out goggles and noise-canceling earmuffs. "For safety," he says.

The goggles are a bit high-school-science-lab, but I smile at the earmuffs, grateful I won't have to cover my ears like a toddler. I set the glasses on my head and the earmuffs around my neck. "Perfect. Thanks."

A tiny smirk escapes as he nods. He grabs a second set, setting everything on the open back end.

"Do you always carry protective gear in your Jeep?"

"You said weapons. I came prepared."

He leaves me for the driver's side, where he opens the door, fiddles around, and sets something in the seat—I don't pay much attention. A moment later, he grabs the case and protective gear, and we start walking.

I lead him behind the barn, where the vehicle graveyard protrudes from the tall grass, and the pond glitters in the low February sun. Ben stops to examine a decrepit piece of plywood leaning against the barn's backside.

"Can this be a target?"

I nod. He totes it to the fence line. Rigging the board against crumbling posts, he checks the surroundings. Rejoining me, he puts on the goggles and the earmuffs, though they're off-kilter on one ear to still hear me. I do the same while he unpacks the gun, loads a clip, checks the safety and the site.

Before aiming, he makes eye contact. Maybe it's the sunlight or the goggles, but his striking green eyes hold my attention. They're a pale, emerald color, making him seem thoughtful, especially the way he zones in on me while asking, "Sure you're okay with this?"

My arms fold, feeling suddenly cold. "Mom would like someone enjoying her gun. I'm fine. Really."

He nods to my earmuffs, nudging his in place with his shoulder. I put them on properly. Then, he aims and shoots in one fluid, sudden movement. My shoulders jump, but I'm glad he does it quickly. I step back, separating from the noise, though it's muffled.

He hits the target six times before lowering the weapon and nudging his earmuffs away. "Want a turn?"

I scoff, pulling the earmuffs to my neck. "You're like John Wick's larger, more intimidating brother. Guns were made for guys like you, but shooting's not for me."

"Your mom liked it. Maybe you will, too."

I groan, thinking of Shadow. "Fine."

He slides the gun into my hand and adjusts my fingers, and my arms, barely touching me. He's very matter-of-fact about it, like someone handing over change. Still, he rouses inner tingles I presumed long dead. That's what happens to unstimulated nerve endings, right? They shrivel and die like unwatered weeds in the hot sun. Apparently not, I decide, when a light touch to my arm inspires a warm tickling parade up my spine—*holy hell*—and I wonder where his hand might go next.

My waist! I nearly choke on a stifled gasp at the hard press of his fingers into my side. "Boots apart. Loose hips. Try to relax."

No chance of that now. His hand leaves my side in less than a second, but I still feel it there—a ghost hand—and it sends my mind aflutter with hazy memories of how sexy-touching felt and how impossibly far off having that again is. And maybe not worth the trouble.

With as few words as possible, he explains the site and how to stand for the best accuracy and comfort.

Anxiety rising over attempting this new, loud, and potentially deadly thing, I ask, "Will it push me back?"

"Say again." He hones in on me as I repeat myself, making me more nervous.

"Expect a slight recoil. Nothing you can't handle."

Knees slightly bent but back straight, I breathe deeply. With earmuffs and goggles in place, I pull the trigger. The force jerks me like an electric current.

The bullet chips the upper corner—*I hit it!* I laugh, shocked that something went the way I wanted it to, *mostly*. Amazed I shot the damn thing at all.

"Good," Ben says.

Two more shots later, my confidence dips. One hits the ground in a dirt explosion, while the other vanishes silently into the woods. Weapon and earmuffs lowered, I say, "It's not as easy as it looks on TV. Mom would be thrilled, though."

Ben slips the weapon from my hand, holding it at his side as he faces me, earmuffs around his neck. "What happened to her?"

I'm surprised he asks me anything, let alone *that* question. "You're the first person to ask me that. Mom had health problems for years, so I think people assumed it was her heart or a stroke in the end."

"What was it?"

"Sepsis." I choke out. Such an ugly fucking word, it hurts sharing it. "Stupid, right? Meds meant to ease her pain and give her a better life chiseled away at her immune system until nothing was left. She spent last year in and out of the hospital battling random infections—things you and I would pop a few antibiotics for—until she couldn't fight anymore."

Ben's green eyes crinkle under the goggles as he stares. I mean, *really* stares. Hanging on my every word takes on a new meaning because *that's* what he's doing—watching my eyes, then lips, and back again. Do they teach that in police school—staring-intimidation tactics to get subjects to talk? It works—the floodgates open, and I can't shut up.

"You expect your parents to die first. You hope for something peaceful, natural, even beautiful, somehow. It was *nothing* like that. For months, caring for her felt like chemical Russian roulette. Drugs kept her alive and did her in—a shitty irony. I couldn't get her better, and, worse, I couldn't take care of her anymore either. She wanted to die here, at home. Instead, she died after five days in the hospital, unconscious and strapped to the bed because she kept ripping out her IV in her sleep. It was slow fucking torture. Nothing felt right about it."

"It's not your fault." My eyes meet Ben's again.

There's a soft moment in the empty space between us that edges on relief, hearing those words, like he's jiggling the lock on the door I'm trapped behind. But my anxiety bitches hate outside interference. *Then, whose fault is it?*

My weird purge makes me roll my eyes and flick my hands at my wrists. "Sorry. That was way more information than you wanted."

"I asked. You answered," he says after a long pause. "How do you feel now?"

"Better," I blurt, surprised, my shoulders sinking with the word.

"Good," he says. "Comfort level with the Beretta?"

"Um, that's better, too."

"Let's practice more, if you're ready."

A few silent turns and two emptied clips later, we return to his Jeep, where he tosses the protective gear into the lockbox and goes to the driver's side door again. He fiddles with his ears, making me curious.

Toting the arsenal to his Jeep's lockbox, I see small, gray devices behind his ears, each connecting to a clear wire that vanishes inside his ear canal—hearing aids. Not only does this surprise me—*why would a thirty-something need hearing aids?*—but I feel like an asshole. He must've removed them for the earmuffs. He wasn't being weirdly intense, only focusing on me to understand what I said.

My anxiety bitches won't let anything go, either. *What's wrong with me—baring my soul? Confessing my failures with Mom? And thinking him creepy for listening?* I worry I've said or done something offensive without realizing, as if I go around flagrantly insulting the hearing impaired. That's not me, *at all*, but my anxiety takes over, and there's little I can do to stop it.

With my parents' arsenal, minus the Beretta, safely locked in the metal storage container in his Jeep and *that* house blissfully safer, I should relax. Standing by the kitchen table, I fidget. And he watches me —this guy has zero qualms about eye contact or silence, which is either beautifully confident or plain awkward. I should say something, but all that comes to mind is... *thanks for touching me without cringing and making me remember I have working lady parts.* I clamp my lips shut and tuck my hands behind me.

"Can I have one of those?" He points to the covered cake plate with last night's cupcakes.

"God, yes. Great idea." I try not to look too excited or relieved as I dash around the kitchen. I offer coffee, but he requests milk. He sits at the table where I bring him a vintage *Smurfs* glass of milk and a Blue Willow plate featuring my orange and ginger cake with whipped cream and candied orange rinds.

Not one for garnish, he picks off the rinds. He finishes the cupcake in two bites, cheeks full and crumbs littering the table. He nods before pointing to the cake plate a second time. I serve him two more—my Cinnamon Toast Crunch swirl and my experimental cherry chocolate merlot—I may have been a little tipsy by then.

He says nothing but doesn't need to. He eats like a caveman—happy for every enormous bite. Watching him fills me with a long-forgotten pleasure. And confidence, given my upcoming meeting with Jason Ford. He finishes them, even the merlot-basil one, and sucks the crumbs off his fingers as he glances at the cake plate again. He considers asking for the last one but hesitates. Locking eyes, I grin with delightful satisfaction, and for an easy second, he smiles back.

CHAPTER

Ten

THE LANTERN CREATES strange shadows across Mom's galley bathroom. The hot water meets the cold air making a ghostly fog, damn eerie, and shaving my chill-bump-covered legs forces cursing.

Coffee'll help. After tending my injuries, I dress—jeans, light sweater, rubber boots—and go to the kitchen.

A low rumbling grabs my attention—my dumpster delivery. An hour later, the storage pod arrives. Alice Harvey might look like a serial killer, but she gets shit done like a mafia boss. Though requiring the bulk of Mom's sock money, the storage container and dumpster are essential for progress.

Only they don't inspire the progress I expect. I'm strangely bothered by how the gleaming metal boxes obstruct the field views and hide the grass. The idea of filling them makes me anxious—no surprise. So, they loom impatiently, waiting for action that doesn't happen.

So, I work on my hutch instead. I set up an old radio and get into a good rhythm with the music. When Will and Max show up, the first coat is nearly finished. The blue hue soaks into the wood, thirsty for more.

"Looks good, Miss Lena," Will says as Max returns comics to the KEEP table.

"Thanks, I think so, too."

We continue sorting boxes from the barn. Despite the satisfying thuds of dumpster-tossing, Will and Max aren't quick to trash anything.

They test each appliance, toy, and tool, salvaging anything useful. They create sections for wood, screws, nails, and other reusable items in the carport.

I enjoy the boys. They play and bicker like Lucas and me when we were kids. A tractor dispute prompts a full-blown rusty-nail battle across the yard. They hang a dartboard in the carport and "test" each dart multiple times. They're a happy diversion from the tedious work.

Joe Jones arrives with a flatbed truck and two helpers. I hand over keys and documents while an aching pit forms in my stomach. They're just cars—metal, plastic, and rubber. And Joe'll put them to better use than being oversized lawn decorations. But when Joe takes the light green Lincoln, bothersome tears speck my eyes—no more Pickle Mobile. While reason reminds me that the dumpy thing hasn't run in twenty years, it's damn sad seeing it go.

Dot rolls up in the MINI Cooper without Mrs. Moore.

Lighting a cigarette, she calls to me. "Aw, the groundhog has finally emerged from the den. You don't look like shit today."

I wince. "Where's Mrs. Moore?"

"Eh, the ol' gal sent me instead. Cataracts are acting up. She's got a little headache. No biggie."

"And you're here because…?"

She shoves the cigarette against her lips and ducks into the car to retrieve a stack of mail. "You forgot your mail again, as Aunt Barb suspected."

Dot joins me in the carport, where I introduce Will and Max. "I know the Harvey boys. We play football after church sometimes."

She shoves the mail pile at me. On her arm, she's written a small to-do list in ink. *Check mail. Ask how she's doing. Get leftover casserole dishes. Be nice.*

My shoulders slump. *Mrs. Moore delegated me to Dot?*

"How 'bout a round of darts, boys?" Dot flicks her cigarette into the dirt drive.

The mail spills on the table. A puffy yellow package catches my attention. I grab it, ripping it open. Seed packets spill out. Broccoli. Swiss Chard. Lettuces. Peas. Radishes. Arugula. Cauliflower.

I unfold the paperwork. A small booklet is titled *A Guide to Spring Gardening.*

A letter explains:

Thank you for your subscription to The North Carolina Gardening Club. Enclosed, you'll find seeds ideal for cool-weather gardening. These hearty species thrive in the changeable temperatures, so plant in early March. In April, you will receive your summer garden seeds, followed by your fall garden in August...

I don't finish the letter but find a folded receipt with a gift message.

My Sweetest Lena,

Let's get the garden going. I'll supervise while you do all the work. Ha! It'll be fun, like the old days. Everything you need is right here. Let's do whatever it takes to make this a happy place for you again.

Love,

Mom

A crying outburst explodes from me, the likes of which are rarely, *if ever,* seen in a grown woman. *Sunny's and now this?*

I eye the date on the receipt. She signed up for the garden club days before my birthday and her last hospital trip. A deep breath escapes between sobs.

The boys gawk blankly like I've shorted out their circuit boards.

Dot cusses and gets on her phone. "Aunt Barb, we have a problem."

"There's no problem." My whiny assurance barely sounds coherent through my bawling. I lean against the table, letting the packets and papers topple. Will races over, gathering what falls.

"Boys, Aunt Barb says to take her inside, make her some coffee," Dot says.

"No, I'm fine. Please, just leave me alone."

Dot's head cocks in a challenge. "Aunt Barb says that if you don't let us help, she'll call her church ladies for a full-on prayer circle."

A dozen prim and proper versions of Alice Harvey checking Mom's china labels and running white-gloved fingers over dusty surfaces—no thanks. "Fine, but wine'd be better."

"Now, you're talking."

Once on the couch, Dot equips me with tissues and a blanket while checking her phone. *Is Mrs. Moore feeding her instructions?* After checking the wood stove, Dot barks for the boys to bring in wood.

They get the flames roaring and stack enough wood on the hearth for the entire night. With thanks, I tell them to take the Nintendo and Atari home for testing, which sends them racing to the barn and skidding away on their ATVs.

Dot fiddles with the remote controls.

"You don't have to stay. I'm really fine now."

"You're many things, Lena, babe, but fine? Hmm." She finds the news and, satisfied, sets the remotes near me. "I don't like it, either, but I'm under orders. Find a way to deal, huh?"

The sooner I stop crying, the sooner she'll leave. But headlines aren't distracting me from imagining Mom, giddy about my future gift and all her beautiful hopes for me. Would she have snuck a birthday card from Sunny's and scribbled a cryptic message about it arriving late but exactly when I need it? I would've guessed a mail-order groom, and, eyes wide, she would've said, "Is that possible?"

Dot hands me chardonnay in the poop emoji mug. *Touché, Dot.*

Then, she shuffles back and forth on her boots as the TV catches her attention.

Political firestorms in the wake of President Trump's impeachment acquittal.

Harvey Weinstein's rape trial.

An international pandemic called COVID-19.

"Let me know when you need a refill, huh?"

Dot retreats to the kitchen, where she fiddles with my leaky faucet. I don't care—anything's fine as long as we aren't talking. Tomorrow, I'll call Mrs. Moore and insist that I don't need to be checked on, especially not by Dot. She exits the sliding glass door and returns with a toolbox. I gulp my wine.

But with the fire blazing, the blanket curled around me, and emotional exhaustion setting in, I relax, *eventually*. Her kitchen noises comfort me strangely. The place feels better with people (even Dot) in it, highlighting what I've known for a while. I'm fucking lonely. Like *insanely* lonely. Like straight-jacket-in-a-padded-room lonely. Even *with* Mom, I was lonely—too busy and overwhelmed to bother connecting.

Caregiving is a lonely endeavor, anyway—a shitty irony since you're with someone all the time. Taking responsibility for another human means shoving your needs aside and, often, forgetting yourself completely. That's what I did—*I couldn't help it.* Friends, lovers, *Netflix*, hell, normal conversation—I went without what could've made my life better because I didn't have the time or energy.

Dot steps into the living room, wiping her hands on a dishtowel. She nods toward the news report on COVID. "Aunt Barb thinks we'll be forced into quarantine."

"Wait, what?" Lonely *and* ill-informed.

"Lockdown's already happening in other countries to prevent the spread. I expect it'll be like swine flu and Mad Cow's disease. No big deal. But Aunt Barb talks about the grieving families and hospitals overrun with very sick people—she's worried, damn near paranoid. Between you and me, that's the real reason she wants to stay home more."

Staying home more? The prospect pushes me for a refill.

Eventually, Dot leaves, taking the leftover casserole dishes to distribute at church. I watch her go through the window over the kitchen sink. Once she's out of sight, I try the faucet.

"That bitch fixed my leak," I breathe out, half-smiling.

Joe returns in his Bronco. Two girls spill out of the backseat, carrying tackle boxes and fishing rods. They wave before racing to the pond. With a Tupperware container of last night's baking, I join them.

"Jade and Josie, y'all say hello to Miss Lena Buckley," Joe says. Jade's the oldest, taller by a foot, and her long, teal box braids sway when she turns to greet me. Josie's tight curls frame her round face like a halo, and her honey-colored eyes gleam behind gold frames, just like her father's. She looks sheepish, but meets my eyes for a moment before they both recite a *hello, Miss Lena Buckley*, like I'm a schoolteacher. I reveal the desserts in my plastic bin.

I catch Joe's eyes. "Is this okay?"

"Dinner and dessert. Fine by me."

"Dessert first." Jade grabs a chocolate eclair, eating half before Josie makes her choice—a strawberry shortcake. Joe opts for a lemon tart.

"That's the best cake I ever ate." Jade reaches for another, prompting her little sister to do the same.

I laugh at the crumbs on their shirts and the icing on their cheeks. The girls run around the pond, taking turns on the saddletree swing. They return to their fishing poles when their dad catches a catfish. Now, it's a competition.

I think of Mom's note with the seeds, and suddenly, it *is* a happy place again. Like magic.

Back inside, the eerie loneliness returns. I add Mom's seed note to my growing collection.

Dream something better

Things will get better

Let's do whatever it takes to make this a happy place for you again.

Then, I turn on Hallmark, *only* because nothing on that channel will ever make me anxious. Beautiful people, perfect homes, and delightful, *successful* careers—it's annoyingly unrealistic. *Or is it?* Maybe I'm the anomaly on the outskirts of a Hallmark world. Life in Malibu or even Asheville could be Hallmark-y, and one must be my new happy place. Maybe.

CHAPTER
Eleven

AS IF MAKING A DARING ESCAPE, I leave the house before sunrise. I worry over possible delays to my Asheville meeting—traffic, a flat tire, a flock of slow-ass geese crossing the road, my shit-luck, generally.

But an easy trip puts me safely within range of The Bean Machine without cutting into my time-buffer. So, I risk two detours—to a salon for my too-long, dirty blonde hair to be tamed into a touseled bob that grazes my shoulders, and to a mall for a new outfit and backups, just in case. I stock up on everything, even underwear. Though guilt-ridden for spending the money, I *must*. I can't pull off a nice, sophisticated city look with my worn country-casual clothes, and I need the confidence.

I feel validated over my shopping spree and makeover when I arrive at the restaurant. The Bean Machine radiates immaculate coolness. *So, this is where the fabulous people hang out.*

"One?" A waitress beams, like I've just made the best decision of my life.

With an hour to spare, I nod. "Yes, please."

She leads me to a window table. The energy on the city streets is mimicked inside, a busy kind of beautiful. The waitress recites so many coffee options, I'm surprised she remembers them all. I order a skinny vanilla latte with a pinch of cinnamon.

When I tell her I'm not very hungry, she recommends a muffin— blueberry or apple crumb. I accept the blueberry. When she delivers it, I thank her. "Um, will you also let Jason Ford know I'm here? I'm Lena Buckley, and I'm awkwardly early for our meeting. I'm happy to wait."

"Of course. Enjoy." She bobs away.

When Jason Ford emerges, I nearly knock my coffee over, standing up to greet him. He mirrors the cool vibe of his restaurant in his black chef's jacket, blue jeans, and Chelsea boots, and a handsome grin that's as playful as it is warm.

He couples his hearty handshake with a surprised once-over. "Wow, you aren't frumpy at all."

Air catches in my throat as my mouth drops.

"Sorry. That came out wrong." He winces, embarrassed. "You aren't what I expected. I mean, you're lovely."

"Thanks, so are you. Did Alice call me frumpy?"

"Well, you know Alice. I'm just relieved you don't have the back-woods farmer vibe I expected since she recommended you."

I laugh. "Well, thanks for risking it. Your restaurant is stunning."

He points to my picked-at muffin. "What d'you think of that?"

Nerves prompt me to lie and say it's good over fears that he baked it. Telling the truth that his muffin sucks might earn me a new Lena-Buckley record—fucking up a potential dream job in ninety seconds by offending the chef. But I can't lie about a damn muffin. "Dry. Skimpy on berries. Needs a crumble on top."

Jason's beard curves into a relieved grin. "I'm stuck in a bad relationship with my supplier. Everything used to be so delicious, but now it tastes stale and unimaginative. I'm desperate for a change."

"You're hoping for something better. I know the feeling."

"Making everything in-house would be better, for a start. How about a tour?"

He interviews me as he shows me around the restaurant, but it's more of a conversation. Funny stories. Favorite movies. Worst kitchen mishaps. We're like old friends catching up. Anxiety threatens to derail me, making me second-guess every word I utter, but staying in the moment rather than in my head helps. *Not today, bitches.*

Our talk lasts over an hour before he asks, "What do you want to bake, Lena?"

I grab an apron from the hooks he showed me earlier. "I take requests. Don't be shy. What would you like?"

His dark eyes widen with a surprised smile. He rubs his beard as he thinks. "Southern biscuits with honey butter."

My lips curl into a happy grin as I tie the apron strings behind me. "What else?"

"Baklava. That's my favorite. And a decadent chocolate cake."

"Is that all?"

Jason laughs. "Wow! I love your confidence. Need anything before I leave you to it?"

I glance around his exceptionally organized kitchen, knowing nothing'll be hard to find. "Nope. I got this."

I bake flakey Southern biscuits with luscious honey butter. My baklava is crispy, sweet, nutty, and melts in my mouth. I make a dark chocolate cake with hints of raspberries and basil, a milk chocolate mousse between the layers, and a smooth milk chocolate icing with a dark chocolate ganache drizzle.

After cleaning up, I post pictures of my creations. *Sweet success*, I type with strange optimism. It feels like an out-of-body experience. *Nothing ever works out for you.* Maybe not for *Nervous Nellie*, but my Asheville doppelgänger kicks ass.

"Oh, my God." Jason gives an orgasmic eye roll, sampling my creations. He shares with his staff, and they offer the same glorious reviews while my confidence meter reaches an all-time high. *I could seriously get used to this.*

After dinner, I follow Jason to my lodgings. I assume he's put me up in a nearby hotel, but we pass by all the big names. He takes country roads and finally pulls into a short driveway beside a cabin. Twinkle lights brighten a screened-in front porch. It's a two-story log house tucked into a lavish mountainside garden.

While I gawk, Jason shrugs. "You can't come to Asheville without staying in a cabin. It's a requirement."

"It's too much."

"Nonsense. It's my uncle's rental. It was available. You'll love it."

Jason leads me inside an eclectic, open living room. He grabs remotes from a bowl and clicks on lights. Strange but lovely art covers the walls. Bear-themed knick-knacks grace the rustic mantelpiece.

"Make yourself at home." He hands me the keys. "I'll take you to breakfast before you leave… Unless you'd be interested in staying an extra day?"

"Oh, um, do you want to sample more of my bakes?"

"Absolutely, but the test is over. The job's yours if you want it."

"Really?" I let out a giddy squeal. "Thank you, Jason. I'll, um, I'll have to think about it."

"Definitely let it marinate. Alice mentioned you had a lot going on, and it's a big move, anyway."

"Yes." My eyebrows crinkle. "Then why the extra day?"

His brow pyramids on his forehead, questioningly. "For fun? I enjoyed having you there today, and I'm picky about who shares my space. We might be kitchen soulmates if we give it a go... Does that sound weird?"

"Well, you're related to Alice, so..." I chuckle.

A healthy laugh escapes him. "Wow, fair point."

"It's not weird. It's nice. It's just..."

"Obviously, you didn't plan on two nights, so it's okay to say no. But I thought it might be fun to work the lunch rush together. I'll pay you, of course. The job offer stands either way, and we'll discuss details at breakfast."

House worries flood me, but I nod before he finishes talking. "I'll stay. I'll definitely stay."

After Jason leaves, I tour the house. I open the local wine he's left for me with a working corkscrew I find in the first drawer I look in. *I could get used to this.*

I try savoring my success, but it's impossible with anxiety rushing in, overwhelming me. *What about Malibu? How would I tell Lucas? Would I screw this up like everything else?* I take in the empty cabin around me.

Damn lonely. Why does it feel so damn lonely?

Even so, I spend the entire next day in great company. We work side-by-side for ten hours. Over a sizzling grill, he tells me about his husband Chris, how they started The Bean Machine, and about Asheville. I share about my life, too, including the Malibu offer.

"I get the dilemma, but how can you be happy working in a place you don't love?" Jason smiles coyly. "But, maybe I'm biased." He motions to the burgers I'm flipping. "Have you ever considered being more than a baker, *Chef* Lena?"

"I only want to get into a kitchen again, however I can. I've missed the energy."

"Yeah, your giddy-vibe's drawing attention." Jason nods toward a hunky beer delivery guy. He makes eye contact with a flattering grin.

I gape while Jason laughs. "That's another good thing about Asheville... lots of opportunities."

Despite my amazing day, I wake up that night in a total panic—sweaty, shaking, panting. It takes me longer to realize that I'm in Asheville—not at home, failing to wake Mom while calling an ambulance. Plugging my phone in across the room before bed prevents another nine-one-one mistake. Still, it's a double-frustration—panicking here, where I can't blame *that* house for triggering me.

Over breakfast, Jason offers a jaw-dropping salary, at least by kitchen standards. *With* benefits. He promises time for the transition and a month-long stay at the cabin while I house-hunt. And given my other offer, he gives me a few weeks to decide.

Driving home takes forever, paradise to purgatory. Glimpsing that better life makes me eager to swap the wood stove, the lumpy couch, and the damn mice as soon as humanly possible.

Unlocking the side door, I find an envelope taped to the glass. Cash accompanies a note.

Proceeds from the sale of the following... Ben Wright lists the firearms he's sold, but it doesn't matter. He's replenished the money spent on my makeover, assuaging my guilt.

The house is bitterly cold. Mouse droppings litter the floor. I curse the plug-in mouse repellents that aren't working until I realize there's a good reason. The power is out. The house retaliated in my absence like a spoiled child denied companionship. I restore the tripped breaker, grateful it comes back on and that my perishable food maintains a suitable temperature—the power wasn't out long.

I busy myself—cleaning, sanitizing, and unpacking. But a strange sadness sets in. I go for wine, frustrated that on the heels of my first success in damn near forever, worries overtake my elation. *Nothing ever works out for you.* Grief, isolation, fear, self-doubt—they're all sneaky, vengeful bitches, like a clique of mean girls tearing me down the second I feel good about anything. Or for no reason at all. And they're in full form tonight.

Distraction helps. So, I bake, hoping the residual heat will warm the house. I work until it's late, and I have enough treats to feed a small army. *What am I going to do with all this?*

I don't know, but I tuck them in airtight containers before crashing on my damn-lonely couch.

Twelve

UP, showered, and caffeinated early, I call Alice. I thank her for connecting me with Jason and promise to have everything done in a few weeks, wherever I end up. She'll have the paperwork ready. Bulldozers, too, I think.

Then, I call Ben Wright. "Hey, it's Lena Buckley. I got back from my trip last night and found your envelope. I just wanted to say thanks."

"You're welcome, ma'am."

"Um, you should take a cut, Ben. I meant to tell you to keep half the money for your trouble."

"It's no trouble, ma'am."

"Of course, it is. Finding buyers, making sure they're not psychos, leaving me cash—you deserve some reward for your valiant efforts."

"It's no trouble."

Is he annoyed? An awkward silence takes over. Last night's binned treats make me remember his big bites and full cheeks.

"Let me do something, Ben. I went on a baking spree last night. Cupcakes, cookies, danishes—a smorgasbord of sweet yumminess. Would you and your colleagues enjoy them? I'd bring them to your station. It's not much but—"

"Okay."

"Okay?"

"Okay. I'll text you the address. Bye, Lena."

Rush hour traffic makes my downtown trip slow-going. The radio reports increasing concerns over COVID. *Maybe Mrs. Moore's right to be nervous.* I turn the station. Traffic stress is enough.

Walking down city streets, arms full and in high-heeled booties, I trip over the uneven sidewalk, nearly losing my bins.

But it's not the sidewalk that I trip over. A shabbily dressed man curses, rising from the tree he's leaned against. He gives me a hard, annoyed stare. "Kick my shins, no one wins."

"I'm sorry. I didn't see you. Are you hurt?"

Uncomfortably close, he peers over my bin tower. "The invisible man, I am. Is that your tale, Miss Vicki Vale?"

Is that a Batman reference? "Um, no. I couldn't see my feet for all my treats." I shrug at my weak rhyme.

A quick grin pokes his cheek, but falls when he looks behind me. "Nothing to fear. Ain't no trouble here."

Awkwardly, I turn, finding Ben quick-stepping toward us. His stoic, hard-nosed expression matches his formal look, especially with *Lieutenant B. Wright* on his silver name tag. *So glad I wore my new clothes.*

He gives my new friend a raised brow. "Problem, Mr. Deakins?"

"There's no problem except my clumsiness," I say with a friendly smile. "I tripped over his leg."

"Up to your old tricks, huh, Mr. Deakins?"

"It's Shakespeare." The man bows to me. "I'm a poet, and everyone knows it." To Ben, he says, "A hipster, not a trickster."

He retrieves his coat by the tree, dragging one foot behind the other, a pronounced limp—not caused by me.

Ben fishes money from his wallet and hands it to him. "Breakfast's on me."

Shakespeare's baritone voice booms, "My pancakes'll be flappy. You've made me so happy." He pockets the money, eyeing us together. "Your lady friend is lovely and bright. You've done well for yourself, Officer Wright."

I hand Ben my containers and open one. Shakespeare bows when I give him a chocolate cherry cupcake and peanut butter cookies. "Fill me up with your delicious baking, and my heart is yours for the taking."

"Could you use a cane?" The words spill out, though I fear pointing out his disability might upset him.

His big eyes widen. "It's a shame not to have a cane. You got one?"

"In my car. Will you be here in a few minutes?"

"What can I say? I'll be here all day." He laughs, returning to the tree.

I chuckle, impressed by Shakespeare's on-the-fly ability, before turning my attention to Ben. His blank look and green-eyed stare inspire my weak smile and an uneasy "Hi."

"Ms. Buckley."

His ultra-seriousness makes me laugh again—probably not the best response, but there's a strange charm to his formality, like he's one of the Royal Guard at Buckingham Palace, and I'm duty-bound to try and crack him. "How about calling me Lena?"

"Yes. Okay. Lena."

I point to the bins. "Do you want help inside with those?"

He nods, so I grab half the bins and walk, easily this time, toward his building.

Ben's gem-like eyes narrow. "You cut your hair."

I shrug, the tousled ends brushing my shoulders. I expect him to say something else, but he doesn't.

"Was Shakespeare trying to trick me?"

"Only to get your attention."

"Why?"

"You're pretty." He says it like it's a fact, but I want to argue. That's not why Shakespeare nearly face-planted me against the sidewalk. He must've wanted to laugh at my clumsiness. Or record the whole thing for *YouTube. Cupcake lady nosedives into concrete.*

I stand there, stunned. And Ben waits, watching patiently, and perhaps critically, like Superman using his X-ray vision on my thoughts. Finally, I forego debating and scoff. He almost looks amused, but with him, it's hard to tell.

Mom and her crime dramas come to mind when walking into the station. *Look Mom—the real thing.* That it resembles an ordinary office, only with uniforms and utility belts, may've disappointed her. He leads me to a large break room where we line the containers on the counter by the coffee. I remove the lids, luring nearby officers.

Ben dutifully introduces me to anyone who asks, but doesn't explain more than necessary. *Lena Buckley, baker, acquaintance.* He's not one for chitchat. But the way he fails to engage in *any* conversation, even with his co-workers, makes me think I've misstepped. *My parents' arsenal and now bothering him at work—get a clue, Lena.* So, to spare him any further annoyance, I tell him I should go.

A slight furrow shadows his brow. Is that disappointment? It's gone before I can decipher it, and he nods curtly."I'll walk you out."

Shakespeare meets me on the stoop and follows me to my car. Ben comes along, too—an unnecessary protective measure, but he probably can't help it.

The Pilot trunk looks like an organized medical rummage sale—Mom's walker, canes, wheelchair, and unused diabetic equipment. I even collected her reading glasses, blood pressure cuffs, and unopened boxes of gauze and bandages.

Shakespeare chooses a cane. He grabs reading glasses and bandages. Then, he rushes off as if afraid I'll change my mind.

"What're you doing with all this?" Ben asks.

I close the tailgate. "My pharmacist friend Norman suggested I donate Mom's leftovers to the senior care center. So, I'm going there next."

Ben's stoicism slips with approval. "They'll be grateful."

"Well, it's just collecting dust at my house. Though it's sad, seeing it go. It's close, right?"

He gives me precise directions. "When you leave the center, take Twenty-Third to avoid traffic if heading home."

"Yes, thanks for the tip. It's good practice, driving during rush hour. Whether I move to Malibu or Asheville, traffic'll be an issue."

"Traffic, yes, but also mudslides and wildfires in Malibu. Violent and property crimes are rising in Asheville." He pauses. "Bears are also a problem there."

"Good to know, thanks." I laugh while he stays impassive. *He's an odd duck, but who isn't, really?* "And thanks for not letting my baking practice go to waste."

"Bring them anytime… if you want… while you're still here."

It's endearing, the choppy way he says it, and a broad smile wraps my face. "You're sure it's no bother?"

"I'm sure." Though his deadpan expression raises questions, I stop making assumptions—they're unreliable anyway—and decide he means it.

"Yes, okay. I'll text you. Stay safe today, Ben."

"Thanks… Lena."

His excellent directions get me to the senior center in minutes. An orderly named Myles Drake helps me unload my donations. He smiles when I tell him he has a movie-star name.

"It's a soap opera name. My mom loved her stories."

"*Days of Our Lives* was my mom's favorite. Not many soaps left these days."

"Soap audiences are dying off." He nods with a vacant expression, glancing at my trunk-full.

Maybe he's lost his mom, too. "Does your facility accept homemade treats for the staff and residents?"

"Store-bought stuff only." He recites the rule like roller coaster announcers before the ride starts. But his rigid shoulders sink with my look of disappointment. He looks around as if worried someone's watching. In a low voice, he says, "Unless it comes from relatives."

Catching his paranoia, I glance around, too. "I don't have any relatives here."

"I do." He tells me about his grandparents and two great-uncles, and how he works there to get a discount and help care for them. "The food's good, but they skimp on desserts. Can you make a good brownie?"

"Oh, yeah. I make kick-ass brownies."

We add each other into our phones on the street corner like we're doing something clandestine.

Driving away, I'm elated. It's silly, really—being happy about my *tiny* acts of charity this ONE morning. It's all *so small.*

Still, I haven't felt this fulfilled in ages. It reminds me of brushing Shadow's coat for the first time—it's something *I* can do despite all my limitations. And damn, it feels good.

I think of Joe Jones and his social worker wife, Olivia, helping orphans learn life skills and earn cars. Mom's Explorer or Dad's truck might be someone's ticket to going to school or getting a better job.

And Ben Wright. He's so committed to service that it doesn't occur to him to ask for anything in return. *It's no trouble.* I bet he says that often.

I've missed the world outside my country-caretaking bubble. I want to donate more, do more, give more, make one thing better for as many people as possible. The prospect fills me with delighted excitement.

So, for weeks, I keep doing it, scrounging for grocery money in couch cushions and old purses, like it's a new addiction I feed with flour, sugar, and eggs. And miraculously, I always have enough.

I create sweet comfort foods, classics with a twist, posting every-thing on social media for instant feedback. Jason Ford becomes my most frequent commentator. To sweeten his offer, he promises me the lead on our upcoming menu. That he trusts my abilities enough to relinquish control makes me feel insanely valued.

And I share my desserts with *everyone.* The boys take them home for snacks. Dot says my espresso brownies are like crack, which is probably the best compliment I'll get from her. I take farm-themed cupcakes to Gloria, her staff, and students. For Shadow, I experiment with oat and honey horse treats with peppermints in the middle, earning his eternal affection. Batches go with Joe to work and with Olivia to the group home. Ben assures me there are never leftovers, and his co-workers seem happy when I show up. Shakespeare thanks me for deliveries with sonnets. I deliver trays of scrumptious brownies to Myles Drake, covertly a block away.

I love my new routine.

Day after day, I don't leave the house without a dozen somethings to take to someone. When their faces light up, something inside me lights up, too. And that damn loneliness moves aside for something stranger. Aside from missing Mom and feeling anxious about where to go and moving altogether, I am—unequivocally—happy.

ONE MID-MARCH WEEKEND, Joe teaches me to fish. Well, not *really*. I *know* how, just like I *knew* how to ride before Gloria's lessons. I only need a refresher.

While the girls play and his wife Olivia sips wine, he instructs me. A thrilling thirty-second battle earns me one respectable catfish to add to his four. We set up a pond-side workstation and fillet them. Then, he sends me to the house for cast-iron skillets, dishes, and ingredients for battering the fish.

It's perfect timing—our impromptu fishing and cooking lesson, taking my mind off my nail-biting deliberations between Asheville and Malibu. While Jason and I have communicated easily, I don't get the same vibe from Root & Bone. In a curt email, Brian explained that I'd wash dishes and rotate through kitchen roles before settling into my permanent position—whatever he decides that to be. While I don't mind grunt work, his response emphasized that letting me work there is a favor to Lucas, and proving myself will be twice as hard. Still, Malibu offers security I can't get elsewhere and, more importantly, family. And I long for that connection.

Back at the pond, Joe and his girls have constructed a fire pit using sticks, bricks, and an old grate from the barn, professional-level making do. They drag tattered lawn chairs from the shed that I hope still work and set up a campfire circle.

"You're welcome to come inside the house," I say, hoping they don't think it's off-limits. "Might be easier to cook." *Maybe.*

Joe smiles. "We've got everything we need, Lena."

I'm reminded of Mom's seed note. *Everything you need is right here.* He starts a fire and warms the skillets on the grate. Together, we prep the fish for frying. It's wonderfully rustic.

I return to the house for paper plates, utensils, napkins, and dessert. I slip into my comfy cardigan and grab a throw blanket for Olivia. I also get chips and tartar sauce. Hands full, I step outside to a vehicle coming up the driveway.

Ben Wright's Jeep stops beside my Pilot. He hurries over, taking the plates and napkins before I drop them. He's wearing a long-sleeve t-shirt that accentuates his broad shoulders. *Hello, muscles. It's nice to see you.*

Arms full, we face off in a strange silence. His tough-guy face doesn't hinder my elated smile. After seeing him so often for dessert drop-offs, I'm used to his stoicism, and it's a pleasant surprise that he's here again.

His green eyes circle my face and then what we're carrying. "I probably should've texted."

"No need. You're always welcome."

"I, um…" He glances at his Jeep. "I'm returning your bins."

"Oh, I could've gotten them next time." *Like we've been doing.* "That's… sweet."

"I thought you might need them." A tiny crease appears between his brows. "And it's a relaxing drive."

"Ah, using your Jeep as an escape pod, huh?" My cheesy grin widens. "Glad I'm not the only one who does that…. You're just in time for our fish fry. Hungry?"

"Yes, ma'am."

"Well, well…" Olivia laughs as we join the circle. "Lena's caught herself another fish."

I introduce everyone, and it's odd—*I have friends again.*

"It's been a long time, Officer Wright. Remember me?" Olivia shakes Ben's hand, laughing.

"Yes, ma'am. Good to see you again, Mrs. Jones. How's Lucy?"

"Still a rascal, but good. Wants to study cosmetology."

Ben nods. "That fits."

"Who's Lucy?" I ask when neither explains.

"Lucy was a neglect call Ben responded to years ago. Her mom hadn't been home in days. He took care of her until I got there. Only I got caught behind a terrible tractor-trailer accident on the highway." Plopping into her chair, Olivia shakes her head. "How long did it take me, Ben?"

"Two hours."

"When I arrived, they were painting each other's fingernails. Was it hot pink?"

"Rockstar purple, actually."

Olivia giggles. "He'd also fed her, cleaned up, and let her dress him in a pretty pink boa and tiara."

"You dressed up like a princess?" Jade snickers.

"And he'd braided her hair!" Olivia coos.

"No!" I gush, trying to imagine it.

"A French braid. So cute!" Olivia says.

"Do they teach you that in police officer training?" I ask, smirking.

"No, my twin sister Becca taught me."

"You have a twin sister?" Jade asks as little Josie moves in beside her. "Is she as tall as you?"

"No."

"Do you fight with her?"

"Sometimes."

Josie giggles. "Bet you win."

"Sometimes."

"Do you arm wrestle her?"

"Not often."

Josie laughs. "Bet you win that, too."

Ben shrugs. "Sometimes."

"Enough, you two. Leave it to my girls to interrogate a police officer," Joe says. "Who's hungry?"

I fetch another chair, which Ben promptly takes from my hands and sets beside mine. Between chatting, I sink my teeth into the most delicious fish I've ever tasted, forcing me to close my eyes and moan a little. "This is fu—freaking amazing."

Joe chuckles. "And right from your backyard."

I imagine stepping away from the mixer for an affair with a cast-iron skillet. A hundred ways of cooking fish montages in my mind, along with succulent accompaniments. Potato salad in the summer. Slow-cooked green beans with ham hocks in the winter. Cole slaws and cream sauces. Maybe Jason's right about expanding my chef-horizons.

Over dinner and prompted by Olivia, we engage in a pleasant discussion about Ben's work and the diversity of calls he responds to, everything from traffic control to well-checks to noise complaints, and hearing him talk, strangely, makes me think of junk drawers. Tackling one means a thousand decisions, mostly small ones, and it's easy to get stressed over getting it right. In his work, Ben makes thousands of decisions a day—ones that matter. My burden feels light by comparison, and I doubt he'd call his a burden at all. But a privilege, probably, like the caring.

And that's how he talks about his job, serving and protecting—like it's a privilege.

I ogle him, a bit enchanted. It's the first time in a dozen encounters that he's said more than a few sentences at once, telling me that he economizes, saving words for what he feels strongly about—a Ben-quality I really like. So, to encourage it, I say what I'm thinking, "Wow, Ben. You're blowing my mind a little."

"Mine, too. That earns you more wine." Olivia refills his red Solo cup.

"Thank you, ma'am."

Oh, my God! I'm having a wine party! A real one!

Bored, the girls run circles through our chairs before Jade stops at Ben's side and ogles his left ear. "Whoa! Check it! He's got gadget ears, like Grandpa!"

"Girls! Enough!" Joe says.

Ben glances over, maybe gauging my reaction, and I meet his eyes with a warm smile, not minding how he holds my gaze.

Olivia breaks our eye contact with, "So, what's the deal with you two? You seein' each other?"

Ben shifts his feet, staring at the fire. "I'm, um, assisting Ms. Buckley, I mean, Lena, with her parents' firearms."

He says it in a funny, spitting way, like he's nervous.

"Ben's been a lifesaver handling that problem."

Olivia grins coyly. "Bet he can handle your other problems, too."

"Holy hell, Liv. Cut it out." Now, *I'm* uncomfortable, to her delight.

"Why? You could do worse than a guy who earns a steady paycheck and doesn't mind playing dress-up with a four-year-old. Right?"

My mouth gapes. With all eyes on me, my anxiety grows. "Okay, he's clearly a catch, not that he wants to be caught, or caught by me, or that he isn't caught already, and anyway, I'm moving, remember?"

"You ain't gone yet," Joe says.

"Are you caught, Ben?" Olivia asks with a wide grin, eyebrows bouncing. I can't deny being curious, though I've assumed him happily attached to an uptight but gorgeous supermodel, tall, thin, and ultra-fit. They do marathons and bodybuilding competitions together. Okay, maybe I've thought about it too much. So, his answer comes as a surprise.

"No, ma'am."

"He's caught in an awkward conversation," I snap. "We both are."

It's laughed off, and Joe changes the subject, *thank God*. Before long, Olivia shares a knowing look with Joe, and they round up their girls. "Let's get home before they turn into icicles out here."

Ben and I stay by the fire. We sip wine and stare at the moon's reflections against the water. Mom's tree sways in the brisk March wind.

He says little while I share my childhood adventures around the pond. Lucas and I pretended we had our own Loch Ness Monster. We'd leave gifts along the bank. Then, we'd creep around with old cameras to catch never-before-seen pictures of our magnificent beast.

And about the canoe—a fun pastime until we saw *Friday the 13th* and feared dead bodies might grab us and pull us under.

Fears often steal pleasures.

Tired of hearing myself talk, I ask, "How do you know Alice Harvey, anyway?"

"I assisted Mrs. Harvey in a ten-sixty-five. Um, armed robbery."

"*You* assisted *her*?"

"The suspect attempted to rob Mrs. Harvey at knifepoint in the parking lot of Independence Mall. She pepper-sprayed the assailant, disarmed him, and zip-tied him to a light post to await my arrival. When I arrived, she was lecturing him on making better choices."

"Damn, Alice is more of a mafia boss than I thought. I suspected she was packing something in her purse, but I pictured a butcher's knife."

Ben nods like he understands. "She's formidable, and she appreciates contacts. Since the mugging, she's asked for my assistance with background checks on church nursery workers, and well, now—"

"Me—the woman standing between her and a bigger farm. Sorry I'm one of her Herculean labors." I give Ben a curious look. "They could've helped me. It's strange, right—referring me to you?"

"Yes, but I don't mind, whatever their motives."

Silence settles, and for once, it's Ben who breaks it. "Have you decided?"

I cut him a confused glance.

"Wildfires or bears?"

I chuckle at how he puts it. "Um, no." I blather on about Root & Bone versus The Bean Machine, Malibu versus Asheville, and even Brian versus Jason. "Once again, Ben, I've given you way more information than you wanted."

The fire crackles. Owls hoot in the trees. When Ben finally speaks, his voice almost startles me. "Home is the place where you can be yourself. Where feels like home?"

What first comes to mind is here. *No, that's impossible.* Then, the answer moves through my mental fog. For the first time since closing the bakery and losing Mom, I know *exactly* what to do. *I think.*

My eyes crinkle, catching his in the firelight. "Gosh, Ben, that's helpful. Thanks."

"You're welcome."

Silence takes over again, but I don't mind. The crackle and glow of the fire, the cold air on my cheeks, and the symphony of barn owls in the trees bring an uncommon peace. Well, that and the fact that I don't feel pressured to talk. It's nice—togetherness in silence.

The evening stretches, and it gets late too quickly. At my nudge to end our night, Ben extinguishes the fire and helps carry stuff to the house. He offers to help wash dishes, but I politely refuse, thinking of my subpar kitchen.

At his Jeep, he doesn't get in right away but stands there, brow wrinkled in contemplation.

"I enjoyed that," he says like words escape him.

"Me, too."

Very businesslike, he reaches out. I smirk, amused that he wants a handshake. My palm presses against his, and he holds it there, midway between us. His hand swallows mine, but I like how dainty it feels nestled there, my icy fingers soaking up his warmth.

His thumb drifts over mine. "I enjoy you."

I exhale sharply, a cheesy grin stretching over my face. His three little words inspire a tidal wave of confused delight. I've never felt *enjoyed* by anyone. Tolerated, yes. Loved, sure. But enjoyed? *Like chocolate cake or an awesome movie or jeans that fit just right?*

What do I say?

"*Um, okay, thanks, weirdo.*"

"*That's nice,*" followed by an awkward hand pat.

Or the robotic, "*I enjoy you, too.*"

But Ben doesn't expect a response. He lets go, smiles slightly, and gets in his Jeep.

Later, I realize we totally forgot about the bins.

Fourteen

TODAY'S LESSON makes me question Gloria's mental stability. Mine, too, for starting this in the first place. "You want me to canter? I can barely trot. Cantering's for teenagers with blasé attitudes and fewer butt chunks. Besides, Shadow's too old for that, too." I give Shadow a neck-pat, knowing he has my back in this argument.

"Don't give *me* that too-old nonsense. Come on, Lena. You can do this."

She explains leads, which seems like tapping your head and rubbing your belly simultaneously. When a horse canters, he puts his strongest leg forward, leaving the weaker leg with less responsibility. A good rider tells the horse which leg to use, exercising the legs equally.

"Squeezing your leg against Shadow's side tells him to canter. Once you get started, squeezing both legs means go faster. Got it?"

"Um, no. It's too complicated."

"You're makin' it complicated. Stop overthinking. Let's just do it." She slaps Shadow's ass, springing him into action. An awkward trot shifts into a clumsy canter. I'm a pebble bouncing on a kid-filled trampoline.

Half the arena later, she orders me to walk. I pull the reins, and Shadow slows.

"We can do this all day," Gloria warns, hands on hips, "and it'll leave you sore and ornery. Or you can take control of your situation. Start with a right lead."

The last thing I need is to go home feeling like I've spent the last hour in a paint can mixer at a home improvement store.

I take a breath. Square my shoulders. My left leg squeezes Shadow while my right hand tugs the rein. I rise out of the saddle to push Shadow forward.

Strangely, it works. He gallops into the canter, and I stick with him, finding the rhythm. Gloria's devious cackles echo across the arena.

We circle the fence line. I squeeze my legs together, and Shadow picks up his pace.

"What'd I tell ya?" She calls out. "You need to stop overthinking and focus on what you want to do."

Yeah, yeah, yeah. I circle the arena again, my fears giving way to exhilaration. I'm a queen, racing across English countrysides. Strong. Powerful. Rebellious, even. The knights protecting me can't keep up. Shadow and I could run away together, escaping all the fences penning us in. If I can do this, then...

Shadow grunts.

"Okay, give 'em a break."

I loosen my legs, sit heavy in the saddle, and bring us to a walk. I rub Shadow's neck. "Good boy."

She strides over with a snide grin. "Maybe next time, you should go where *I lead you* instead of hemmin' and hawin'."

"Yes, ma'am."

Between walking breaks, we practice leads well over the hour allotted. Gloria takes a picture—Shadow and I look like equestrian rock stars. Later, I post it: *Things are moving fast, but Shadow and I like keeping things exciting.*

Though Ben's crazy-good advice should've been enough, learning leads pushes me forward. Choosing Malibu isn't taking the lead but the backseat. It'd be like using my strongest leg for an easier ride and less responsibility when my weakest one has never set out on its own before and needs the damn exercise. I need to stop overthinking and do what *I want* in a place where I can be myself.

I choose bears.

The next morning over coffee, I email Jason Ford my acceptance, absolutely giddy with my decision.

Of course, that giddiness quickly fades once the email whooshes away, and my spirits sink over what I must do next.

A seasoned procrastinator, I make breakfast, sort through boxes of

Reader's Digest Condensed Books, and start laundry—all urgent matters. I research homes and apartments in Asheville. I think of Ben, smiling over his *I-enjoy-you* remark. I stare at my phone, debating.

I shrug and text him.

> What if Lucas doesn't understand my choice?

Not expecting an answer anytime soon, I set the phone down. But the teasing ellipsis appears before the screen turns dark again.

> He will in time. You'll feel better once it's done. Bears, then?

I chuckle, taking a deep breath.

> You're right, and yes, bears.

> Good. Bear attacks are extremely rare. Asheville's lucky to get you.

My eyes pinch as I smirk.

> Thanks for that and the advice.

> Anytime.

> Stay safe today, Ben.

> Always.

I straighten my back—Asheville *is* lucky to get me. I'm an excellent baker and a pretty decent person, too. Why not take the lead and choose the place where I think I can be myself?

I call Lucas. He pops onto my screen with his classroom whiteboard in the background. "Things are getting crazy here, sis."

"Crazy?"

"COVID crazy. We're fine, but it's spreading like mad here. Luna and I are days away from getting an unplanned school vacation. It's a mess." He holds up an enormous jug of hand sanitizer. "This is my new best friend. How about you?"

"It hasn't reached this side of the state. Yet. One upside to country life, I suppose. Do you have time to talk?"

"Sure. What's going on?"

Just say it. "I've accepted an amazing job offer." I offset my blow with gratitude and outline my reasons—logical, well-thought-out reasons. "Though I'd love being with you, Asheville's my chance for real independence with a boss who already values my abilities."

"You're blindsiding me, Lena. I've arranged everything. We added the pool house suite for you."

"No, you planned for the pool house, anyway—that's what you said. Besides, I never asked for anything, and it's good news, right? I *don't* need to be taken care of, Lucas."

"Like you didn't need a college degree? Or help with the bakery? Or marriage advice? This sounds familiar, Lena. You're chasing a dream that'll let you down in reality."

"No, not this time. Asheville's the right thing for me. It's what I want."

He looks constipated. Annoyed. "Okay, Lena. Let's be smart. Brian's flexible. I won't tell him this now. With this Coronavirus madness, who knows when it'll be safe to travel anyway? There's time to try Asheville—"

"*Try* Asheville? Wow, you don't think I can make it on my own."

"I think..." he says slowly, "... things haven't worked out before, and it's wise to have a backup plan."

I gasp as if sucker-punched. "I screwed up a marriage and a business, but that was ages ago."

"Before that, you never liked working for other people."

"No one likes working shit jobs, Lucas, for little money and less respect. This isn't like that."

He sighs as if tired of my excuses. "Here, you'll have us if things don't work out for *whatever* reason. What will you have in Asheville?"

I almost say bears, but don't.

"I understand wanting independence, Lena. But let's keep Root & Bone in our back pocket, huh? It's smart, given your history."

Once off the phone, I grunt. "That didn't go the way I expected."

Though I feel better for telling him, I'm blindsided, too. Doubts prowl around the outskirts of my confidence, ready for attack. *Is Lucas right to be so damn discouraging?*

I get a glass of wine.

My phone pings. It's Jason—a video message. He's in his chef's garb at the grill, burgers frying. "Lena, got your email. I'm thrilled. We'll make plans once this COVID stuff settles down. Okay? Can't wait until you get here. Oh, and the beer guy asked about you." He winks. "We'll talk soon."

The recording ends, and I'm in tears. First, Ben Wright *enjoys* me, and now this? It almost takes the sting out of Lucas' discouragement. *Almost.*

Making that decision creates momentum. For weeks, I take the lead, pushing forward with the house. With the boys' help, I get rid of Mom's shabby recliner and the two unsalvageable living room couches. We throw out every mattress and box spring, all too old for good use. The crowded house empties, leaving it strange and unfamiliar. Colder, too. It's no longer a home but a warehouse.

Though trash predominates our barn exploration, we find lovely treasures, too. I delight in my grandmother's milk glass in white and jadeite and Mom's metal signs—Coke, Budweiser, RC Cola, and a large sign that reads: *Low Flying Planes.* The more we discover, the less I want to throw away.

The leftover sock money goes to bills, but I reserve enough for the storage unit and dumpster rentals. I cancel Mom's hellishly expensive cable, leaving me reliant on local channels and her DVDs for entertainment. Things are tight. Things are *always* tight. But I do my best to stop overthinking and stay future-focused. The Bean Machine. Jason Ford. Baking my ass off. *Everything'll work out this time,* I tell myself over and over.

CHAPTER
Fifteen

"YOU CAN'T RIDE SHADOW TODAY."

I stare at Gloria blank-faced, sure I don't hear her correctly.

"He worked a little girl's birthday party." She points to a small paddock near the tacking station.

"What the hell?" My jaw drops. Multi-colored ribbons hang from his pink-dyed mane and half-tail. Pastel handprints dot his gray body, and glittery pink polish covers his hooves. He gives me a side-eye. He looks furious.

"I'll clean him up." I'm desperate to save him from his nightmare, but Gloria grabs my arm, shaking her head.

"I'll take care of him later. You can't ride him, anyway. He's tuckered out."

"I had dibs, Gloria. Surely, you have other horses you could've tortured."

"Shadow's perfect for kids. Besides, you can't be a one-horse rider. You need to experience a different horse."

My eyes narrow. "You did this on purpose."

"With the stay-at-home order coming, our lessons'll be on hold. Best make this a good one. Huh?"

Turns out, Mrs. Moore was right to worry about COVID. Within weeks, an *oh-by-the-way* news report morphed into the story of the century. Travel bans, closures, and now a stay-at-home mandate starting on Friday have North Carolinians on edge.

Strangely, I feel more bothered about cheating on Shadow. *Could be denial.*

Gloria pulls me away from Shadow's nightmare. "Come and meet River."

River, a gorgeous reddish-brown thoroughbred with long legs, walks over when he sees us coming. He needs no bribes to get his halter on and doesn't resist when I lead him. He nibbles my hair lightly, like he's flirting. Tacking up goes easily; River lets me do whatever I want.

Several hands taller than Shadow, River's like riding in a jacked-up truck instead of a boxy car. We walk the arena, warming up for our lesson. We steer clear of Mya practicing jumps on Patriot, not Diesel this time, and a little girl riding a plucky pony named Cocoa Puff.

The sitting trot. The posting trot. River's responsive, even hyper-sensitive to my movements. He wants to please me—a vast difference from Shadow's over-it-attitude. *Maybe change isn't so bad.*

I get the correct lead, and River transitions easily into a canter. But River's height and speed unnerve me. Rather than Shadow's barrel-like midsection, it's like I'm straddling a balance beam. *Is the saddle slipping? Or is it me?* I don't think about what I'm doing—squeezing my legs for a better grip—but River's lovely little jog changes to a full-blown, balls-out gallop.

"Whoa!" River doesn't listen.

"Everyone stop!" Gloria yells to the other riders. "Lena, loosen your legs!"

"I'll fall off!"

"You're sending him the wrong signal! Get control, Lena!"

"I can't!" I scream, hoping she'll rush over and work her juju on him. Of course, *she can't.* No one should ever get in front of a runaway horse.

River rounds the arena like he's a race car on a speedway. I hang on, barely. *Holy shit! I'm going to fall off this horse!* My heart palpitates, imagining face-planting into the earth—a sudden, back-breaking, concussed end to my whimsical horse-dreams.

Mya and the little girl blur as I race by them. My legs clench tighter. *What if he jumps the fence? Or jumps anything?*

River turns tightly, scraping my left leg against the fence.

"Fucking hell" bumbles out, like my skin's being peeled from my bones. River whinnies while I yank him away from the fence line into the arena's center, toward the jumps.

"Holy shit!" I call out as he barrels toward the first jump, full speed.

I lurch forward as he goes airborne, slapping against his neck and slipping offside.

A unified gasp from the bystanders backgrounds my butt sliding to River's side. Holding on by one stirrup, the reins, and his neck, I lift into the saddle as he takes the second jump. He clears it easily, despite his uncoordinated cargo.

In our clunky landing, I hear Gloria. "He thinks y'all are having fun! Run him in circles! Wear him out, Lena!"

He's having fun? Really? The idea offers strange comfort. River doesn't have murderous intentions—he wants to show me a good time. The fact that he wants to impress me and have fun—not throw me off— makes me want to meet his challenge.

I grip the reins, lift my ass, and lean into his rhythm. I steer him in tight circles—shortening our joyride to half the arena. A smile pushes through my terror. This high, this fast—it's suddenly exhilarating. Now, I'm flashing a daredevil grin, taking River's speedy turns with an expert air. We do donuts, tighter and tighter.

"That's it!" Gloria calls. "Keep circling. He's getting tired."

River slows, only now I'm revved up, wanting more. I round the entire arena for an epic last lap before River brakes in exhaustion.

Onlookers clap and hoot. Gloria grabs River's reins as I slide off, nearly collapsing under my noodle-legs.

She pats my back. "Excellent riding, Lena. It got crazy, but you didn't panic."

I didn't panic? How's that possible? Now on my feet, I'm dizzy, even disoriented. I lean over, hands to my knees, adrenaline pumping.

"That was amazing." Mya rides over, holding her phone. "I got most of it. I'll tag you on Insta. You're Lena Buckley, right? My dad showed me your Shadow posts. Pretty cool."

I just survived a near-death experience. *And a teenager thinks something I did is cool?* The universe *has* turned upside down.

My weak smile fades, leaning over. Head spinning, I shift into panic-mode as my thoughts play catch-up. Flushed, sweaty, heart-racing, hands and knees shaking—it rushes over me.

Gloria pats my back. "You okay, honey?"

"Fine." *Not fine.*

"Get some water. Sit down a spell. Check that leg. I'll calm River down."

My scraped and bruised leg isn't so bad, especially with my panic-induced full-bodied tremble taking priority. I plop onto a bench with my water and phone. My mouth suddenly goes dry, and I chug my water as my phone chimes. Mya's tagged me in a post. I watch her video, if only for the distraction.

A thirty-something woman about to have an epic fall off an out-of-control horse—I wince at imagined laughter and criticisms when people watch it: *what the hell is she doing on that horse?*

My anxiety spikes again. *What will it take to get Mya to delete it? Money? Tearful begging? Peppermints?*

But the movie changes. A strange confidence takes over. My body works with River, our donuts kicking up dust. I see the me I *want* to be —a ballsy take-charge woman who doesn't fall off, who runs horses instead of letting horses run her, who impresses teenagers. I share the post without a caption. I don't know what to say, and my fingers are too shaky, anyway.

Once I return to something resembling normalcy, I care for River. Then, Shadow, too. His heinous makeover turns to odd colors on the stall floor as I wash it away, like oil stains in sunlight. I squeegee the excess water so he doesn't get cold and then brush out everything, even the knots in his tail.

Back to his beautiful self again, I release him into his paddock. Then he lies down and rolls around in the dirt. I smirk and snap a pic. *That's my Shadow.*

The day after my epic ride, days before quarantine, Dot shows up.

Why should I expect Mrs. Moore to listen to me? She never listened to my Chemistry excuses.

"Lena, have you stocked up on supplies?" She says it script-like, but I don't see cheat notes on her arm this time.

I stop the final coat on Mom's hutch and hold my dripping paintbrush over the can. "Mom was a packrat. Of course, I have supplies, but I'll be fine, anyway. You don't have to do this, you know. Just hang out, smoke a few, and return to Mrs. Moore with a good report."

She wags her black-nailed finger. "Babysitting you isn't fun for me, either. But Aunt Barb's good to me. She promised your mom she'd look in on you, only she feels too immunocompromised to do it herself. So, please, hold your shit together while I'm here, okay? If you so much as shed one fucking tear, I'll call Aunt Barb's prayer circle myself."

Her brashness counters all the gentle, sympathetic treatment I've suffered through since Mom died, making my appreciation for her uptick slightly. "Fair enough."

Her head jerks in a nod. "Do you have toilet paper?"

"Yes. Mom bought a case from Sam's Club every time we went. I've got eight cases stored, along with paper towels and more canned veggies than I can eat. Do *you* have supplies?" I nod to the screened-in porch surrounding the back door, which houses supplies, freezers, and the utility room with the water heater and breaker box. "Take whatever you need."

Dot tosses her cigarette and makes a wide, awkward sprint in that direction like I'm stashing cigarettes in there. I laugh when she emerges with a case of baked beans, toilet paper, and a joyful grin like she's just hit the motherlode. Stashing her goods in the trunk, she retrieves a small paper bag and hands it to me. Hand sanitizer and three home-made, double-lined face masks—black, leopard print, and tie-dye.

"Aunt Barb made you choices for different outfits. Meow." Dot claws at me. "She made mine outta my old band t-shirts. I wore my Aerosmith one yesterday like a freaking bandit."

"Thanks, but masks seem extreme. Right?"

"Aunt Barb wants us to wear them in public. Doctors only recommend them for vulnerable groups, but we'll all be wearing them before long. Best be prepared." Dot inspects my hutch. "You need at least two more coats, Lena."

"Anything else?"

She runs through a mental list, ticking items on her fingers. "Um, only the store. Aunt Barb wants us to go today—not wait until the last minute."

"What? Together?"

"That's optional but preferred." She grins like the Joker hatching a plan for Batman. "You'll cramp my style, but it'd make Aunt Barb proud, us joining forces. So it's worth the annoyance." She gives me a critical once-over. "Maybe."

Rebellious twinges peck at me, like when Mrs. Moore assigned too much homework. I'm not going grocery-crazy like everyone else before bad storms or snowflakes. *And with Dot? Like I need a chaperone.*

"Consider it carpooling," Dot says. "You can drive. It'll be like I'm not even there."

I doubt that. But a committed Boy Scout leader, Mom would side with Mrs. Moore. BE PREPARED. *And so what if Dot tags along?*

"Fine." I gather the leftover money from Ben—a piddly $87.00, which means forgoing Sunny's.

Walmart's a brightly lit hell-pit. Lines stretch to racks in the clothing section. Carts race in an unhinged frenzy. Everyone radiates pure frustration, more than usual. Like it's a hunting expedition, my leopard-print mask fits. But only a handful of elderly folks bother wearing them.

Dot grabs her own cart. "You get your shit. I'll get mine. Race you to the front." Then, she scuttles off like a sea crab.

A cart full of toilet paper passes me, followed by a woman wearing a housedress and slippers pushing Miller Lite cases in hers. *Is the good beer already gone, too?* I rush to the grocery section. The toilet paper is gone; the paper towels are dwindling, and several people eye the tissue boxes with careful consideration.

Holy shit.

I post a pic: *Um, what?*

I scavenge, stocking up on baking stuff, coffee, cream, chicken, fresh vegetables, and cleaning supplies—as far as my $87 will stretch. Not far, even here.

Dot beats me to the front, and her cart looks as though she's scooped full shelves into it, willy-nilly. "Let's get in line."

Checking social media alleviates the forty-minute wait. My post gets attention. I've gained many new followers lately, thanks to my equestrian and charitable endeavors. Friends report toilet paper shortages, while others joke about the flimsiness of facial tissues.

Ahead of me, Dot reads women's magazines. "Says here, if you have a stick up your butt, you should try meditation. Maybe you should give it a go, Lena, babe."

"Any advice on how not to be annoying?"

She laughs. "I'll check. I'll also look for cures for crying fits… for you."

"Ah, thanks. What about fashion advice for Billie Eilish-looking hobbits?"

Dot grins like this is a compliment, and I enjoy our little game. "You worry too much." She holds up her magazine. "I'll see if they have any advice on that… oh, they do. Herbal tea'll do the trick."

A huffing sigh escapes me, puffing out my mask, but I'm smiling underneath it. Having her company for this overwhelming task is nice —not that I'll tell her that.

My total comes to $85.77. I'm officially broke.

CHAPTER
Sixteen

QUARANTINE'S OKAY, no big deal, *really*. I only have myself to worry about now—at least that's some relief with COVID reddening the map as it spreads. So, I force the same attitude with the stay-at-home order that I had with Mom. *This is what I have to do right now. This moment isn't all moments. Make one thing better.*

I make *many* things better. Finishing Mom's hutch and a long sideboard makes me feel like a badass archeologist, saving forgotten treasures from ruination and deeming them museum-worthy. Or at least show-stopping centerpieces for my new place in Asheville. *My own, working place—I can't wait.* The storage unit fills with bubble-wrapped and packed collections of Mom's best china, silver, and crystal serving dishes, making me long to host parties and dinners like she once did.

I tackle books next. Mom believed strongly in an at-home library, though her collection ended up as glorified dust-collectors as information-gathering became search-engine-easy. Leafing through novels, a five-dollar bill falls to my feet. I spend an entire day with the books, earning $47. *Did Mom tuck money inside the books as rewards for reading them?*

I move her urn into the living room, where I've sorted the books into piles. "If you'd let us in on your game, you could've turned us into voracious readers, Mom."

I take a picture of the cash tucked into the books and post it: *Real page-turners.* I let Mom in on my joke, laughing.

Days pass, and the house empties with my progress. But the blank spaces give me heebie-jeebies, like walking through a ghost town. So, Mom's urn comes with me, room to room. *Not sad—but practical.* Talking to myself feels better with a visible target.

I text Lucas, asking for updates and sharing house discoveries. He responds dutifully, politely, but a wall has wedged between us over my Asheville decision. So, we never communicate long.

Ben reaches out every few days. Scheduling dessert drop-offs changes to random texting.

> Target has cleaning wipes and toilet paper. Are you running low?

> Do you have a working thermometer?

> There's a BOLO for a perp attempting to infect people with COVID. Avoid Walmart today.

I always respond with something snarky but grateful, and our conversations fizzle fast. He usually ends it with something like,

> Let me know if you need anything.

He's sweet and practical, and there's always a point to his communications.

So, I temper his business-like messages with personal ones.

> How are you feeling?

> Work must be so stressful right now.

> I hope you're taking care of yourself.

And just like in real life, he answers positively but with as few words as possible.

> No symptoms.

> Busy, but manageable.

> Yes, thanks.

Between terse Ben-conversations and household projects, I bake. I fine-tune recipes and send Jason pics. We FaceTime over kitchen experiments. He shows me how to spatchcock a whole chicken while I delight him with my artsy icing techniques. It's a fun, easy respite from the solitude. But as the weeks drag on and the novelty of being quarantined wears thin, our sessions dwindle until we're emailing only.

When I need a break from the increasingly creepy house, I take long walks around the property and spend many hours in the carport. There's always something to keep me busy, which helps ease the loneliness.

A little.

To stay informed, I watch local stations. At night, when I can no longer stand how the news primes my anxiety, I watch Mom's DVDs. I rekindle my love of the classics—*The Iron Giant, Clue,* and *Anne of Green Gables*. Mid-watching *The Never-Ending Story,* I tell Mom that the destructive nothing sweeping across Fantasia is like this pandemic, stealing our peace and leaving us empty.

The Harveys keep their distance. Mrs. Moore calls but doesn't even send Dot anymore. The pond and remaining old cars sit dormant. I don't play bakery-delivery-girl anymore because dropping off danishes and cupcakes isn't an essential service. *It should be, right?*

A wave builds in what's absent. Whatever I was before—anxious, depressed, lonely—the pandemic quadruples the intensity. Worse at night, panicked nightmares rouse me every few hours, and I struggle to relax just to go through it again. And again.

Stay busy. Make one thing better. Mom used to say, *this too shall pass.*

But like everyone else in the world, I wonder… *will it?*

As days run together, there's little hope that anything'll change soon, and my anxiety threatens constantly. When carrying her urn around like a baby starts feeling pathetic, I return her to the kitchen. Her *dream something better* note lies flat against the counter. I fix it, propping Ben's note beside her, too.

Things will get better

But now I'm no longer sure.

Working in Mom's room, I get teary over the smallest things: coins, batteries, and flashlights. I remove the thick, burgundy curtains, making dust clouds. I open a window near her desk, letting in fresh air and rain sounds. Then I plop down at her desk.

Fountain pens. Flashlights. Pill vials—none filled with pills. The pictures around her desk make me smile. Dad, Lucas, and me in a photo booth making funny faces. Lucas and I in our Sunday best with Easter baskets in our hands. The three of us riding horses.

I save Mom's unused school supplies for Olivia's group home. Mom didn't do back-to-school shopping in August; she kept a stash year-round—part of her be-prepared mantra. The trash bag full of coin wrappers will prove useful for the large, plastic cheese-puff container filled with change in the corner.

My shoulders slump, estimating the time it'll take to roll all those coins.

But I need the money.

"Why does everything have to be so hard?"

"You're making it hard," I almost hear Mom saying.

Two coin-filled vases bookend a row of notebooks. I grab a heavy binder and flip it open. Coins are tucked into plastic sleeves. Some have scrawled notes in Mom's handwriting. *Lincoln Wheat 1946.*

I look it up on my phone. The penny's worth a whopping fifteen cents, in good condition—this one isn't. I try again with a 1943 Canadian Penny. Three cents.

"I'm a penny pincher, Mom, like you always wanted."

"A penny saved is a penny earned," I can almost hear her say, along with her other penny-isms. *"You're worth every penny… You're as bright as a new penny… A penny for your thoughts, Lena?"*

"My thoughts… hmm… I'm a bad penny. I always turn up. I don't have two pennies to rub together."

Exasperated, I huff. The more I do, the more my work expands. I try dozens of coins—a solid representative sample of the ones she featured —with the same abysmal results.

Should I save myself an enormous hassle with a trip to the coin machine? Her squeaky desk chair moans as I twist in it. Mom toiled over these coins. Did she do all that work for a measly few cents profit? Or was it merely something to do?

Maybe it was another bitch-slap of her mental deterioration—her imagining a value that wasn't there. I feel bad for her. Bad for me, too. And I'm glad her urn isn't in the room to play witness to my sappy undoing.

I remember her waking me up, flashlight in my face. *"Lena, what're you doing on this couch? Why aren't you in your room? Is Lucas up, too?"*

Her confusion scared me. Disorientation meant an infection—that's how infections show in the elderly, doctors told me, like I should've known. Not with fevers or coughs or anything obvious, but with dementia—a sneaky bitch. Maybe her confusion was worse than I realized—so much was, in the end.

Especially at night. A blurry montage of Mom's crazy wake-up calls streams my thoughts. *"Lena, where's my little red wallet... who moved my magnifying glass... why are you here... did you make the cupcakes for Lucas's class party? You remembered Frederick's peanut allergy, right?"*

My head shakes with the stupid irony—she remembered the allergy of a random kid from Lucas's third-grade class but not what year it was. She should've had professional care. I wasn't enough.

I turn away from her coin-covered desk to the sliding glass doors. The rain pats the decrepit porch outside, a soothing drum beat. It's a lovely spot—the rain glistening on Dad's hand-laid brick walkway; the patchy grass about to be lush and green; Mom's azaleas prepping for blooming season. I close my eyes and feel her there. With me. *She is, right?*

And being here really isn't so bad.

A weird thud jerks my shoulders to attention. As I travel through the house, a thumping noise grows louder, instigating my panic. *What the hell is that?* Turning into the living room, I scream when the empty bookshelf falls forward and smacks the floor. Rain pours down the dirty wall behind it. Mushy, broken bits of drywall flutter as the rainwater spits through the ceiling's edge.

A race for towels and buckets ensues. My bare feet squish into the shag carpeting as I makeshift a catchall for the hole. Then, I get Dad's ladder and duct tape. Forming a shabby patch, a duct tape lattice affixed to the dry parts of the ceiling diverts the water, somewhere.

With no other ideas and unable to tarp the roof in a rainstorm, I sop up the wet carpet and watch anxiously for more damage. Frustration forces more tears since, like everything else, I shouldn't pay to fix it and don't have the money, anyway. It's the never-ending story with this house.

CHAPTER
Seventeen

DARKNESS SETTLES. The rain stops, and my duct-taped patch holds. Still, I imagine the roof caving in... or the electricity shorting out... or the floor collapsing... or several other equally devastating scenarios that could leave me homeless with nowhere to go during a stay-at-home order.

A noise outside makes me jump. *Another house disaster?* But hearing nothing else, I grab the poker to stoke the fire, shaking my head at my sensitivity. *It's been a rough day.*

Then, a gentle rap on the door prompts a full-bodied scream. A hulking shadow hovers behind the glass. Gripping the poker, I flip on the patio light.

It's Ben.

His black mask ties behind his neck like a bandana, like he's a bank robber from the Old West. I yank the door open as he steps back. He's the first person I've seen in weeks, and it hits me that there's only so much nothingness a person can take.

My smile is a mix of warm welcome and relief. "Should I put my mask on?"

"No. It's okay. I'm exposed to many people. I don't want to put *you* at risk."

Romance in the time of COVID, I think, with hefty sarcasm. Wait... *is this romance?*

"I'm sorry I scared you." His bright eyes pinch at the bridge of his nose. "Are you okay?"

"Fine." I lower the poker. "You've just ended an impressive marathon of zero in-person human interaction, Ben. It's good to see you."

"You, too." He holds up an envelope. "Money from more sales and a permit for the Beretta." He hands it to me.

"Thanks. That'll keep me in wine and ramen for a while." I mean to be funny, but Ben's eyes crinkle.

"Are you short on supplies?"

"No, I'm kidding. Mom hoarded essentials. I have plenty to share if you're low. I *even* have toilet paper." A playful wink accompanies my grin. "Do *you* need anything?"

He shakes his head.

"Thanks for asking, though." I cock my head. "Have time for wine?"

He checks his watch. "It's wine o'clock."

The poker clanks to the cement patio. My hands go to my dropped mouth. "Ben Wright! Was that a joke?"

"A bad one, but yes."

I laugh like it's the best joke I've ever heard. "Ben, I wasn't sure you had it in you."

"Next time, I'll make it funnier."

"The wine should help."

Remembering my duct-taped ceiling, I suggest we sit outside. I whip through the kitchen and return to him, hands full. He pulls the towel from under my arm and dries our chairs before tugging his mask down. Finally settled, we sip quietly, each waiting for the other to say something. I give in—no surprise.

"How's work?"

"Busy." He hesitates before elaborating slowly. Ben has a deep but soft and calming voice—very *Iron Giant*. "Fewer traffic accidents, but more domestic disturbances and thefts."

He tells me about their extra precautions. Though masks are new, he's always worn gloves in the field. Safer that way, he says. With many people out of work, robberies have increased, and he expresses frustration over people who don't lock their cars.

I'm pleased he's opening up. Building a friendship with Ben is like a long hike in the woods—if you make it to the scenic overviews, the payoff is well worth the effort.

The more he talks, the more I like him—not sure that's a good thing.

"How did things go with Lucas?" he asks.

"He reluctantly accepted it, sort of, but not really."

Ben stares into his wine glass. "Sounds like my family when I enlisted. They expected me to go to college. My sister Becca was especially upset."

"She didn't want her brother in danger."

"That, and she always thinks she knows what's best for me."

"Lucas, too. They mean well, I suppose. In what branch did you serve?"

"Army. Ranger. Ten years." His words come out awkwardly, as if talking about himself goes against his nature.

"Wow, that's amazing. Service *really* is no trouble for you," I smirk. "Did you ever regret going against their wishes?"

"No. Never." He pauses unsurely. "Even with the cost."

"Your hearing?"

He looks surprised. "Yes. How'd you know?"

"Soldiers returning from Afghanistan with hearing difficulties was one of *many* news stories that upset Mom. I thought maybe that could've been what happened to you."

He nods. "One explosion too many. It's irreparable and probably degenerative."

"You could lose your hearing completely?"

"Over time, yes."

"Ben, I'm sorry." I shift in my seat to see him better. "What's it like for you?"

"Um, like being underwater." He sits up, shuffling his boots against the patio. "Or like I've been front-row at a heavy metal concert on days I'm overstimulated."

My forehead crinkles, trying to imagine but failing. "Wow, that really sucks."

"It's nothing compared to what others have gone through. I'm lucky, even with the headaches and hearing aids."

"You made a sacrifice that keeps taking. I admire your attitude, but it's hard calling that lucky, I think."

"I was angry for a long time. But my loss inspired gains once I was willing to see them. It humbled me, made me more understanding." A soft smile spreads as he glances my way. "Sign language and reading lips prove useful, too."

"Ah!" I nod, remembering his intense focus during my Mom-rant. "You were reading my lips that day we shot Mom's Beretta."

"Yes. I could hear you softly, but reading lips is good practice. Preparing helps me cope."

"That's smart and healthy," I say.

He looks down, seeming to search for words. "You surprise me. Most people find it awkward to discuss. I like your openness."

My openness often gets me in trouble, I want to argue, but I side-step my negativity for how lovely his simple compliment makes me feel. "Well, I like your company, especially with Lucas and me on the outs."

"Don't worry about Lucas. You'll do great in Asheville. Once you prove him wrong, he'll never doubt you again."

"I hope so. Lucas will happily dish out the I-told-you-so's if I don't, especially if I end up in his pool house anyway." I laugh, but it's not funny. "He's a great brother, really. He wants to protect me. He just underestimates me."

"Why?"

"I'm Nervous Nellie." I blurt, a little shocked at my wine-induced slip. "Um, I was diagnosed with an anxiety disorder as a teenager, so he grew up seeing me through that lens, and my life up until now hasn't exactly improved his view of me."

"What's that like? Having an anxiety disorder?"

That he asks doesn't bother me, but I doubt he'll understand. My heads-up to Mark when we dated proved useless. I had it controlled then, so it was like describing a Yeti-sighting—too rare for concern. But later, when my anxiety-Yeti emerged from hiding frequently, he refused to understand, calling it easily fixable, like my chewed-up fingernails. When he was especially inconvenienced or irritated by my panic attacks, he'd tell me they were nothing more than an attention-getting performance altogether.

A throaty groan rumbles out. "It's hard to explain."

"Try me."

Maybe it's the wine, warming me to talk, or remembering how kind he was with what I told him about what happened with Mom that relaxes me—he made me feel better then. So, why not tell him?

"Um, well, my first panic attack landed me in the hospital, sure it was a heart attack. I was fifteen and completely mortified when the doctor said it was psychosomatic. My head plays tricks on me, convincing me I'm in real distress. My chest tightens, my heart races, my breathing becomes irregular, my hands shake, and I flush with sweat—symptoms that retreat once I refocus and regain control. But even then, my anxiety triggers stomach problems, headaches, exhaustion. And, of course, delightful emotional bullshit, too. Sometimes, I lash out. I'm not fun to be around when it happens."

"Does it happen often?"

"More lately, but generally no. I have flare-ups. Or something emotionally charged might set it off. Usually, I feel it coming and manage it. I don't even need meds anymore—not that there's anything wrong with meds, well, except for their side effects. After Mom... well, I'd rather do without them if I can."

He says nothing, probably not getting it. But what *should* he say, anyway? What's the *right* response to someone admitting to head games so intense her body revolts in protest? There're no Hallmark card sympathies for *sorry you're so fucked up.*

I finish my wine, contemplating another glass.

Finally, he sighs. "It's not so bad, being broken."

"Really? Feels bad."

"It helps us understand ourselves and the world better."

"Gee, Ben. I'd rather go about my merry way blissfully ignorant of the world, then."

"No, you wouldn't." He shifts in his seat. "And you wouldn't be nearly as intriguing."

Once again, I'm stunned by an undeserved compliment. A welcome silence takes over. The cool night mixes with the dampness in the air, creating a sparkling mist around the strange relief I feel that he didn't balk, question, or, hell, demean me for it. Then a chill slips over me, considering the bullshit I've tolerated from others in my life.

"Everyone misses your desserts," he says, eventually.

"I miss bringing them. I can't eat them all myself. I threw out a dozen chocolate cream cupcakes the other day."

"Tragic," he says seriously, though it sounds funny. "You should keep delivering if you're comfortable doing it. No one will pull you over for being on the roads. Governor Cooper's stay-at-home order excludes anyone doing charitable work."

"Really? You think it's okay? I'd hate to cause problems or, God forbid, spread it to anyone."

Ben's eyebrow rises, looking around my quiet farm. *"You'd* be at risk more than anyone else. Sanitize, social distance, and wear your mask, and the risk is negligible."

My head cocks, sizing him up—or trying to. "I don't know how you do it every day. Doesn't it worry you? Being out in the world with the pandemic?"

"No. Anything worth doing involves risk. I'm careful, prepared, and content with the consequences." He sits back, making the chair creak. "But if you're unsure, then—"

"No, I want to. I'm happy to. Do you really think people will still want baked goods from my home kitchen?"

"Your kitchen's probably the safest in town."

I almost say, *"Yeah, as long as mice don't carry COVID,"* but I don't. An obsessive cleaner, I have no worries about sanitation. "It'll be good to get out. I miss going to the city, to the farm, riding Shadow."

"Shadow?"

I show Ben a Shadow pic while my mouth runs like the Energizer Bunny. Yes, I'm starved for human interaction, but I'm proud, too. I'm not even bothered when Ben pulls up my wild ride on River and watches it.

My phone dings when Ben follows my account. I check out his profile. He doesn't post much—mainly community-related stuff like traffic notices, pics of lost pets, and events—but he has thousands of followers. *Thousands.*

"Wow. I can't believe you stayed on that horse."

"I had to. With Lucas in California, I have no emergency contacts— none I'd burden, anyway. It kept me up that night, panicking over who I'd call if I broke my leg or worse. Such a silly thing to lose sleep over, but after Mom, anything health-related triggers my anxiety."

I take a breath. "Sorry, Ben. As usual, I've told you way more than you wanted to know." I bury my face in my hands. "Yikes, why do I do that to you?"

"You haven't."

"I Haven't?"

"You haven't told me more than I wanted to know. I asked. You answered. You're honest—I like that."

A gasping exhale escapes. "You might be the first."

His lips part to say something, but he hesitates, his brow pinching like he's unsure how to deliver his thought."Call me, Lena."

"Oh, I wasn't fishing for an emergency contact."

"I know. But I'm here."

"Thanks. If I get thrown off a horse, I'll call you to be my caregiver, though, I warn you, you won't enjoy me long under those conditions."

"I'll take my chances."

He stays another two hours. We talk and laugh, and it feels good— the resurrection of another thing I've missed. It's not just the company, but there's something about *his* company. Even in our silences, I feel better, and the nothingness fades behind this unexpected friendship.

CHAPTER
Eighteen

BEN MEETS me outside the station the next morning, looking impressive, like always, and I can't deny the pesky butterflies fluttering when he says, "Good morning, Lena."

"Hey, Ben." My black mask hides my smile but matches my backup new outfit, nicely completing my city look. I hand him three large dessert bins. Though I stayed up until the wee hours baking, I barely feel tired, like I've stockpiled energy. Or maybe it's the excitement of getting out of the house.

"Thank you, ma'am."

"It's no trouble."

His eyes narrow at my Ben-like response like he's smiling under his mask, and it pleases me that I've amused him.

"Wait, there's more. You drink coffee, right?" I extract the travel mug wedged precariously in my bag.

He nods, admiring the blue-gray Coleman thermos.

"My dad was a truck driver. That thermos saw him through many long trips. You should have it."

"Oh, Lena, I couldn't—"

"I insist. He would've liked you, and your quiet, responsible ways. He'd love you to have it."

"Thank you. I'll take good care of it."

"I don't doubt it. I made you lunch, too. Or, um, dinner if you already have lunch packed." I extract a paper bag from my extra-large purse.

He looks confused.

"Too much?" My face scrunches. "I couldn't help it. I found basil in Mom's overgrown flower bed, so I made pesto. It's a pesto chicken biscuit with tomato, bacon, and mozzarella, and sweet potato chips."

"Thanks. I look forward to it."

Hands full, we go inside to drop off the bounty. We arrange the bins in the break room, where officers greet me by name while helping themselves. It's good returning to my usual routine despite the unusual differences—masks, plastic desk shields, and sanitizer stations. Every encounter is a calculated risk. But it's one worth taking if it's something I can do for others, and small compared to the risks they take every day. Cupcakes and danishes may be an insignificant perk, but it's something I can do, my brand of caring.

A suited man, fifty-ish, makes a grand entrance into the break room, greeting everyone and filling the room with noise. With hands on hips, he pushes his jacket back, revealing the gold badge hooked to his belt. He corners us near the coffee bar.

"So, you're the lady with the nice cakes, huh?"

I mask-gasp while my eyebrows shoot up. He laughs like it's okay to sexually harass a stranger because it's only a joke. But I don't find his remark funny. At all. To make matters worse, his voice is thunderous. I back-step, knocking into Ben behind me.

"Detective Gentry, this is Ms. Buckley. She's—"

"Detective Ed Gentry," he booms, cutting Ben off. He sticks out his hand, but then remembers social distancing with an annoyed grunt. "A pleasure to meet you, dear."

"Thanks, I think," I manage weakly.

"How'd you get so lucky, Benny?" He gives me a creepy once-over. "Let me guess, you let her do all the talking, huh? She talks too much, and you just turn 'em off, I bet." He motions to Ben's ears.

My mask hides my shock and anger. *Mostly.* Over my shoulder, I see Ben's brow furrow and his eyes narrow, like he's trying to control himself with this guy, who may be a superior, and I'm appalled for him.

"Oh, don't worry, honey. Benny doesn't mind a little joshing." Gentry goes on, voice still raised, "I bet he plays the hearing card with you all the time, doesn't he?"

"No. Ben doesn't make excuses, and why would he? And you don't have to be so loud. We hear you just fine."

"Oh, yeah, with those military-issued boom boxes in his ears, he better. That's our tax money at work, right there. Man, they sure do coddle you boys these days." He shakes his head and eyes the treats.

Coddle? The word stirs my inner rage, kicking up my heart rate.

Casually, he turns away. I reach for a red velvet cupcake—the most colorful—to ram *accidentally* against his pressed, blue Oxford button-down. I inch closer, raising the cake in my hand.

Gentle fingertips tiptoe around my side, one strong finger and then the next, halting my mission and making my heart skip for a new reason. His fingers wrap my waist just above my hip on the left side while he eases the cupcake out of my right hand, disarming me. We're close to each other. *Really* close. Like Jennifer Grey backed against Patrick Swayze before he spins her out in *Dirty Dancing* close. *God, too many old DVDs lately.* It's my fault—pushing into Ben gave him nowhere to go. It's more nerve-wracking that we don't correct our social distancing slip-up. We share a curious, bemused glance over my shoulder, and I wish he could see the coy smile inching up my cheek.

"I'm happy for you, Benny." Gentry pulls down his mask to shove a danish into his mouth. "We've had our differences, but every man deserves a full belly and a warm bed. You've got both with this one. Never thought I'd see the day." He belly-laughs. "But, you know. The whole world's gone crazy."

Polite, little Lena should leave well enough alone; the guy's an asshole—not the first or the last. But nerves already primed, polite, little Lena takes a backseat, letting my pissed-off side take the wheel.

Matching his volume, I ask, "Did you say you're a detective?"

Gentry bounces on his feet, exposing his gold badge again. "Yes, ma'am, just like on TV."

"Wow. You have an authoritative vibe, too. Are you in charge of other detectives?"

"Uh, oh, Benny. She may be a badge bunny." Gentry laughs.

Ben doesn't share his amusement, but his hand, still resting above my hip, tightens like his hold on me may be the only thing holding him back from this jerk.

Gentry clears his throat. "Yes, I'm a senior detective."

"So, you're a dick, right?" It's a fun word to say—*dick*—with its strong consonants and monosyllabic simplicity, and I say it that way, as if teaching someone else. *Repeat after me... DICK...* and overemphasize the hard K at the end. Chuckles, gasps, and whispers fill the break room. "Right, Ben? Don't people call detectives dicks?"

Ben nods, the corners of his eyes crinkling slightly. "Yes."

Gentry takes in the stifled laughs and gaping stares from around the room. "Um, that's—we don't use that word anymore."

"Well, it deserves a revival, just for you."

Gentry pushes out a weak smile. "Damn, Benny. She's a talker. Opposites attract, I guess, but you've got your work cut out with this one."

"She's right. You are a dick."

"Oh, he's not *just* a dick, Ben." My head cocks at Gentry. "He's the head of dicks. Wow. A bona fide dickhead. If the department gave a prize to the most dickish dickhead, you'd win for sure. Actually, it's a crime that your colleagues don't remind you more often of your dick-headedness, especially since you clearly deserve the title."

My small audience laughs while Gentry's genial expression falls. He puts his hands up submissively. "Okay, enough of the dick talk. You kiss your momma with that mouth?" He laughs, but no one joins him.

Having made my point—*yes, too well*—my flight tendency kicks in. *What the hell have I done?*

I grab my purse and make a quick exit. I don't breathe again until the front stoop. With no one nearby, I pull down my mask and take deep breaths. *Shit, shit, shit.*

Leaning over the concrete handrail, I try controlling my breathing. My heart rate soars, my hands tremble, and I can't calm down. My mind spins with replays of what I did and what I should've done. Nothing, probably. I try imagining what Mom would say, but knowing she'd never get passed the dick thing, I can't. Redirection proves impossible. *Damn it.*

I need to get to my car. To get away. To go home, where, at least, I can freak out in private.

"Lena."

Shit. It's my fucking ridiculous bad luck. I share my panic disorder with Ben only to spiral into exactly what I claimed was under control less than twelve hours ago. It's like my anxiety heard my blasé remark and retaliated.

"Lena," he says again.

I spin, leaning against the railing. Ben's eyes crease as he studies me. I want to apologize—*profusely*—but I can't. I hide my shaking hands behind me, but there's little I can do about my frenzied breathing or flushed face.

Taking his own calculated risk, Ben pulls his mask down. Then, he steps close and holds his hands out. "May I?"

"I'm fine," I huff with attitude.

"Please." He motions for my hands. "It's okay."

Ben doesn't look angry or disappointed. Still, I want to run—to shove him away and never see him or this place again. I hate what I just did. I hate that I told him about Nervous Nellie, my issues, all of it. I hate everything.

Only I can't do anything but extend my trembling hands.

My breath catches with his gentle, careful acceptance of my hands like they're some delicate thing entrusted to him. His fingers ease over mine to my palms. His grip tightens slightly before turning them over.

"Close your eyes. Breathe." His thumbs move to my wrists. Pressing into the inner sides, he makes circles. In front of me, shadowing the sun behind him, he massages a thumb-sized spot under the base of each hand, but off-center—weirdly specific.

A beach memory stirs, getting caught in a wave as a kid. Unable to get my footing, it barreled me over, smashing my face into the sandy bottom. Dad latched onto my wrist and yanked me out. With that first breath came gratefulness and relief, and he held on until my feet were safely in the sand again.

Today feels the same way, surfacing into the world again. And so does this. His touch feels like captured lightning, resurrecting inklings, feelings, warmth all over me. My breathing eases while my heart rate keeps its hurried pace. *He's touching me. On purpose. And it feels really good.*

"Um, you're—this is—um, what're you doing?"

"Helping?" Ben folds my fingertips into his, running his thumbs gently over my palms. At the fish fry, he held my hand and said he enjoyed me. *Not anymore. Not like this.* My eyes flutter open with a curious, pained look.

He shrugs, his fingers returning to the same spot on my wrists. "It's a pressure point. It's supposed to ease anxiety."

I pull my hands away completely. They aren't shaking anymore. My forehead lines crease into formation. "Um, did you Google anxiety tricks or something?"

"No." His face pinches unsurely. "Becca was in a bad car accident in high school. She couldn't drive for a long time. Even being a passenger made her anxious. She'd rub her wrists like this, back and forth. She said it helped. Did it help?"

My suspicious attitude strikes again. "Yes, thanks."

"Good." He moves to the lower step, bringing us shoulder to shoulder. Then, he bursts out laughing. "A prize for the most dickish dickhead?"

He laughs so hard, I think he might tear up, and it's a lovely, unexpected prize. *Ben laughs?* Better yet, it moves my panic aside like a footnote.

"I'm so sorry, Ben. I fucked up. Will it cause you problems? I'll apologize to him. I'm good at apologies, usually."

"No. That's unnecessary." He smirks, sizing me up. "I don't think you could get through it, anyway."

"I'd *make* myself if it'd help. I'll even throw in light flirting—that should tell you how bad I feel about this."

"You have nothing to apologize for, Lena. I mean it. I'm glad I stopped the cupcake assault. The dick-thing was much better."

I cock my head, scrutinizing him. "You really aren't bothered? I feel like you should ban me from your workplace forever. Post signs with my face that say, *beware the foul-mouthed dragon.* Or worse, that I've earned a spot on your never-want-to-see-again list. I wouldn't blame you."

"You're funny." His lips curl up his left cheek as he takes me in, and those pesky butterflies resume fluttering in my stomach. "It's my fault, anyway. I usually handle him, but the appalled look in your eyes made me curious. I had to let it play out."

I gasp, feigning offense. "Better be careful, Ben. That's risky."

"Worth it." He nudges my shoulder with his. "It's a good day, Lena. It was sweet, actually. You're sweet." Our eye contact lingers a little too long.

"You are, too." My eyebrows pinch. "Thanks for, um, taking me in stride."

"Anytime."

I leave Ben thinking of calculated risks again. For the first time ever, someone witnessed my anxiety disorder in action and didn't make me feel worse for having it. And that he had a strategy at the ready, well, that means Ben Wright thinks about me.

He's got me thinking about him, too. *Shit.*

CHAPTER
Nineteen

AFTER I LEAVE BEN, I deliver another lunch and treat bin from my gigantic bag to Shakespeare. Then, at the Pilot's tailgate, he has his pick of Dad's old clothes. He takes his favorites, including a very poetic-looking Indiana-Jones-style hat, before calling his buddies over to take the rest.

Shakespeare insists on a masked selfie with my trunk and his friends in the background and posts it with poetry. *Her beauty and kindness make us grin. She helps us remember that love always wins.* Though I could do without the praise, I appreciate seeing Dad's things in use again.

Myles Drake meets me outside the senior center, wearing full medical garb. He aims a thermometer at my forehead and questions me about symptoms. Other senior care facilities have been hit hard, and everyone's on edge, he explains. Still, he takes my brownies and chocolate chip cookies with a grateful sigh.

"With no outings or outside visitors allowed, they need something to cheer them up." He wipes the surfaces with a cleaning wipe.

"Oh, could you use this?" I show Myles an old radio, extra batteries, and a stack of CDs—music and audiobooks. "It's a little old school, but maybe the residents would like it?"

"Super cool." He pulls Lysol from his pocket and sprays the surfaces. "This'll get them away from the news for a while. You've made my day."

"It's no trouble." I think of Ben. It *is* a good day, even with the dick-drama.

I drop off cupcakes, books, and school supplies to Olivia's group home. Waving off my protests, she posts a picture on the county's account, thanking me. "It's more for us than for you. Giving's contagious. Maybe you'll start a trend, huh?"

I'm no trendsetter, but I don't argue. She's the charity-expert—not me. But I can't help but feel proud of doing something that could inspire others.

Deliveries done, the leaky roof must be dealt with, though.

As I peruse the hardware store's patching supplies, my phone alights with Lucas's face.

"Are you out?" He's almost frantic. "You shouldn't be out, Lena."

"I'm not at a party swapping spit with people, Lucas. I'm at the hardware store buying Flex Seal. What's wrong?"

He hangs his head. "Drew tested positive for COVID."

Oh, my God! What if Lucas gets it? And Luna? I should be there. I need to go, take care of them, help. How can I? Drive across country? During a stay-at-home-order?

A deep breath fills the silence between us. *Stop overthinking.* I put down the can and duck out of the store. Around the building, I remove my mask. "It'll be alright. Drew'll muscle through this. Are you and Luna okay?"

Lucas nods. "He traveled to San Diego for work. He quarantined after he got back, so Luna and I are fine." He gives a tired sigh. "It's scary, you know?"

"Yes, I know." I get him talking, pressing him for details about Drew's symptoms. The more he talks, the calmer he gets, like Mom used to do with me. Before long, he jokes about Drew's cabin fever, grateful they have the pool house to quarantine him in.

"Is there anything I can do?"

He sighs again. "What can you do? If you were here, we could handle this together. I really wish you'd reconsider."

"Lucas, you've got this. You're a certified neat freak. As clean as you keep your house, that virus doesn't stand a chance. Follow the doctor's instructions, and you'll be fine… and if you ever *really* need me, I'll be there, even if it means driving across the country wrapped in plastic. COVID be damned."

This earns a laugh. "Well, if anyone could rock a plastic frock, it'd be you… I want you here, but it's probably for the best. For now, anyway. Root & Bone's closed."

"Sorry to hear that, but I'm sure it's temporary. Things will get back to normal soon."

Lucas scoffs. "What's normal anymore? I can't remember."

"Me, neither," I breathe out, thinking about Mom.

When the call ends, I lean against the building, hidden worries surfacing. *Breathe. Just breathe.*

Lucas is my last family. My only *real* emergency contact. Losing Dad, then Mom—my life umbrella, people who have protected me from the storms, has diminished until it's nearly gone altogether. And it's always raining. *Always.* With his family now in crisis, I feel guilty that I provide no shelter for him when he's been so generous with me. Maybe Asheville's selfish.

At home, I find Dad's ladder and climb to the roof. The leak occurred where the vaulted ceiling meets the lower level in front, *I think.* I spray the afflicted area with a thick coat, shaking my head. I'm pulling the same half-assed fix-it job my father would've done to save money on real repairs. But I have no choice.

Inside, I remove the soggy duct tape, blow dry the wall, and re-tape the gaping, chipped sections—another half-assed patch. Fans dry the shag carpeting while spray air freshener rids the living room of its damp, musty odor. Mostly.

Hours later, I reapply the Flex Seal and repeat this process until the last can is empty. On the final coat, the afternoon sunshine burns my shoulders. The yo-yo weather of March has surrendered to the increasingly hot sauna of April.

Not only will the sun bake the roof into submission, *I hope*, but spring means less hassling with the wood stove. I used to joke with Mom about celebrating it—a spring solstice meets Burning Man. We'd dance around a campfire of unused firewood while chanting grateful songs that our clothes would no longer reek of charred wood. The time gained from not having to stack wood, carry wood, and maintain the fires justified a party, I thought.

Of course, we never did it, even when we could've—too busy keeping up to fuss with weird, over-the-top celebrations.

I stand on my roof perch, superhero style, taking in the front yard. The live, rooted Christmas trees my parents bought every year stretch higher than anyone expected. Mom's magnolia tree looms near the dilapidated fence, littering the lawn with its thick, waxy leaves. The cherry blossoms look inviting, like pink candies. It's a beautiful place—when kept well. My thoughts are interrupted by a truck rumbling up the driveway.

What's Jack Harvey doing here?

I round the roof and descend the ladder as he exits his truck. He wipes his sweat with his dirty pocket towel before slipping on a hospital-style paper mask with dirt smudges on the strings.

"Whatcha doin' on that roof, little lady?"

My eyes narrow. "Patching my leaky roof."

He scratches his head as if he can't imagine it. "Well, ain't that somethin'. Good for you."

"What can I do for you, Jack?"

"How 'bout some of that delicious coffee?"

"Sure." While I prepare the coffee, he tours my den. My leopard print mask sits next to Mom's urn, and I put it on.

"I see whatcha mean." He laughs at my duct-taped wall. "You've got serious water damage."

Duh, I want to say, but don't. "The patch should work temporarily."

"You're making good progress. Feels downright empty in here. My boys miss helpin' with the treasure hunt."

"I miss having them. Will and Max are great."

"Well, Will's got asthma, so Alice is extra cautious. They're drivin' her crazy, on purpose, I think. She'll send 'em your way soon."

Jack's heavy frame makes the chair creak. I deliver his coffee along with a cream cheese danish. His eyes widen as he lowers his mask, and he attacks the pastry as if it might sprout legs and run off his plate.

"Dang, girl. That's the best danish I've ever eaten."

"Thanks, Jack. So, what can I do for you?"

He eyes the cake plate like Ben did. I serve him another one, happy he's enjoying them.

"This dang pandemic's put a kink in our plans, huh?"

"It's delayed them, for sure." *Wait, is he backing out?* "Um, but it'll work out. I'm just stuck here longer than I hoped."

"Oh, I'm not worried. In fact, let's get the ball rollin' anyway." He pulls papers from his overalls and pushes them to me. I scan the contract as he talks. "I know you've got to stay until, well, you *can* leave. But I want the deal done, Lena. Even with you livin' here, I can work your fields."

"You want me to sell you the house *now*?"

"Well, by Friday."

My eyes dart to his. "That's days away."

"Does it matter?" He bites into his second pastry. "With the money in hand, you can hit the ground running once the travel ban lifts. It'll help with expenses… Rent on a new place or, I don't know, a little shopping spree. Get yourself some new clothes for that fancy job of yours."

My eyes narrow as I scan the papers. "You're offering me $225,000?"

"A bonus since you're doin' me a favor." He points to the field between our properties, where Mom's garden once bordered the horse pasture, and the shabby swings tilt precariously. "I'll start with that side and work my way around. You got twenty-five acres, but you only need the house. Upping the deal seems fair since you'll be wakin' up to tractors in your backyard."

"The contract mentions nothing about me staying here."

"My lawyer kept it simple since we don't know how long this virus'll last. We're neighbors. You have my word—stay as long as you need."

"Would I pay rent?"

"Course not."

I peruse the paperwork with a sinking, uneasy feeling. The idea of a huge jump in my bank account urges me to sign. *Right fucking now.* Jack Harvey sees my growing anticipation and pulls a pen from his shirt pocket.

I don't reach for it.

"This deal expires Friday. If we draw up new papers and drag this out, I'm going back to the original price."

"So, if I don't sign by Friday, I'll lose $25,000?"

"Exactly."

Snap judgments concerning money rarely turn out well, something I learned with the bakery. Though pulled to sign and be done with it, I hesitate. *Why wait until Friday? Why not wait until Friday?*

"I'll think about it, but I'm sure I'll bring the signed papers by your place on Friday."

Disappointment shadows his face. He *really* wanted to walk away with my signature, which feels presumptuous.

He nods, rising from his chair. "You'll love workin' for Jason. He gives his employees health benefits and retirement plans. That's why he charges five bucks for coffee and ten bucks for avocado toast. Anyway, he's excited to get you on his team." Jack points to his empty plate. "Put that on the menu. Charge seven or eight bucks for it."

"Thanks. I'm excited, too. I'll see you Friday."

"Come by early so I can get the papers to my lawyer before lunch. Okay?"

Jack leaves, and I return to the roof to check my patch.

Satisfied, I sit on a safe part overlooking the yard and imagine a different landscape. The grass churned into fields. The fence, the swing set, the outbuildings, the barn—all demolished. Blank spaces taking over like there was never anything here at all. It's everything my parents built coming to nothing.

Despite its problems, this place has always been an umbrella, too. A shield when the world outside heightened my anxiety. A rest stop when school and life got to be too much. And finally, the safe haven I returned to when my marriage fell apart. It's harder than I thought, letting go of the only real home I've ever known.

CHAPTER

Twenty

STILL SUN-BAKING on the roof next to my Flex-Sealed patch, my phone chimes. A text from Ben:

> Everything's delicious, and the dickhead's been quiet.
> The entire department's indebted to you.

> Sure you have to move?

I chuckle, pushing my pesky emotions aside.

> Yes, but I'm open to more wine nights and curbside deliveries until I leave.

> Looking forward to it.

> Me, too.

If the house doesn't crumble around me. I run my fingers along the sandpaper shingles, outstretching my legs. It's risky, having a sit-down on the precarious roof, but it stirs memories of stargazing with Lucas when we never worried about things like structural integrity. And, what better place to contemplate Jack's new offer, where I can get a bird's-eye view of what I'm handing over?

Still, many deep breaths later, and I'm no closer to any decision.

Worries for Lucas, Drew, and Luna predominate, anyway. I fumble with my phone.

Ben, I forgot to ask… what's a badge bunny?

The ellipsis shows up, but disappears. My phone rings.

"You don't want to know," Ben says.

"Oh, please tell me. I need the distraction."

"Something wrong?"

Tell him everything's fine. He really doesn't want to know, anyway. "Um, my brother-in-law has COVID. His symptoms are mild so far, but Lucas is upset and worried, all the things he should be."

A silence lingers, making me rethink sharing. *One nice evening and a dick-show turned panic attack doesn't make us besties.*

"I'm sorry. That's troubling news." His words are soft, dandelion seeds floating on a breeze. "Tell me how you are."

This strikes me funny. *Why ask about me? What about symptoms or treatments or launch into a COVID talk generally?* A million other things are so much more important. "Oh, I'm fine. Worried, of course, but fine."

Ben responds with a slow, "Hmm," before saying, "A badge bunny is a cop groupie. I have no firsthand knowledge—not that I'd ever put myself or someone else in that position—but apparently some women find those in law enforcement…um… attractive."

"Ha! I'm sure Detective Gentry likes to think so. I'm glad I called him a dick."

"Your turn. *Fine* can't be the appropriate adjective for what you're feeling."

I smirk at the way he puts it. "Helpless because there's nothing I can do. Guilty because I'm choosing Asheville over family. And…"

"And?"

I take a breath, staring into the gleaming magnolia tree. "And I'd rather it be me."

"Why you?"

"I'm nonessential. In the world or *any* inner circle. If the pandemic has a death-quota to meet, why not take me over a nurse or teacher or someone with family who needs them? It's sad enough—good people dying—but the devastation left behind in losing them… and now with

Lucas at risk…I wish I could trade places." I take a deep breath, my anxiety bitches threatening an attack. "Sorry. I overshared, again."

"No, you haven't. I feel the same, and the collateral damage of my loss would also be minimal."

"Your family, your *twin*, would beg to differ. And you help people every day."

"We're all expendable." The words slip out in a labored sigh, as if it's a lesson stuck on repeat. "But living as fully, honestly, and generously as we can honors the lost, an endeavor that loses its momentum when we struggle over things we can't change. Besides, your family wouldn't want that for you, either."

"That's, um…" My Flex-Sealed patch gleams in the hot sun. *This isn't what my parents want for me.* "You're right." I swipe tears I'm glad he can't see. "Gosh, Ben. Broken *and* expendable—it's like we belong on *The Island of Misfit Toys*."

"Yes, but at least we're in good company."

Once inside the house, I sign the papers. The pen jitters in my fingers with each stroke, as if electrified by my nerves.

For two days, the document sits there, open and signed, begging me to grow comfortable with the idea.

Dream something better. Mom's words circle like dead leaves spun up in the wind. They stay with me—a broken record. It's what Mom wanted, and there's no full life for me here.

Jason Ford. Asheville. Baking my menu in a fabulous restaurant. *That's* dreaming something better.

Patching roof leaks with Flex Seal? *Not so much.*

Friday morning, I shower, shave, and even dab on make-up like I'm, I don't know, an ordinary girl or something. I put on a dress—an anomaly that hasn't happened since Mom insisted on church, one funeral aside. Besides, my usual wardrobe lies in a dirty heap on my couch-bedroom floor. Laundry has taken a backseat to bigger life issues, as it must, sometimes.

Over coffee, I stare at the papers. Handing over the contract will be cathartic. Closure. No more indecision. It'll make *everything* better at once.

Rain specks the patio outside the sliding glass doors. I don't finish my cup before finding a light sweater, grabbing my mask—leopard-print, *meow*—and keys. I slide into my rubber boots and tuck the contract under my sweater to keep it dry.

"I'm doing this, Mom," I say to her urn.

Drops turn to splotches on the drive to the Harvey's farm, saturating my windshield and making me rethink the dress. I park beside Jack's truck, mask up, and race to the front porch as best I can in rubber boots. Already soaked, I ring the doorbell. Bright purple lavender in a patch next to the house catches my eye while waiting. Lavender pots decorate the porch in all corners—a purple explosion.

Alice greets me, tucking a mask on behind her ears. "Oh, bless your heart, Lena. We weren't expecting you so early."

A phone-glance reveals it's barely after seven. Even so, Alice is in full form, right down to her laced-up pumps, pantyhose, church dress, and bright red lipstick. A ruffled, polka-dotted apron completes her fifties look.

"Sorry, Alice. I didn't realize how early it was. Here."

Her eyes widen as she peeks inside the pages. "Oh, Lena, that's wonderful! Jack'll be over the moon."

"Well, I'm excited, too. Thanks for connecting me with Jason. He's awesome, and his restaurant—well, it's the perfect job for me."

Her grin falters slightly—not the reaction I expect. Patting me on the head while patting herself on the back feels more in line with the Alice I know. "Um, well, no need to thank me. None *whatsoever*."

"Sure, there is. Your boys are wonderful. Ben, too. He's, um, well, a surprise. Wish I could take him with me." I step back. "Anyway, thanks. I'd better go."

"Lena, wait. Wanna stay for coffee?"

"Oh, no. Thanks. I've got, um…" I wouldn't *entirely* mind spending time with Alice; I'm *mostly* convinced she isn't a serial killer. Only handing over the signed contract isn't complete until I leave. "I, um, have errands, so I best be off." My brush-off sounds too peppy, but Alice doesn't seem offended.

Her hand goes to my damp arm. "No matter what happens, you've done a good thing, Lena. Good for us, but more importantly, good for you."

Her remark strikes me as funny, but most things about her do. I assume she's referring to the pandemic, as it's made everything so uncertain. I wave goodbye as she slides the folded contract into her apron's pocket.

I dash through the rain to my car. *It's done. It's finally done.* A ginormous weight topples off my aching shoulders.

A solo party at home serves as my celebration. I crank music, day-sip chardonnay, and bake, dreaming better things now possible. *Is it weird fantasizing about a fully-operational, organized kitchen? Or seeing my name on a paycheck again?* Weirder still, I know I've made the right choice, *for once*. Things haven't worked out before, but they will this time. They must—why wouldn't they? *It's done, finally done.*

Late afternoon, a call from Jason stops my baking frenzy. Hands sticky with icing, I switch off the radio and tap the speakerphone with my pinkie.

"Jason, I'm glad you called. I can't wait to introduce you to my Cheerwine cupcakes, and I have more good news, too."

"Lena, wait. We need to talk."

Fuck. It's the death voice. The delicate twinge to his words stabs at me with aching familiarity.

"I can't hire you. Not now. The dining room's been closed for weeks. I'm losing money and employees. I don't know if the restaurant will survive on curbside takeout, let alone be lucrative enough for a pastry chef again."

He tells me how sorry he is and how talented I am. But my ears fill with water. The house is a fishbowl, and I'm drowning in it.

I should've seen it coming, *of course*. My foolish shortsightedness sharpens my sinking feeling. *How come it never occurred to me that the outside world could affect my world? How come I still think I'm in my own bubble?*

My silence prompts him to sigh. "I hate this. I'm so sorry. It's a hard call to make. Alice and Jack kept telling me to put it off, wait, and see what happens. Alice wanted me to wait until after the weekend at least, so I wouldn't ruin it, but it seemed wrong to delay. What's a weekend anymore anyway, right?"

I say all the right things to assuage Jason's guilt and end the call.

Practically panting, I brace myself against the counter. *Oh, my God, what've I done?* I can hardly breathe. *Nothing ever works out for you.* My legs weaken as everything feels heavier. Trembling and flushed, I sink to the floor between the island and the stove. *No house. No job. Nowhere to go. Well, nowhere but Malibu, when it's possible. And forced to watch the oaks and magnolias, old Christmas trees, even the barn brought down and churned into nothing.* My chest tightens with my raging heartbeat and tornadoing thoughts. Even the money provides zero consolation for this latest fuck-up. *I've lost everything. Again.*

I picture Lucas's knowing expression. *Good thing we kept Root & Bone in our back pocket, huh?* He'll say this is another example of my shit decision-making, that Malibu's what's best for me.

And he'll be right. *I did this.* I just sold Mom's property to asshole liars. How could Alice let me ramble over Jason's perfect job, knowing I'd lost it already? Jack's "generous" push to sign by Friday—they knew Jason was rescinding his offer, so they got their deal in place, urgently. Motherfuckers!

I get up, wipe my hands, and slip into my rubber boots. Mud puddles spin up in my race from the driveway.

"Stupid, so stupid. They tricked me!" I rage, spraying mud up their drive. If they lied about the job, they could've lied about everything… letting me stay… keeping Mom's tree.

I don't bother with the doorbell but pound instead. I slip on my mask, hoping my eyes flash my anger. She opens the door, wiping her hands on the same ridiculous apron she wore earlier. Our eyes meet. She knows exactly why I'm here.

I have this grand plan, but my tongue-lashing doesn't come. She folds her arms over her chest, waiting—almost daring me with her cocked-up eyebrow and pursed red lips.

The blue contract sticks out of her apron pocket. Guess Jack lied about needing it by lunchtime, too. I snatch it like a seasoned pickpocket. She gasps, mouth dropping. She tries taking it back, but I rip it into quarters, shoving the bits into my soggy sweater pocket. Her *oh-shit* expression is hella-satisfying. She looks like a cartoon character with smoke puffing from her ears.

"Big mistake, Lena. That's the best deal you'll get. Maybe the only one, too."

"I don't care. I'd rather have no deal than a dishonest one. You tried pulling my home right out from under me, *knowing* I have nowhere to go."

Alice's face softens. "I'm sorry things didn't work out with Jason. That surprised us, too. But don't be so dramatic. You'd have the money to go anywhere once it's safe to travel. And there's always Malibu."

"You lied! What would you have done, huh? Evicted me?"

"No, of course not. But it's not like you want to stay, right? It's not our fault the job fell through, and we didn't want more delays. Call it a neighborly nudge. We want the property, Lena, and you don't, so what's the problem?"

"You manipulated me! That's my problem. Fuck you, Alice."

I go home, drenched and crying like a baby. Not that it matters. I've lost my dream job and, oh, $225,000. No one would begrudge me a few tears. I walk inside and hear a familiar trickle.

Oh, the roof's still leaking. *Of course, it is.*

Twenty~One

THE CONFUSING LIVING room water feature draws me in—staring is better than screaming. The leak's not as bad as it *was*, trickling through the duct tape seams. I kick pots into place to catch the water, glad I didn't bother putting them away. *Nothing ever works out for you.* I almost laugh, adding Flex Seal to that impressive list.

There's tapping at my door. Alice or Jack, probably—the last people I want to see.

But it's him.

He steps back when I slide the door open. His black mask highlights his crinkled, green eyes. I'm sopping wet, which must be confusing since I'm inside. *Most* houses are dry on the inside.

I'm a mess. Eyes surely red and puffy from crying. Worry lines permanently etched on my forehead. Butt chunks more pronounced in my wet cling-wear.

Ben looks at me. *Really* looks at me. Cares about my eyes, ass, and everything else melt away. Maybe I imagine it—this strange connection —but I suspect he sees me exactly the way I am and somehow likes me, anyway.

His eyes narrow. "Is it Lucas? Your brother-in-law?"

"No," I breathe out with some relief. My anxieties diminish with his question. "It's just a shit day. Hell, it's a shit everything, a shit year." I stop talking, afraid I sound whiny, and try composing an explanation, sure he'll want details.

But he moves forward, concerned eyes locked on mine. "What can I do to make it better?"

I chuckle, gasp, and nearly cry together. It's strangely intoxicating that someone wants that for me. He makes me feel cared for, like whatever my answer, he'd do it.

But would he? What comes to mind is risky. It's a different world now, one of covering up and keeping distance. My frustration, sadness, and longing meld into exasperation. I run my hand through my damp hair and then motion helplessly to the space between us.

My silent tantrum brings him closer. He pulls his mask off, shoving it into his pocket. "It's okay."

I meet him in the rain in one step, pressing up on my toes and magnetizing my body to his. In fairness, I hesitate before kissing him, sure he'll protest. *I'm sorry if I've given you the wrong idea,* or *I'm in love with someone else, not into losers, or just not interested.* Or worse. *Stop! What are you doing?*

But he doesn't hesitate, cupping my wet cheek and letting his thumb drift over my lips like they're a delicacy. A bemused relief passes between us with our mutual acceptance, like sailing easily over a hurdle once thought impassable. His other hand tightens at my waist, urging me closer while my fingertips skip across his chest.

And holy hell, it's a kiss *years* in the making—and it shows. *I can't believe I've lived without this. I remember kissing. I love kissing!* He's damn good at it, too—a surprising perk given his quiet nature and my terrible luck. Kissing has always been this beautiful idea that, in execution, leaves me wanting. Not this time. His sweet gentleness couples with a toe-curling intensity from his unrestrained touches to his strong lips, like every kiss is the first and last together, desperate with longing. Our affection is full, powerful, and lovely.

Ravishing his lips, his hands skate over me, and my nerve endings creak open with every fiery touch. If not for the pouring rain, strengthening with us, I'm certain the blaze would consume us where we stand.

His lips never break from mine as he moves us inside and closes the door, shutting out the rain. *Practical is still sexy.* He kicks his boots off near mine and peels me from my wet sweater. It splatters to our feet, torn contract and all. Then, his fingers travel my neck, along my cheek, and into my hair. Like the cupcakes, he devours me. I savor each of his nips, licks, and kisses. I relish being so wanted. I *need* this. *This* is for *me.*

His hand slides up the back of my bare thigh, bringing my dress with it, and he lifts me gently. As my ass meets the table, my legs spread and curve around him, pulling him closer. Along my neck and collarbone, his strong lips and tongue make me whisper a quivering, "Ben." The heat swimming in my core, spreading out all over, feels unbearable. I don't remember the last time I felt like this—I'm not sure I've *ever* felt like this.

Tugging at his shirt frees it from his pants, allowing my hands to slip over his bare stomach. *Oh, my God.* He is *all* muscle. Eager to explore the hard lines of his body, I let my fingers roam. But he flinches as my hands rise—a tiny reaction he quickly covers with zealous kissing and pressing harder into me. *Are my hands too cold? Or is it something else?* I retreat to his shoulders, over his shirt, desperate for whatever he's willing to give me.

The table creaks and wobbles. *Will it hold me? Hold us?* It's our family dinner table. We played intense Monopoly games here and did homework and… *shit. No, no, no. I will not let my anxiety ruin this moment.*

Breathless, I pull away. "My room, now."

My room? That's a joke.

Still, we travel through the house, passing unfinished cupcakes and bumping into obstacles between kisses. In my room, dirty clothes litter the floor, and blankets hang haphazardly across my couch-bed, but Ben's eyes are fixed on me. The back of his legs hit the sofa, and with a gentle push, he's seated. His bulky hands grip my thick thighs, edging me toward him and encouraging me into his lap.

Straddling him, my dress hiked up to my hips, I ache against the bulge in his jeans. Our lips crash together, and soon we're a flurry of tongues intertwining. His fingers dig into my hips, pressing me deeply into his erection, and I rub myself against him, each thrust sending shockwaves through my most sensitive parts. It's a little astonishing how damn good this feels, how good *he* feels, how good *we* feel together. Breathless laughs escape between kisses, as if we're both giddy over finding this one beautiful thing we've been missing. Our frenzied exploration feels gorgeously all-consuming.

And yet, odd thoughts begin to trickle in. Mom rolling past the couch with her walker flashes through my head. *Lena, where's my purse? I can't find my little red wallet.*

I kiss him harder.

Mom, it's late. Go back to bed.

Who's the mom, and who's the daughter? I'm supposed to take care of you, not the other way around. It must be here somewhere. I need my wallet, Lena.

Okay, Mom. I'll help you look.

I shift from his lap and pull him on top of me. His weight feels good, but he moves sideways like he might crush me. I reach for his belt buckle, as he locks eyes with me and traces my face with his fingers, slowing things down in a good way, *I think*. I like looking at him. His ruggedness, even his long scar, gives him character. There's sincerity in his sternness and, strangely, gentleness in his roughness. My lips drift into a smile as his finger slips over them. His hand travels down my neck, across my collarbone, and down the front of my dress. The slower pace makes way for unwanted memories to break through again, even when I kiss him.

Lena, what're you doing on the couch? Why aren't you in bed? You've got school in the morning.

Mom, it's okay. I'm not in school anymore. Remember?

Her frustrated, confused face blinks through my mind.

I shut my eyes to block it out. *Why can't I keep my focus?* This *can't* be happening. "I want this." I cringe, realizing I said that aloud.

"Me, too." He kisses me softly, searching my face. "What is it? Tell me what you need."

I'm surprised he cares. The men from my past were usually too focused on themselves to notice my anxiety, let alone take the time to consider my needs. He slips the hair from my eyes and tucks it behind my ear, eyes never leaving my face as I try to explain. *But how do I?*

"Um, I just need… fresh air. Let's go, um, to the barn."

"Are you sure about this? We don't have to—"

"I know. Bear with me, Ben. Please."

We're soaked by the time we reach it. Against the cleanest brick wall, I tug him to me. Kissing comes easy with the cool air, the raindrops tapping the roof, and Ben's warmth pressing against me. This *might* work.

I shut my eyes, blocking out pesky memories. Hide-and-seek games with Lucas. Horses peeking through stalls. Mom wanting so badly for us to love riding like she did. *Focus, Lena. Focus.*

Only something's lost now. While he could easily take me against the wall, and *maybe* he's working up to it, his determination has waned. Between kisses, I take in the slight pinch between his eyes, and I feel his uncertainty. This isn't what he wants—or at least not the way he wants it. And unable to escape my mental chaos anyway, it's not what I want either. *God, what am I doing?*

Kissing becomes crying. I bury my face against him—embarrassed but still starved for his warmth and closeness. *What's wrong with me?* This place haunts me, and its ghosts will have *none* of this. Only it's *just* a place. And this bullshit is *all* in my head. *Am I such a failure, inside and out, that I can't succeed at something so basic?*

College, bakery, marriage, Mom, Asheville, contract, Flex Seal, and now sex. Nothing ever works out for you.

His hands tighten around me, and barely above the rain sounds, he says, "Is it me, Lena? Did I—"

"No, you're lovely, Ben. It's me. I'm sorry."

"Don't be. I'm here, *whatever* you need."

Damn, damn, damn.

I stay against his shoulder for the longest time. It's been *forever* since someone's held me, and never like this. I feel like I could stay here as long as I want, and he'd never pat my back—*there, there, dear*—or pull away. He doesn't tell me everything'll be okay, either. He just lets me be. Strangely, the longer I indulge, the tighter his grip, like maybe he needs this, too.

Finally, I let him go, but I don't know what to say. Something like, *sorry to play musical make-out rooms with you, only to use your shoulder as a giant tissue for my emotional outbursts. It's okay if I end up as a funny anecdote you share with your friends.* Only words don't come.

His eyes roam over me, taking in my wrinkled, damp dress with a gentle twinge of amusement. "So, this is you in a dress." An appreciative smirk eases up his cheek. "I like it. A lot."

My eyes meet his. "Another joke? That's pretty good."

"I promised my next one would be better."

I swipe my wet cheeks, chuckling nervously. "Forgive me for taking emergency contact to a new level."

"No forgiveness needed. I enjoyed it. But are you alright?"

"I'm fine." *But am I?* Attacking a man at my door with pent-up kisses isn't like me. I fold my arms, hesitant to articulate my disastrous life to him because, *hello*, where do I start? I sigh and rub my arms.

"You're cold." Ben waves toward the house. "Come on."

We walk together, but apart, across the lawn and up the patio. Once inside, I go for the wine while he heads to the wood stove.

Ben stacks logs inside, tucking kindling in between, and starting the fire. It's endearing, the care he takes, and I imagine he's like that with most things in his life. Meticulous, careful, exact. Watching him puzzle it out, I curl up in a chair close to the stove, wrapped in a blanket.

Finally satisfied, Ben closes the wood stove. "I have to go. Will you be okay?"

"Oh, um, of course." I force a smile. This isn't what I expect. *At all.* But like Asheville, I should've seen it coming. "I didn't mean to hold you up. You *should* go."

An obligatory peck on the forehead later, he lets himself out.

It's no wonder he leaves. This place might as well be a carnival's House of Oddities. *In this exhibit, you'll see the rare Lena-Wildebeest. This creature attacks mercilessly, only to stop suddenly for room changes and bouts of crying, leaving her victims disoriented and scurrying for an escape.*

"God, I can't believe I dragged him to the barn."

Sadness overtakes snark. I fold into myself. *What kind of sad-sack loser can't even make out without having a breakdown?* Whatever bottom-barrel-low I hit before deepens now, like I've clawed through the barrel and into the earth it sits on. I'm a worm tunneling into the abyss because I no longer know how to find the surface.

And worse, I don't care. Better nothing than my endless bullshit. Better the abyss than the barbed-wire loneliness tearing through me, inch by fucking inch, gutting me.

I gulp the wine, doubting I'll ever see Ben again. The thought aches more than it should, but, you know, it's been one of those days.

Twenty~Two

DARKNESS TAKES OVER. The trickling stops, and the water pot levels out. The heat from the wood stove burns my face, drying me out. I stop crying. There's nothing left anyway.

On hard days with Mom, I used to play a mental game where I'd set aside all the bad things—the things I couldn't control, change, or make better for her—and focus on one thing we could look forward to. It was something ridiculously small and insignificant, usually, but just enough to drag us through to the other side.

An after-dinner dessert. *"Let's have tapioca pudding tonight with whipped cream and a chocolate drizzle."*

Getting home after a rough day of doctor's visits. *"We'll be home soon. You'll feel better at home."*

Watching her favorite crime show, *Nightshift*, and teasing her about her crush on the actor, Matt Kirby. *"Who needs sleep around Detective Mike Storm?"*

Morning after a long, aching, sleepless night.

But she's gone, and all I have is me, and I can't come up with something to look forward to when every good thing that happens shoves me back on my ass. The landing is rougher each time, the mud thicker, and getting up again requires an increased effort when my energy is all but gone.

I'm weak and tired and over it. So, in my blanket in front of the fire, I stay there, wallowing, because I don't know what else to do or what other thoughts to think.

My phone pings across the room, but I hesitate. *What if it's Lucas? And things are worse?*

It pings again. And again. I rush from my huddle.

It's Ben.

> Come to the pond.
>
> Please.
>
> Lena?
>
> It's okay.

I scoff. *Nothing's okay.* But he's back, and that's weird. Curiosity drives me into my rubber boots.

I shuffle across the yard, wearing my blanket as a cape. His Jeep isn't next to my Pilot, like usual. Rounding the barn, I see he's parked in the field, backed up toward the pond. A bonfire brightens the water's edge, where we had our fish fry. He stands between the two, waiting.

What the hell is this?

His shadow moves around the makeshift campsite. Then, a spark, a long, ascending whistle, and a pop answer my question in the most gorgeous way. The sky alights in colors—bold and brilliant—before sprinkling like fairy dust down to the water.

Fireworks? He brought me fireworks?

He sets off another as I move closer. Blue and silver sparkles brighten the sky, the pond, everything, stirring laughter in my delight. I nearly lose my blanket cape, racing through high grass in my rubber boots.

I stop at his Jeep's open tailgate as another explosion hits the darkness. Green, gold, red, and purple lights umbrella down, illuminating Mom's tree as if dressing it for a surprise party. The dark, dreary field is an incredible theater featuring brilliant, sparkling performances as the colors boom, dance, and fade to make way for the next.

It's never looked so beautiful here. *Never.*

Ben moves beside me, smiling sheepishly as another bursts into center stage—all gold this time, like a heavenly spillover. We share a glance, laughing, as it brightens our faces. The speckled nuggets drizzle before vanishing.

He motions to the back of his top-down Jeep, urging me to sit and enjoy the show. Cross-legged, I huddle in the blanket, swaying side to side with the Top Forty music softly playing over his Jeep's speakers, and loving how he's turned this day—*this day of all days*—into a party. Dazzling me with one animated rainbow after another, he glances my way with every bright burst, watching me watch them. Through laughter and smiles, I make color and distance predictions, and we break out in childish cheers whenever I get it right. My earlier nightmares become forgotten understudies to tonight's headliners, losing me in the dream. *It's a happy place again.*

Stranger still, he did this *for me. When has anyone made such an effort on my behalf? Ever?* And it's such a shockingly beautiful gesture, I'm certain I'll tell this story when I'm old, an incredible highlight in an otherwise average life; that I'll die remembering this. *The night Ben Wright gave me fireworks.*

Nearly an hour passes in shimmering performances. I'm in awe at its conclusion, eyes locked on my evening's surprising savior, and, for the second time today, I've no clue what to say.

Ben hands me a lit sparkler. Its miniature show crackles and dances in my hand. He smiles at my tearful laughter. "Better?"

"Much."

"Good." The stick burns out, so he tosses it into the fire. He sits beside me. We say nothing for a while. That's a good thing about Ben—there's no pressure to speak. Actually, there are *many* good things about Ben.

Watching the flames and the light bouncing off the water is hypnotic. Mom's tree makes cool shadows on the other side, swaying, it seems, to the music. And everything is, mysteriously, okay.

In the silence and beauty of it, I remember one afternoon after I'd just moved back home and meeting Mom in her weedy, overgrown garden. I picked a fat, beefsteak tomato from the vine, and inhaled its distinctive odor. "I love that tomato vine smell."

"Glad you've finally decided to join the living again," she said.

My recent marriage exodus rendered me a mess, cloistered in my bedroom for unlimited tear-fests. I shrugged, not proud. "Thought you might need some help."

The encroaching grass and near-wild plants made traversing the rows difficult enough without the mobility problems brought on by her arthritis, and I could see that she was struggling. She could barely lean down to pick anything without wincing in pain. She nodded, handed off the bucket, and fell into a chair near the garden's edge. I took over in my pajamas and old Nikes.

"We'll get you rubber boots. Walmart has cute ones. Black with little skulls wearing pink bows on their heads." She laughed. "Sassy and dark, like you."

"I won't be here long enough for boots." I huffed over the renegade tomato plants and then the acre-sized garden. "Why go through the trouble of a garden if it hurts you to keep it up?"

"Because I love it, and it makes me happy. It's worth the struggle." She pointed her cane at hidden cucumbers, eyeing me critically. "You were right to leave him, Lena. You were the loneliest married woman I've ever seen."

I laughed sarcastically. "Now, I'm the loneliest unmarried woman you've ever seen."

"Eh, that'll change, one day, if you let it."

Now, sitting on the back of the Jeep on a chilly night with a man who has delighted and encouraged me more than once, I don't feel so lonely anymore. Then, it had been Mom and the garden to bring me out of my sadness. Now, Ben gently tugs the dark veil of mourning away, slow inch by slow inch, and things feel mysteriously okay again.

His arms fold over his chest.

"Are you cold?"

"Little."

I slide closer, swinging half of my blanket around his shoulders. "I can't believe you did this."

"You're having a rough time. Maybe now you'll remember this more."

"I will." Mom would gush. *He's so sweet, and wasn't it beautiful? He's a keeper, Lena. Wow.* But something tells me he doesn't want me gushing with thanks and adoration. "Thank you, Ben."

"It's no trouble." He pauses before asking, "Do you want to talk about it?"

"I lost the job in Asheville."

"Damn, Lena. I'm sorry."

"Let's not talk about it. I'd rather you explain where you got fire-works during a stay-at-home order."

"I confiscated them from some kids in the park." When my mouth drops, he adds, "Weeks ago. It was for their own good. Promise."

He tells me about it and other funny stories while I laugh and bask in how the shittiest day turned into such an unexpectedly beautiful night.

His sweet gesture stirs other possibilities. *Maybe things aren't so bad. Maybe this place isn't either.* I imagine grainy, short images, like an old movie reel. Ben and more fireworks. Joe's girls racing around the pond like Lucas and me when we were little... swinging on Mom's tree... horses in the fields... a vibrant garden. Maybe it could be beautiful again.

As it gets late, the fire fizzles, but we're warm, cozied together. We snatch up conversation so the night won't end. I've never been so starved for anyone's company, not even my ex-husband's. I blame the pandemic. Or my dire situation. Or maybe the house is emitting toxic fumes.

But, it's Ben, too—a thought that intrigues and saddens me together. With my future so uncertain, this feels risky and irresponsible.

Even so, I can't help but smile when Ben says, "It may not be the right time to say this, but losing Asheville will lead to something better. I know it."

"Normally, I wouldn't believe you, but fireworks, Ben? I can't help but feel hopeful now."

"Good." His hand slips around me, tugging me closer. "I'm not ready to lose you, anyway."

Unable to hide my pained expression, I twist to face him. "Ben, you shouldn't—I mean, you can't..." I take a breath. "I still have no idea where I'll end up, you know."

"I know." His smile widens as he shifts toward me. "But you can't move until you meet more of my colleagues first."

I bust out laughing, thinking of Detective Gentry. "Holy hell, Ben."

"My rookies need to be put in their places."

I lean into him, giggling.

"My great uncle is a total misogynist, so you'll have fun with him."

"More jokes? What's gotten into you?"

"I wonder." He closes the blanket around us, pocketing our warmth into a cocoon. "We need more nights like this, too."

I'm about to argue that tonight is a lovely anomaly and remind him of earlier, when I turned a fun time into a breakdown, proving my incapacity for normal things, let alone something as delicate and complicated as, well, whatever this is...or could be. But his forehead rests against mine while he locks our hands across my lap. "You're cold," he says, rubbing them. With his breath against my lips and my skin warming with his touch, I save my arguments for another day.

He kisses me, soft and sweet, like it's impossible to be this close and not mingle lips. "It's getting late, but I like this."

"A few more minutes?"

"Yes." Another kiss. "At least." And another. "I'm glad this happened. Not your bad day, but everything else. It's, um, pleasant—being close to you."

I chuckle at the way he says it. "You, too. Makes me nervous how easy it'd be to get used to this."

"Agreed, but I want to, anyway." And another kiss.

I sigh against his lips. "You and your risky propositions."

"Yes, but worth it, I think," he says.

Mom's words stick on repeat. *It's worth the struggle.*

His lips tangle with mine again. "Let's just be honest with each other and see what happens."

"Honesty, huh? You say it like it's easy," I say.

"It's worked for us so far."

My eyebrows pinch—he's right. I've been bare-all honest with him since we met, and, slowly, he's let me in, too. No one sets out to lie—I hope—but it's easy to muddle the truth over unrealistic expectations and fear of judgment. That's why I've always hated dating. It felt like a game of pretend, with people hiding behind well-designed masks, too afraid to show their true selves. I used to play that game. And I lost.

With Ben, games and masks aren't necessary—a fact that's both refreshing and frightening.

Many just-a-few-more-minutes later, the fire fizzles out in a string of smoke. With quiet resignation, we part. He takes my hand, helping me down from the tailgate, and escorts me dutifully to the passenger seat. After a slow drive over the bumpy terrain, he meets me there again, opening the car door with a lazy smile. I slide out, blanket and all, and he shuts the door quietly behind me.

I expect him to say something odd, like after the fish fry. Maybe I've moved up in his esteem to earn an *"I like you"* or a sassier *"I look forward to you attacking me again soon,"* though neither feels like an upgrade from *"I enjoy you."* But, for once, his expression says enough. He looks sweetly befuddled as if I'm a weird, dramatic painting he likes but can't decipher and isn't sure he wants hanging over his fireplace without understanding it first.

Finally, I say, "I can't remember a better night."

"Me, neither."

"Thanks for turning my day around."

"It's no trouble. Fireworks for fireworks."

I chuckle lightly, glad he sees what happened between us in a positive light. Room changes and tears aside, there *were* sexy moments. Damn sexy. Hot, even. And I don't regret it. I feel like *me*. The *real* me. I went after what I wanted, and, thanks to Ben, it turned out better than I hoped.

Ben takes me in with his all-seeing look before grabbing my blanket-cape and easing me toward him.

I inhale sharply. "I don't know about this."

"I know." He kisses me, warming me all over, like sunshine on the beach after being in the ocean too long. He pulls back slightly and smiles when I try kissing him again. His lips graze mine before leaving me altogether.

"Goodnight, Lena." He lets me go.

CHAPTER
Twenty-Three

I WAKE UP SMILING—A surprise considering my jobless, contract-less, and roof-insecure situation. I shower, start laundry, and mix a batter for peppermint horse treats to sneak to Shadow and his paddock-mates.

Sliding the treats into the oven, my phone rings. The FaceTime request makes my heart race. "Lucas, is everything okay?"

"Drew's fever broke," he says, standing at his espresso machine, "and his appetite's back, though he can't taste much. He's getting better, but it's been a nerve-wracking few days." He shakes his head, tipping his mug at me. "I don't know how you did it so long with Mom—this constant alert."

A little gasp escapes me. *I wish I knew.* "Well, I'm happy he's doing better."

"One more week quarantined in the pool house, and we'll all be in the clear. For now." He takes another sip. "Please tell me what's going on with you. Anything?"

"Yes, actually." The whole story starts to spill from me because I want to tell him about last night. I *rarely* have anything good to tell Lucas. And geez, it's fireworks—if that isn't brag-worthy, what is? Besides, it'd be fun talking about boys like the old days.

But to get to the good part, I have to go through the bad, and we get hopelessly derailed.

"Wait a minute. You tore up a deal for $225,000? Are you kidding?"

"That's not the point. Just listen—"

"Lena, you overreacted."

"No, I didn't. They manipulated me—"

"It wasn't their place to tell you you'd lost the Asheville job. You should've known that would happen. It's happening everywhere."

"Maybe it shouldn't have been a surprise, but it *was*, okay? And if the Harveys lied about that, then what else? He could've evicted me, Lucas."

"Is that such a bad thing? You sleep on a fifty-year-old couch. The toilet's liable to fall through the floorboards the next time you sit on it. A push out the door is exactly what you need."

"I didn't ask for a pandemic, Lucas. You think I'm *trying* to stay here?"

"Yes, because you *have* to move, and you're preventing it. It was a good deal—the best you'll get for that dump—and you let it slip through your fingers." He stops to run a hand through his hair. "You're self-sabotaging. It's the bakery all over again."

"No, it isn't. Stop holding the bakery over my head. I'm not the same person. I'm kinder and stronger, and, damn it, I'm smarter, Lucas. I refuse to be manipulated or rushed or made to feel like I don't know what I'm doing because my bakery failed..." I stop to grunt. "... four fucking years ago. You put this, this... *dump* in my hands, so I'm handling it *my* way."

"Well, that was *my* mistake because *your way* means you'll be there forever. You've made one bad decision after another. Turning your nose up at Root & Bone. Putting all your hopes in Asheville. Ruining the deal with the Harveys. What'll happen when the house becomes unlivable? What then, huh? Guess it'll be my pool house, after all."

"No, it won't. I'll figure it out, *like always*. And stop acting so fucking high and mighty because you *gave* me the house, okay? I didn't ask for it or anything else. *Ever.* If you want your half, take it, especially if you'll stop bringing it up the rest of my life. This is why I don't want Malibu. Your generosity isn't a gift; it's a life sentence. If you can't be support-ive, then don't be anything. I have to go."

I hang up on him—something I never, *ever* do—and immediately regret it. He's going through enough already. But I can't fix my mistake yet. *Have I made bad decisions? Am I self-sabotaging? What* will *I do when the house caves in?*

I take the horse treats out of the oven. They're overdone, but Shadow won't mind.

"I need a plan," I say as if one might matriculate from the dust in the air.

A memory stirs, something Mom said whenever I needed help with homework. *Start with what you know.*

With the stay-at-home order extended and a phased reopening of businesses after that, it will limit employment opportunities. Even the best restaurants will struggle. Money from the sale of the house won't last long if I can't find a job to support myself. "I need to live here for the foreseeable future."

What would've sent me into a frenzy a month ago doesn't now. I smirk, remembering *fireworks,* and think it'll be okay. Somehow. Mysteriously. I've made it this far.

I bin the treats, grab my keys, and head to the farm.

Horses dot the landscape, sharing their paddock space with pecking ibises. Shadow centers the field, swishing at flies with his half-tail. He gives me a side-eye before turning away.

Seeing no one around and hopeful Gloria won't mind, I step through hellacious mud puddles from yesterday's rain and enter the gate.

He retreats until he sees the open bin and something in my hand. Shadow munches while letting me love on him. His velvety coat is warm in the April sunshine. I lay my head against his neck.

"I've missed you, Shadow."

He helps himself to another treat from my open bin and then farts to let me know he appreciates it.

A roaring ATV disrupts us. Up the lane, Gloria speeds toward the paddock.

Busted.

She greets me at the fence, hands on her hips. "You shouldn't give 'em treats unless he earns it. Fancy a ride?"

Within the hour, we mount our horses. In the saddle, I inhale deeply, like I haven't breathed in weeks.

"You did everything yourself this time," Gloria says as we mosey toward the trail.

I smile. I hadn't noticed. After several hilarious, slightly disturbing virtual dating stories, she asks me how everything's been going.

Losing the Asheville job rounds out my report. "I cook and clean, and there aren't many promising opportunities now that don't involve a drive-thru."

"You do more than cook and clean, Lena. You learn fast and can handle tough situations. You're nice to talk to, and you love caring for people. You don't need a job. You need a calling. Something that'll use *all* your talents."

I smile, wondering what that would be like—a *calling* instead of a job. *Dream something better.* Mom's words shove me into a daydream. I'm in a gorgeous kitchen cooking delectable desserts and savory dishes to share with whoever stops by—and *everyone* does. The Jones family visits for fishing and food. The Harvey boys bring friends over for snacks. Mrs. Moore and the church ladies stop by for tea and cookies. I use Mom's china and silver tea services, sparking lovely conversations about the good old days. My online friends pop in whenever I post something amazing, which is constantly. I host families for tractor rides and fishing and picnics in the grass. Anyone in need of a good cup of coffee stops by on a whim, and everyone feels at home.

And when I want to get out, I round Wilmington with lunch and dessert drop-offs to my usual spots.

Then, when the kitchen is clean and the oven off, I ride horses and play in my garden. I sleep well, I'm never bored, and I'm always ready for company.

That *full, honest, generous life to honor the lost* that Ben mentioned holds the beautiful vision together, like glue solidifying the dream into something real. Even more amazing—it happens right where I am, at Mom's house.

"Let's go to the arena and get our canter on," Gloria says as we near the barn. "We could use the exercise."

With the arena to ourselves, we do our own things. She calls it "Go as you please."

I practice trotting and work up to a canter. We take sharp turns, cutting across the diagonal, kicking up mud, and making Shadow grunt with exertion. I eye the low jump in the center and go for it, remembering how I stayed on with River.

Shadow and I sail over the rail easily. Though not far off the ground, cresting the jump feels like flying.

"Good boy." I slow him to a walk, laughing and patting his neck.

"That's what I call going as you please!" Gloria claps from her horse.

"You're a natural! Shadow hasn't moved that well in a decade, the ol' coot!"

Shadow and I jump the rail again. This time, Gloria snaps a picture as Shadow and I are mid-jump. I post it with the headline: *Go as you please.*

"Things aren't all bad," I say while untacking.

"Oh, yeah?"

"I don't know. I maybe, sort of, met someone."

"What? During a stay-at-home order?" She tosses a brush at me. "Talk about burying the lead! Tell me all the juicy details."

I don't tell her *everything*. Some things, I don't know, feel sacred. But I gush about Ben and fireworks like I wanted to with Lucas.

Her girlish grin widens as if watching a lovely movie. "If you don't fall in love with him, I will!"

"It was a night I'll remember forever, but I'm not getting too excited."

"Dang, Lena! Why not?"

"I'm a wreck. No job. No money. No clue where I'll end up. Things like this *never* work out for me. And being alone is better than going through heartbreak again. I'm fucking tired of being sad."

Gloria gives me a hard stare. "Never give up on love, Lena. It's a shit-thing to do to yourself. Mr. Fireworks wants a chance with you. And, girl, you should let him have it."

My anxiety bitches assure me nothing else good can come from *that* risky proposition, however sexy and sweet Ben is.

But going as I please, no matter what Lucas or anyone else thinks, stirs other, safer plans. The words echo in my head on the drive home, reminding me of Mom's message in the seed packet. *Let's do whatever it takes to make this a happy place for you again.*

It *is* a happy place. It can be *my* happy place. Maybe other people's, too.

It's a frightening, anxious, exhilarating thing—building a new dream. But, with the world on hold, what else can I do?

Twenty~Four

BUT GOING as I please requires funding. *Must find job.* A glance around my dilapidated house forces an amendment—*must find well-paying job.*

I cold-call every food-related business within thirty miles. Bakeries, grocery store delis, restaurants, hotels, cafeterias, assisted living centers —anyplace that cooks for people gets my resumé. But between temporary closures, reduced hours, and closed dining rooms, most tell me they're not hiring. Some even admit they're barely scraping by. *Yeah, me, too.*

Frustration leads me outside, where everything is lush and blooming and goes on regardless of what's happening in the world.

Planting Mom's seeds feels like the perfect middle finger to the Harveys and Lucas. It's a bold move that says *I'm staying... at least long enough to plant, cultivate, and harvest a huge ass garden, so back off, bitches.*

As the middle-finger-garden idea materializes, so does the equipment to do it. Knocking over a tower of boxes in the barn reveals a wheelbarrow full of gardening tools.

"Everything I need is right here, huh, Mom?"

After mowing the high grass, I try the tiller. The patchy earth where Mom once had her garden churns with new promise as the tiller's blades dig in and upturn the dirt. *This might work.* In true middle-finger-garden spirit, I sing *Hot Girl Bummer* as I go, a song that seems to be on the radio every time I turn on the car. *"Fuck you, and you, and youuuuu…"*

Late in the afternoon, with the large patch of dirt nearly ready for planting, Ben shows up, surprising me. Yes, he gave me fireworks, but things always look different in the daylight, and such sparkle fades. I thought he'd tally the pros and cons of really "seeing what happens," and find me not worth the effort. *I still can't believe I dragged him to the barn.*

He meets me in the plowed rows with a critical once-over. Sweat and dirt accessorize my shorts, tank top, and Dad's work gloves, while mud crusts the edges of my rubber boots—not my *best* look.

He glances at my semi-neat rows and then his eyes find mine again, crinkling with the tiniest glimmer of amusement. "Staying then?"

"For now."

He retreats to his Jeep, removes his button-down shirt for his dark undershirt, and grabs gloves from his cargo area. When he returns, he eases the hoe from my hands.

"Do you always carry work gloves in your Jeep?" I ask.

"Yes." He looks curious, like *doesn't everyone?*

I move the wheelbarrow to collect the weeds I've churned up. "What else do you keep in there, you know, aside from goggles and earmuffs?"

"First aid kit. Hand sanitizers. Extra masks. Digital thermometer. Flares. Bolt cutters. Chain—"

"Chain? What for?"

"In case someone's stuck in the mud or sand," he says with a quirk of his shoulders.

I smirk. *Duh, Lena.*

He goes on, "Bungee cords, blanket, small chainsaw, and duct tape."

"Gosh, Ben. Sounds like a hit man's shopping list. Why the chainsaw?"

"Downed trees in the road."

"You're ready for anything," I decide with a sigh.

"I like to be prepared." His eyes narrow, glancing at me. "I also brought over beer and pizza."

"I think I like you, Ben."

"Good. I know I like you."

I press my lips together, trying to contain my blushing smile. I pick weeds from the dirt, tossing them aside. "I bet you were a Boy Scout."

"Yes. Eagle."

I gawk. "Mom would've *adored* you."

"I wish I'd known her."

"Eh, she would've made it creepy," I say.

"Creepy? How?"

"She would've played matchmaker. Hard. Especially with an Eagle Scout. She was a troop leader for years. She would've arranged for you to come over for some chore. Then, I'd find you under the kitchen sink, and Mom would wink at me, like *yeah, you can thank me later*. Then, she'd ask awkward questions like, *'Lena, doesn't Ben have wonderfully muscular arms?'* or *'Ben, wouldn't Lena benefit from a little lip gloss?'* Then, she'd disappear into her bedroom with her coins, leaving us alone to attack each other, but we'd be too embarrassed."

"I see where you get your determination," he grins. "Did she do that often?"

"What? Play matchmaker?"

Ben nods.

"The last year or so, yes. She was desperate to see me settled. But not when I was young. She keenly voiced her disapproval of the boys I brought home then." I stop sifting through dirt to laugh. "She'd decide they were not right for me over the smallest, silliest things."

"Like what?" He leans against the hoe.

I rise from my dirt pile, hands resting on my hips. "He wears too much cologne. His hair's too long. His pants are too baggy. He doesn't shake hands right."

"There's a wrong way to shake hands?"

I take my glove off and extend my right hand. Ben does the same, gripping mine firmly. A butterfly flutters in my stomach.

"That's the right way." I take my hand back and grab his again, fingers only. "That's the wrong way."

"I don't like that either."

"Of course not. Any self-respecting Boy Scout knows how to shake hands." I shrug, my smile falling. "No one was ever good enough. Fast forward to my failed marriage, living with her, and my life going nowhere, and her attitude changed. Then, anything was good enough. No wonder I'm such a mess, huh?"

"She just wanted what's best for you." He grins, puffing out his chest. "Apparently, that's me."

My laughter thwarts wayward tears over missing Mom. "You'd

exceed *any* mom's wish list for a son-in-law. Don't your family and friends play matchmaker with you?"

"No."

"Gosh, Ben. Why not?"

"My sister says I'm too serious and have no personality."

"That's *definitely* not true." But then, I remember *Robocop*-Ben pulling me over and not even smirking at my jokes, and I could see her point.

"Around new people, it is. I'm not easy to get to know," he says.

"Why is that?"

He looks distressed by the question, but says, "It's learned behavior."

"Learned why?"

"As a kid, I trained myself to be quiet and not stand out. I'm dyslexic, but I wasn't diagnosed until middle school because my sister and I hid my reading problem. She drew attention away from me in classes we shared with jokes or questions for the teachers. I limited participation."

"Aw, Ben. That must've been hard, and middle school sucks, anyway. Why hide it?"

His eyes widen. "I was ashamed, frustrated about my inadequacy— faulty thinking, I realized later. Talking less and listening more helped me in school. It's served me well in my careers, too. I don't view it as a detriment."

"I don't either. Chitchat's exhausting and overrated, anyway."

"Yes, but dating's difficult." He motions to his ears. "These don't help."

"Why would your hearing aids matter?"

"They're off-putting to some. The more a date notices or asks questions, the more it bothers her, usually."

"So, if she makes a big deal, then it is a big deal?"

"Yes. Or the subject's ignored, like it doesn't exist. That's happened with some dates. Other women handle it passive-aggressively. The worst example was when a woman I liked raised her voice, spoke more clearly, and answered questions for me on a date."

"Holy shit, like you're a child."

"I've also been rejected outright for my... injuries," he admits slowly, "which is more honest than pretending to be okay with them, I suppose."

"But it must hurt more," I say, sad for him.

"Yes." His eyes pinch as he looks away from me, like he could be reliving those hurts in the moment.

"I'm sorry."

"It's okay." Ben nods. "My sister says I'm a trifecta of social awkwardness. I come across as unfriendly and deficient with my scars and hearing aids. I'm no Prince Charming."

"Charm's overrated, too. It's their loss. Your hearing aids help you hear *AND* weed out assholes, so they're not a detriment, either."

"Agreed."

I slip my hand back into my glove. "But, yes, dating's all chitchat and pretense, so it must be difficult."

"I'm spared from matchmaking, at least."

"That's good. Mom propositioned doctors, nurses, therapists, random strangers in the elevator, anyone and everyone. Her meet-my-daughter spiel embarrassed the hell out of me."

"Did it ever work?"

"Ah… no. Her delivery kinda sucked. *This is my daughter, Lena. She lives with me, but that's so she can take excellent care of me. She's divorced, but that means she thinks for herself. She didn't finish school, but bakers don't need college. Isn't she beautiful?*" I laugh at my spot-on Mom impression, but it falls fast.

"Yes."

I glance at Ben. "Yes, what?"

"You *are* beautiful." His eyebrows crease, and he starts hoeing the ground again. "And you are not your circumstances."

But that's how I feel—broke, jobless, house poor, hanging on by a weak, fraying thread. Sure, there's more to me than problems, but it's hard to get past them, too. And what's left, well, doesn't feel like enough.

Then, I imagine young-Ben struggling with something he couldn't control, and it certainly didn't make him less than. Even now, he could choose bitterness and anger about his scars and disability. But Ben is more than his circumstances. They're merely footnotes to his beautiful existence. So, maybe my self-image is faulty thinking, too.

I smirk, rolling my eyes. "I really want to argue the beautiful thing, but I'll just say thanks."

"Good. It's not up for debate."

"Well, otherwise, your honesty is refreshing. I like learning about you."

"I've enjoyed learning about you since your speeding confession—that's refreshing honesty." He laughs slightly. "*You* can ask me anything, anytime."

He says it like he's establishing a rule—one that I, apparently, started the day he pulled me over. The memory makes me chuckle. "Don't get confessions often?"

"Ah, no. The heavy rubber boots excuse was also original."

I laugh, nodding. "Well, you can ask me anything, too. I mean, not that I don't talk enough without prompting."

I continue tugging grass clumps out of the churned dirt at my boots, but Ben hesitates. "Okay. What happened with us the other day? I thought you were enjoying it—I know I was—but then something changed."

I deflate a little. "Sorry, Ben. I still can't believe I dragged you to the barn. That ranks high on my list of craziest-Lena moments. I made things between us so awkward and disappointing."

"I didn't feel either of those things, but I want to understand."

"I couldn't relax," I say softly.

"Why not?"

My shoulders bounce with frustration. "The short answer is that I couldn't get out of my head long enough to enjoy myself."

"What's the long answer?"

I bite my bottom lip before taking a breath. "Fine. The long answer… I struggle relaxing in *that* house on a good day. Mom's around every corner, and now the house is falling apart just like she did. Those last months, I called nine-one-one so often that they knew me by name. I still wake up most nights, grabbing for my phone… I, um, even called recently, *after* she died, forcing the entire cavalry to show up for a fucking nightmare. That mishap tops my crazy list. I was on high alert *all* the time—I still am, like I can't turn it off. I thought… engaging with you like *that* might break me from it. But bad memories crept in, distracting me and intensifying my anxiety, no matter where we were or how much I… enjoyed you." A gasping breath escapes. "And I did, Ben. I do… enjoy you. But…"

I shrug, wiping a wayward tear with Dad's glove, surely getting dirt on my face. I tug them off and let the gloves fall to the ground to clear my tears better. "I got in my own way, and that won't change… If that's why you're here."

No joyrides on this crazy train.

I await his quick exit—he'll remember something he has to do while slowly back-stepping to his Jeep—because no one wants *this*.

The broken part of me wants to see him go, to scare him away, never to be seen again, because it would be a relief—it's safer and easier not having the added pressure. I like him enough to be worried about breaking his heart or him breaking mine. My anxiety bitches love destroying relationships with their nonsense, feeding my worries. It's a battle I'm too weak right now to win, and it's difficult justifying the mental effort, especially since nothing ever works out for me, anyway.

But he stays still, looking perplexed.

"Sorry. *Again*. I'm sure you didn't want the long, *long* answer."

"I want the answers, whatever the length." With the hoe perched between us, he waits until my eyes meet his. "Lena, I've never wanted to know someone more. I've never *wanted* anyone more… but I'm here to spend time with you, that's all. Two friends, hanging out, enjoying each other. Until we're both all in, that's all it should be."

All in? That'll never happen. I'm not all-in material, certainly not for a guy who, very clearly, has his shit together at all times.

I take the hoe from his hands. "That's what I'm saying—nothing'll happen. You *really* shouldn't waste your time. Maybe dating's hard, but trust me, it'll be easier than this."

He nods, eyeing the uneven dirt mounds. "You're right. I didn't realize there'd be gardening."

My eyes catch his, and a laugh rumbles from me. "Oh, it's all tears and hard labor around here."

"Sounds like every date I've ever had… We said we'd see what happens, right?"

We did say that. I hear Gloria in my head. *Mr. Fireworks wants a chance… let him have it.* My pained smile slips into a nod before I decide that the first step in seeing what happens means getting back to work on this messy attempt at a garden.

But he grabs the hoe between us, wrapping his fingers over mine and gently demanding my attention. My eyes latch onto his—they seem softer than before, as if between the sunlight, sweat, and honest conversation, he's lost a little of his usual rough edges.

"That alarmed feeling will go away, Lena," he says. "Traumatic events end, but getting over them takes time. That's where the real struggle is—in the aftermath when survival shifts to living again. It's not easy. It's too quiet. Too much time to think. But it gets better. You've lived in crisis mode so long that your head hasn't caught up to your change in circumstances, yet. But it will. I promise."

I would normally scoff at someone trying to tell me what's wrong with me, but his firm grip over my hand and his disarming gaze hint that he's experienced something like this, too. *Wait, like PTSD? That's for soldiers, not caregivers.* But maybe he's not *entirely* wrong. That would explain the nightmares, the surge in panic attacks, and this strangling current of unease that seems to shadow me. How can I argue?

Though I want to… *I'm fine. Really. Fine.*

A strange smile pushes through my tears as I wipe my face again and try to latch on to the comfort he's offering. "Any way I can skip through all of the tears and panic and move the process along?"

"Yes. By doing what makes you happy." He tugs the hoe from me completely, sporting a sly grin. "And hanging out with me as much as possible."

Laughter breaks through, sweet and easy. "Gosh, Ben. You and your risky propositions."

"It's worked so far." He looks over at me. "If you're okay with me showing up."

"Yes. Okay. If you want."

We finish clearing out the grass clumps and making mounded rows. Then, I plant the seeds like Mom did. I poke holes in the mound with a broken broomstick handle, drop the seeds inside, and cover it with my boot. I plant every seed from the packets because if you're planting a middle-finger garden, you should do so with fervor and gusto. Anything less would feel half-assed.

We link the semi-working hoses to the spigot on the side of the house and douse the gray earth mounds with water. Our job done and stomachs rumbling, we have dinner on the patio, willing the plants to grow through the damp, dirty mess, hoping for something good to come from our efforts.

The surprising thing is that something good has already come from it. Over beer, pizza, and easy conversation, I realize that I haven't connected with someone like this in an excruciatingly long time. I feel closer to him now than I did when we had our lips and hands all over each other. Closeness is a risk but also a comfort. He not only accepts whatever state I'm in, but he also seems to understand why I'm in it. It's validating.

And, if I'm honest, extremely sexy.

So when it gets late, and we face off in an awkward silence at the sliding glass door—me about to go inside and him about to head toward his Jeep—I linger, hopeful for contact but unsure what that should be. Maybe he wants to kiss me—I can't tell. It's probably best he doesn't. But still.

Then, he does the perfect thing. His hand grazes my cheek as he leaves a breathy kiss on my forehead.

"It's been a good day." Then, he smiles, says goodnight, and gets in his Jeep.

IN AN EIGHTIES MOVIE, this would be the cheesy montage where nothing mind-blowing happens, but small, good things accumulate slowly.

Like growing weirdly accustomed to quarantine. First, going out into the world was a tremendous gamble, like skydiving. But now it's the new normal. We've gone from being skittish meerkats, peeking from our burrows, to scurrying haphazardly from one hole to another in a busy race, dousing ourselves in sanitizer at each port.

I limit my outings, combining grocery shopping with Shadow visits and baked deliveries. I social distance, wear my mask, and sanitize my hands. It's rote memory now, like buckling my seatbelt, and they're such slight inconveniences against the larger threat. If it can save lives, why the hell *wouldn't* I do it?

And staying at home, even at *that* house, isn't so bad.

I clean out the entire upstairs. I toss old schoolwork and embarrassing love letters, but not before laughing at their requests to *check this box*. Giggling, I post a pic—sparing the sender's identity, of course. *If you've ever received or sent one of these, click this box.*

Norman writes back: *Your posts are the only reason I go to social media anymore. Keep 'em coming.* Another friend echoes his sentiment: *Thanks for the break from all the pandemic news and political rants. Your posts are a fun relief from the madness.*

If junk drawers and funny finds give a momentary reprieve, then why not? It's another small thing I can do. Besides, I'm gaining a following—not Ben-level yet but growing.

While upstairs, I try flushing the toilet and discover it works. The triangular shower works, too. Finding no sneaky leaks, I realize I stopped using it because of the extreme temperatures, not disrepair. With no central heating, a bum furnace, and old, single-paned windows, the upstairs is an ice cave in the winter and a sauna in the summer. Soon, I'll be reduced to cold showers only, and even then, I'll sweat. But I don't care. *A fully-functional bathroom!* I do a happy dance across the blue linoleum floor—one that doesn't bend underfoot.

I clean out the downstairs bathrooms, shut off the water to both, and close their doors until I can afford to get them fixed properly.

When that will be… remains a mystery. Diligent job hunting occupies my mornings, but offers little hope. No one's hiring, and with millions now out of work, I understand why. Still, it's a downer to my montage.

On the upside, though, there's Ben.

He shows up every few days. He joins me in whatever I'm doing—refinishing furniture, sorting boxes, baking, yard work, whatever. Then, we water the garden, eat dinner, and talk until it's late.

Ben is strategic, a discovery made over old board games. When I ask why he keeps his Monopoly money stacked in a pile instead of spreading it out like a normal person, he says, "So you'll have difficulty assessing my net worth."

He beats me at nearly everything but never gloats. And he's not unmerciful, proven over laser tag—his favorite game that we've rediscovered in the clean up so far. We spend many evenings in red-lasered shootouts around shed corners and behind old cars. Despite my home advantage, he always bests me in a shooting game. But he gives me extra time to hide and misses easy shots on purpose to keep my spirits up.

We take long walks around the property. We talk about insignificant but amusing things like what tree animal we'd rather be or which superhero's most likely to turn evil.

Ben doesn't rush—not to move, speak, or even judge. He's an intentional slowpoke, unless we're playing laser tag—then he's the fucking Flash.

We spend many rainy afternoons in the carport, hovering over intricate salvaging operations and filling Mason jars with what shouldn't be thrown away. Flipping through thousands of books recovered from the barn for money bookmarks doesn't bother him either. He's a good sport about everything, making me question his sanity. Mine, too… as if Ben's an imaginary friend I created to fight loneliness.

Wait… *Is he? Am I Sixth-Sensing myself?* Bruce Willis's social awkwardness fits, but Ben manipulates objects, wears different clothes, and brings food. My warped subconscious couldn't pull off such an elaborate enterprise. *Could it?*

I don't even care. We're in a pandemic, and imaginary or not, I need the company. Ben eases into my life slowly, and whatever we're doing, I find it easy to be present with him instead of stuck in my head—a good thing.

And a surprise since Ben's not a talker. More proof he's not imaginary—if I made him up, he'd be a better conversationalist. If I'm not talking, we go hours in silence—our best stint is two hours twenty-two minutes. And yes, I always break it. While he volunteers random factoids *occasionally*, like the proper thing to do with old license plates we find or how to clean rusty tools, he reveals little else without me asking directly.

With his ask-me-anything rule in place, my favorite Ben-question becomes, *"What are you thinking?"* And he's quick to grant me access, sometimes mid-thought. Usually, it's something about work or his family, but I enjoy catching him off guard and testing his honesty.

Over Connect Four… "You made a bad move. I'll win on the next turn."

Over an experimental jalapeño potato soup… "Too much pepper. Not creamy enough."

Over losing at Clue… "No motive. No witnesses. This is nonsensical crime anyway. But I'm glad you won. It increases our chances of playing again."

Over catching him staring in the garden… "Um, well… You in the garden may be the sexiest thing I've ever seen." His eyebrows pinch. "Aside from you… in a dress… in the rain."

His admission makes him as nervous as it flatters me. He focuses on weeding rather than my reaction. And not wanting to embarrass him, I smile and do the same.

One night, stargazing in his Jeep by the pond, he uses a phone app to show me constellations. We lean in, shoulder-to-shoulder across the console to better see the images overlapping the stars behind it. *Lyra.*

Orion. Ares. Ben reciting the names with his *Iron Giant*-voice makes me think less about stars and more about how comfortable this is.

"Do you think we'll still hang out like this when things go back to normal?" My question blurts out over the top of him, saying *Cassiopeia.* His head shifts toward me, and I realize I've practically made his shoulder my pillow. I inch away and catch the funny look he gives me.

"You're my normal… my *new* normal," he says.

While I gnaw my bottom lip and try to figure out what to say, he smirks, brow cocked, and returns to the stars. "Ursa Minor. Little Bear." His hand grazes mine as I chuckle.

Then, one rainy afternoon under the carport, we sort boxes from Lucas's old room. We find his *Garbage Pail Kids,* including my nemesis *Nervous Nellie.*

I muse over her dark corner and gnawed hands. "Look, it's me."

"You?"

"Mom and Dad called me *Nervous Nellie,* so when Lucas found the card, it became *my* card." I hold it next to my face. "A decent likeness, I think. I used to bite my nails until they bled." I flutter my long nails with my other hand. "I broke that habit with help."

Ben looks bothered. "How?"

"Well, Mark called me disgusting—a baker who bites her nails. So, he gave me these thick rubber bands for my wrists, and whenever I did it, he snapped the band. It worked, eventually."

I slip the card into the keep pile, but Ben grabs it, holding it up with a stern expression. "Lena, never think of yourself this way again—I mean it. I don't see you this way. Anyone who loves you shouldn't either. You aren't a damn Nervous Nellie or anything like her. You're strong, brave, kind, and beautiful, and you sure as hell don't cower in *any* corner. You should burn this and get angry at anyone who calls you that."

Holy shit, I hit a nerve. Hard. I look at the card, hating the nickname and everything associated with it. And though I know in my heart, *truly,* that my family never *meant* to hurt me, it did anyway. And I let it.

He drops the card between us and takes my hands. His thumbs run over the delicate under-skin of my wrists, softly erasing the sting of the rubber band snaps from years ago. "Hurting you wasn't helping you. You deserve better. He didn't love you, Lena… and he was an asshole, anyway."

"You're right. It took me way too long to see it, but I know he didn't love me. How could he?" I nod toward the card. "That's how he saw me, too. In the end, anyway. Nervous Nellie's hard to love."

"She is, but you aren't." His fingers slide into my palms, folding my hands in his tightly. "You aren't *Nervous Nellie*. You're *Lovable Lena*."

My mouth drops in a gasp, dazzled. "Damn, Ben. You win the prize for the sweetest thing anyone's ever said to me." *Lovable Lena today, but that'll change. Someday.* More fitting L-descriptors stream through my head. *Loser... lackluster... laughable...* But I push my anxiety bitches aside. "I hope that's *always* how you see me. I kinda like having you around."

"You win the prize for the best understatement. You *love* having me around."

Though we laugh, our comfortable friend-zone dissipates the longer our hands tangle, especially as his fingers slip softly over mine.

"My saracastic tendencies are pushing me toward a rebuttal, Ben, but how can I say how useful you are for heavy-lifting and food-delivery after the whole *Lovable Lena* thing? You've backed me into a sincere corner."

"Better say what you're really thinking, then." He leans closer, whispering like it's a secret.

"Yes, I love having you around." My cheeks flush as nerves rise, and my hands fidget inside his. "But I hate it when *Nervous Nellie* crashes our party... like now. You're right. She's not good for me."

"Let's burn her." His stoically delivered solution makes me laugh. "Seriously. She doesn't belong—not in your life, not with us."

Us? Is that the right pronoun? I shake off us-thoughts, wishing I could burn my anxiety bitches, too. "Yes. Let's get the metal barrel from the barn."

I tell him about the Burning Man slash Spring Solstice celebration I always wanted to do with Mom, so for the ceremony, we go big—why not? As Ben puts it, "We don't believe in half-ass-man-ship." In the drizzling rain, we drag the barrel close to the carport. We use Lucas's old schoolwork as kindling and get the flames going.

I hold the card over the barrel, strangely hesitant. *It's just a damn card.*

"Do it. Murder her. Make her dead to you."

I laugh, letting it go drop-the-mic style. "This is weird, but I love it. Let's burn more things."

Ben grabs the other *Garbage Pail Kids*. "What about these?"

"Well, they *are* mean and totally problematic."

"For good reason."

I sigh and take a breath. "Okay."

Ben smiles and drops them in. We lean over, eyeing their curling edges as they turn to ashes. It's crazy satisfying, especially considering the Harrys, Lotties, Seymores, Jeds, and countless others who suffered over the caricatures as I had.

"What else?" Ben says.

"Um, I don't know. What would you burn if you had it with you?"

He pauses thoughtfully. "Um, my discharge papers—I wanted to be a career soldier. Oh, and somewhere I have a completion certificate for an Improv class."

"Improv? Why would you ever take Improv?"

"You aren't the only one with an ex who tried to fix you. She thought it would make me less socially awkward, especially at parties."

"Holy hell, it's a wonder you survived the trauma."

"The relationship didn't. Worst hours of my life, and I've been in combat."

"Aw, Ben, you may take the prize for worst ex, even with my rubber bands."

He grabs two beers from his cooler. We clink the cans together as he smiles. "Things are definitely better for us without them."

I take a sip. "For the record, I'd love to go to a party with you."

"You would? Really?"

"Hell, yes. We'd make a game out of it, betting on the other guests. Who'd get drunk first? Double dip? Say something inappropriate? And, we'd have secret signals to rescue each other from boring conversations. We'd leave early and spend the rest of the night drinking and talking about people. It'd be a blast."

Ben considers this. "I've never wanted to go to a party more."

"Let's hope we get the chance to someday. For now, those are really good contributions to our fire-barrel."

"I'll bring mine next time." He mimics the drop-the-mic motion over the fire. "What else do you have?"

"Be right back." I speed-walk to the house through the rain.

Upstairs, I retrieve a dusty tomato box from my old room, another from Mom's bedroom, and something from the kitchen table. Returning to Ben, I edge the boxes onto a table.

From the top box, I grab a wad of papers. "Mom's medical paperwork. You need a cryptology degree to decipher it and saint-like patience to keep track of it all." I toss the first handful into the barrel.

"I have a box like this I'd like to burn."

We take turns tossing statements into the barrel until the box empties. Watching the numbers and procedures turn to ash fills me with satisfaction.

I follow it up with what I grabbed from the kitchen table. I hold the crumpled remains of the Harvey's contract since dried out, but still antagonizing me.

"The deal I lost on the house." I toss it in with a light shrug. "Another thing I'm better off without… *I think.*"

We celebrate with another swig of beer. Then, Ben nods to the tomato box. "What's that?"

I lift the lid and retrieve my wedding album. "Mom and Dad paid a small fortune for these. What a fucking waste. He didn't want them. Not even one." I flip through the book, catching glimpses of smiling faces and fancy clothes. "The most I ever looked at them was here… after it was over. I don't want them anymore."

Ben's eyes dance over my face. "You win the prize for the best contribution to our fire barrel."

"Are you curious? Want to see them first? It's the *prettiest* I've ever been."

"No, it isn't." Our eyes lock as he shakes his head. "That's not you anymore, anyway."

The album thuds as it hits bottom. The impact sends ash into the air and wakes my anxiety bitches. *What am I doing?* Those are memories— very expensive memories—of a man with whom I once shared a life. *What kind of cold, callous bitch throws that away?*

But Ben watches me, and I can't take it back. I don't want to. Mark moved on with his life, leaving all Lena-memories behind, so why should I be the fucking historian and solitary patron of *The Wrecked Marriage Museum*? I toss in more exhibits, relics of my dead relationship. Loose pictures. Dried flowers. Ticket stubs. And finally, the card he sent after Mom died—a nice gesture, though he only signed his name, first and last, as if I wouldn't remember him. I watch the Hallmark sympathies curl and char until the card vanishes altogether.

"This is a good day." Ben nudges my shoulder. "What're you thinking, Lena?"

"I feel empty."

"Better to feel empty than burdened with bad reminders."

"Yes. Maybe. I don't know." My shoulders slump with regret. It's a fucking miserable shame to list entire years of my relatively short life that I want to be eradicated from history. The loneliness resurrects, watching my previous life turn to ashes. I force a small smile as his eyes capture mine. "This is… long overdue. It *is* a good day."

"But?"

"But—no surprise—I'm overwhelmed, soul-sick over losing Mom and even Mark, oddly. I don't love him anymore, don't miss him. We never belonged together. But it's a shame all the time, energy, and heartache I wasted on us." I shrug lightly. "The fire-barrel can't take away me being an idiotic love-fool."

"Giving your heart to someone, wanting to be loved back—that's not foolish. It's brave and hopeful. You just picked the wrong guy." Ben smirks. "You should've held out for an Eagle Scout."

My laugh catches in the smoke, forcing a cough. "You're right. His knot-tying skills were shit."

"Red flag. I bet he didn't shake hands right, either."

"Nope. What was I thinking?"

We lock eyes, laughing, until our giggles fade. My hand goes to Ben's chest—not sure why—but my fingers rest over his heart. "I don't mind it when you're quiet, Ben, but I love it when you talk. You're a delight. I hope you know that."

"I do, actually. My mom tells me that all the time."

"I'm being serious."

"So, am I." His hand curls over mine. "I'll talk more. Your smile is an excellent incentive."

Of course, I smile again at the way he puts it. "Thanks for helping me fire-barrel my baggage."

"You're welcome. The emptiness will pass now that you've made space for better things."

He's right. I don't need any bullshit reminders—they're burned into my brain, anyway.

Later, lying on my couch-bed, I notice that the house feels better without those things in it, lighter even, like it's been purged of bad energy.

Me, too. I fall asleep dreaming of a montage of better things to fill up those empty spaces.

CHAPTER

Twenty~Six

OUR CHEESY MONTAGE crashes to a stop when Ben shows up the next day.

I *really* don't expect him. A day or two usually gaps his visits, so I do what I *don't* want him to see—ridding the house of Mom's soiled linens and stained clothes, things that wouldn't get clean no matter how many times I washed, bleached, or scrubbed them.

He takes in my ridiculously expressive face. "You're not delighted."

"I'm not Lovable Lena today."

"Why say that?"

I don't race to hide the unsightly pile *like I want to*, but shrug defeatedly. "Her meds upset her stomach, and she was on corticosteroids for her arthritis. A lovely side effect was thinning skin. Her arms looked like tissue paper, and her skin was so fragile that any little thing made her bleed. And she accepted those shit side effects but refused strong pain meds because she feared getting addicted."

A sarcastic laugh escapes me. "*Her* anxiety over addiction kept her from real relief when she took a dozen pills daily just to live, and was still in chronic pain regardless. It's hard to move, or hell, even breathe when everything hurts. Not accepting *real* help meant more suffering."

I toss the blood-dotted sheets into the dumpster. "And we never had money for new stuff, so… It's not a crime scene, Ben. I mean, not *really*."

He follows me to the carport and opens another box in my queue.

I slap it closed. "Please, don't touch any of this."

165

He steps away, hands raised.

"Why do you do this, Ben? You deal with people's fuck-ups and miseries all day. You don't need someone else's dirty laundry." I motion toward the dormant barrel. "Or emotional bullshit—and there's way too much of that around here. I don't get why you show up. Don't you have a million better things to do?"

"No." He hesitates before meeting me where I am. "What bothers you? Remembering how tough it was or me seeing it?"

"Both. This is… too much honesty. Dealing with it's bad enough without worrying what you think. I'm not asking, either. It's better not to know this time."

His firm grasp of my hand breaks my mental spin cycle and forces my eyes to his.

"You took excellent care of your mom, Lena. You made the best of a difficult situation, and she understood and appreciated everything you did for her."

"You don't know that." I try pulling my hand away, but he doesn't let me.

"I've never taken responsibility for anyone, but I've witnessed the entire spectrum of care. With some authority, I can say yours lacked nothing. You did all you could, Lena."

"It wasn't enough."

"It was more than enough. She wanted to be here, in the place she loved, and you made that possible for as long as you *reasonably* could. You did everything right." Ben squeezes my fingers. "*Nothing* was overlooked or mishandled—not with two strong, determined women sharing the house. She would've told you so. Right?"

Yes. Repeatedly. A weak laugh splits through my tears. "You're right. Her bluntness was legendary. But… she wasn't herself… and I couldn't handle it. I just feel so guilty, like it's my fault. If I'd done something— *anything*—differently, would it've mattered? Or been better? Could she still be—"

"No. There was nothing you could've done, Lena. *Nothing.*" His firm tone puts a quick end to my spiraling. "You never failed her. You saved her until she couldn't be saved anymore. That's the truth. I wouldn't say it otherwise."

"I know you wouldn't. Sorry, Ben. I'm glad you're here. You just caught me off guard, and I didn't sleep well, and—"

The MINI Cooper scoots up the driveway. I pull my hand from his, swipe my cheeks, and toss a quilt over the boxes.

Dot emerges phone-ready, and I hear the click of her camera. "Aunt Barb's not going to believe this. Whatcha got there, Lena?"

"This is Ben. He's my gun guy."

"I'll say." Her villainous laugh and roaming eyes make me block her view of him before realizing how silly I must look. She laughs again, pulling her mask down to light a cigarette.

"Ben, this is Dot. She's, um, well, her aunt is… I mean, was Mom's best friend, and Dot's her surrogate to check in on me."

"Nice to meet you, ma'am."

"Muscles and manners. Nice one, Lena." Dot winks.

"So, what is it this time? Want to raid my pantry again?"

Dot consults her inner palm. "Mabel Cunningham's orange Rachael Ray casserole dish is missing. She railroaded Aunt Barb's virtual Bible study over it."

"I handed over the dishes, Dot."

"Eh, Mabel's convinced you have it."

"She's a hundred years old, so maybe she's mistaken. I would've noticed an orange dish. Why is it such a big deal anyway?"

"It's not. But the last thing she needs is Mabel ruining her only social outlet bitching about a casserole dish." She sighs heavily, shaking her head. "Lena, babe, Aunt Barb's still spinning over losing her BFF, and now she's afraid to leave the house. Maybe we can fix this small thing for her?"

My shoulders slump. I'm reminded of my mantra to make one thing better, and regret my shit-attitude. "What can I do? Buy her a new dish?"

Dot grins. "Another Walmart run's tempting, but any chance you overlooked it?"

"I doubt it. I cleaned out the fridge."

She stubs her cigarette against her boot and tucks what's left inside the pack.

"I'll check the house," she decides, dashing awkwardly across the lawn before I can argue, not that I care, really.

Ben searches the tables, even in boxes I deemed off-limits. But, again, I don't care. Everything inside me sinks over never considering how Mrs. Moore might be suffering, too. *I'm not the only one who lost her.*

Dot sprints from the house, and damn if she isn't carrying an orange dish.

"Fuck," sputters from me.

"It was under the Tupperware in the cabinet," Dot says.

"I'm sorry. I'll, um, pop in tomorrow to apologize and check in on her… Would it freak her out?"

"Eh, maybe, but she'll be happy to see you." She chuckles, pointing at Ben and me. "Especially to hear about this surprising development. Bring brownies. Wear your mask and be prepared for a full Lysol-ing at the door."

She ducks into the MINI Cooper and leaves. I huff, feeling bad about the stupid casserole dish, about snapping at Ben, neglecting Mrs. Moore, about everything.

Ben turns to me. "Escape pod?"

I gasp like it's a novel idea. "God, yes."

"I'll drive," he says, smirking.

Moments later, we're on country roads in his Jeep, top-down and music playing. We don't talk but soak up the sun and warm breezes. Expertly zipping through Wilmington traffic, Ben drives to Carolina Beach. At the North End, where off-roading is permitted, he pulls up to the booth separating the road from the beach. With the beaches closed, there's no attendant, and cones block the path onto the sand. Ben assures me he has permission—not that I ask—before driving us through. Then, he kicks the Jeep into four-wheel drive and eases onto the sand.

Where the ocean funnels into the Intracoastal Waterway, currents crashing, Ben stops. We stand on the shore, taking in the chaotic beauty. *The beach always makes things better.* Mom called it a scenic reset-button.

"It holds you right where you should be—in the moment," Mom explained once. *"It's called the present for a reason… it's a gift."*

Mom-isms aside, we could agree on the beach. The salt air restores my lungs, making my breaths deeper. The chilly ocean breezes blow the day's negativity away. The water nips at my rubber boots, friendly-like. Worries leave me, and here, it's easy letting them go. A weird peace settles over me, about Mom and everything else.

I slide my hand in his, but he pulls me close instead. Wrapped up together, I rest my head against his chest.

"Still just your gun guy, huh?"

I gasp, edging away to see his face. "No, not at all! Sorry, Ben. Dot flusters me, and I-I honestly don't know what to call you, though gun guy's confusing and oversimplifying…"

My voice trails off with a sudden awareness of how close we are—our warm embrace has lingered and intensified. His strong hands tighten around my lower back while my hands slip up his chest and wrap around his neck. His gaze circles my face and the smallest grin creeps up his cheek as he takes me in, reminding me of how sexy it was, kissing in the rain. He inches closer, leaning into our tiny pocket, and then, like he's reading my mind, his lips take mine with gentle authority, telling me that we're *more* now.

My toes curl in my rubber boots at the full-bodied tingling his lips inspire. It's poetic, his delicate intensity as if he's stringing his movements into a soft, sweet serenade. Something strange, lovely, and frightening has built over dirt, junk, and a fire barrel. There's depth to us now, and Ben's done playing in the shallows. *But am I?*

Leaving me breathless, he pulls back. "Definitely oversimplifying."

"A little."

"This is good. Right?"

"Yes. I think so. It's scary good." I shrug, disoriented by my muddled feelings and that sweet kiss. "Sorry, Ben. It wouldn't be me without *some* anxiety."

"What makes you anxious?"

What indeed? It's the beach and Ben—neither an appropriate cause for runaway anxiety. *Nervous Nellie* is gone, and if ever there was a good reason for that bitch to heed her eviction, it's definitely Ben.

"Anything. Everything." I lean in for another soft kiss. "And suddenly, nothing at all. You always make me feel better, Ben."

His brow creases while his fingers press against my back. "I know you struggle, and you don't see yourself the way I do, but I wish you could. Lena, you're my best friend. More than that. You make me happy… and I haven't been able to say that… not for a long time."

He tucks a breeze-blown lock of hair behind my ear before tracing my cheek with his fingertip, and his sincerity sinks in, shoving all my anxious feelings aside—*they can't be trusted anyway*. But Ben can. His hands slip around me again, holding me there, and he watches me with a strange adoration, like nothing on earth could please him more than this. I'm hard-pressed to imagine anything better myself.

My hands roam up his chest, along his neck, and skim the gentle roughness of his cheeks. Smiling, he kisses me again, tugging at my lips in a sexy, playful way before noticing my tears.

I try laughing it off. "Sorry. It wouldn't be a true Lena moment without *some* tears."

His thumbs move softly under my eyes, removing the dampness. "We're us. You and me. We should be whatever that is and never feel bad about it."

"Damn, Ben… That's, um, perfect. You aren't helping my tears, though."

"Tell me why you have them."

"You make me so frightfully hopeful… And I'm a mess. No job or good prospects, no money, barely a house—This is an all-time low for me, and yet… I've never felt better and not just about, well, whatever this is, but everything. It scares me to death, Ben, dreaming up lofty ideas about my future again."

"What ideas? Tell me."

My eyes roll, dropping more tears. "You'll think it's ridiculous."

"Tell me anyway. Let me decide what I think."

Changing the subject feels safer and more like me. But his hopeful look and wandering fingers scramble my anxiety bitches. They don't know what to attack first—our leveling-up relationship, my far-fetched future, or this sweet moment when everything meets in our affection. It feels so safe being in his arms like this. And telling him may rid me of the burden—if it's a bad idea, I won't do it, and I'll figure something else out.

"You'll tell me *exactly* what you think? No sugar-coating or sparing my feelings?"

"I'll be excruciatingly honest."

Though I want to bury my face in the sand as I tell him, I lock eyes, unwilling to miss his reaction. The first five seconds will tell all. "I'm thinking of turning my parents' place into a business—a working farm and bakery café."

Ben being Ben, he reveals little in my pause but appears more amused than concerned. *He likes it?* Now more nervous, I leave his hold on me, flicking my hands at my wrists.

"Um, so I'd expand the garden to supplement my kitchen and make picnic baskets. Mom's old quilts are perfect for families to sit around the pond or wherever. Or they could eat at the café once dining rooms reopen. I'd refinish tables and chairs from the barn and use Mom's china and tea sets. I'd bake delicious desserts and make kick-ass coffee and cook fish or whatever the hell I want, even horse treats. Because I'd have horses, too. And chickens. Maybe goats or sheep, too, because why not? Fishing… fireworks… tractor rides for the kids… maybe pumpkins. Or strawberries for picking. Or a corn maze."

I take a hurried breath, still flicking my hands. "I want to create a retreat. When I cared for Mom, Mrs. Moore came over and relieved me for a few hours… but I never knew where to go. The mall. Grocery store. Whatever. I needed time to myself, desperately, but I squandered it with bullshit errands when I should've taken a walk or fished or laid on a blanket under the sun or sat in a rocking chair on the porch." I stop to laugh. "It's funny. All that time, I could've had that in my own backyard, but I was too busy and overwhelmed to see it… It's far-fetched and too much, *I know*. It's okay if you think it's a bad idea. How would I do it, anyway? I don't even have a fully-operational kitchen."

"Lena…" Ben catches my hands in his like two spastic butterflies and keeps them captured between us, running his thumbs along mine.

Here it comes. A consoling letdown.

"It's not ridiculous." A smile curls his lips. "You'll give people a place where it's okay to just… be. What's better than that? I love it."

"Really?"

"Yes. The garden. Your baked deliveries. Letting people enjoy the place. It's a business version of what you do already. Right?"

"I guess so, only bigger and more complicated and definitely expensive, and I've failed one business already."

"That makes you more qualified. You're less likely to make the same mistakes. You're good with people, too. I've never had more fun or felt more welcome anywhere."

"That's because you're you."

"No, it's because you're *you*. When your heart's in something, you hold nothing back."

Worry lines crinkle my forehead. "That's where I go wrong, Ben. Too much heart. Not enough of everything else. That's why everything falls apart."

"No. Not this time. It's a beautiful place worth restoring and an incredible idea worth believing in. With everyone on the hunt for safe outdoor activities, the timing's right. You should go for it. Absolutely."

I hunt for the slightest hesitation, but there isn't one. His sincere, excited look makes me think he's not only jumped aboard my idea-ship but grabbed a paddle. *And hopefully, a life jacket.*

Up the driveway after dark, his headlights catch the garden. Green shoots line the rows, peeking from the earth like waving hands. *Hello, little friends.* Practically giddy, we rush across the lawn for a closer look. Okay, *I'm* giddy, while Ben's mildly amused. Of course, we've seen sprouts already, but not in full force. It's like every seed grew and shot up by inches since we left the house.

"God, how long have we been gone? It's a *real* garden. Can you believe it?"

His cocked eyebrow says, *of course.*

"Nothing ever works out for me, Ben, especially around here."

"I wonder which'll be more challenging… restoring your parents' place or your belief in yourself." He smirks at the promising greenery. "Times are changing, Lena."

CHAPTER
Twenty~Seven

TIMES *ARE* CHANGING. I'm changing, too. Letting Ben in has left less space for my anxiety bitches to play. My *nevers* become *maybes*, and it feels like my nothing-ever-works-out life is veering off in a better direction.

Days after the beach, I find gardening and farming books stored separately from the in-house library. I pour over pages most nights, jotting down ideas. Ancient cookbooks lead me to experiment with old-school stuff like loaves, savory pies, and, *yes, fucking casseroles*. I plan ways to provide a simple but diverse menu without being stuck in the kitchen all the time.

Ben sends me links about local gardeners, farmer's markets, innovative farms, and even the oddball recipe, like jalapeño mac and cheese. *Must have mac and cheese.* His encouragement becomes a must-have, too, helping me stay focused and, more importantly, hopeful.

When the restrictions lift on the stay-at-home order, Joe comes to collect the other vehicles. Though I cried over the Pickle Mobile months ago, I don't get teary as the rest disappear, maybe because it's not an end but a new beginning.

With Lucas, too, when I call to apologize. Though health-related texts fly between us often, nothing's been the same since our fight. So, I breakdown and FaceTime him.

He's playing dress-up with Luna. He looks like the *Monopoly* guy in a red top hat, monocle, and a suit vest. Luna prances in a red, beaded flapper dress that trails on the floor. I bust out laughing as he tips a tiny porcelain teacup in my direction.

"Oh, my God. How do I take screenshots while FaceTiming? This moment should live forever."

"Don't worry. Drew's already posting some."

"He's doing better?"

"Yes, our household has the all-clear for now. How's everything with you?"

"Good, actually, but I'm sorry for getting upset last time. I shouldn't have hung up on you."

"No, it's my fault. I should've supported your decision about Jack's offer. After talking with Drew, I think you were right to back out."

"Um, thanks. That means a lot."

"Well, I took what you said to heart. You're always welcome here, and you don't have to work at Root & Bone, either. I get it's not exactly your cup of tea." He tips his teacup again.

"Thanks, but I'm okay. *Really.* The house needs work, but it's not so bad. I started the garden again. I'm baking, making friends, riding horses, and finding treasures."

"Treasures? Like old books and doilies? If you say so."

"I can be happy here, Lucas. It's what I want."

"Okay, then. Your house, your choice. We support your decision." I feel he wants to say, *"You'll come to your senses one day"* or *"We'll be here for you, watching it blow up in your face."* Almost as bad, he asks, "How are things on the job front?"

Hmm… 10 million people out of work… highest unemployment rate since the Great Depression… businesses closed or operating at reduced capacities… headlines jumble in my head. "Oh, fine. I check new listings every day, and I've applied everywhere. It's a waiting game."

"No bites yet?"

"I got hired at a pizzeria, but the owner backed out days later. His employees came down with symptoms so he closed temporarily."

"Geez, that makes two jobs you've lost in all this."

"Third time's the charm." I flash my best smile.

Luna stops to rest against Lucas's shoulder. "Auntie Lena looks pretty."

"Not nearly as pretty as you," I say.

She twirls in her flapper dress, flitting off again.

"You *do* look happy." He says it suspiciously, as if me and happiness can't go together.

"Um, well, I am." My breath catches in my throat as it washes over me. "Incredibly happy... actually."

"In that house, it's hard to believe."

"It's not all problems. Everything I need is right here," I say, remembering Mom's note. "But it'd still be nice to have the money to fix things properly."

"Maybe you'll uncover a real treasure to fund that, too."

"Yeah, right. Mom's pennies might turn into doubloons." *Or I'll find a Picasso in the attic like Ben predicted on the way home from the beach. What would Lucas think of my farm and café idea?*

"Well, it's a Monday afternoon, and I'm playing the Mad Hatter with Luna, indefinitely, so anything's possible."

Except finding a decent job.

As if reading my mind, Lucas says, "If you're truly serious about staying, working a drive-thru or waiting tables at half-capacity restaurants won't be enough, Lena. You need a salary, not a wage. And benefits. When was the last time you had health insurance?"

"I'm seeing someone." A sharp wince follows my escaped words, a knee-jerk reaction to curtail another brotherly lecture. My anxiety spikes, fearing his reaction. *Ugh, it's Mark all over again. No wonder you want to stay. What'll you give up next, huh?* Only I can't keep it in any longer.

"Does *he* have health insurance?" My face pinches while he laughs. "Tell me about him."

Like with Gloria, I don't share *everything*—so much is sacred. But Lucas lights up with my Ben stories, especially when I explain how he understands my anxiety and, well, the fireworks.

"He sounds wonderful. A big, strong, silent type, huh?" Lucas goes to his laptop and narrates his way to social media to check Ben out.

"Damn, are those his arms, really? And shoulders? He's handsome, Lena, in a tough-guy way." Lucas chuckles, taking his phone and holding me next to the screen. "Yes, you look good together."

"Thanks. I should've told you sooner."

"I just followed your boyfriend," he says, looking devious. "Why didn't you?"

"I didn't want you to think I was making bad decisions again, like with Mark."

Lucas's eyebrow shoots up. "Mark was a tool, Lena. You're *way* overdue for a new guy—a good guy."

"Yes, Ben's definitely that."

"Good." Lucas tips his glass toward me. "I'm thrilled about Ben, and the right opportunity will come along. How can I help? Want me to spiff up your resumé?" Lucas laughs, eyeing his computer screen. "Ha! Your boyfriend just followed me back."

Lucas and I work on my resumé via FaceTime for almost an hour before my phone demands recharging, and Luna commands his complete attention. But my thoroughly spiffed resumé fails to offer better results—not in Wilmington. May marks a partial reopening of stores, with mask mandates and social distancing limits, but open doors don't mean new-hires, as companies seem employment-shy given all they've lost already.

But not in Asheville. Jason Ford leaves an excited voicemail two months after rescinding his offer. "Lena, I just got done with my accountant, and guess what?"

Holy shit, he's re-offering the job! He explains that after the initial pandemic slump, he redesigned the menu, tried new marketing, and sped up carryout and delivery. Inspired by my charitable deliveries on social media, he donated family dinners to first responders and hospital staff.

He calls it strange karma—the more he's given, the more business has boomed. "So, risking the longest voicemail ever, I need you. I won't back out this time, Lena. Promise. I want the best, and I'll do whatever it takes to get you on my team. Call me back. Anytime."

Hands trembling, I delete the message. *I wish he'd never called— dangling a sweet-ass carrot I can't have anymore.* Turning down Jason's offer twists the knife already rammed in my gut. I call during his lunch rush when I know he can't answer, like a coward. I leave an appreciative refusal on his voicemail, sparing myself a full-fledged conversation.

Hours later, Jason texts.

> Thanks for getting back to me. I'm bummed but not
> surprised that you've found other opportunities.
> Please let me know if anything changes.

I bang my head against the table. It's hard resigning myself to dishwashing, fast food, or takeout delivery when I could have my dream job in Asheville—with health insurance! Minimum wage isn't enough

—is it ever? The college degree I forfeited for Mark would offer a better chance—one that might support me and *that* house. And though Ben isn't the *only* reason I want to stay, I fear slipping into the same trap.

So, the pressure builds—a vice clenching my chest. And everything going on in the world turns it tighter.

The in-police-custody death of George Floyd launches protests across the country, including Wilmington. One sickness fades behind a darker, more incomprehensible one.

Ben shares his frustrations in a sigh like an exhausted, uncensored newscaster. "He couldn't breathe. He said it. Over and over. How could any good cop, or hell, any decent human being, let this happen? I don't know how much longer I can stay a member of a system that's so broken."

One night, I tell him, "You should teach, Ben." His surprise prompts more explanation. "It wouldn't solve everything, but maybe it could make a difference locally. Law enforcement needs instructors who care about change. That's you."

He looks surprised. "A white male teaching about racial injustice?"

"No. A dedicated police officer teaching about ethical, correct policing."

"Teach, huh? After all the trouble I caused my teachers?"

"The best teachers understand troublemakers. Plus, your lessons would be in as few words as possible…you'd make a *great* teacher."

Though he says little else about it, something hopeful glimmers in his expression, like a tiny seed sprouting in his mind. And that *I* planted it, makes me proud—an unexpected quid pro quo for his belief in me.

A belief that's as whole-hearted as it is pressuring sometimes, the vice clinching with each job rejection and house frustration and made exponentially worse by how my affection for Ben seems to expand expontentially every moment we're together. We are growing close, *real* close, and letting myself have this deep connection with someone again is *killing* me with my heightened anxiety.

Mid-working, sneaky worries arise from nowhere until I debate whether to text him. It's frustrating. And weird. *Why am I so irritatingly needy?*

But with the world the way it is, I worry—*a lot.*

Besides, having Ben-brain means I'm in *serious* trouble. *Relationship* makes me think *sinking ship*, like the *Titanic.* Sure, it seems great *now,* but there's an iceberg out there somewhere. Instincts have me searching for a lifeboat when the mood hits.

That mood hits *hard* when I'm pining over Ben, counting the days since I last saw him and wondering if he'll show up. Or when I finally give in to those worry-bitches, text him, and stare at my phone, waiting. It's always like this…

Is everything okay?

Yes.

Moments later…

Are you okay?

Hating my pushy anxiety, I respond with the blandest of emojis—

So, while I do okay with the world falling apart, I don't do well with other changes, like being in a relationship. And my anxiety loves capitalizing on the pressure.

One late afternoon, we walk to the saddletree. Our sunset stroll has been mostly quiet, so nothing prompts Ben to talk. He motions to the tree swing, so I sit. Gently sending me forward, he says, "I want to tell you how I was injured."

Though my instinct is to stop and face him, he keeps pushing as if it's easier this way. He tells me about the "one explosion too many," a shrapnel-packed IED that ambushed his unit's convoy, injuring him and killing two others. His story becomes this sacred thing between us, *another sacred thing*, and leaves me breathless and heartsick over what he went through—what he *still* goes through.

"I struggle, sometimes. The men lost had wives, children, more to return to. It should've been me."

My rubber boots kick up dust clouds as I jerk the swing to a stop. "Damn it, Ben. That belongs in the fire barrel. Never think it again. I mean it."

My fingers travel his cheek, his scar, wishing to erase those thoughts. "Our heads play mean tricks on us—*I know*. And, yes, we're all expendable and can't control explosions or viruses or anything, really. But, you belong here. With me." I bite my lip. *What am I saying?* "I need you, Ben. You're not expendable. Not to me."

Ben's sweet smile moves fears aside. At my hip, he draws me in. My fingers fall to his chest, where I tug at his shirt to ensure he stays there. His hand wraps around mine between us.

"I need you, too, Lena. I won't think it again."

"Just like that?"

"Not just, but yes." He holds his hand out and mimics dropping it into our fire barrel. I chuckle lightly. "You're the best reason. Every good and terrible thing we've been through makes strange sense now. That's why I told you. I want you to know everything. No holding back."

My words to Gloria on our first ride together when she asked what kind of love I wanted replay in my head. *I want someone who needs me and doesn't make me feel bad for whatever that is... No holding back... above all, honest.* And somewhere between the soft, coastal breezes, swaying Spanish moss, and tangling fingertips, I realize—*fuck me*—I *love* Ben.

CHAPTER
Twenty-Eight

FIVE DAYS PASS. Ben stays busy with extra shifts while I grow frustrated for employment that doesn't come. Mirroring the turmoil, spring weather makes dramatic performances most days.

One evening, under the promise of heavy storms, I treat myself, at least by my minimally-resourced standards. After a long, steamy shower, I dig out my favorite pajamas—a soft, t-shirt tank gown in heather gray. I slept in my clothes with Mom around, so PJs are a rediscovered luxury. I bake over-topped pizzas and pour wine—Pinot Noir to fit the storm mood and calm my nerves. The electricity will probably go out. Hell, the whole place might fall like a sandcastle in high tide.

I place pots strategically on Dad's ladder under my living room roof leak. It *looks* secure, layered with duct tape and coated with white paint, but it's merely a half-assed cover-up to thwart Ben's repeated offers to hire a roofer—*I can't let him do that.* With three more cans of FlexSeal coating the untrustworthy shingles, I hope for a dry, non-collapsing night.

Still, it must be monitored.

Around the TV, I make-shift a comfy, fort-style couch-bed on the floor with layered blankets and pillows. I arm the coffee table with flashlights and old towels. Battery-operated candles create warmth in an empty room. Ridding the windows of their heavy drapes was a mistake, creating strange shadows, and the absence of real furniture adds to the eeriness.

Need more distractions. A hunt through Mom's DVDs produces *Aliens*, an all-time favorite.

By the time the soldiers infiltrate the tunnels in search of the colonists, the storm is in a full-blown rage. The house shakes with each cosmic boom, and weak shrieks slip from me with each flashing, thundering disruption.

Fueled by wine and anxiety, I turn the TV volume up and tackle Mom's coins at the dining room table. Armed with a magnifying glass, I look up each coin in Mom's latest coin reference guide before sorting them into piles: roll or keep. If it's worth more than face value, I keep it. Otherwise, it goes into a mason jar to await a paper wrapper.

"I know why the world's facing a coin shortage, Mom. They're all in your bedroom."

Lightning streaks and thunder rattles the house, making me jump. Water pecks my pots, so I rush to the ladder. Large drops dampen the drywall at the ceiling just south of my painted patchwork. I dab it with an old towel as the power flickers.

I fetch more coins from Mom's lair. She's collected them in a dozen different tins, jars, and even a plastic cheese-puff container that's the size of a boulder and just as heavy. I retrieve her notebooks, too. I rummage like a thief, flashlight in hand. Her side of the house is dank and dark and musty from months without electricity and no way to circulate the air.

The livable side offers sweet relief, though, even without much furniture. With every light on and aliens being satisfactorily destroyed, the house is as warm and cozy as ever, a true shelter in the storm.

But as soon as I think all is well, a noisy downpour drowns out machine gun sounds from the TV. Water drops quicken into the pots. The power goes out, leaving me in candlelight only. Without the TV, fans, or AC unit humming, the eerily silent room makes the storm seem louder.

It's a storm. This happens. It'll come back on.

But lights across the field at the Harvey's place reveal *they* still have power. So, I grab a flashlight and go to the breaker.

The dingy, cobwebbed corner housing the breaker box, water heater, and exposed pipes feels more like a dank basement than a back porch. At the metal box, I examine the panel while fumbling with the light. The offending breaker switch won't reset. And it's loose in its slot as if ready to jump from the sinking ship. A faint metallic smell adds eerie finality.

The entire house is powerless—and nothing I wiggle, switch, or curse restores it. Tomorrow the rising sun will bring the May heat, giving inside-living the sauna-like feel of a sealed car in summer. I wonder which'll be worse—tomorrow's sauna or tonight's eeriness.

With trembling fingers, I text Dot, asking if she can come by in the morning to take a look.

She responds with an "As you wish" GIF from *The Princess Bride*.

I consider texting Ben, even calling him, just for the company. But I don't want my call to turn into a rescue mission. Finding out I'm powerless might fuel his fix-it tendency, and I don't want to trouble him, especially since he's working a double shift.

I refill my Pinot, missing the machine gun fire from *Aliens*, and Ben, too.

As beautiful as our relationship is, feeling this way for someone again is oddly painful, too, like my body's been invaded by an emotional alien—a foreign entity that I want to reject, given the havoc it'll cause. Ben's not a hostile alien parasite, but exploding from the inside out is how losing him would feel. *Remember Mark? All those love-feelings dashed, the heartache, the struggle to escape?* I sigh heavily, imagining how broken I'd be *if... when... if...* that struggle became ours, too.

I set up a lantern and get a battery-operated radio and crank the local station, hoping the noise'll keep the mice away. Wine, music, and coin work create a decent buffer around my increasingly stuffy, vice-clenching reality.

Eventually, I fall asleep hunched at the table and slip into vivid dreams. Making catfish sandwiches and people picnicking on Mom's old quilts and Mom—her younger, healthy self—harvesting yellow squash. *"I can't wait to get these in a pan with some butter,"* she says. People are *everywhere*—at picnic tables under the carport, fishing along the pond bank, kids running through the rows in the garden. It's the *happiest* place, and Mom smiles, hands on hips, as we take it in. She says,*"You should make your summer squash salad and a veggie tart. Good picnic food."* Arms full of beefsteak tomatoes, I say, *"Margarita pizzas, too. Where's Ben?"*

She nods to the field behind me. *"Playing laser tag with the bears."* *Duh, Lena.*

Watching my quirky boyfriend in a tactical standoff with Smokey the Bear, Mom and I break into laughter.

And that's how I wake—laughing. Sunlight streams into the

windows. I peel pennies from my face and glance at the notebook I used as a pillow.

Lena, check this out.

Mom's scrawled writing covers a yellow sticky taped to the front of a red wallet-sized photo album—the kind once carried in purses to show off kids and grandkids to acquaintances before phones made portable picture albums easier. Sharpie-written arrows, stars, and smiley faces decorate the note like a sunburst. In her coin stash, it's the first message to me. *I think.* But after my many Mom-finds, I shouldn't be surprised.

I flip through it—the same little, red photo wallet we searched for at three o'clock in the morning and found on her desk exactly where she left it. Pennies are displayed in makeshift holders, done with index cards and staples, and secured with tape inside the plastic pockets. It looks like a child's elementary school coin project done last minute with zero help from Mom and Dad.

Need coffee. Sighing, I push the mess aside. A headache nips at my temple. *Too much wine, but getting properly drunk can finally be crossed off the list.* I search Mom's kitchen for her ancient metal percolator and then pop open K-cups to fill the basket. I fill the base with water and take it to the outdoor grill.

Waiting for grill to heat and the percolator to, well, perk, I check my phone. Two missed texts from Ben.

> Good-morning, Lena... I'm off-shift soon.

> Everything okay?

Not really, I think, but don't text. With only ten percent left, I tuck my phone away, unsure how to answer.

A plain but beat-up white van races up my driveway. It's Dot.

She slides out carrying two tall cups of gas station coffee. She meets me on the patio.

"The coffee was Aunt Barb's idea," she says before I can thank her.

Her voice is strikingly loud. I wince, rubbing my temples.

"Looks like you had a rough night." Dot leans in, squinting. "Is that a penny?"

I peel the coin off my neck. "Thanks for coming. It's more than a tripped breaker this time. I don't know what to do. I can't afford this house call, let alone anything major."

Dot gives me her best motherly smile that comes off as sinister rather than comforting. She looks like Ursula convincing Ariel to take the deal. "Let's not worry about money yet, okay? Take a load off. I'll have a look-see. Won't take long."

She leaves me. I plop onto the rickety chaise with my dwindling coffee and close my eyes. *Only for a second.*

"Hey, sunshine!" Dot's round head blocks the sun, but she moves to the chair beside me, clipboard in hand. "Sorry to wake you. You look like a worn-out street baby."

I don't know what to say to that. I sit up, rubbing my eyes. My coffee's empty. So, I restart the grill. "Figure out the problem?"

"Your entire circuit breaker needs replacing, along with all the wiring. It couldn't handle the juice you were asking it for, especially in the kitchen. Too many small appliances. You fried it." She shakes her head and chuckles like it's such a Lena-thing to do.

"How much, do you think?"

Dot's dark eyebrow creeps up her forehead. "Ten thou. Ish. And that's a lowball estimate since we don't know what's in those walls of yours. But that's not your only problem. The foundation is cracked, along with one chimney—fire hazard. The roof's toast."

A sigh escapes. *Right, the roof.*

"That'll cost you thirty, at least. Hell, it'll be a few grand just to fix that leaky mess in the living room. There's mold, you know. And you've got rotten floors and a serious plumbing issue. Your furnace is done. The water heater's on its last leg. And let's face it—the shag carpeting's got to go." She shrugs at my gaping stare. "I'm kidding about the carpet. Sort of."

"Wait, you were in the crawlspace? On the roof?"

"Aunt Barb said to take good care of you, especially given your big plans. She's so damn excited about your farm and café idea, Lena, babe. She's been talking about it nonstop since your visit. I'm thrilled, too. My chess club needs a new headquarters."

She pauses, but I don't respond. *Is she kidding?*

"Anyway, I looked at everything. Besides, you needed the nap, huh?"

I imagine Dot touring my house like a *Lifetime* movie stalker, going through my drawers, checking out what shampoo I use, discovering decent hiding places for when she plans to kill me. I refill our cups with the percolated coffee.

"Bottom line, best estimate—how much for everything?"

Dot blows out a puffy-cheeked sigh. "One-fifty to two-hundred'd be realistic to make everything right. Turning it into a business'll be more."

Last night's dream becomes a cruel mind trick now, as if the laser tag bears take a violent turn, clawing us all to shreds. I bury my face in my hands. Holding on to Mom's place is just clinging to the past and far-fetched fantasies I'll *never* see realized. *Can't live here. Can't create a business. Can't survive. And there's Asheville.*

"Buck up, Buttercup. Everything's fixable." Dot lights a cigarette, inhaling deeply. "It's an old house. It's overdue for a reno. But the barn's in good shape. Your mom built it, right? What was her plan for the loft?"

"Plan? It's storage."

"It's wired, even for appliances. Plumbing, too. You've already got a fully-functional bathroom downstairs... with hot water."

"The creepy bathroom? You went in there?"

"A girl's gotta pee. Needs a new lightbulb and a good cleaning... but the barn's a structural, working paradise, compared to the house. It's got great bones, just needs meat. Seems strange she put so much into it for storage."

A memory resurfaces, fished out by her tiny mention. The blank stretch where the barn was to be built. Trucks and materials. Me chasing Lucas around pallets.

"She wanted a clubhouse for Lucas's Scouts... and somewhere I could... practice baking to my heart's content," I say, remembering her words when she explained it.

Dot flicks her ashes. "Creative idea. Barn clubhouse. What happened?"

"I don't know. Maybe she ran out of money. So, the barn loft is livable?"

"Could be. My designer friend, Cherry, loves unique spaces. We could bring her in, but I've got ideas already. The beams and the arched ceiling'd be farmhouse chic. An east-side window would give you a sunrise view of the pond. Imagine waking up to that every morning. And it's way more cost-effective than fixing this." She motions to the house.

"But still expensive, right?"

She shrugs. "Eh, less than thirty, maybe. It's a viable option."

"No, it isn't. I can't even afford to get the power back on, so thirty-thousand, a hundred grand, two-hundred grand—what does it matter? I'm broke. *And* unemployed. I'll be rolling change just to pay my next power bill." I stop for a sardonic chuckle. "Good thing this'll make it cheaper, huh?"

Dot takes a long drag of her cigarette. "It's not the end of the world, Lena."

"No. But it's the end of *this* one." A hard lump wedges in my throat.

My phone pings. Another Ben-text, checking in.

I haven't told him anything about my job-hunting woes, house issues, Jason's second offer, or refusing it. Handling my shitshow life is a solo endeavor—the fewer people involved, the better. I don't want Ben to see my reality taking hold like I *knew* it would, like it *always* does. For once, I don't want him to show up.

My fingers shake as I answer. *You must be tired.* Delete. *I don't need you to…* Delete.

> Hey, sorry. Slept in. Everything's fine. You've been working so hard lately. Take a break from visiting here for a while. You need to rest, and I'm perfectly okay. Let's talk after you've slept.

"That your muscley new friend?" Dot chuckles. "The way you blocked my wandering eyes from properly checking him out was classic, Lena. I get why my irresistible sensuality would threaten you, but please… Big, strong boys aren't my type."

She puts her hands on her hips and gyrates, modeling her sexiness. We break out laughing over her puckered lips and Dot pushing her breasts together atop her three t-shirts and a flannel button-down. "Maybe he can help figure this out, huh?"

A black cloud shadows me again. "There's nothing to figure out. I can't fix what's broken, and I've got an amazing job waiting for me in Asheville. It's a no-brainer."

Her dark eyes narrow under her bushy brows, scrutinizing me. "You sure? Asheville's most-def more your speed than Malibu, but, you know, bears."

Bears? I sink into the nearest chair as reality hits. *College, bakery, marriage, Mom. How can I add this place to that fucking list? And what'll be next?* My whole body cringes as my anxiety bitches whisper the answer —*Ben.*

"Hey." Dot snaps her fingers. "The bears aren't *that* bad. I saw an old generator in the barn. You'll feel better once you have light to count your pennies by. Let's hook it up."

I do what she says. When things falls apart, it's best to stay busy. Several hours pass in setting it up. In her van, Dot drives us to the nearest gas station for a quick lunch and to fill empty gas jugs from the barn.

On the drive home, I say, "How much for today's work?"

"Eh, it's on the house."

"I don't want your charity."

"It's not. Maybe you'd post how quickly I came to your rescue? I've been stalking you a little. You're pretty funny, you know, when your sky isn't falling. Course, when isn't it?" She laughs. "You're pretty funny then, too. Some social media love would really help me out."

"*That* I can do. Once my phone's charged, that is." Having died, it charges in her center console. "I'll take a pic of your business card."

She hands me the rumpled card and takes it back once the picture is taken.

Dot lights a cigarette and puts her window down. "Maybe Asheville's not a horrible idea. But things aren't so bad *here*. For all its problems, this place has potential. And you got people. That's better than nothing. Take a page from your mom's book, Lena. Get fucking creative."

My phone rings, halting my many arguments. We both see that it's Ben, and Dot gives me a stern order. "Answer it."

Too bothered and overwhelmed to argue or resist, I do.

"Lena," he sighs. "You're right."

"Right?"

"A break from visiting your place would be good… Come to mine."

My mouth drops. Excuses line up—soldiers in my head—but I stumble. His voice strums a soft chord in me, lifting the day's tension. Still, all I manage is, "Ben… I don't know."

"Why not?" His voice syncs with Dot's as she asks the same thing. She holds her hands up and mouths, "You should hit that."

I shift toward the passenger door, phone pinned tightly to my left ear.

My silence prompts him again. "What're you thinking?"

I press my forehead against the glass, and I tell him exactly. "If I say yes, I may never want to leave."

"Pack a bag, then."

My heart soars and then sinks, an emotional yo-yo. It's a terrible, awful idea—getting closer when I know I'll have to leave. Distancing myself now will make the changes coming easier for us both.

"Please, Lena. It's just us. Hanging out. As always. Say yes."

His butter-soft voice reminds me of the beach, and that relaxed-effect he has on me takes over. "Yes. Definitely. Yes. Text me your address."

<h1>CHAPTER
Twenty~Nine</h1>

BEN LIVES IN A REAL HOUSE... *a cute house!* Homeownership *shouldn't* be a shocker. People with *real* careers often have *real* houses. But whenever he's talked about his place, I pictured an out-of-the-way apartment, perhaps in a retirement community, where he helps elderly neighbors carry their groceries while checking for security threats. *He might still do that.*

His street ranges from boarded-up shacks to charmingly renovated bungalows. While magnolias and majestic oaks shade his lovely cottage, the yard needs work. Bushes overtake a gorgeous palm, and the grass is patchy. The tired white exterior needs repainting. But the roof looks new and delightfully leak-free, and the paint supplies stacked on the porch tell me he's restoring it himself—efforts surely delayed by trips to the country for farm-work and takeout.

I park behind his Jeep and give myself a once-over in the rearview. Lip gloss, shadow, and mascara are minimal but decently effective. Though I hated taking her fashion advice, Dot talked me into a sundress and wedges instead of my usual jeans and boots. And now, *here,* I'm glad for her brash pep talk. *"This isn't field work, Lena. It's a date. Act like it. God knows, you need the distraction."*

To further insist, she promised to watch over *that* house for the night to give me less to worry about, and when she saw that I wasn't comforted, she tucked my rubber boots into the backseat in case I felt "homesick." Then, she practically kicked me off my own property. She means well, but my anxiety plays up regardless.

With a cleansing breath, I get out, and there he is, waiting for me.

Okay, so it's only been six days since seeing him. I went thirty-some years without Ben Wright; six days shouldn't matter. But we lock onto each other like we're war-torn, time-separated, or otherwise kept-apart stars of a sappy movie. He buries his face in my neck, breathing me in, while his hand scoops my hair and my arms tighten around him.

"I've missed you like crazy," he whispers.

Anxieties dissipate as his embrace hits all my pressure points. "Me, too. It's been a long week."

"Yes, the longest."

But my nerves make a comeback, pulling me away and nearly tripping over my wedges. He grabs my arm, steadying me.

"I, um …Nice place." I hand him a bottle of red I picked up at Sunny's, pointing to the label. *Nineteen Crimes.* "Get it?"

"Yes. A real bottle, too."

"Mom always said never show up empty-handed. Your mom must've taught you that, too. I should've stopped for takeout."

"I'm cooking." He gives me a critical once-over while slipping his hand into mine. "Is everything okay? You seem nervous."

"I am." I sigh. "Sorry. It's been a tough week."

"Tell me."

His sweet sincerity makes me want to. *No power. No money. No choice but Asheville.* But Dot's other advice circles in my head. *"Hey, dummy… Try to have a good time, huh? Your problems'll be here—no sense dragging them along with you."*

I lean into him, giving him a soft, slow kiss. "Oh, come on, Ben. Finally seeing your place is *much* more interesting. I still have no idea if you have any weird collections or shrines or a serial killer's basement."

He laughs, fingers pressing into my waist as he holds me there. "There's no basement."

"Whew." I wipe pretend sweat from my forehead but then chuckle, realizing he said nothing about shrines or collections. "Take me inside?"

He leads me up the porch, holding my hand. A hall tree flanks the doorway, neatly arranged with his work gear, jackets, hats, and shoes at its base. I kick off my wedges beside his boots and set my keys on the seat.

An intoxicating smell—peppery, cheesy, buttery—draws my attention. "Smells delicious. What's cooking?"

"Reubens."

My eyebrow cocks up. "Wow. It's hard to make a good Reuben."

"Growing up, we took turns making dinner. Reubens were my only specialty. Make yourself at home."

While he tends to dinner, I roam the open living and dining space. Everything's recently remodeled, from the dark hardwoods to the scuff-free gray walls. The galley kitchen makes me jealous with its granite countertops and new, fully-operational appliances. Despite the lack of knick-knacks, leaks, and cobwebs I'm used to, it's cozy and inviting.

Ben's a minimal decorator, but his living room wall lures me closer. Pictures are separated by awards and medals for distinguished service and flanked by decorative gold plates from Bahrain, Afghanistan, and Iraq. Formal pictures couple with casual ones—Ben with his family and army buddies.

"Hope this doesn't count as a shrine." He hands me a glass of wine.

"Not at all. There's nothing bad about genuine accomplishments… Ah, your Eagle Scout picture." I eye teenaged Ben with adoring fascination. "Always so serious. You're even more handsome when you smile, you know."

"Hmm, debatable. My sister did this when I moved in. She said I needed a Ben Wall."

"Delightful *and* distinguished—you're incredible. Not that you need a Ben Wall to impress me."

But he wants to, I realize, as his smile grows talking about the pictures. I put faces to Ben's life—his twin sister Becca, the rest of his big family, the soldiers he served with—and it's beautiful. All of it—beautiful. A privilege, even hearing him talk about it. Making me wish I had more family left. Making me wish for a spot here one day.

"Something's wrong. What is it?"

"Nothing." The word pops out automatically, and he's dissatisfied. "Hormones. Allergies. Hormonal allergies. Could be anything. Sorry, Ben." Through a weak chuckle, I shrug toward the display. "Mom would've turned into a hellbent soap opera villain over this. Bribery, drugs, tricky schemes—ah, she would've stopped at nothing to get you to marry me."

"I wouldn't need convincing. More likely, we would've conspired to convince you." His words come quickly—zero hesitation—and I can almost picture him whispering plans with my mother. "Is that what's wrong? Missing your mom?"

A tearful scoff bumbles from my flushed face. *He'd marry me?* "Um, maybe. That and it's *still* really nice learning about you."

"Good." His hand slips around my waist. "Feel free to look around, go through drawers, the medicine cabinet, hunt for strange collections."

After a chuckle, I lean my head against his shoulder. "How 'bout I watch you cook first?"

I pop onto a barstool at the kitchen island, where he sets a cheese and veggie plate. I pick at it absentmindedly while he toasts sandwiches on a hot skillet.

A tower of already-made Reubens sits by the stove. "Ben, how many sandwiches are you making?"

"I thought we'd walk downtown after dinner, give the extras to Mr. Deakins and his buddies."

"Yes, I love that idea."

"You inspired me. Besides, I wanted to practice."

I grin coyly. "Aw, why? You're not intimidated by me, are you?"

"No." His eyebrow perks up. "Well, maybe. I burned the first two."

He serves me a plate and waits as I pick up the sandwich. I take a bite, not expecting much. A Reuben is distinctly personal—the ideal ratios of thousand island dressing, toasted rye bread, swiss, sauerkraut, and pastrami. It's not a one-size-fits-all sandwich.

"Oh, Ben, it's delicious." I moan, surely looking like a chipmunk when I shove another hefty bite in my mouth.

He smiles. "Really?"

My eyes widen. "I love it. You can make these for me anytime."

He lights up, grabbing himself a plate. We sit at the bar, facing each other, as we devour his creation. He opens up about work. Recent events have created undeniable tension. "The department finally realizes it needs to change. We can do better. Hopefully, citizens will give us the chance to prove it. But it's a shameful, tragic reality that it took the loss of innocent lives to get us here."

"It's hard to know how broken something is until it's too late. That's the way it was with Mom. Infections kept getting worse, but I failed to see it sometimes… or maybe I didn't want to. Let's hope the world *really* sees this, and good can come from it."

"Good usually comes from honesty…" He nods, but a curious pinch darkens his brow as he pushes our dishes away. "Um, you should know… I see my ENT this week, my hearing doctor. I suspect bad news."

My hands lock around his across our laps. "Why? What's wrong?"

"More headaches. That's partly why I've limited our visits."

"Ben, I wish you'd told me. I could've helped—"

"No. You've cared for someone the last three years—I didn't want to do that to you. Didn't want you to see me like that, at least, not without discussing it first…. That's another reason I've limited my visits, to delay this conversation."

My head cocks questioningly. It *almost* sounds like the start of a break-up. "I don't understand. Delay what conversation?"

"If it's worse… when it gets worse, the implications will be considerable."

"You'll manage, like always. You shouldn't worry."

"I'm prepared. That's not what worries me."

"Oh. What worries you, then?"

"You do, Lena." His grip tightens against my fingers. "More migraines mean more bad days, less time together, and you feeling obligated to help. If my hearing continues to deteriorate, hearing aids might not help for long. Cochlear implants are obvious and cumbersome." He winces, tilting his head. "They might not work long-term, either, if I opt for the surgery. There's no treatment after that. Everything would change, and not just for me. Anyone close to me would be impacted. *You* most of all."

"You don't think I can handle it?"

"Yes, I do. You can handle *anything*. But… would you want to?"

"You think I won't want to hang out with you if you have to get implants or I have to bother learning sign language?"

"There's more to it than that, but yes. You deserve to know what being together means, no surprises. Deafness is… more likely. That's a burden we'll share, *if* we're together."

If we're together… It *is* a break-up conversation. *Or it could be.* My anxiety bitches rally, as if his confession opens their cages and invites them in for a vote. *This has already gone too far… Asheville's my only option… This is my chance to end it without taking all the blame… It'll never last, anyway…*

My grip on him tightens with my resolve. "Deaf or not, you could *never* be a burden. Not to me. How could you even think it?"

"Our communication *will* suffer," he says. "Even with the best preparations, a thousand unforeseen frustrations will wedge between us. The easy way we are with each other'll be gone. I won't hear you call for me, won't hear you laugh, or… even remember the sound of your voice, eventually. You say you don't mind when I'm quiet, but what if that's all there is?"

We're both crying, but don't realize it until we simultaneously drop hands to wipe each other's tears away. Then, we chuckle over doing the same thing.

"Sorry to upset you."

My fingers linger against his cheek. "You're right—it won't be easy. Sorry I made light of it."

"I need you to understand what you're getting into."

"Are *you* worried about what *you're* getting into, Ben?"

"No. Not for a second."

"Then, why should I? Brokenness brought us together. Losing your hearing will *never* drive us apart. Our easy way'll change, but it won't disappear. We won't let it. Whatever your reality, I'm with you, and I'll try to make it better… like you do for me. As long as you're okay with mine—you are, right?"

"Yes. Always."

God, I hope that's true. "Then, what's left to—?"

He pulls me in with a deep kiss. And all I can think is… *maybe. Maybe everything's okay. Maybe nothing's as bad as it feels. Maybe Ben and I…*

He holds me there for the longest time, even when the kiss ends. His fingertips skim my surface while his green eyes do a deep-dive into all that I'm feeling, it seems, until the intensity leaves me breathless.

"Ben, you promised me a walk," I whisper finally.

CHAPTER
Thirty

OUR INTENSE SPELL BROKEN, we clean the kitchen. A lovely lightness resumes in our laughter and talking. I expect rigidity in the way he wants things, a critique or flat-out rearrangement of my loading the dishwasher or putting things away. This is *his* place, so it should be *his* way. But there's none of that.

He fills a recyclable bag with water bottles and sandwiches. He grabs a light jacket, too, and hands it to me moments after we leave, when the night air prompts me to rub my arms. The Riverwalk's only a few streets over. We walk the parts not under construction, away from the demonstrations near the courthouse.

We find Shakespeare and friends hanging out under the covered dock by the tourist boats—shut down indefinitely thanks to the pandemic. Except for Shakespeare's crowd, it's a ghost town.

"What a joy to see my friends together, taking a stroll in this lovely weather." He tips Dad's old hat.

Ben nods. "Mr. Deakins."

"Hello, Shakespeare. Ben made Reubens. Hungry?"

"Always empty. Never full. That's not the exception. That's the rule." He rubs his stomach.

While we distribute sandwiches, a gentleman at a picnic table waves me over. He points to a bucket filled with carnations, daisies, roses, and lilies, slightly wilted like florist-rejects.

Shakespeare taps the bucket with Mom's cane. "Nothing like flowers on a romantic night. Take what you want to our delight."

Ben pulls out his wallet. "How much?"

The man refuses and gives me a *don't-be-shy* expression, motioning toward the bucket again. I reach for a yellow rose and pull down my mask to catch its scent. He gives me a bushy, raised eyebrow, prodding me. I take a purple Gerber daisy, another yellow rose, and a bright orange lily.

Ben hands him money, anyway. "Please. I can't have another man giving her flowers on our date. Can I?"

Shakespeare laughs, patting his friend's shoulder. "Better to take the bill than cause ill will."

The man nods as if impressed by Ben's argument and tucks the bill into his overalls.

We wish the small crowd a goodnight, and as we leave, Shakespeare says, "Goodnight dear friends. May your love never end."

Down the dock, we remove our masks, and I smirk at Ben. "Thanks for the flowers and for that. I enjoyed it."

"Me, too. May I have those?"

With a funny look, I hand the flowers over.

He twists the stems together in odd ways, tearing off the dead leaves and wet ends. He winds them into a circle. Once intact, he sets the flower-tiara on my head. "Beautiful."

I touch the delicate blossoms, blushing. "You always surprise me. Is this another skill learned from Becca?"

"No. My niece Hailee. She's five." He slips out his phone. "May I? I must show her my work."

"Only if we take one together to post." He looks curious, surprised even, so I shrug. "Lucas made me promise."

"Becca did, too, actually, but I would've been okay to disappoint her." His brow scrunches with concern. "She started a family group chat."

"About me? Why?"

"Speculating about my personal life is a family pastime."

His stoic delivery makes me laugh. "Especially since you keep it a mystery, I bet"

He nods. "Fair point."

I want to scroll every text between them, but resist for my anxiety's sake. *It's best not to know.* I lean against the pier railings, motioning him over. "Let's give them something to talk about then."

He gives me a short kiss before prompting his phone. We take several, forcing cheek-to-cheek grins, but the best one happens by accident—a between-shot when, smirking, he tells me that selfie-related deaths are rising and my laughter over his timing makes me tumble on my wedges, nearly knocking the phone from his hand. The candid shot beats all the posed ones. We both look happy.

We start walking again. The flickering lights off the Cape Fear River and the rhythmic sounds of cars going over the bridge play background to a pleasant evening. The Battleship North Carolina looms impressively on the opposite side while evening boaters cut through the rippling currents in between. His hand slips into mine, and it's like the night of fireworks again—the way everything feels so hopeful.

But I deflate when he says, "Tell me why it's been a tough week."

I scoff. "Do I have to?"

He stops walking and faces me. "Please, Lena."

To satiate him, I pick what I least mind reporting. "The job hunt's not going well. That's all."

He looks skeptical. "Doesn't seem like all."

"*That* house is getting worse by the day. I need a good job to afford repairs, but the pandemic's put a freeze on most hiring."

"Most?"

"Well, there's always fast food. Or Waffle House—they seemed interested. Oh, and the Front Street Brewery manager felt sorry for me, so her cousin offered me third shift at Circle K on Market Street."

Ben looks almost aghast. "Convenience store employees are more likely to be victims of gun violence than cops. I'm not telling you what to do. But no. Please."

His compulsive protection brings a smile to my angst. "Well, that's my best paying offer. The rest are minimum wage, and I can't survive on that. Not here. Not anywhere. Certainly, not in *that* house."

"You'll find something better. The hiring slump is temporary. I know people. I'll ask around. Do you need money? I have plenty set aside. Let me handle some bills until you—"

My head shakes before he finishes. "No, please. I appreciate it, but you can't rescue me. It's not right or what I want. And I'd feel worse, anyway."

"You should never feel bad about accepting my help." His face scrunches like he's perplexed by the Lena-puzzle. "I'd do *anything* for you, Lena."

"That doesn't mean you *should*." My head droops, feeling guilty over what I've left out, and pained in his sincerity in holding nothing back. *He really would do anything.* I force an uneasy smile. "Forget I said anything. I'm fine, really. Only venting." I step closer, resting my hands against his chest. "It's a lovely night. Let's not ruin it with my bullshit, okay?"

"We need to talk about this, though."

I laugh strangely. "We have, Ben. We can check it off the list now. Lena's shitshow life… check."

"Please. It's important."

"Another time, okay?" I point to my floral headband. "I'm the queen, right?"

"Always." His hands lock behind me. "We'll table it, for now, but I need one thing from you."

My grip tightens as I flash a coy grin. "That sounds promising. Hope it involves those lips and your exceptional kissing skills, Ben Wright."

He laughs. "Your diversionary skills are even better."

My shoulders sink. "I'm sorry. What is it?"

"Tell me you see us as *together*. I need you to say that you're not alone anymore."

Shit. Of course, I'm alone. Always alone. It's my state-of-being. Anxiety bitches don't count as companions, do they? No one else sticks around long. I won't either, not with that house falling apart and Asheville waiting for me. I shift away involuntarily, but he holds me in place, eyes fixed.

A crease forms between his eyes. "You can't say it, can you?"

I groan. "Of course, I can. I'm not alone anymore."

A heavy sigh escapes him. "I wish you believed it. Why don't you believe it?"

My attitude melts with his disappointment. "I want to but… Do you ever feel like we're living in this beautiful bubble that'll pop?"

A long moment passes, his eyes jumping from me to the river over my shoulder and back to me again. "No. This isn't a bubble. It's a universe with us at the center. It'll keep expanding, the more we put into it. All we have to do is be together, and that's easy."

The lovely way he puts it elates and saddens me at once, but I want to believe it. I fall a little more in love with him then, as if, like sleep, I sink into another level—light to REM to deep. Tears slip out with my words. "I'm not alone anymore."

His grin returns, full-on. "Yes. That's it."

"Sorry, Ben, but I don't make anything easy. Mom always said I was too intense, complicating everything with my crazy."

"Stop using that word. You're not crazy. You're honest. Besides, you don't waste your beautiful intensity on anything you don't care about." He smirks. "You *really* care about me."

Tears fall as if sad-sack-Lena can't help but show up. My over-thinking has always been this awful detriment, a disease I hide desperately, like young-Ben covering up his dyslexia. That he sees honesty and beauty in it makes me wonder if it's a defect at all. Maybe it's just who I am.

And whatever I am, Ben knows it. Likes it. Wants it, even.

Ben traces my cheek. "Things aren't ideal for you now, but we're in this together, whatever our realities."

"I did say that, didn't I?"

"Yes, and please say you mean it. For me, there's *nothing* better than being with you, Lena." He pauses, a tiny pinch between his eyes. "That's what I want… *you and me*… for as long as our universe allows. I predict forever."

"Ben… damn it. For a guy who says so few words, how do you come up with exactly the right ones? Our own universe? *Forever?* That's the sweetest and most devastating thing you've ever said to me."

"Devastating?"

"Yes, devastating. I'd hoped for a no-tears evening with you. You're turning me into a mess, but in the best way." I slip my fingers under my eyes, hoping my minimal mascara isn't making train tracks down my cheeks. "I usually don't cry on dates… well, I have a few times, but never in a good way. Please don't put this on your sister's group chat."

"Of course not. I only share what's sharable. The rest is… sacred."

Sacred? Like the fire-barrel? Or that day under the saddletree? One word shouldn't matter, but it's an earthquake, breaking down the last of my defenses. *What's between us is sacred. Ours alone. Holy shit, we really are an us.* The stone-like fortress around my heart cracks—a surprise since my walls are feats of mental engineering. That's what years of failure and loss do—fortify defenses, so the next time a battle rages, you might be protected.

But river breezes sweep around us. Streetlights flicker in his eyes, *fireworks*, and we hold each other like there is nothing else, forcing my fortress to crumble… at least to crack enough to pull him inside.

He leans his forehead against mine. "What're you thinking, Lena?"

I laugh through my drying tears. "Gosh, good timing, Ben. Only how badly I want to kiss you and how impossibly far away your place feels right now."

His lips meet mine in a frenzy, sending us to the pier railings. He presses against me so tightly we aren't two people, but one, and it's scary, the intensity of how much I want him.

Splashing interrupts our entanglement. Below us, a gator bobs in the murky water, glaring like he's just spotted dinner if he only could reach it. We laugh at the unusual distraction.

Ben says, "It's a juvenile. The white and yellowish bands fade when they get older."

"I didn't know that. He's cute." I take a picture to post with a clever caption later. "Who'd win in a fight? Gator or shark?"

"The larger of the two."

I pull him along the boardwalk, back the way we came. "What if they're the same size?"

Ben outlines their strengths and weaknesses but can't decide. It's nice hearing him talk and holding his hand as we walk.

Our steps slow at the driveway, and we take strange turns leading one another toward the house between random thoughts about sharks and gators. He tells me a shark has multiple rows of teeth while I say a gator has the strongest bite.

"And the longest body… and arms, however short and stubby." I pull him to the front steps.

"Gators need air. Sharks don't."

"Sharks need water. Gators don't. *Jaws* scared the hell out of me as a kid," I laugh.

"Did you ever see *Lake Placid*?"

"Yes, I have both DVDs at home. We should plan a shark versus gator night next time." *Next time?* My anxiety bitches try for a comeback, bum-rushing me with thoughts of *that* house and Asheville.

But on the first step, his hands circle my waist, turning me toward him. His face, once thought so stern, almost cold, blankets me with reassurances. My anxiety bitches can no longer compete with how beautiful and comfortable and loved he makes me feel.

Still, he says, "We'll have many other nights like this, if you're even *slightly* unsure."

"I'm not." I rise to the next step. "I've never been more sure about anything. Are *you* unsure?"

"No." He takes one gigantic step to the top, making me laugh. I meet him there, leaning closer.

But under the porch light, he hesitates again, brow crinkling over words that won't come.

"What is it?" I kiss him softly, hoping to encourage him.

Eyes locked, he takes my hand, guiding my fingers under his shirt. The first time we were close, he flinched at this and diverted me. Now, I understand with strange clarity that I wasn't the only one dealing with pesky anxiety bitches that day. His reluctance makes sense as my hand discovers the reason. Fire and shrapnel from the explosion marred his skin like razored sandpaper. He's scarred. His chest is covered in old wounds, craters and divots over what should be smooth and muscular. *Ah, Ben.* My fingers trace his skin's uneven texture. Tears escape—I can't help it, imagining him bloody and shredded. *He must've been in so much pain.*

Ben hangs his head. "I should've told you. I wanted to. It's not easy… It's okay if you want to stop."

"Why would I want to stop? I hate that this happened to you, but it changes nothing for me. This is *you*, Ben, and you're exactly what I want." My hands skip over his marks as I whisper, "No holding back."

Deep kisses press me against the door. He fumbles for his keys, dropping them and making us both laugh. And moving, or rather, stumbling inside the house, we leave the last of our worries at the door.

Thirty-One

KEYS AND PHONES spill onto the seat of the hall tree like unwanted debris, weighing us down as we shuffle inside. With the door closed and the world locked out behind it, I fist his shirt in my hand and say, "Let me see."

His eyes leave mine only to pull his shirt over his head. I look at him. *Really* look at him. His scarred mosaic captures the pain of that day forever, and I wonder what it's like for him, reliving it with each glance in the mirror. But there's depth to it, reflecting both his brokenness and his resiliency. It's survivor art, and that makes it the loveliest thing I've ever seen.

I say nothing. I don't need to. His cares fade with my eyes, fingers, and lips moving over him with zero hesitation. The more I touch and kiss him, the more I reassure him as he's done for me time and time again, the more intensely he answers with frenzied kisses and teasing hands until he seems desperate.

Hell, *I'm* desperate. He's the sexiest, most alluring man I've ever encountered, scars and all, and I ache for more of him.

We litter the hallway with shoes and clothes and flowers falling from my hair. It's hurried and frantic, as if waiting this long has supercharged the air and created a tornado around us.

But once in his room, between breathless kisses, he whispers, "Lena, I want you *slowly*."

Slowly? That's been us from the start—achingly so. But the way he says it—hungry but intent on savoring—makes me flush with desire even more. There will only be one first like this for us, and it won't be rushed or ordinary.

We shed what's left of our clothes, undressing each other until it's us and nothing else. Standing at the foot of his bed, not touching, in full view of each other, I can't help but question why it's not awkward. *Nakedness is always awkward, right?*

But it's too inevitable to be weird, like the last page of a book reaching its happily ever after—we were meant for this. And time and togetherness have softened this final vulnerability into just another thing between us.

With a shaky breath, he says, "I can't think of the right word for this… for you."

A chuckle escapes. "I think it's *naked*."

"No. We've always been kind of naked… It's something like *beautiful*, but that isn't enough."

Eyes locked on mine as he moves closer. His fingertips trace my brow and float along my cheek. He leans in, his lips lingering near mine, but resisting like he's afraid the moment our lips touch, he'll devour me, when his plan was to savor each taste.

"I've wanted you for so long, imagined this a million ways." He scoffs slightly, his breath hitting my lips. "I never came close to getting it right… God, Lena… You're breathtaking."

"So, are you." Light from the hall reaches us here, at his bed's edge, and lets me follow the muscular curvature of his thick arms and tight stomach. Maybe it's atypical to say this, but he's beautiful, and it's a feat keeping my hands off him. *This is for me. And I am all his. He is exquisite…* that's the word. And other words—*want, desire, need*—take renewed positions as if I've never known what they meant until now. I *want* him. Though it's no mind-blowing revelation, its strength and depth surprise me. It's unfamiliar energy in formerly familiar territory. I've never *wanted* someone like this. I *want* him… mind, body, soul. Everything.

Watching me take him in, he seems relieved. "You make me feel good about being… seen. No one ever has before."

A gasping chuckle escapes me. "Then we're even. You've made me feel that way from the first moment we met."

His incredible arms slip around me, tugging me close, skin to skin, and his forehead rests against mine. My fingers drift along his cheeks, catching the gentle struggle behind his narrowed eyes. He almost looks emotional.

"You make me feel better, Lena. Not just better but..." He hesitates, his fingers drifting feather-like up my spine. "But... whole, like I'm myself for the first time. I, um, just want you to know how damn lucky I feel right now. There is no one in the universe I'd rather be with than you. Naked or otherwise."

He stumbles over his words in a perfectly lovely way that makes me even more desperate for him. I grin at the heart-tugging sweetness of it, emotion welling up. "*Our* universe," I correct weakly.

"*Our* universe," he says with a smile.

"Best kiss me then," I say breathlessly. "Kiss me and show me how lucky we both are."

A wild kiss bridges the tiny gap between us. As generous as he is with his lips and tongue, it's his big, strong hands that enflame my pleasure centers the most as they move slowly over me. Fingertips dance over my back before slipping over my cheeks and lacing through my hair, tugging me closer. Then, down the front of me, sliding over my chest, my breasts, the hard tips of my nipples, across my stomach, and lower still, every touch in reverence, every touch lighting me on fire for him.

His lips travel down my neck, nibbling and tasting me. "Tell me," he breathes against my skin. "Tell me what you like, what you want."

A confetti cannon of warm shocks bursts and spreads through my core to every end of me. Holy fuck—his words push me to the very edge, like I might orgasm on the idea alone. And what I want spills out from behind an unlocked door, suddenly yanked open. "Hands, lips, tongue, and teeth, I want you all over me. I want your face between my legs... for you to explore me, to take your time, to *enjoy* me. And I want to do the same with you. Discover you with my hands and mouth. Every muscle. Every vein. Every scar. I want to know you better than anyone ever has. To tease you and taunt you with my lips and tongue until you can't fucking take it anymore. I want to see just how far I can take you in my mouth," I say, my hand sliding over his impressive length as he groans and his chest heaves at the touch. "I want to bring you to the damn edge. Until you're desperate for me. Until *I* can't fucking take it anymore. I want you inside me. Bare. Nothing between us. Slow at first, to feel you deeply, like I already do in my heart. I want it to build, just like we have—slow and steady, together, and then every-thing surges at once. I..."

My voice trails off as he lays me on the bed, and I wonder if I've said too much. He peers up from my chest, smiling deviously, but looking pleased. "And? Go on."

"Um, that's it, I think. For now," I say with a nervous chuckle. "Is that okay?"

"Better than okay. It's perfect, exactly what I'm thinking, but..." he says, coming up to my lips and nibbling my bottom one. "Only I'm at the damn edge already."

"Me, too. We should get to it, then," I grin.

And he does. Ben takes his sweet time with me, doing everything I ask but his way, making me feel wanted and beautiful with each touch and lick and nibble.

This is *nothing* like I've had before. This is movie sex. Once-in-a-life-time sex. The kind of sex that makes me realize that everything before was perfunctory and one-sided, and not knowing any better, I let it be.

Not *that* woman anymore, I'm an eager archeologist excited to uncover every treasure, like sex has regained its virginal intrigue and hidden mysteries. Delicate gasps escape often—the new me is a moaner, apparently. When he makes me come the first time… and the second… I cry out with blissful surprise, not expecting the intensity of it —the full-bodied, emotional satisfaction of it.

Not only that, but *I'm* the badass sex goddess I've always imagined myself to be. Eventually, I take over, exploring him with the same gentle intensity he's shown me and building this gorgeous pressure between us. When I take him first with my mouth and second inside me, his raspy, "Lena," and his flexed muscles only heighten my need to feel him deeper. To take as much of him as I can. On top of him, I roll my hips, one glorious wave after another, while his hands grip mine midair, supporting me with every move.

Soon, he sits up with me on his lap, locking his arms around my back, guiding me with sweet pressure, and bringing his face to mine as if we were too far apart. He smiles, watching me, and it's so good I want to laugh, cry, and scream all at once. And then, it happens for us both—a double prize that feels so mind-shatteringly lucky that I wonder if one of us is faking. Um, we're definitely not. It's like getting a two-for-one out of a vending machine. Only a million times better... and, well, maybe not the rarity I once thought it to be. He is *really* good at this. And I'm pleasantly surprised to learn that, *ha*, so am I.

We stay there in a giddy sex trance, sweat peppering his brow and me trembling. He's unraveled every hard, twisted knot inside me and, finally freed, my loose strings encircle him, pulling him closer. Our heads lean together as our breathing slows. I run my fingers along his face, down the uneven terrain of his scar, and over the stubbled roughness of his cheek while he watches me with sweet admiration, dragging his fingers up and down my back, pulling me tighter as they go.

"What're you thinking, Lena?"

His question inspires a soft smirk—*of course, he asks me that*—but I struggle over my answer like I'm searching my mental files to identify something foreign. "I'm not thinking. I'm just… happy."

He takes in my surprise and says, "Strange, huh?"

"Extremely… and I want more. More of this. More of you." An anxiety spike comes with my confession, worried I sound demanding and insatiable—*Nervous Nellie* meets *Lustful Lena.*

But Ben smiles before kissing me and running his tongue over my bottom lip. "Good. That's what I'm thinking, too."

It's then that I decide to tell him everything in the morning—Jason's new offer, Dot's report, no power, no chance to make the farm and café happen. It's only fair, given his honesty with me. And if we make the decisions ahead of me together, then maybe there's still a chance we can stay that way. *This* way.

But that's tomorrow's problem, especially when he says, "Shower with me?"

My lips coil dreamily while the dying embers of my desire reflame with surprising vigor—*who am I?* My eyes widen like it's the best idea anyone has *ever* had.

"Yes, excellent idea, Ben."

Wavy strands fall over my eyes, and he sweeps them aside. "Want anything first? Water? Wine? Truffles?"

I laugh over him playing host, but I'm more amused by, "Truffles?"

"I thought you might want something sweet." He smiles sheepishly. "And I may have been somewhat overzealous in my preparations at the grocery store. Don't get your hopes up. They won't be nearly as good as what you can make."

"They'll be the best we've ever eaten… based on how the rest of the night has gone."

"Fair point," he says with a laugh.

I peel myself away from him and slip into a robe hanging on the backside of the door. "What else did you get in your overzealous preparations?"

He pulls on his boxer briefs and shares his hilarious grocery list. He pillaged the grocery store like a seasoned Eagle Scout—determined to be prepared. Truffles and ice cream in case of a sweet tooth. Chips and salsa, if not. A toothbrush, in case I forgot mine. A cooking magazine to read before bed. Chamomile tea, in case I couldn't sleep. Scented candles for ambiance, though he forgot to light them. Tampons, *just in case*. And everything I need for a shower, floral scents in my usual brands, so I wouldn't smell like him after using his—a hopeful contingency, he admits.

Giggling, I imagine my tall, imposing boyfriend sniffing candles and pondering over feminine products. "It's nice to know I'm not the only one guilty of overthinking."

"I, um, may have done some recon in your bathroom." His broad shoulders bounce in a shrug. "You always make me feel at home. I wanted to do the same."

We sidestep flowers and shoes in the hallway. Holding my hand, he leads me to the kitchen and extracts a small bakery box from the fridge. We share chocolate truffles and wine between kisses and conversation. It's light and easy and fun.

Part of me had hoped that in coming here, I'd discover some nagging, bothersome thing about him that would make leaving for Asheville easier. I wanted doubts and misgivings—anything that would get me to say, *"Eh, it wouldn't have worked out between us anyway."*

But as I chuckle over his grocery store confessional, loving the comfortable way his hands play hopscotch on me—arms, fingers, waist, back, cheek, like he can't stop touching me—there's nothing I don't like. He is perfect. And it's killing me.

Done with wine and truffles and mid-chatting about nothing in particular, his sudden, deep kisses move us toward the shower, me tripping over one of my wedges as we do our strange kissing-dance down the hall. He lifts me onto the counter by the sink.

"Don't move," he says, kissing me again. He starts the water in the oversized shower and sets out thick, white towels. Peony and lavender body wash and shampoo take up a corner of the tub next to a pink loofah—the *women's* products he promised. He retrieves the grocery store candles and uses them in lieu of the bright bathroom sconces. The flames flicker in the mirror, warming the sterile whiteness of the subway-tiled walls.

Though I love it, I say, "You don't have to romance me."

His eyes crimp curiously as he moves between my legs and pushes the robe off me. "I'll *always* want to romance you."

The word *always* stirs the unwanted bits of my life, like dust particles flying into the air. But I pay them no mind, not with Ben's lips playing a delicate teasing game with mine and his hand moving up my thigh.

Our shower time doesn't leave me with anything to count against him, either. Quite the opposite. We shampoo each other's hair between laughs and kisses and touches until, finally, the water turns cold, forcing us out.

Back in his bed, we go for each other again, ravenous and single-minded. And it doesn't get old. Each time brings us to another level, surpassing the last, like some fun, beautiful game we'll never want to stop playing.

But late into the night, tiredness takes over. Wrapped against his chest, I've never felt so content. I think of how I felt on the tree swing at Mom's saddletree—finding that elusive peace and comfort is easier with Ben around.

Just as sleep begins to take me, he leans closer and says, "I love you, Lena. I *really* do. I have for a while. That's hard for you to hear. I know. Harder still for you to say. So, don't say anything. Just know it. Know that I love you, Lena. No matter what."

My head pops up, but a sweet, slow kiss thwarts my stunned, breathless reaction as if he planned it that way. Then, he lies against the pillow, smiling and satisfied. I curl closer, bringing the blanket over us and using his shoulder as a pillow. He nestles me to him, lips grazing my forehead. And I think *this is Ben*. Perfect and perfectly broken, Ben. My best friend. My best... everything. And it feels like the last time, the only time, anyone will love me like this.

So, the words come out as naturally as air. "I love you, too."

Slipping in between anxieties over this new reality and the one that awaits me at home, sleep finds me, eventually.

Shit! Where's my fucking phone? Jerking up, my hands scurry around me. I hear it, *know it*, though I don't see it—Mom thrashing in bed as tiny aliens scuttle beneath her thin skin. Their toothy grins poke through her crippled joints. She wails in pain, screaming for an ambulance. Layer by layer, I search. *What is this? The Princess and the damn Pea? I just saw it. It's here, somewhere.*

"What is?"

The quiet voice confuses me. *Had I said my thoughts aloud? And who answered? An EMT? Why isn't he helping her?*

Toneless, his words become clearer when he says, "What are you looking for?"

"My fucking phone."

"Lena, stop."

I yank the comforter at my feet, shaking it out. *God, how many blankets are there? She's dying.* I reach for the sheet, but my arms lock at my sides. I wriggle against the alien's grasp, but it's too strong. "Let go! She's dying!"

"Lena, wake up. It's a bad dream." The voice is sterner now, forcing my attention.

My eyes adjust, and the strange room dumbfounds me. Furniture. A real bed. Quiet. No screams. No moans. No Mom. *I'm too late. She's gone. It's too late.*

Ben's soft voice cuts through my distress. "You're safe. There's no one to call. There's nothing you need to do. You don't need your phone." He delivers instructions in a gentle monotone, like the announcer before an amusement park ride. *Keep your hands in the vehicle at all times.* "Everything's okay. Just breathe."

A glance down reveals arms—not alien tentacles. I relax against him, glad he can't see my face for the tears of embarrassment leaking out.

His grip loosens, but he holds me there, saying nothing. *What's there to say, anyway? Sorry, Ben. Night terrors feature in this girlfriend package. There's no time or money refund, but trading in for a less dysfunctional model is highly recommended.*

But my snarky, embarrassed thoughts diminish in his comfort. The steady rise and fall of his chest lulls me. My hurried breathing slows to match his. He runs a hand over my sweaty brow, sweeping hair away from my face, cooling me.

I twist in his arms to see him. "Sorry."

"No apologizing. This is just you right now." He kisses my forehead. "At least we'll never be boring."

"Gosh, Ben. I'd quite like boring." I pull away from him for the bathroom and splash cold water on my face and wrists to calm down. Can't blame *that* house for this one. Not entirely, anyway. I push those thoughts aside for Ben's words. *This* is *just me right now.* Will he hold me through the rest of my nightmares, too? And will I get to hold him through his?

I return to bed, my heartbeat normalizing with my resolve to come clean in the morning. He's already drifted off, and I try not to bother him as I sneak under the covers. But he curls close as soon as I'm settled, tugging me against him and absorbing my coldness into his sleepy warmth. His lips graze my shoulder with light kisses as he nestles me. And, once again, he deserves credit. *Damn, it.* Calming me and not making a big deal afterward, he makes me feel completely accepted, securing his *I-love-you* like a contract he'll never break. *I'm not alone anymore.* The words not only ring true but bang and reverberate, making me believe it's true.

Thirty~Two

LIGHT WAKES ME, sneakily edging through the blinds, the hair over my eyes, and even my eyelids. On my stomach, I shift to my elbows, surprised. I slept hard. So hard, I *feel* rested. It's been years since I've slept like this. *Fucking years.*

Ben's not here. Bed space being another odd-thing-missed, I'm sprawled like a human pancake, spread wide. *Shit! In my bed-greediness, did I push Ben out?*

On the bedside table, a glass of water holds last night's flowers, trimmed to fit. With a groggy smile, I roll over. My bag sits on his dresser, along with an Army t-shirt, neatly folded. My discarded clothes lay across the end of the bed. I pull on the t-shirt with a bad feeling. *How long have I slept?*

In the kitchen, he hovers over a breakfast operation. I wince at his microwave clock. It's after nine! "Aw, Ben, why didn't you wake me?"

My distress softens with Ben's enormous grin. He meets me mid-kitchen, slipping his arms around me and nearly lifting me off my feet. I laugh—I can't help it—before he kisses me and says, "Good morning, Lena. Sleep okay?"

"Too good. After.. Been up long?"

His seriousness returns in a quick nod. "My internal clock wakes me at five every morning, regardless of my wishes." He lets me go to flip bacon while I target the coffeepot.

"Well, I'm glad it wasn't me—kicking you out of bed."

"No. For you, I stayed an extra forty-five minutes. I like watching you sleep."

"Okay, stalker." My coy smile widens as I sip coffee and check out his stovetop. Pancakes and eggs keep warm under aluminum foil while the bacon crisps. "You didn't have to go to all this trouble, Ben."

"It's no trouble." He gives me a funny look. "Breakfast is the most important meal of the day."

I smirk, glancing at the hall tree by the door and finding it tidied. "Seen my phone?"

He bobs his head toward the kitchen bar, where my phone sits face down, plugged in by the outlet. "Charging." He fills my hands with condiments and utensils before I reach it. "Let's eat on the porch."

A small settee corners his screened-in porch giving us a street-side view, and it's hypnotic watching the cars go by. The day promises to be a hot one, but his shaded lot has captured the morning chill, holding it tightly. Even the noisy Carolina wrens fussing overhead add to the peacefulness, activity highlighting my stillness.

Not to ruin it, but I want to confess, fill in the blanks I skipped last night to finish my warped *Mad Lib* with words like *powerless, unlivable, and unsalvageable*.

But Ben cuts me off. "Move in with me."

My breath hitches. "What?"

"Move in with me."

I pause for an absent punchline. "No. Why ask me that?"

"It's what I want. My place makes sense. *For now.*"

My eyebrows triangulate on my forehead. "Ben, you're punch-drunk on sex. Me, too. Last night was… incredible. The novelty will wear off, and you'll see it's a bad idea."

"You and me, together as much as possible—how could that be a bad idea?" His green eyes lock on mine. "I'd never ask on a whim. I've given it ample thought."

My skepticism breaks through the sweetness of his offer—I can't help it. "Um, it's too soon. Too… reckless. This is our first breakfast together. Seems risky, committing to them all just yet."

"Does anything fail to meet or exceed your expectations?"

I chuckle at how he says it. "No. Definitely not. But there're rules against impulsive relationship decisions like that."

"We make the rules. And it's not risky or impulsive, considering how I feel. You have my heart, might as well share a home, too."

He really means it. Moving in? Really? A thick lump lodges in my throat. "Why now? Why so soon?"

"Why not? My place isn't huge, but we'll make it work. Your mom's hutch'll fit—your other refinished pieces, too, if we're creative. I'll clear out cabinets for your kitchen supplies and build a pantry on the back porch. We'll put a garden in the backyard if you want to supplement the one at your farm. Moving in means you can take your time with the restoration, and you wouldn't have to settle for some shit-job. You could hold out for something good… or, better yet, focus on the farm and café entirely. Work there during the day. Come home to me at night."

"Um, you really *have* given this thought," I say, a little breathless with surprise.

"Yes." His serious expression reinforces his determination. "Nothing's perfect, but it'll be close. Don't you think? Even what's bad will be better with us together."

"Uh-oh, Ben. You're starting to sound like Shakespeare." I chuckle, and the irony sideswipes me—I'm nearly homeless, too, and Ben could be my ticket out.

"Hmm. Don't hold that against me." He studies me, fingers strumming mine while I consider it. "I promise, it'll be *our* place. We're equals. It wouldn't be like it was with Mark."

"I know… I'm not thinking about him."

"What then?"

This time, I struggle to put words together. I want to say yes. *So badly.* I can't think of anything better than living with him. And that he doesn't know how grave my situation *really* is, inclines me to accept. This isn't charity or some knee-jerk reaction to keep me from moving. He doesn't know I have to yet. *I could say no to Asheville. To selling.* The vice clenching my chest releases. I could go at my own pace with the repairs and make non-desperate choices.

Or is this just another one? My anxiety bitches nag me to think it through. *Ben never rushes. Why rush this?* "You have me spinning, Ben. It takes you months to invite me over, but one night to ask me to move in?"

"After last night, are you really surprised?" He smirks, bridging the short gap between us by pressing his forehead to mine and letting his hand roam up my thigh. Last night rushes over me like a hot wave, making me flush and get flustered at once. "Say yes, Lena. I promise— living here, you won't feel pressured about anything. Not the house or job-hunting. It's what's best for us."

He sounds like Lucas. And Mark. Even Mom. *At least stay until you can get back on your feet, Lena.* I fluctuate between gratitude and suspicion. *It's perfect timing… too perfect… but he doesn't know… does he?* Then, like a puzzle piece snapping into place, I remember my phone.

A bowling ball of bad emotion strikes something inside of me. Desperation pulls me away from him and draws me into the house. I snatch my phone from where he's put it. Missed notifications clutter my screen like an open diary, secrets spilling.

Dot:

> More bad news, Babe. The generator conked out. It's like this place is cursed. Hit me back, pronto…

Jason Ford:

> Of course, the job's still yours if you want it! Call me after the lunch rush and we'll…

Lucas:

> Got your message. Drew and I will help you get the power back on, but get more estimates first. One estimate is never…

I stand between the front door and the porch steps, twitching with fresh anxiety. I hold up my phone. "You saw these?"

"Yes."

"Never pegged you for a snoop, Ben."

"Never expected you had something to hide." He sighs, furrowing his brow. "Why not tell me?"

"I planned to, but *this* is why I couldn't. I don't want you handing over money or keys. My situation sucks, but it belongs *to me.* I can't believe this is why you asked me to move in! And instead of confronting me, you used a strategy on me?"

He hesitates before saying, "Yes, only because I knew you'd never ask."

I scoff, wiping tears. "Well… you *almost* had me. Nice trick, riding on the coattails of my dishonesty with your own."

"I would've done the same if you'd told me outright. I *want* you here. There's nothing dishonest about it."

"Oh, only the part about us being equals. You asked *because* you know I'm desperate. How would it ever feel equal with you playing the hero and me the damsel in distress? You manipulated me, and I don't need your fucking charity, anyway."

Heart racing, anger surging, hands flicking at my wrists, an urge to escape jolts through me, sending me inside. In his bedroom, I trade his t-shirt for last night's clothes, still draped on the bed.

He stands in the doorway, watching me cyclone for my things. "Lena, it's not charity. Can't moving in together be what we want *and* solve your problems simultaneously? What's wrong with accepting my help? You asked Lucas for money."

"Yes! I did! After two glasses of wine while sitting in the fucking dark—not my best moment. I won't take it." With my open bag in hand, I stop at the doorway.

Ben doesn't move aside. "Your house has no power. You *need* a place to stay. That's a fact."

A sardonic smile eases up my cheeks. "Thanks for the handy dandy recap, but I'm fully aware of my situation, and I don't need anything from you. Let me by."

He hesitates. "Why are you so angry?" His question disarms me a little, especially in how calmly he asks it. "I only want to help. Can't we talk about it?"

"There's nothing to say." A shaky breath brings more tears. "I'm taking the job in Asheville. Selling the house."

A puzzled look is replaced quickly with resolve. "Okay. If you want Asheville, we'll move to Asheville."

My breath sticks in my throat. "What? You'd move for me?"

"Yes. I love you. I'll follow you anywhere, Lena."

"I'd *never* ask you to do that. You have a life here. Your family's here. Your career. You can't give that up for me."

"So, it's okay for you to make sacrifices for the people you love, but not okay for me?"

"This is different!"

"How?"

"You have shit to lose. You haven't been through this before… and you're not the broke, unemployed, nearly homeless one. If things were reversed, you'd hate being reliant on me. Right?"

"Likely, things *will* be reversed one day. I'm positioned to help *now*. Once your career takes off, you'll have the financial upper hand. Wouldn't you provide for us if I couldn't do my job anymore? We support each other. That's how this works."

I laugh like he's told a funny joke. "How would I *ever* be able to support you, Ben? Look at me. I can't even take care of myself. You need someone you can rely on, and that's not me. You deserve better, *so much better*, and I'm sorry."

I push by him, but he edges into my path again in the living room. "Wait. You're denying my help, my home, *and* my willingness to move? What's left, Lena? Are you… breaking up with me?"

The words hit me like bricks dumped on my head. "Um, yes, I— that's the best thing."

"That's… unacceptable."

"It's not up to you!" My bag falls from my shaking hand, but I scoop it up quickly and race for the door. *I hate this. Hate everything. Must get out of here.* I grab my wedges, but too flustered to put them on, shove them in my bag. I reach for the doorknob, but his hand falls on mine, stopping me again.

"Did I ever tell you how they discovered my dyslexia in middle school?"

The randomness forces an awkward, "Um, no."

"I kept pulling fire alarms."

"I don't care. Let me go, Ben."

"Please, just listen. Two minutes." He pauses, and I say nothing, but I don't move. "Becca and I weren't in the same classes, leaving me vulnerable. I couldn't do what my teachers wanted, making me seem belligerent. My grades suffered, upsetting my parents. So, whenever the pressure felt too great, I pulled the alarm to escape it. Momentarily, it was a relief, but it wasn't a viable solution long-term. And it got me in trouble."

"Why are you telling me this?"

"You're pulling the fire alarm, Lena. You're panicking. That's all this is."

A montage of shameful me-moments streams through my head when overrun with anxiety surges, I lashed out at the people closest to me. Panic first, apologize later has always been a shit-system, one I don't want to resurrect. But I'm too far gone, long overdue for an escape. *He pushed me. Made this worse. Made me panic.*

"Whatever our realities, remember?" he says slowly.

My own words coming back to bite me in the ass—no surprise. But it triggers flashbacks of my last sleepless days with Mom—every second, an anxious deliberation between wait-and-see and call nine-one-one. I broke in the end. I called. Mom died anyway. Nothing I did or hoped or wanted mattered, except that she didn't get her dying wish to be at home. Now her place is doing the same—crumbling to pieces until it breaks me and dies, anyway. The same will happen—*is happening*—with Ben and me. *How could I ever hold my part of us together?*

My eyes fall away from his. "I shouldn't have said that. My reality is a shitstorm no one deserves but me."

He takes a timid step toward me. "The shitstorm doesn't matter. You love me… that's your reality, too. *Right?*"

A long breath forces a damn tear-waterfall. I want to deny it, but how can I?

"Lena, please. Fight through what you're feeling now and get to the other side. This is your panic talking. Not you. In a day, a week, a month, a year, these problems won't matter. But losing each other will. That's not what you want. It's not what I want."

His words kick up therapy memories like dry leaves in the wind. *This moment isn't all moments.* Whispers from Mom's bedside stir, too. *Please, don't leave. Stay with me. Fight through.* "What I want *never* matters. Panicked or not, my reality's the same. It's better this way… It's over. I mean it."

Pushing by him, I scuttle barefoot down the porch steps.

"How can you say that? After everything? After last night? This is why nothing ever works out for you. You won't let it! Unless it's all been bullshit, and last night was just… you feeling sorry for me."

My feet scrape against the concrete path coming to a stop. His tone paralyzes me. He's fucking vitriolic, and I've never heard that from him before. I spin around, nearly tripping over my feet. I want to see his anger and bitterness, so leaving is easier. *He hates me. He really hates me.* But that's not what I find when we lock eyes.

With the same tearful desperation, I say, "No! Never! It wasn't like that!"

"Then, what was it? You said you *needed* me, Lena. When did that stop being true?"

"Ben…" My panic retreats like a spent wave the longer we take each other in. "It hasn't, but—"

My phone rings in my hand, making me jump. Though the worst time to take a call, I do it without thinking.

"Honey, Shadow's not doing well." Gloria's serious tone makes my heart skip. "The vet's comin', but I thought you'd—"

"I'll be right there."

Thirty~Three

NOT SHADOW. *Please, not Shadow.* I clench and unclench my hands before pressing my inner wrists, back and forth, massaging my pressure points. My seatbelt strangles my neck as I stare out the passenger window. But catching racing glimpses of neon-pink azaleas, lanky pines, and bursting palmettos doesn't quell my ongoing panic. "I can't believe you talked me into this."

He side-eyes me, business-like expression fixed. "It's a public service, considering how you drive when you're upset."

A weak smirk pushes through, remembering my near-tickets the day we met. I fist my fingers again. Ben's right hand slips over them, squeezing softly. I enclose his hand between mine, tightening my grip. "This won't change anything."

With a short sigh, he says, "Right. Break-up still in effect. No talking about us. This is about Shadow. I got it… We're almost there."

Outside the passenger window, fields give way to pines before Gloria's bright red barn comes into view. I scan the paddocks. Shadow rolls in the pasture, kicking his legs and biting his side.

Ben barely has the Jeep in park before I slide out and rush to the field. I don't bother with the gate but bend between the straps of the electric fence, speed-walking with a desperate, sinking gut feeling.

Gloria puts her hands up. "Lena, best give him space. He's been thrashing."

My rubber boots slide to a stop. *Fuck. He's hurting.* "What's wrong with him?"

"Colic, likely."

"Colic?" The term reminds me of Luna's infancy. "Like in babies?"

"No, it's an abdominal problem in horses. See how he's bloated and nipping at his stomach."

He writhes abnormally, like a snake after its head's been chopped off. His agony reminds me of Mom, unconscious in her hospital bed, but still trying to rip out her IV.

Ben looms behind me, catching Gloria's eye. I motion over my shoulder. "Um, Gloria, this is my… This is Ben."

"Nice to meet you, ma'am."

Gloria gives a half-hearted smile. "Mr. Fireworks, right? Wish it could be under better circumstances."

"Yes, ma'am. I'm at your service, if I can help."

"Well, aren't you a tall drink of water on a hot day?" Gloria points to the lot over our shoulders. "Vet's here. How 'bout we see if she needs help carrying her equipment?"

Gloria and Ben leave me with Shadow—not that there's anything I can do. He wriggles and kicks in sudden bouts, seizure-like, making it impossible to get close.

But Doc Evie maneuvers behind him and administers a mild sedative. She gets him to his feet as the medication takes over. As Shadow relaxes, I move closer, standing by his lowered head and rubbing his nose. She takes vitals and examines his engorged belly. Then, she puts a tube down his throat.

"Sand colic," she says, like a judge reaching a verdict.

Gloria nods knowingly, but my hand goes up like I'm in school. "Explain, please?"

"It's the coast. There's sand in the grass and hay. Ingesting too much leads to an impacted bowel. Worst case, the impaction causes the intestines to twist or knot, meaning surgery but given Shadow's age and the expense, well…" Doc Evie shares a glance with Gloria. *Surgery isn't an option.*

"The next few days'll be critical," Doc Evie says.

Gloria nods. "We need to get Shadow moving, pooping, and back to his ornery, farty self again."

My eyes dart between the two more-knowledgeable women. "How?"

Doc Evie adjusts Shadow's tube and inserts a liquid. "Mineral oil might help. Check him every twenty minutes or so. The discomfort causes anxiety, so if left on his own, he'll lay down too much for relaxation. But this causes the intestines to knot, if they haven't already. I'll leave you with pain meds, but don't feed him his regular diet."

"What can he eat?" I ask.

"I usually do a bran mash," Gloria says. "It's not his favorite, but he'll eat if he's hungry enough."

My mind spins. "What about natural food remedies? Can I make something that'll help?"

Gloria pats my back. "Lena's peppermint horse treats are a big hit around here."

Doc Evie nods. "Anything with an oat or bran base is good. Peppermint, ginger, and dandelion help digestion."

"What about for his anxiety? Can he have chamomile and lavender?" I ask.

"Absolutely." Doc Evie looks surprised. "The anti-inflammatory properties of chamomile make it good for this problem. CBD oil helps with relaxation and pain relief. I'll give you a list of appropriate doses. Anything will help, *if* he'll eat them."

"I'll do my best. Yes, I'd like a list."

Doc Evie and I discuss it while walking toward her truck. Using the back of a prescription pad, she jots natural ingredients and amounts needed to affect a large animal. Meanwhile, Ben and Gloria try walking Shadow. He lays down each time, too pained to try.

Doc Evie leaves. Gloria offers her most comforting smile as I rejoin them. "He's been through this before, but I've never seen 'em so bad. No one'd blame you for sittin' this out. It's too soon after your momma. I'll take good care of 'em and call ya if anything changes."

"I'm fine. I'll get supplies and then—shit, can I use your kitchen? Mine's, um, out of order."

"Sure, honey."

"Thanks. I'll cover the night shift."

"*We'll* cover the night shift," Ben says, standing beside me.

Driving away, I see Shadow thrashing again, tickling my panic. With no time for experimentation, I need to get Shadow's naturally medicated treats right. I make a mental grocery list while concocting recipes. Anxiety slugs through my veins—a constant undercurrent rather than a sudden spike, like it was with Mom at the end. *It's too much. All this. Too much.*

"Where to?" Ben asks.

"Um, your place. I'll get my Honda. That way, you can—"

"Lena, I'm staying with you. Where would you like to shop?"

"Sunny's." It comes out in a defeated huff. I'm too preoccupied to argue.

At Sunny's, we mask up. He pushes the cart while I peruse the produce section. Ben says nothing as the cart fills. I splurge on expensive rice and coconut flour—*easier on the stomach*—as well as coconut oil, fresh peppermint, oats, bran, ginger, and chamomile. I grab apples and carrots for sweetness. But they don't have fresh dandelion greens or lavender—two must-haves for digestive relief and calming.

At checkout, I stand, guard-like, at the card machine. Ben doesn't offer to pay, and it's a relief, swiping my card.

Rolling through the parking lot, Ben asks, "Where to, now?"

"The Hemp Farmacy... and I don't know. Sunny's didn't have fresh lavender or dandelion greens."

"Use social media. Someone might know where to find them."

"Good idea." I prompt my phone while he loads the Jeep. *Does anyone know where I can get fresh lavender and dandelion greens? I'm baking treats for a colicky horse.*

By the time I purchase the highest concentration of CBD oil at the Hemp Farmacy—another expense cutting harshly into my reserve—there's an answer. *I have both at the farm. Stop by anytime.*

"Shit. Not Alice Harvey." I scroll through the other responses, hoping for an alternative. But no.

Beggars can't be choosers. I can almost see Mom's signature look—a critical smirk that says, *"Maybe you shouldn't use the F-word on your neighbors. Hmm?"*

Yeah, yeah, yeah. "My place and then Alice's... Are you sure we shouldn't just swing by your house for my Honda? This is going to take all night, and—"

"I understand. Stop worrying about me. Focus on what you have to do."

"Don't you have to work soon? Or tomorrow? This is—"

"Lena, I want to help... If we're over, then consider this my last wish."

"Fine... but no more last-wish talk. Don't jinx Shadow."

"Understood."

"Do you have pen and paper?" It's a long shot. Ben's Jeep interior looks fresh from the lot, tidy and clutter-free. But he opens the center console revealing a plethora of supplies. A baggie of loose change. Tissues. Cleaning wipes. Hand sanitizer. And a small notebook with pen attached to the spiral. I tweak my horse treat recipe with Doc Evie's suggestions.

At *that* house, Dot's fixed the generator—*for now*, she warns. She's at the kitchen table, boots propped, watching *Friends* reruns on an old, battery-operated TV from the barn.

"What the hell, Dot?" I blurt, eyeing her interesting set-up. A damp flannel hangs on the sliding glass door, drying. A network of extension cords trailing to the generator outside power lights and fans aimed at her and the tussled fort-bed. A cooler and hotplate sit on the counter, along with enough convenience store snacks to feed many trip-weary children.

"You said to make myself at home," she says.

Did I say that? "I thought you were just keeping an eye on things. Why stay here when you have Mrs. Moore's place?"

She groans. "We need space. She blames me for you backing out of your farm and café idea, as if it's my fault. Maybe I didn't have to hit you with everything at once, but would you want your doctor only giving you half a diagnosis?"

"No, it's better to know the place is a lost cause."

Dot prompts my laptop. "I never said that. I'm working on a detailed estimate for you, just in case."

"Don't bother." My eyes catch Mom's urn and the note-shrine around her.

Things will get better

Everything you need is right here. Dream something better.

They no longer inspire Hallmark-esque optimism, but jab sharply at my self-worth, what's left, anyway.

Even worse, I'm ashamed as Ben's eyes roam the place. My fort-bed in the living room, the crumbling and stained dry wall held barely by my ridiculous patch-job, and the coffin-like stuffiness and darkness in the kitchen. Even with Dot's fans, the place feels dank and still—nothing like the warm retreat of the old days, or, hell, even the make-do coziness of months ago when Ben first showed up. It's a damn embarrassment. No one should live like this.

Maybe it's good—him seeing how bad it is. *He must understand now.*

I fill Dot in on my horse emergency while rummaging the kitchen. I dig out my extra large, mini-muffin tin and other baking tools Gloria may not have. I fill a small box with baking staples from the pantry. I change into farm clothes—worn jeans and a tank top—while adding my cushy sweater and extra clothes to my overnight bag.

The drive to the Harvey's farm is beautifully silent. The radio doesn't even distract me from rehearsing apologies. *Never mind that fuck you, Alice* is the best I come up with, but it doesn't matter. The intense standoff I expect is thwarted by her meeting us in the driveway. Seeing us together prompts a wide grin as she circles the Jeep. She hands me a large wicker basket full of beautiful purple lavender and fresh greens.

"Figured you'd be in a hurry," she says. "Is this enough?"

"Plenty. Thanks, Alice."

Her arms fold over her paisley dress. "Well, we're neighbors. Hope it helps. Colic is no picnic."

"Look, about last time, um, I'm really—" An abruptly raised hand stops me cold.

"Lena, honey, time and tide wait for no man. Neither does a colicky horse." Her red lips curve into a wide grin. "Beg my forgiveness later… when y'all return my basket. Alright?"

Though the basket might as well be another casserole dish, a relieved smile busts through my tension. "Thanks, Alice."

At Gloria's farm, Ben helps carry supplies inside, and I take over her lovely, working kitchen. It takes hours to get it right. I create human samples first. Once satisfied with its yumminess, I adjust the amounts for higher-dose horse versions. On Ben's notepad, I scribble changes as I go. The first horse batch comes out with a wave of honey and lavender. With a smirk of success, I look up from the muffins to see that no one's there. Ben's gone. The cottage sits quiet and empty.

With the warm treats, I race to the paddock, scanning the grazing horses. But Shadow's missing. Circling the property, I find him bucking angrily in the same small paddock where he recovered from that kids' party. Gloria tugs his lead rope, yanking him into submission. But he pulls back before toppling to the ground and snapping at his gut. He lays on his side, head down.

I rush over, tapping my bin as I get closer. Curious, he stands and ambles to me. The treats, covered in apple bits, carrot shavings, and honey, are impossible to resist. He nibbles it from my hand and nudges me for another.

"That's the first thing he's eaten in twenty-four hours." Gloria shakes her head. "And he's been as ornery as a bridge troll. He's hardly taken any steps."

"Well, these'll calm him. They're filled with natural relaxants."

Gloria peers into my bin. "And your usual tasty magic, too, looks like."

I rub Shadow's nose. "Let's hope it helps."

I hand Gloria a smaller sample, and her eyes widen as she chews it. "If he doesn't eat 'em, I sure will."

As if to argue, Shadow digs into my bin for another and gobbles up two before I manage to close it. His exuberance tickles me, and my glimmer of hope for him brightens. *Maybe it'll be okay.*

Gloria captures our treat exchange in a picture and fiddles with her phone. "Saw your post. Best let everyone know you got what you needed, and maybe someone'll have advice for us, huh?"

"Can't hurt… Hey, have you seen Ben?"

She laughs, nodding over my shoulder. Ben stands like a club bouncer, arms folded and shoulders back, as he watches us from the fence line. Behind him, a blue canopy has been erected, shading three pop-up chairs, cooler, and a camping table covered with snacks and supplies.

"He calls it Shadow Watch Headquarters."

"What? He did that?"

"Yep. He left for a bit and returned with gear. We agreed this'd make the best spot, close to the barn. He brought food, too. I like him, Lena. He's a quiet fella, serious, but actions speak louder, anyway, and he's saying a lot. Don't ya think?"

"He shouldn't have gone to all this trouble."

"It ain't trouble when it's love, honey," she says, patting my back.

Gloria takes a break at her house, leaving me to walk Shadow. But with his pain centerstage again, he's a stubborn ass about it, pawing the ground in irritation, sputtering, neighing, and swishing his tail at me. Yanking and pulling, he protests as vehemently as a toddler mid-tantrum, stomping his feet angry-faced at his mother. I want to back off, but I don't.

Mom had dark, pain-induced moods, too. Pain makes people act differently. Horses, too. Shadow doesn't mean to be a dick now, so I deal with him the same way I did with her.

"I love you, Shadow. I'm with you, and I'll do whatever I can to make it better." Tears surface with the words. A glance at Ben, and I feel even worse. Worried that Shadow might sense my bad feelings, I shove them aside. He lets me love on him as if he understands everything. Or maybe it's my calm voice. Or the treats kicking in. It's hard to say, but Shadow and I walk the perimeter when Gloria returns an hour later.

Our success fails to produce the positive results we want—stomach gurgles, gas, or poop. His calm, easy moments change to terrible discomfort that brings him to the ground, thrashing with irritation.

Shadow eats more treats for dinner. Gloria and I press our ears to his belly, listening.

She shakes her head. "It may already be too late. If his intestines are already knotted, this'll get worse, not better."

"It's not over yet."

Gloria points to Ben's headquarters. "Take a break, huh? He's standing, so maybe he'll fall asleep. I'll order pizza." She retreats to her house.

"You're good with him," Ben says when I join him.

I smirk lightly as he hands me cold water from the cooler. "Shadow Watch Headquarters, huh?"

"Every mission needs a base of operations."

"I appreciate it." A sigh rattles out. "You know, you would've been a godsend with Mom around… if I could've relaxed enough to let you help."

"I'll remember you said that. I wish I could've been there. This must be similarly difficult. Thinking about her?"

"Too much."

"You're a warrior, Lena, stronger than anyone I know. It's good, thinking about your mom. You're fighting for Shadow the same way. If it's in your power to save him, you will. If it's not, you'll be grateful for every moment you tried."

I resist tears. "Damn, Ben. You're making me regret breaking up with you."

"It was the wrong move."

"Not my first or last, surely." My chuckle fades as anxiety pushes through. "Not that this'll change anything."

"So you've said."

Shadow grows antsy again, urging me from rest. I struggle with Shadow's lead rope. *So much pain. I hate this.* But Ben falls in next to me to help control Shadow, and I remember him thwarting my panic attack on the stoop outside the station. *Do horses have pressure points?* I find a *YouTube* video on equine massage therapy for colicky horses, and Shadow watches with us, weirdly. *I wonder what it's like in Shadow's mental world.* While Ben holds his lead rope, I follow the recording's instructions. If my hands bother him, he shifts away. But he stays put when it feels good—and mostly, he does. Finally, he falls asleep again.

But each rest gets shorter as the night wears on, and Shadow's pain intensifies. His thrashing and neighing jolt us to his aid like an alarm that grows louder with every ring. Even worse, my heart speeds up tenfold each time, priming me for panic.

Body trembling. Breaths short and hurried. Flushed with an exorbitant heartbeat. Gloria forces me to her place for a break. I stand over the bathroom sink, cleaning myself up while trying to calm down.

Splashing cold water on my face and running it over my wrists helps, but tears start anyway.

Losing Mom... that house... Ben, soon, too... And now Shadow.

Ben awaits me on Gloria's front porch. Without a word, he wraps his arms around me while I cry.

CHAPTER
Thirty~Four

HOURS BLUR INTO A TEDIOUS, but familiar routine, one I barely survived with Mom. Shadow gets antsy. We calm him with treats and massage, try to walk him, and when he falls asleep, we rest at headquarters or alternate breaks at Gloria's cottage. It's grueling, but not unbearable. There's comfort in our threefold partnership, in taking turns and never shouldering the effort alone. That's the unfamiliar part, and it's my fault I didn't have that with Mom—I *never* asked. And it's why Lucas was so quick to leave *everything* to me—that's how I seemed to prefer it.

Not anymore, I decide, closing my eyes. But people think many things in the middle of desperate nights.

Ben and I fall asleep sometime in the gray-quiet of early morning—Gloria takes a picture to prove it. Side-by-side in canvas chairs, we're wedged against each other like bookends—me curled to his chest and him resting his head on mine. He fists the blanket close to my neck to prevent me kicking it off. We wake to sunrise cutting through the majestic pines and pinging Instagram notifications from Gloria's post: *No matter how long the night, the day is sure to come.*

I sigh against him. "Mom used to say that. Often toward the end. It's a cruel joke, how everything gets worse at night."

"Let's hope that's the worst of it, for his sake."

I peel myself away from our warm pocket, running my eyes over him. "Thanks for staying. As bad as this is, you've made it better. And you didn't have to… Don't have to." I smile lightly. "It's okay if you go. You can't man Shadow Watch indefinitely."

Ben shifts, leaning against his knees, his expression almost pained. "I'm not leaving you, Lena."

His decisiveness brings instant tears. "You don't think he's going to make it."

"I don't know," he says quickly. "But I'm not leaving."

I nod, forcing a laugh. "That's above and beyond ex-boyfriend responsibilities, Ben."

"Yeah, I know." He kisses my forehead, brushing wetness from my cheek with his palm. "I'll order coffee and breakfast. Where's Gloria?"

I shrug, hearing the distant rumble of an ATV. "Taking care of her other one-hundred and six horses, I think."

Morning through afternoon offers no relief for Shadow. But daylight makes it better. *Slightly.*

And worse, too, because daylight brings texts… Dot telling me the generator conked out, *again*, and Jason Ford asking when to reserve the cabin, and Lucas wondering if I've gotten another estimate yet. I tell Lucas never mind and put the others off for now. But in quiet moments between Shadow's fits, the outside pressure returns, twisting the knife already lodged there. It's all bullshit. Wanting to stay, but knowing I have to go. Loving Ben, but knowing I'll leave him. Hoping Shadow'll get better, but knowing…

Maybe it's the exhaustion, but the fight with Ben sticks on a vicious mental replay, each time worse than before as my thoughts exasperate it. *We yelled? We screamed? Did his hands fist? Did mine? That's not even us.* I imagine a tumultuous, aching future, another fight and him cursing the day we met for all the pain I've caused him. *What a waste of time and energy,* he'll think about me, *hating* me. *Lovable Lena* morphs into something dark and cruel in his head… *Lena the bitch, the failure, the irredeemably broken.*

Tears surface with zero effort, like dew on leaves, as I struggle with Shadow. "Come on, boy. Just a few steps."

He putters, snapping his neck away from me.

"Let me have a turn," Gloria says, appearing behind me. I hand her the lead rope and rub my raw hands. "Where's your boyfriend?"

"Making some calls… and he's not my boyfriend." Though I go for a professional, *oh-by-the-way* tone, it comes out in an awkward tremor, like saying it shakes my foundation.

Gloria's eyes me with hawk-like precision. "Does *he* know that?"

"Yes. I'm moving to Asheville after all. I don't have a choice. So, logistics…" I shrug, too tired and bothered to explain more.

Gloria clicks her tongue, turning Shadow in a circle. "Logistics? I don't buy it. If you love each other enough, logistics can be worked out. Do you love each other?"

It's not that simple, I want to say, but don't.

She nods. "That answers my question… Now, tell me why you *really* broke up with him."

"My family home's impossible to salvage… or live in, anymore. If I stay, I'll have to move in with him, be a parasite, mooching off his generosity indefinitely because I'm incapable of supporting myself here, and dependency isn't fair to either of us. If he comes with me to Asheville, then I upend his life. His family's here, his career. I can't do that to him. Ben deserves better. An equal. Someone who won't turn his life upside down."

Gloria gives me a funny look. "But he's willing to do those things? To turn his life upside down?"

"Yes, he said he'd do anything."

"And you broke up with him for it? Lena!"

"How could I let him risk everything for me? He needs security and stability—the opposite of me. If I really love him, why would I ruin his life?"

"Oh, honey… Why assume you'd ruin it? He certainly doesn't think so." Gloria sighs, her friendly face curving into a sympathetic smile. "I get it… You don't think you're worthy. That's the real problem here."

I grunt. "No, that's not it. If that were true, I wouldn't have let things get this far in the first place."

Gloria scoff-chuckles. "Are you kiddin'? My therapist would have a field day with your misguided perceptions. It's like you're seeing things through broken glass. You fought this thing from the start. The man gave you fireworks, for goodness sakes, and what did you say… you weren't getting too excited?"

"Well, it would've been foolish to get excited then. It was too soon."

"And now? I don't know many guys who'd drop everything for a horse. Do you?"

"He's worried about me. That's all. And when this is over, I'll leave and, well, he'll get over me."

"You need to get over yourself. Why're you fightin' so hard against him?"

I want to argue, but she's right. I have fought against him. Not expecting him to show up. Distrusting it when he did. Pushing him away. And how slowly, carefully he eased into my life anyway, like I'm a bomb requiring surgical precision to diffuse.

Gloria twists Shadow around again, and he complies, as if interested in our conversation. "Remember what you told me about your ex? That you ruined the perfect marriage? That wasn't true. You left a man who didn't love you. End of story. But your broken-glass-perceptions convinced you that it was your fault, that you're unlovable."

My eyes close tightly as Ben's voice echos in my head. *Lovable Lena.*

"It's just not true, Lena. Not to him." Gloria shakes her head. "You and Shadow are the damn same—so clogged-up with bad stuff you can't enjoy yourselves. You're too constipated."

An impacted bowel seems an inappropriate metaphor for my relationship skittishness. Shadow thwarts my arguments, toppling and rolling in discomfort again.

The night hours haze by. Shadow thrashes more and shows no signs of improvement. My treats lull him into a brief calm, *maybe.* But it's an agonizing nightmare overall. *So much pain.*

After a rough, sleepless night, the gray morning brings agonizing clarity. Gloria's hands go to her hips. "I'm callin' Doc Evie. He's suffered enough. Better a peaceful end than lettin' this go on."

Then, she leaves us there alone.

The sun crests the tall pines surrounding the farm, specking us with warm bands. Ben watches from the sidelines while I plop beside Shadow in an exhausted stupor. *I thought I'd have more time. God, why can't I have more time? There's never enough fucking time.*

My last coherent conversation with Mom involved winter Hallmark movies she wanted to watch—real thought-provoking cinema like *Love on the Slopes* and *Snow-Kissed Getaway.* *"And don't forget the new mystery… you like those. Oh, and add wine to the grocery list. We need a wine night."* Such a damn shame—wasting final words on subpar movies and wine I was too anxious to buy when I should've told her I loved her, that she was an amazing mother, and that I'd be heartsick without her.

I sob in Shadow's ear, whispering the same things I did to her. "Please, don't leave. Stay with me. Fight through."

Only he doesn't. And I feel selfish for asking like I did with Mom when *wait-and-see* shifted into *it's-too-late.*

As Shadow deteriorates, my hopes go with him. *I won't ride again. I won't own horses. Or have a farm. I never should've started this bullshit in the first place. I'll go to Asheville, and let work fill the emptiness. It's better, being alone.*

But as I hold him and our brief but beautiful history replays, I know that's not true. *Lena, fight through what you're feeling right now and get to the other side.* I run my trembling fingers along Shadow's ears and through his mane, recalling everything he's taught me—lessons I wouldn't trade for anything. To go at my own pace. To stop overthinking. To take the lead. To go as I please.

In our quiet meadow with the sun hitting our backs, I tell Shadow how much I love him, everything he's taught me, and how fucking sad this place, my life, the world'll be without him. His ear pivots toward me as I talk and his occasional grunts assure me he understands.

Only I don't. The genre of my life changes, *once again,* with this devastating blow. From a sappy comedy of errors to a tragedy. I'm not *Bridget Jones' Diary.* I'm some weird indie film that's awkward to witness and ends badly. Probably with a murder by disgruntled house cats. *Shit, I'm not thinking straight.* The glass isn't just broken; it's shattered.

My closed eyes release fresh tears. *He's dying. Can't wake her. It's too late.*

Footsteps rouse me to the world again. Ben's hand squeezes my shoulder. "The doctor'll be here soon. It's better for Shadow this way."

"I know." Everything I felt beside Mom's hospital bed rushes back like I'm there, reliving it, surging my panic and tears alike. Making the decision. Turning off the machines. Waiting. And then… nothing is ever the same again. "But that's the shittiest part—realizing death is better, and actually *wanting* it for them."

"Come with me. We shouldn't stay for this."

Shadow putters tiredly, as if we're party guests who've stayed too long. I rub his nose while he gives me his annoyed look—I'd be annoyed, too, dealing with someone's freak-out on my deathbed. *He's right. I can't watch someone else die.* I slip out from under his head and stand up. Shadow whinnies, disturbed by my sudden movements.

But the mother of all panic attacks rises with me, making me dizzy. I keep thinking *he's only a horse.* But no one's *only* anything, and whatever he is, he matters to me. Near hyperventilating, I put my shaking hands on my knees as nausea sets in.

Ben's hands grip my waist, holding me steady. "You've done all you could, Lena. Just slow down and breathe."

"This is why… Ben." My words escape in breathless gasps. "Why I can't stay… You'll leave… That's what'll happen. It *always* happens."

"No. Not *always*. Stop thinking and breathe."

Anger joins my panic, preventing reason. Ben tries rubbing the pressure points on my wrists, but I slap him away. "See? I love Shadow, but here we are. Why did this have to happen? Why Shadow? Why me?"

"Why not you? Or Shadow? Shit just happens, Lena. You know that."

"No. This isn't shit-just-happens. This is shit-*always*-happens. I probably jinxed Shadow by riding him. I destroy every good thing!" *Losing Mom. Losing Ben. Losing Shadow. Losing, losing, losing.* "This is so fucking unfair!"

Startled by my wild, tantrum-like shriek, Shadow pops up, lets out a fart cacophony, and unloads a manure-tower from his backside. We gape as the plops continue spilling—a sewer pipe finally unclogged.

Gloria races over. "Lena! You scared the shit out of him!"

Laughter replaces my panicked rage. *Did he do that to end my ridiculous tantrum?* "I-I can't believe it. What does this mean? Is he going to be okay?"

"Yep. That's all the proof we need!" Gloria grabs his lead rope while Shadow moseys away from his massive pile as if nothing's happened.

Ben and I stand there, stunned silent. Or, at least, I'm stunned, and Ben's probably waiting for me to get over myself. And I do. I *really* do. Everything clicks into place and I realize, *what the fuck am I doing?*

"Okay, yes, I pulled the fire alarm… I'm so sorry, Ben."

"You're forgiven."

"Just like that?"

He side-eyes me, brow cocked. "Yes."

I turn toward him, hands fidgeting. "But I damaged our universe, right? What can I do to fix it? Don't you want gushing apologies and promises never to do it again?"

He steps closer, taking me in. "All I need is you, Lena."

The *no matter what* part of his love etches into me with his sincerity. *He means it.* He holds nothing against me. No one's ever been so accepting—least of all me. My Lena-disappointment list whips out easily whenever the occasion calls for it, and often, for no good reason at all. But Ben has no such list. And lost in his stare, I imagine he never will.

Doc Evie joins Gloria in the field to examine him. Disinterested, Shadow moves away, turning his ass toward them, swishing his half-tail. *Back to his old self.*

His newest Lena-lesson solidifies in my thoughts—*maybe things work out for me, sometimes.*

CHAPTER

Thirty-Five

WHEN WE REACH Ben's place, we're zombies. Ben looks downright pained and doesn't say much, not that either of us wants conversation. It's been a grueling few days. After a bare-bones shower, we relent to exhaustion, climbing into bed just after noon.

But a shift soon wakes me. Ben sits on the edge, face buried in his hands.

"What's wrong?" I touch his back when he doesn't hear me. When he turns, I ask again.

"Nothing. Headache. Go back to sleep." He squeezes my fingers before leaving.

The sun creeps around the edges of Ben's blinds. We haven't slept long. I wonder if Ben's slept at all, considering his distressed expression since arriving home. I roll over, thinking he'll return after meds and water. But many minutes pass without movement or sound, and I can't lay there any longer.

My breath hitches when I find him—in the hallway bathroom, propped against the tub beside the toilet, lights off. I use the dimmest flashlight setting on my phone to create a lantern by the sink, providing enough indirect light to see without hurting him. My cold hands go to his hot face, and he squints to see me.

"I'm okay," he says with a labored breath. "Go back to bed." The effort makes him gag. He pushes me aside and hovers over the toilet. Beyond coughs, nothing happens, but the agony is real enough. This

235

isn't a headache, but a wicked migraine, probably brought on by lack of sleep.

I dampen a washcloth with cold water and set it against the back of his neck as the dry heaving continues. I ask if there's anything he needs, but with his hearing aids on the bedside table, he doesn't hear me. Witnessing his affliction hits me harder than him explaining it ever could. The hearing loss, headaches, uncertainty—I try imagining what it's like, living with the damage done while expecting more to come, and how it must chisel away at the security he's worked so hard to build. And how days like this must make him feel completely at the mercy of anything that might trigger it.

I sit with him for the longest time, rewetting the towel every few minutes to keep it cold and holding it to his forehead. When the dry heaving seems to have stopped for good, I get a large bowl from the kitchen and coax him to bed. He's resistant, but exhaustion makes him finally agree. I place the bowl on his bedside table, just in case the nausea returns. Then, propped by pillows against the headboard, I ease him closer to me.

Head in my lap, he closes his eyes. I massage his temples, increasing the pressure slowly. As my fingers press his brow, his forehead lines soften. His shoulders relax as he sinks into it. Into me. I take my time, slow, meticulous movements, hating his pain but loving that I get to do this for him.

It brings up Mom memories, of course, but not bad ones. Times I actually got it right. Massaging her hands when she ached. Fixing happy food when she seemed sad. Telling a joke when things got too much, like she often did with me. My broken-glass perceptions skewed that, too, making the worst moments so large they hid the good ones. *It wasn't all bad.*

Tears speck my eyes as another memory resurfaces—Mom nauseous over a new medication, and me holding her hair back as her breakfast made a violent return into the plastic pitcher I held for her. Between vomiting, she said, in a voice so weak it was almost child-like, "I'm so glad you're here, Lena."

Vomit-duty doesn't rank high on my list of things I want to do, but I remember thinking I was glad, too, that there was nowhere on earth I'd rather be than with her, helping her through it.

And now, that's true again. I smile, remembering Ben's words. *Even what's bad will be better, with us together.*

Fingers soft and strong, I move through his hair before rubbing his neck and along his ears. My fingertips slide across his forehead, skating his scar. I trace his hairline, his jaw, even delicately skimming his eyelids. *This is what I want for the rest of my life.* Not Ben in pain, of course, or me dishing out pain relief, but all of it. I want to be the one he comes to for everything.

He feels the same, I realize, with pangs of idiocy over our fight. He's quick to hand over money, keys, and go sleepless for a horse, all for my sake, not because I'm pathetic or desperate or less-than but because, in his eyes, I mean more than anything, whatever I am.

My resolve forms in this quiet moment and grows stronger with every touch along his pained brow. Mom wanted me to dream something better… and *this* is it—not just being independent, but someone I love depending on me. *The farm and café must happen.* For me. *And* for Ben. It's no longer about taking care of myself but us both. And my best hope for that is the dream he helped inspire and that we'll build together.

Somehow.

I rub his head until my fingers are sore, and his rhythmic breathing assures me he's asleep. Then, I doze off, too, upright and hands at the ready on his forehead.

In a dark sky, I wake to tingling legs. Ben's rolled to his side, nuzzling my stomach with his arm wrapped behind me, like I'm a body pillow. Though amused by his tight grip, I shift him away and curl behind him. Holding him close, I find sleep again easily.

The next time I wake, the room is twinged gray, and Ben's watching me. His wide-awake attention prompts a groggy chuckle. "Is it five?"

"5:25."

I scoot closer, hand going to his cheek. "Ah, you're cold."

"I showered. Cleaned up."

"All better then?" I ask, running my fingers along his clean-shaven cheek and touching the damp ends of his hair.

"Yes, thanks. You helped a great deal, though I'm sorry for putting you through that."

"No apologies, Ben. I'm glad I was here. Is it always that bad?"

"Sometimes worse."

"And now?"

"When it's gone, it's gone… Until it comes back."

"I want to move in… if you'll still have me."

"Yes. Good."

"And when the house is livable, you'll come with me?"

"Gardens, picnics, and fireworks, then?"

I laugh at how he puts it. "That's the plan... How it'll happen—I have no idea, especially if there're any more disasters."

He casts me a funny look. "What's another disaster? You've handled tougher ones before."

My leftover confidence scrapes together with the causal, easy way he says it. *He's right, damn it.* If the house delivers another sucker punch, who cares? It's all fixable and matters little against what I've gone through already. Hell, even the last few days make a broken house feel easy comparatively, and we got through that.

Surviving, making do, making things better—*that's* what we do. It's *who* we are. It's who we *all* are these days.

"It's worth every hardship if it makes you happy," he says, tucking wayward hair behind my ear.

Mom's words in the garden sweep through my thoughts. *It's worth the struggle.* And how the sickening loneliness I felt then has gone now that I finally let it.

"Will it make you happy, though?" My eyes pinch, scrutinizing him. "It risks us both, and you're already facing enough uncertainty. I don't want my dream to become your burden."

"It won't." He scoots closer, hand resting on my hip. "It worries you —taking my help, staying here, depending on me. But for the life I want, *you* are required, Lena..." He smirks lightly. "But preserving the place where we fell in love—of course, that'd make me happy."

"Okay. But I'll come up with a solid plan—no tapping into your savings or going into debt."

"Then, how will you fund the repairs?"

Mom-memories flood me, starting with her clubhouse idea and matriculating down to small things. Wallpaper paper dolls. Felt door clings. Legos in Maxwell House cans. "I'll get creative. I have a barn full of antiques and a carport of refinished furniture. I'll start with selling things and see how much I can raise. Who knows? Maybe Mom and the house'll come through for me like it has for horseback lessons and dumpster money and, gosh, giving me a reason for a gun guy."

He presses against me, fingers running up my back. "I'm really glad you needed a gun guy."

A light giggle emerges as his fingertips tickle my skin. "I could get used to this kind of wake-up call."

"Good. It's what I've wanted to do since my eyes opened."

In his arms, I melt and grow stronger at once. Not because he's turned some key to unlock me, but *I* did. I've softened into a mushy pile of vulnerability, which is the strongest thing anyone can do, really, though it doesn't sound like it. Being a broken mess has broken down my walls, too, making love and everything else possible. Good things happen, even in the worst times—maybe especially then because that's when we appreciate them the most. I can't imagine a day I won't be grateful for loving and dreaming with Ben Wright.

CHAPTER

Thirty-Six

AT *THAT* HOUSE the next morning, I arrive to Dot lounging on the patio chaise. She wears boxers, a tank top, and boots and smokes a cigarette. *She's still here? What're the squatter laws in North Carolina?*

"Aunt Barb's still pissed at me," she says, bypassing a greeting. "Sweet, old ladies shouldn't hold grudges, but she's got a vengeful streak. Teaching chemistry for so long turned her into a mad scientist. I mean, hell, there's probably a limit on how many times you can safely smell formaldehyde. Right? She gave me the silent treatment for a week over smoking in her car *once*. Imagine how long it'll be for me *scaring you away*." She raises her fingers for air-quotes. "You don't mind me crashin', right?"

"Um, no. But you can tell her I've changed my mind. I'm keeping the property and turning it into a business… eventually."

Dot pops from the chaise so fast, she knocks it over. "Ah, can I take credit for convincing you? It'd go a long way."

"Sure. You did, anyway. You got me thinking about the barn loft."

"Super-sweet." Dot holds up a hand and darts into the house through the open sliding glass door. Normally, playing open house to the elements and critters would bother me. *Not today.* Even with her fans at full blast, the inside is oppressively hot.

She sifts through mail and magazines on the table, avoiding my messy coin stacks. She pulls out a stapled pile, and hands it to me. "Here's the estimate I wrote up while you were horsing around with

Shadow. Printed it at Aunt Barb's to prove I was trying. The barn loft's in there, too."

It's broken down in categories and color-coded based on priority. Though surprised by her professionalism, the numbers are a bigger shock.

I leaf through pages, amounts jumping out at me like bullies on a playground. "Um, thanks."

"Don't get your panties in a bunch, Lena. We'll start small."

Amounts blur in my head as they rise, hundreds to thousands to tens of thousands. The barn loft alone tops thirty-five-grand, and that's keeping it basic—one full bathroom, bottom-line appliances, few windows.

"I'll have to think about it… and raise money, somehow." The stack of unpaid bills next to Dot spills over thanks to her elbow. "And, um, I owe you, too. For setting up the generator… and the estimate."

"Nope. Those are freebies. So is my diligent housesitting. Your social media love won me three new appointments this week. I owe you."

"Well, you're welcome to stay. I'm moving in with Ben… but it still doesn't seem right—not paying you anything."

"You know what your problem is, Lena? You know, besides being strung tighter than a cable on the Golden Gate Bridge. You're the first to help someone but the worst at accepting it. If I say it's a freebie, it's a freebie. The appropriate response is *thank you, Dot.*"

"Thank you, Dot."

"You'll pay me plenty once work gets underway."

"Let's hope so."

A long walk around the property, idea notebook in hand, doesn't stir many creative answers to my money problems. In the carport, I research refinished hutches, buffet tables, and other pieces like the ones I'd restored. As expected, bespoke furniture might score me thousands and provide a hefty deposit toward home improvements. So, I take hundreds of pictures to create online advertisements at Ben's place later.

I hate the thought of selling them, though. Watching the Pickle Mobile leave felt pathetically sad. Seeing Mom's gorgeous hutch—my flagship piece—put in the back of someone's truck, never to be seen again, will be a sharper, deeper gut-wound. But it's the quickest way toward progress, even if Ben said we could make room.

I get a lot done—busyness usually helps. By late afternoon when Dot returns from patching things up with Mrs. Moore, I'm properly packed for Ben's place. A suitcase, my laptop bag and notebooks, Mrs. Moore's church cookbooks, and a bin of coin books, unsorted change, and coin wrappers fill my Pilot's trunk. I plan to stay up late sorting and rolling while feeling grateful for Ben's air conditioning.

The change jingles as I bump and curve out of the driveway. It'll be a long night—one that probably won't pay off much, especially considering the hole in my reserve.

At the driveway's end, I don't go right toward Wilmington, but left, remembering what Mom used to say. *You can solve all of life's problems on the back of a horse.*

"Riding a horse won't solve my money problems, but visiting Shadow'll make it better." I glance at the seat beside me, as Mom's image fades, and I don't feel as bad, watching her go.

Shadow enjoys a leisurely day in the paddock as the Pilot kicks up dust down the lane. The farm looks quiet, but when I slide from the car, I hear muted giggling.

Around the barn's backside, Gloria and Doc Evie lean against ATVs looking giddy holding red Solo cups. They remind me of sharing playground secrets with my BFF in middle school. Well, except for the liquor bottle resting on Gloria's steering wheel.

Gloria waves me over. "Lena, perfect timin'." She pours me a cup without asking. "Me and Doc Evie think your special baked treats helped Shadow with his tummy troubles."

"Gloria gave me a sample, and it was surprisingly tasty. How did you come up with the recipe?"

The whiskey burns going down, but doesn't prevent me from gushing an answer, ending with, "I amended my peppermint horse treats to accommodate the extras, and added flavor with what I'd want. Apples. Carrots. Honey. But Shadow's easy to please."

Doc Evie looks skeptical. "Normally, yes, but animals lose their appetites when they're feeling bad, just like people, especially with digestive issues. I'm still amazed that he ate them."

Gloria chuckles. "He couldn't resist Lena's bakin' magic."

"Would you be interested in making them on a regular basis for my practice?" Doc Evie asks. "For dogs and cats, too?"

A chuckling sigh bumbles out—I nearly snort. "Really?"

"We use packaged holistic treats, and they're beneficial, but it's difficult getting pets and livestock to eat them once they're already struggling. The freshness and quality of your treats are clearly better. I'm sure my patients would prefer them, and they'd feel calmer for their treatments… I'd want a batch for each delivered every Monday to start, and we'll see how it goes."

"Um, yes, definitely. I'll do it!" My head spins with plans. "I don't know what to charge, though."

"Bill me later, once you figure it out." She hands me her business card.

"I wanna batch every week, too. Some of my babies could use a chill pill, like Diesel. Hard to ride horses who're scared of their own shadows. You can deliver mine after you hit the vet's office. I'll get the word out to other farms, too." Gloria pushes her Solo cup toward me. "Cheers to new partnerships, huh?"

Our cups make an awkward clink—not nearly satisfying enough for me. Excitement kicking in and bubbling over, I do a happy dance in my rubber boots in Mom's honor. A horse has helped my money problems, after all.

Thirty-Seven

A DAY LATER, I slip from the Pilot at the Harvey farm feeling very nervous. *Maybe this isn't such a great idea.* It's quiet. Too quiet. But with Jack's truck and Alice's minivan in the driveway, I know they're home.

I grab the nine by twelve Pyrex of hot and creamy macaroni and cheese, made fresh this morning—*yes, a fucking casserole.* And Alice's basket, now filled with cut flowers, thanks to my new friend downtown.

With some impressive hip action, I close the car door and turn toward the house, but a clanking sound draws me to a nearby outbuilding. Jack Harvey hovers over a workbench, pounding something metal with a hammer. Lethal weapons cover the walls and hang eerily from the ceiling. Lead pipes, wrenches, and ropes—*what is this, Clue?* I don't find guns or candlesticks but machetes, pickaxes, hammers, and hundreds of stabbing or blunt force trauma devices. It's *Texas Chainsaw Massacre* in here.

"Holy shit," sputters out at the sickles and scythes in the corner.

Jack whips around. We lock eyes. I probably look a little deer-in-the-headlights and nervous. He tosses the hammer onto his table, grabs his sweat towel, and plasters on the cheesiest grin.

"Well, I'll be! The Prodigal daughter returns." He chuckles heartily, wiping his sweat.

I don't know what to say to that but hold up the casserole dish. "I brought mac and cheese."

"There's nothing quite as neighborly as mac and cheese. Come to the house. Alice and the boys'll be delighted."

Alice greets me at the door with an aggressive side-hug. The boys race downstairs, sharing their news—*Miss Lena…* this and *Miss Lena… that*—before taking the casserole and rushing into the kitchen. Their warm reception surprises me, considering my fully-intended "fuck you" to Alice and backing out of the deal.

"Aw, what pretty flowers." Alice takes the basket and loops her arm in mine to lead me into the kitchen. I'm hit with fragrance—pleasant but overpowering. I've interrupted an impressive operation involving several bubbling pots and measuring tools.

"Am I smelling lavender? Rosemary? And, what is that? Ginger?" I ask as my brain identifies them.

"I'm experimenting." Her curt tone halts further discussion. She puts on an absurd, rainbow-colored, cat-dotted apron. Each cat has a unique body posture—playful, scared, shy—as if the apron should be titled *Cat Moods* and should come with a subscription to *Cat Digest*. She wipes her hands on the ruffled print as she gets plates and starts coffee.

The boys attack the casserole dish, extracting huge helpings into bowls before excusing themselves for Playstation.

It's a normal-looking kitchen, *mostly*. The toaster, teapots, salt and pepper shakers, even the onions and potatoes don bright, hand-knit cozies. The vase she uses for the flowers has a bright pink cozy, as if to keep the water warm. *What the hell, Alice. And what's the odorous experiment going on?*

Seated with food and coffee, I take a breath. "I'm sorry for my reaction over losing the job with Jason and for what I said, Alice. I lashed out when I should've calmed down and thought things through. I was upset about my situation, and I took it out on you."

"Well, we accept, Lena." Alice purses her bright red lips. "We're sorry, too. Maybe we manipulated things a teensy bit, but only because we thought you were dead set on leaving. We got a little carried away."

"We thought getting outta here ASAP was what you wanted, too." Jack slurps coffee. "Greasin' those wheels made sense. We would've found you another job if you needed the help. Leaving you high and dry never would've happened."

"I know. I shouldn't have gotten so angry."

Alice shrugs. "Who knew you'd get bit by the country bug, huh? We had no idea you were thinkin' about stayin'."

"Well, a few months ago, I couldn't wait to get out of here… Even last week when the power went out and Jason re-offered the job, I didn't think I had a choice."

"Wait, what's this now?" Alice's measured breaths don't hide her confusion.

I tilt my head, scrutinizing them. "You didn't know about Jason's new offer?"

An annoyed glance passes between them. Alice grits her teeth and straightens her linen napkin, like she wants to tear the thing to shreds with her bare hands. "Well, isn't that a nice surprise? I must call my nephew and congratulate him for turning things around."

"And give him grief for not telling us. So, you get your dream job after all, huh, little lady?"

"No, I turned him down. It's not my dream anymore." With another deep breath, I say, "I'm restoring Mom and Dad's place, and turning it into a business."

Alice cocks her head like I'm a puzzle that has her stumped. "Bless your heart, Lena. You're a Tilt-A-Whirl—up and down and spinning all the time."

Jack laughs, reaching for a second helping. "She's makin' me dizzy, that's for sure. What sorta business?"

Though nervous telling them, my plans gush like a river freed from its dam. Any disappointment over them not getting the property is hidden in their excitement—*they genuinely seem happy for me.* "It'll take years to get it started. The house is in bad shape. I'll be selling off antiques just to get the power back on. But the investment's worth it, I think."

"Well, I'll be a monkey's uncle!" Jack's heavy cheeks glow red for all his smiling. "Saddletree Farm and Café. Got a nice ring to it! Your folks'd be tickled pink!"

Alice nods, swiping under her eyes like she's afraid her mascara will run. "So will everyone else! Givin' people a place to make memories together… that's as precious as the family legacy you're workin' to protect. You're a little turtle finally peeking outta your shell." She cackles like a spastic witch. "Funny how you've always snubbed your nose at our humble casseroles, and now you're the poster girl for coun-try-dreaming, and gallivanting around town with cupcakes, cookies, and casseroles, too."

My eyes narrow. *My nose-snubbing wasn't that obvious. Was it?* "I wasn't snubbing my nose at your casseroles, Alice, just getting fifty at once."

She waves her hand. "Oh, please. I hate getting casseroles, too."

Jack jabs his fork toward his plate. "Not this one, though."

Alice smirks. "*Most* casseroles mean people are feeling sympathetic, probably for a good reason. No one wants that. Only, it's how we show we care. We do what we can for each other, like you with your mom, and now with everyone else."

I nod. Caring for Mom, Shadow, or anyone who'll eat my food—I get making something better in whatever small way you can, even if it comes in a casserole dish.

Alice grins like I'm her cult's newest recruit. "Anyway, who knew country life would agree with you?"

My eyes crinkle, though her words strangely brighten my darker, snarkier places. "I'm glad you like the casserole."

Jack gives me a teasing look. "It's not poisoned, is it?"

"Not today."

"Alice saves her poisoned ones for annoying relatives," Jack grins.

A laugh blurts from me. My respect for Alice and Jack spikes, especially in the loving looks they give each other, like any moment might inspire ripping their clothes off or breaking into a waltz or, *you know,* killing someone together. Only this time, I know *exactly* how they feel.

"So, what does Ben think of your fancy ideas?" Alice asks, as if mind-reading. "Don't forget who brought you two together."

Jack waves his full fork. "Oh, yeah, Lena. Ben's got it bad."

A cheesy noodle catches in my throat. "Um, when did you talk to Ben?"

They share questioning expressions. Alice says, "Oh, months ago. A friend of mine was falling for an online scam and I had to intervene."

I smirk. "Let me guess. You called Ben?"

"Of course, I did! He met with her, gave her a gentle talk about not clicking links or buying strangers giftcards, and she listened by the end of it, I think."

Jack nods. "He tried, at least."

"Anyway, before he left, he said, oh my gosh, the sweetest thing ever. What was it, hon?" Alice taps her fingers.

"I don't remember, only it was sweet, Lena. Funny how a serious guy like that can be so mushy."

"Nearly brought me to tears. It's on the tip of my tongue..."

I huff, ready to beat their heads together until Ben's words rattle out. I'm curious what my quiet, stoic *RoboCop* Ben would divulge to Alice, *of all people?*

"Oh, I remember!" Alice perks up. She likes this—having information I want. "He thanked me for bringing you two together, which I appreciated."

She gives me a mental *wink, wink,* but I don't bite. "And?"

"He said," she pauses dramatically. She might turn *me* into a serial killer. "Whenever I see her, it's like coming home. Lena makes everything better."

Now, I swipe under *my* eyes to catch my mascara. "That's… um… well, exactly how I feel about him."

"I knew it!" Wide-eyed Alice turns to Jack. "Didn't I tell ya?"

"You told me. You should play the lotto, hon, with those psychic abilities," Jack laughs.

"I'm not psychic, just had a hunch." Her dark eyes meet mine again, and she gives me a funny look. "You know we could've handled your parents' arsenal, Lena, but I had a feeling about you two."

"Why? Because we were the only single thirty-somethings you knew?"

"No, because Ben's had a rough time, too. His combat injuries, PTSD, survivor's guilt. His family and work've seen him through it. But he hasn't been happy until now. It's like he couldn't find his place until he found you."

"Me? Wait! How do you know all this?"

Alice looks shocked. "His Aunt Janie's in my knitting circle. I don't add *just* anyone to my contact list. My goodness, Lena! I never would've recommended him without making sure he wasn't a serial killer or something!"

Jack laughs. "Alice knows everyone 'round here, and if she doesn't, she knows who to call to find out about 'em."

"He needs someone as kind-hearted as he is—a gal with warmth and humor, so he feels at ease and opens up. And, I imagine, he's the track to your Tilt-a-Whirl, right? He's calm and diligent and probably keeps you from tilting over. I'm right, aren't I?"

Laughing, I shrug. "Well, I still tilt over, but he's good at helping me back on track." *I owe Alice for my love-happiness? Really?* Still, I thank her for bringing Ben and me together—something she'll mention on every occasion for the rest of our lives, and, even crazier, I'll never mind.

"Ugh, now that I've bared all to you… please, tell me. What're you experimenting with over there?" I point to the pots still simmering on the stove.

"Might as well tell her, hon. It's what we were plannin' to do with your land." Jack leans back in his chair. "But we'll figure somethin' else out."

"Lavender Fields Forever. That's my business. Like the Beatles song. I make lotions, soaps, candles, bath salts, and face masks."

"That's awesome, Alice." I mention my lavender-laced horse treats and how her supplies helped save Shadow. Then we get into a long discussion about lavender's million uses. It's a little strange, but I'm okay with it, even when she suggests experimenting together and calls us Herbal Mad Scientists.

"I'll put in a standing order for lavender and dandelion greens, if you can spare them," I say. "I'll need them for my side-business."

"She's got a half-acre patch for her herbs, but we wanted to go bigger. She sells out with every vendor she's got—even *with* the pandemic going on."

"People need comfort and self-care now more than ever," she chimes in.

"Her online sales are through the roof. Only we can't risk takin' space from our money crops—not with the boys going to college next year," Jack explains, topping off our coffees.

"I'm doing just fine with the space I have. It's a blessing in disguise —not running myself ragged with all that extra work." She stands, scraping her chair behind her, and her slightly pinched brow reveals that she's letdown, even if she's happy for me. "Anyone want dessert?"

"Wait… Why does it have to be all or nothing?" The question spills out from my Mom-memory file—something she asked when I left college. *"He wants you to give up everything you've worked so hard for or he won't have you at all? Why can't he compromise? That's not love. That's control, Lena."*

I shake off bad ex-thoughts, and stand, too, nearly knocking my chair over. My hands flick at the wrists as nervous energy pumps through me. "I don't need twenty-five acres. Not now, anyway. Would you be interested in a partial land lease? Say ten acres? I need the income, and you need room to grow—win-win. I wouldn't mind being surrounded by purple fields."

Alice stands silently, like a cat's stolen her tongue. She breaks into a wide, hopeful grin, turning to Jack. He beams, slapping his hand on the table. "Well, that's the best idea since sliced bread! You got yourself a deal, little lady!"

Thirty-Eight

THE BEST VERSION of any *Choose Your Own Adventure Book* requires the smartest, bravest, and sometimes weirdest choices to prevent detours and dead ends. That's where I am—knocking over the dominoes in my *real* story. Not the one I tricked myself into following. It's not a nothing-ever-works-out life, but a beautiful universe, expanding as I go.

And, yes, I'm sorting kids' books under the carport, and saving all the *Choose Your Own Adventures* for Luna.

That is, not to say there won't be pitfalls, I think, staring at the impressive gallery of my refinished pieces. I scroll the responses to my listings, halfway hoping no one's interested. But so many people answer the ads, I'm overwhelmed.

To sell or not to sell?

Mom's hutch brings in bids over my asking price without even being seen. I should be ecstatic, but my shoulders slump. Transforming the hutch was therapeutic—my first big undertaking after Mom—greasing my rusty capabilities. The rest busied me during the height of the pandemic, filling me with hope for my future place where I'd salvage these family treasures. It's not just a shame—letting them go—but feels like a self-betrayal, given all the work I put into them. But I need the money.

Rumbling engines interrupt my overwrought sentimentality, luring my attention toward the field. Will and Max race through the trees on ATVs like nights atop their trusty steeds. They stop outside the carport.

"You're here."

"Mom says we can help as long as we social distance and sanitize." Will holds up sanitizer from his pocket while Max motions to his mask, dangling around his neck.

"We're driving her crazy." Max grins.

"On purpose, a little," Will says. "She said you were selling things today, so we wanted to help… You okay?"

"Better now, thanks. It's just… It's hard letting go, no matter how much I need the money." My fingers trace the hutch's smooth surface, mimicking my brush strokes. A glance at the pod container reminds me of everything I've already packed—Mom's milk glass, crystal serving pieces, china sets. "It's depressing, trading heirlooms and decorative showpieces for electricity and a new roof, like swapping wine for water."

"Don't start with what you love," Max says. "There's plenty here you don't care about, right?"

"What about these? Old guys love rusty crap like this." Will points to the table of antique tools.

"The older, the better." Max nods, examining the collection.

"You really think they'll sell?" I ask, as we search our phones for like-pieces. We find similar tools selling for hundreds, even thousands, depending on condition and rarity. "Wow, you're right. Everyone has their own sentimental collections, I guess."

"The old guys'll give you a fair price. They'll also bore you with stories about the old days, so you'll earn every penny." Will laughs.

"Yeah, post some pics and see what happens. I bet Grandpa shows up." They chuckle while Max cues up social media to advertise our wares.

Will points to the crowded lamp table. "Mom suggested selling the hurricane lamps, too. She'll share pics with the ladies in her clubs."

"Yes, definitely." The boys are right—the things I treasure don't have to make a mass exodus, at least, not yet. "I'll keep the large blue one and the two small, white lamps, but let's post the rest. There are more lamps in the barn if you want to dig them out."

The boys bicker about driving the tractor before settling the dispute with rock, paper, scissors.

As we blanket social media with stuff for sale, Dot's pep talk comes to mind. I *do* have people here. It's a strange realization, given how alone I used to feel. I've created a circle I didn't have the energy or understanding to initiate before. I wish I had, though, for Mom's sake and mine. As this year has repeatedly proven, we need each other. And, there's nothing wrong with accepting help or the occasional casserole. The old me believed I had to do everything myself. But the new me knows that the best, most important dreams that truly make the world a better place happen *with* other people, a weird symphony of parts meshing together to create something beautiful. I can't do it alone. And even if I could, I wouldn't want to.

A gaggle of elderly gentlemen arrives by lunch, including the boys' grandfather. Though we're outside, we all wear masks and keep a respectful distance. The tools sell quickly, thirty here and fifty there. One guy pays me two hundred for some old axes, while another offers the same for a single saw. Will and Max supervise an impromptu auction when two guys want the same hand drill; it sells for eight hundred.

Lamp customers stream in, too—a surprise given the bulbous fixtures' antique look. The carport becomes a strip mall as people peruse the tables. Antique dolls, old cameras, and even books become impulse buys for my customers.

Our small efforts domino into others. Timeless Treasures, an antique shop downtown, messages me about consigning my silver tea services, soda crates, and art deco clocks. I make an appointment with the owner for tomorrow and pack the items he wants to see in the Honda.

By the day's end, I've earned over four grand. Elated, I give the boys money for helping and promise a portion of everything they help me sell going forward—for their college funds.

With all quiet again, I secure the carport and retreat inside. I pack more things for Ben's place and turn off the generator. I grab my bag from the kitchen table, knocking over Mom's red coin wallet. *Lena, check this out.* I have no idea why—maybe because it looks like a wallet—but I drop it into my bag. It should join the rest of Mom's collection, presently occupying Ben's dining room table.

That's where many hours pass—at Ben's table, surrounded by coins, lists, and my laptop. On a master list, I jot income—proceeds from the land lease and antique sales, along with a projection of earnings for the animal treats, a number that continuously gets erased and rewritten. On another list, I take the crumpled receipts from the groceries for Shadow's treats, and estimate what it'll cost me to make more. It's painstaking, trying to figure out a reasonable profit without asking too much. Between jottings, I look up coins, making a third list, identifying them and their potential values, another difficulty since I'm no expert on conditions. Even so, pennies here and pennies there add up to little in the end. And every glance at Dot's estimates highlights the cavernous gap between my small efforts and getting anything done.

Even so, it's been a good day. I'm no longer lost in the swampy land of indecision but moving steadily forward with concrete goals in mind —a freight train rather than a sputtering engine, heavily burdened and eking uphill. The more choices I make, the easier it is to make them. And though I wish my dream could be a reality sooner rather than later, it's amazing to think it's possible at all.

Ben arrives home, and I greet him at the door with a kissing attack, making him laugh and lift me off my feet. Sure, one day the novelty'll wear off and kiss-heavy greetings will become an occasional thing. But maybe not... and certainly no time soon.

After dinner, we walk downtown, holding hands and basking in river breezes. He shares about work and Detective Gentry's latest offenses. I reveal that the boys and I are becoming seasoned hagglers over my parents' antiques.

"I wonder what Mom'd think—me selling off her precious things for another business idea."

"She'd love it, Lena. You always said she loved having people there. You're carrying on her tradition in a much bigger way." His eyes lock on mine as we stop on the sidewalk outside his place.

"Yes, I hope so." I force a smile, but my worried face refuses to hide. "I want this to work *so badly*, but I feel... desperately unqualified. I don't know what I'm doing ninety percent of the time. I expect that'll go up *if* I open for business." I stop to laugh. "Please excuse my preemptive worrying... It's something I do."

He takes me in thoughtfully, slipping his hands around my waist. "No one has it all figured out. But, if you're worried, learn everything you can. Talk to people. Do your research. Knowledge builds confidence."

"Ben, you're a genius!" I gasp, eyes widened by the lightbulb blinking to life in my head. "And the best way to learn is from someone who's done it! Maybe Jason Ford would be open to a consultancy. I could teach him my recipes, maybe train someone for him, and he could mentor me about running a successful business. I could go for a week or longer if he likes the idea. What do you think?"

"It's brilliant, as long as he doesn't convince you to stay."

My fingers walk up his chest. "Maybe you could come, too, if it falls under the follow-me-anywhere thing."

"It does. I'd love to get away with you."

"I *almost* can't wait to call him and pitch the idea." I smile, slipping my hands around his neck and pressing against him.

Ben gives me a soft, short kiss before we take slow steps toward the front porch. "Don't worry about what your mom would think. She left you with a property full of treasures for a reason… Maybe this is it. When Saddletree happens, you'll know she approves."

Tiny tears well in my eye-corners at the idea that Mom had method in her hoarding madness. As if she knew her *Choose Your Own Adventure Book* had a sequel featuring me and everything she left behind. Could she have had an intuition about my future hopes, even before I did? I don't know, but Ben earns a warm smile and a teasing kiss for suggesting it.

Thirty~Nine

THE FOLLOWING MORNING, I drive us downtown. While bars are still closed, shops beg for customers. Since it's a nice day, spring careening into summer, many masked patrons oblige. I park street-side next to Timeless Treasures.

We don our black masks, like bank robbers. I carry the soda crates while Ben grabs the large box of silver tea sets and clocks.

The man at the counter doesn't look up from his magazine as we enter, but he slides his blue mask over his nose. "Let me know if I can help you."

"Nice to see you again, Mr. Morris," Ben says.

He glances over his reading glasses and slaps the magazine on the counter. "Ben Wright! What a pleasant surprise!"

"I helped him with a break-in once, and he helps me with Mother's Day presents," Ben tells me.

We move through the long glass counters and curio cabinets. Dolls, knick-knacks, silver sets, jewelry, records, dining sets, teapots, lamps, crystal vases, and candlesticks—a retail version of my carport.

"Who's your friend, Ben?"

"Lena Buckley, my girlfriend." He gives me a smirking side-eye. I can't help my cheesy grin.

"Oh, heavens. I finally get to meet Miss Lena Buckley!" The man's eyes crinkle.

I stop in my tracks because he acts like he already knows me. *Did he see my breakdown in Sunny's? Do people talk about that?*

"*The gal about town turning frowns upside down.* That's what Shakespeare says. I rarely listen to that fool, but my nephew Myles tells me how you feed everyone's sweet tooth over there."

I smile at Ben. "From the senior care center." My pride swells at the unexpected recognition, and that Ben's not the only one with connections.

"What can I do for you?"

"We messaged about consigning my antiques?" I set the crates on the counter.

"Oh, yes. Millennials love these crates and clocks. I like the silver myself. That's what you can always count on, you know? Silver, gold, and currency." He sorts through my items, seeming to tally numbers in his head. "I'll buy your items outright, or you can set up an account to consign. You make a little more money consigning, but it takes longer."

He makes an offer for the lot, but I decide to consign. He has a primo location for foot traffic, and given his inventory, I have more to show him. He sets the soda crates aside and brings out paperwork.

"Okay, Miss Lena Buckley, I'll need your ID."

I dig through my bag for my wallet. "The last time I dug this out was for you, Ben," I say, smirking as I rummage. I accidentally snatch Mom's red coin wallet, too, setting both on the counter. The coin wallet flaps open. I pick my driver's license out of its tight holder, handing it over.

Mr. Morris eyes the red wallet with a crimped expression. "What's this here?"

"Oh, sorry. That's nothing. Mom's coins."

About to retrieve it, Mr. Morris stops me. "May I take a look?"

I shrug, nodding. "Mom collected everything, but she obsessed over her coins. I haven't found any worth much more than face value."

Mr. Morris flips through the small, ragged collection. He holds the booklet open in the middle to share a scribbled note jammed into a flap. "Did you see this?"

"No." I lean forward.

These are all for YOU, Lena. I treasure you, ha! Time to get on to better dreams, girl.

Tears dot my eyes as they roll. I hold little hope these featured coins will be worth more than a fast-food dinner *if* I'm lucky. Still, I'm sad that she wasted time make-shifting gifts for me as if she owed me.

Mr. Morris says, "May I remove the coins from their, um, protective cases?"

I swipe my cheeks above my mask. "Of course."

Ben hands me a handkerchief, and I dab my leaky eyes. "You know, Ben, this'll surprise you, but I *never* cry. I've gone years without a single tear, and this year, I can't stop. Good or bad, I'm all waterworks now."

"For good reason," Ben says, his fingers making circles on my back.

"It's been a year for tears, anyway." Mr. Morris pries the staples holding the index cards together. He lines the coins along his counter, examining each with a magnifying glass.

Eventually, Mr. Morris leans back on his stool. "I'm afraid more tears are coming, young lady."

I wave my hand. "Oh, it's fine, Mr. Morris. I don't expect them to be worth anything."

He grabs a magnet from his desk drawer. Then, he uses it on one of Mom's pennies. It doesn't attach.

"In 1943, the mint switched to steel pennies because they needed copper for the war. But a handful of copper pennies got made by mistake from the leftover copper in the machine. Steel is magnetic; copper isn't. That's a 1943 Lincoln Cent. *Copper.*" He waves his hand over the four other pennies. "All these have value. The 1969-S Lincoln Cent with that funky overlapping of the letters there... that's about twenty, and she's got two of 'em. The two 1970s ones, around three apiece. But this 1943 copper penny... you're looking at a couple hundred."

Surprised, I tally the numbers. *That'll buy more than one fast-food dinner. It'll buy groceries... at Sunny's!* "Wow! Two or three hundred? That's great."

Mr. Morris chuckles. "I'm speaking in thousands, young lady. Two or three hundred thousand. More, probably."

"No. No way. They're fakes. They must be." I should've checked Mr. Morris' Yelp reviews before driving downtown. I imagine one-star reports about the *"crazy owner"* being *"prone to illusions of grandeur"* or perhaps a *"tendency toward bad pranks."*

"They'll have to be authenticated, but I've been doing this a long time," Mr. Morris says. "You stand to make a pretty penny off these pennies."

What the fuck! And a penny-ism, too, like Mom's whispering in his ear? I hide my fidgeting fingers behind my back. "No offense, Mr. Morris, but you're mistaken. We aren't rich people. Sitting on a fortune while our toilets break and the lights flicker—that's *not* us. We lived dollar to damn dollar." My voice shakes with my hurried breaths. "Mom would've told me."

Deadpan, Mr. Morris says, "I can't speak to that."

"What else proves these coins are valuable? More information would be helpful." Ben squeezes my hands behind the counter, assuring me everything's okay. And it is, only my head games pick up, bouncing me mercilessly between *this can't be real* and *what if it is.*

A coin tutorial ensues. Mr. Morris shows us pictures online with auction prices. He explains color, luster, die casts, and even the tiny flaws that prove authenticity. I'm in Mrs. Moore's chemistry class again, suffering through things way over my head and anxious for the bell to ring, so I can race outside and breathe again. *Just breathe.*

Ben caps off Mr. Morris's hour-long lecture by turning to me. "It's true, Lena. Your mom left you a fortune."

With me besieged by waterworks, it's no wonder that Mr. Morris retreats to the backroom to give us "time to talk things over."

Ben faces me, pulling his mask down and revealing a wide smile. He tugs mine off, too, taking me in. Leave it to me to be distressed about hitting the jackpot, but my frustration over her having this *all along* makes me want to scream.

But Ben laughs.

"It's not funny."

"It's very funny. You wanted her approval. I say you have it."

"Okay, yes, the timing is funny. But damn upsetting, too. How could she have had this and not replace the oven or one broken toilet? We could've had *Netflix*! She could've had better care. A physical therapist. A doctor who'd do house calls. We could've installed a ramp and gotten her a motorized wheelchair! She struggled *every* day. Why didn't she make things easier for herself? Easier for both of us? It doesn't make sense."

"It makes perfect sense, Lena. She had everything she wanted. She wanted this for you."

I lean into Ben with a sigh, tears still slipping down my cheeks. "But it doesn't feel right."

"That's because she's gone." He lifts my chin with his finger and locks eyes, smiling. "You deserve *every good thing*, Lena." He says the words slowly, making them sink in. "Between you, me, and your mom, everything'll work out exactly as it should. Let go of the rest and be happy with me."

I laugh, slipping my hands around him. "God, Ben, she would've loved you."

"Yes. I shake hands right."

"That, and you have superior Lena-loving skills."

He gives me a short kiss, chuckling. "Yes. That's easy."

Not so easy—imagining Mom's up there, pulling my life-strings like she once tried with her meet-my-daughter spiels. I don't *quite* believe *that*. Even so, she's my posthumous fairy godmother, waving her penny-laden wand over my pumpkin-life to turn it into a lovely chariot moving forward. And somewhere, my parents are having a big laugh and probably doing an awkward-looking happy dance.

With the coins in Mr. Morris's hands to authenticate and auction, I could—*easily*—spend the days thereafter in a tizzy. But I don't. *Lena, try enjoying yourself, for once, please.*

I go as I please. I spend time with Ben. I work with the boys. And I go to Gloria's farm to ride and help out. I ride Shadow when I want things easy and River for more oomph. Mucking stalls, slinging hay, and cleaning tack prove therapeutic—helping me clear my muddled head. The more I do, the more I let go and think *I can do this*.

But calling Lucas sparks a minor panic attack. Sure, he'll be thrilled about discovering Mom's coins are a treasure, especially when I promise him half of the bounty. *It's not all keychains and doilies after all, huh, Lucas?* Splitting the windfall is only fair, given how generous he's always been with me, and maybe it'll butter him up for my farm and café idea.

What will he think of me starting another business? At our parents' dilapidated farm in the middle of nowhere? During a pandemic?

He answers my call lounging poolside, watching Luna swim. I see a tropical drink on the table beside him. *Good timing.*

Everything gushes out in one large, excited clump, ending with, "Resurrecting this beautiful place and sharing it with others is my dream. Saddletree Farm and Café will be a retreat for everyone. I can make things better, Lucas, for other people and me, too. It's what I want."

"Aw, Saddletree? I love it." He sips his fruity cocktail. "Sounds amazing, but how will it work?"

"In some ways, it already has."

Mouth already running, I tell Lucas about the Jones family and the girls racing around the pond and fishing. I explain my baked deliveries across the city. And about my garden and interest in savory cooking. I even share how it all came together for me on the back of a horse, making him laugh and, surely, think of Mom.

Finally, Lucas says, "If you'd suggested this years ago, I would've called you crazy. Not now. People are desperate for safe, outdoor activities to do with the kids. You have our full support. Oh, and it's all yours, Lena. I meant it when I turned over my half."

"Lucas, I couldn't possibly—"

"She wrote the note to *you*, Lena. Let's not argue. Now, tell me more about your plans. Have you considered hosting school field trips? Once things go back to normal, that is. Luna loved her trip to the apple orchard."

Once things go back to normal… I repeat on a mental loop. *What's normal anymore?* And yes, while the world slides back into its old grooves, slowly, and everyone sighs in cautious, guarded relief as they find their normals again, I'm beyond grateful that my old normal isn't my life anymore. And never will be again. That nothing-ever-works-out-for-me life is over.

The more I reach for every good thing, the more reachable those once-elusive beauties become.

MY GOOD VIBES dwindle somewhat upon meeting Dot's designer friend Cherry. She's a petite, pale woman with long, dark curly hair and a perky fashion sense with her chunky necklace, oversized earrings, and cherry-themed dress. The cherry barrette in her hair is a little much, and I wonder how often she references herself this way. She carries an iPad with a pen, giving her a professional air that contrasts wildly with Dot's oversized overalls and backward hat.

She shakes my hand the *wrong* way, but it fits her dainty demeanor. I thank her for coming, and she breaks into tears—a full-blown sob-fest. *What is she doing? This isn't Sunny's.*

Before I ask what's wrong, Dot jumps in. "Let's get right down to business, shall we?"

Since Dot ignores Cherry's crying and Cherry says nothing, I go on like it's not happening, which feels weird. "I want to renovate the entire property."

"Whoa!" Dot exclaims, patting Cherry's back. "That's great news. Isn't it, Cherry? You've done the right thing, calling us in, Lena. I'll make everything work while Cherry makes it beautiful. Right, Cher?"

Cherry sobs in strange agreement. Over her shoulder, Dot mouths, *"She's fine. Sorry,"* before saying aloud, "Where shall we start, Lena?"

"The barn loft. We love your idea of transforming it into a home. And now that things have changed for me—"

"What's changed? Aside from, you know," Dot pauses to wink, "getting yourself some hellishly overdue action from your muscle-man?" Dot stifles her laugh with a glance at Cherry's ongoing waterworks. "Not that anyone needs a guy to improve their situation. *At all.*"

I give Dot a puzzled look. "Turns out, I've inherited more than mice and bad circuit breakers. I've come into a little money, so I want upgrades."

A little money is an understatement. Mom's coins were quickly authenticated, and since such a collection doesn't show up every day, like—*yes, Ben*—a Picasso in the attic, the auction sparked much interest. After the auction house, Mr. Morris, and the government got their cuts, my bank balance exploded to over $300,000—not a Mega Millions jackpot, but life-changing money, all the same.

Dot lights a cigarette while we walk to the barn. "Cherry loves designing unique living spaces. Ain't that right, Cherry?"

She hugs her iPad like it's her lifeline and nods.

On our barn tour, they take measurements and make notes. Cherry snaps pictures and sketches layouts on her screen while asking questions. I show her my rough sketches, too, and she doesn't turn her nose up at my idea-scribbles or my unprofessional spiral notebook.

When Cherry drifts to a safe distance, Dot whispers in my ear.

"Sorry about the waterworks, but Cherry's husband just left her for a waitress named Olive—"

"He doesn't even like olives," Cherry cries across the room.

Dot whispers softer. "Her husband's in real estate. Cherry set aside her architecture and design aspirations to do all his staging. Now, she's out of work and brokenhearted. Double-whammy. She needs this, Lena."

"We *all* need this... and I'm used to tears, anyway." *Though not used to someone crying more than me.*

I engage Cherry on ideas for windows and a gourmet kitchen. She offers insights about maximizing the space and using eco-friendly materials.

"I've made a list of accommodations I'd like for Ben. He's hearing impaired." I hand my research to Dot. "Could the loft be livable by the time we return from our trip?"

"Oh, where are you going?" Cherry asks.

I hesitate to tell her. Two *surely* romantic weeks with Ben in a luxe cabin could prompt more of Cherry's broken-hearted waterworks, so I'm delicate. "Asheville. A good friend, Jason Ford, owns a café there.

He's teaching me how to run a successful business while I help him design his dessert menu and train his staff." A jolt of pride over my consultancy plan with Jason rips through me, as it does every time I think of our upcoming trip.

Dot's black-nailed fingers go to her hips. "We'll do our best to give you a home to come home to… just don't come back early."

Next, I lead the ladies through the house.

"This'll be the café," I explain, twirling through the kitchen and living room. "I'd like an open chef's kitchen—we can expand to the back porch. I want multiple ovens, fridges, and a large display case."

"How about French doors at the front and back and a wide wrap-around porch for extra seating?" Cherry adds, swinging her pen. "It'll maximize your capacity while still providing a homestyle experience… How do you feel about porch swings?"

"Who doesn't fucking love a porch swing?" Dot says, her eyebrows cocked.

Dot's serious expression makes me laugh. "I'm a fan."

After looking at Mom's bedroom and the ones upstairs, Cherry suggests suites with their own bathrooms. "In case you ever want a bed-and-breakfast," she explains, breaking down again.

We take tall wine glasses to the back patio. Cherry's tears dry over talk of a wood-fired pizza oven and refinishing more furniture to go into her designs. Dot suggests getting some materials from her buddy at the Habitat for Humanity Re-Store to recycle and support a good cause.

"I love that. A modern farmhouse should have an eclectic mix of old and new," I say. "It's an enormous undertaking. I need talented help to see it through. Are you guys up for it?"

"I'm down. There're a lot of guys out of work, so this'll be awesome for them, too," Dot says.

Cherry's eyes twinkle. "It's a major project, but I'm happy to be a part of it." The words spill out in a sob.

Maybe it's the wine, but it's surreal—sitting at a rickety patio table with these ladies making plans. Dot, Cherry, and I are the same—starting over with whatever we have left and making this place part of that story.

I hold up my phone. "We should share this journey. Let's build all our businesses by publicizing the transformation."

"Yes!" Dot stands up. "People love before-and-afters!"

Cherry wipes her eyes. "It'd be nice to share something positive."

"Let's start right now." With our masks back on, we huddle together. I snap a few selfies, pick the best, and share them on social media: *Cheers to mighty partnerships and the amazing transformations to come.*

Those transformations get underway without me. A week after finalizing our renovation plans, I stand in the carport with Will, Max, and Dot, sipping coffee and handing over extra keys.

"When the cat's away, the mice will play." Dot laughs.

I roll my eyes. "If the mice play while I'm away, that's on you, Dot. You're in charge."

She gives me a wicked grin. "I'm going to take housesitting to a new level."

"Don't do any weird shit in my house, Dot."

She laughs but doesn't make any promises.

Will says, "What do you want us to do, Miss Lena?"

"Yeah, it'll be strange working without you," Max says.

"I trust you guys. Keep selling what we've agreed on," I say, motioning to the sorted antiques. "Unless Cherry sees something she wants to use... she's working on blueprints and designs. She might pop in."

"Oh, yeah, she'll be around," Dot says with authority. "This project's the only thing taking her mind off her misery. Hope you boys don't mind tears."

They chuckle, glancing at each other and then me. "We're used to them," Will says.

I smirk, going back to my list. "The loft is ready for you, Dot, but there are more boxes and furniture in the house that need clearing out before work starts there."

"I'm going to tear that place down to the studs." Dot slaps her hands together like she's about to feast.

"Not until I get back. The barn'll keep you busy enough." My hesitation over *that* house makes little sense. But I can't let Dot at it, not yet. Though it's technically been mine since January, it won't feel that way until I make it my own. That can't happen without me—no matter how hard it may be to see it torn apart.

"I know, I know," Dot says, flicking ashes off her cigarette and dripping with disappointment. "No demolition until you get back... Oh, shit! Is that laser tag?"

My nerves kick up as she and the boys plan a little fun before getting to work. Though I fully trust the boys and, *mostly*, Dot, two weeks is a long time to be away. I stare at the house like a worn, shabby comfort blanket that'll unravel in my absence… or go up in flames… or get chewed on by mice. *Can I relax enough to leave it?*

Ben's Jeep rumbles up the driveway, stopping next to my Pilot. We lock eyes when he gets out, sharing a smile. *Hell yes, I'm ready.*

Meeting him at the Jeep, I plow into him for a giant embrace with unbridled enthusiasm, as if I didn't just see him a few hours ago. He laughs, lifting me off my feet like he missed me, too.

"Can't wait to get away with you," he whispers in my ear before loosening his grip.

"Me, too." My feet land on solid ground again, and I take in the over-packed Jeep. A cargo rack attached to the hitch carries a cooler and a waterproof bag held down with bungee cords. "Wow, Ben. You look very prepared."

He leans down for a short kiss. "I stocked up on supplies."

After a brief scan through the plastic window, I ask, "You got my luggage, right?"

"Your *one* suitcase, computer, and recipe bin?" he says with a funny look. "Yes." He points to my things, packed like it's a scientific feat of engineering, and he believes the Jeep might be off-balance if the weight isn't evenly distributed.

"What more do I need? I have you, and you've clearly thought of everything. I like your impressive packing skills."

A coy smirk appears on his lips, briefly, before he gives me another kiss—a teasing, lingering kiss this time.

"Hey, how 'bout packing up that PDA, huh? Save it for the cabin," Dot says, flicking ashes. "Time to get this show on the road."

In our awkward circle, the small crowd looks to me expectantly, but my stomach ties in knots.

Ben nudges my shoulder. "Ready?"

I take a breath. "Yes. Maybe. I think so."

Dot waves her arms. "Dang, Lena. We got this, okay?"

"I'm only a text or call away if, for some reason, you don't."

Ben's hand finds mine, squeezing gently. His comfort gets lost in my growing anxiety, though. I turn to the house. "Um, I forgot something."

It's unnaturally warm inside the house, stuffy and oppressive, and dim. Boxes filled with dishes, pots, pans, and other kitchen appliances monopolize the space. Mom's urn—the only item not boxed up—sits in its usual place, a central tower overlooking the madness.

Tears drip from my eyes, pissing me off. *This is not the time for this.* "What am I going to do with you?"

Ben joins me minutes later. Once again, he takes in my pathetic display. "Everything okay?"

Enough with the tears already. "She was my best friend… I mean, before you."

He smirks as if that's no secret.

"It feels weird, leaving her here."

"We can bring her. There's room in the backseat."

I shake my head before he stops talking. "No. I appreciate it, but that feels even weirder… She always wanted this—me living the beautiful life she knew I was meant to have. Only it hurts that she's not here to see it. To live it with me."

"But she is, in a way." Ben's eyes pyramid at his brow before he says, "She's in everything you do, Lena. I never met your mom, but I know her—you've made sure. You keep her around… even though she's gone."

Ben's words bring to mind all the times she's been with me, even though she wasn't. In my escape pod. In my choices, my conversations, my horse adventures, hell, even my dreams. That won't change.

My hand rests atop her urn as a deep, almost quivering breath escapes. I think of holding her hand at her hospital bedside, her fingers pressing against mine before she stopped breathing. Guilt, regret, loneliness—my usual bullies don't show up for once. Only sadness over missing her, as it should be.

"Goodbye, Mom. Love you." I smile at Ben. "I'm running off with my Eagle Scout, but I'll be back. Don't worry. I'm in excellent hands."

He chuckles, setting his hand over mine. "Yes. I'll take good care of her, Mrs. Buckley."

I laugh, wiping away tears with my free hand. I curl my fingers in his, taking them away from the urn. "Gosh, Ben. I love that you take my weirdness in stride."

"I don't think it's weird."

"Ha, talking to an urn on the counter? Come on."

"It's honest. Not weird. And who cares, anyway?"

With a kiss, I lead him to the door, smiling at the way he puts things.

Back outside, my team awaits. I rattle more instructions as Ben tugs me to the Jeep. "Mom's on the counter. Don't move her unless you have to. You're welcome to talk to her. She likes it. And boys, please, take care of my garden. Anything you harvest, take home to your mom. Okay?"

Ben opens the passenger door, nudging me inside. Amid goodbyes and quickly vanishing nerves, I leave home.

Damn lonely. As we arrive at the hillside cabin, the words repeat in my head, ghost-feelings from my first Asheville trip.

The loneliness was my fault. *Partly.* I failed to reach out when I needed it most. After losing everything, I wanted to hide, and caring for Mom gave me a good reason.

Those lonely feelings are distant, strange memories now, disappearing in laughter as Ben points to the bear decor gracing the living room mantle and says, "See? Bears are everywhere here."

Forty-One

FROM THE DRIVER'S SEAT, Ben eyes my fidgeting fingers. "Don't worry. There's always our cottage."

"It's good having a back-up plan, I know, but me, not worry?"

After two amazing weeks in Asheville, it's no wonder that my anxiety bitches rally now—they've had little to latch on to lately with me surrounded by loving, encouraging people, housed in excellent conditions, and baking my heart out in a functional kitchen. The only hiccups have been the occasional nightmare and Dot's increasing evasiveness when I call, forcing me to think something's wrong. *Something's always wrong.*

I imagine it'll look like a nuclear test site—the barn reduced to its frame with wires and pipes loose and hanging out willy-nilly, a junk-yard of discarded bricks and drywall, and, *worse, that* house a pile of rubble because Dot got antsy with her sledgehammer. "Gotta tear down to build up, Lena, babe," she'll say. Back and forth, I attack my wrist's pressure points while a mysterious tension thickens with each roll of the tires toward home.

Everything looks the same pulling into the driveway—abysmally unremarkable. The sagging house, the overgrown former Christmas trees, the droopy magnolia—it's like we never left. But Jack Harvey has churned the earth on my property's outskirts, showing some progress. So does the roughed-up lane Ben navigates over. Truck tires have engorged the driveway, riddling it with uneasy tracks that force me to grab the *oh-shit* handle above the door. My breath catches rounding the bend by the garden.

"Holy shit! What the hell is that?"

Ben doesn't answer but skirts the Jeep into its usual spot while we gape.

Dot opens my door, donning a car salesman's smile. "Good trip? You look good. Feeling good?"

"What did you do?" I slip out, gawking at an unfamiliar structure.

"Nothing… I took some small liberties. No biggie."

No biggie? About to give Dot a stern vocabulary lesson, starting with her misuse of *small*, I'm side-swiped by Ben. His hand locks in mine while he stares ahead. "Wow."

Damn right, wow.

The barn's now a magazine-worthy dream home. I said I wanted upgrades, but never imagined this. The once dull, rust-colored bricks are white-washed, creating a speckled, weathered effect—barn meets beach. The lighter makeover highlights other new features: the refurbished gray barn door, the zigzagged staircase next to it, and the black railing surrounding the second floor. An upper-level wraparound deck has been constructed, overhanging the downstairs walkways, where the horse stalls open to the outside, and no longer sag like overburdened shoulders. A black-doored entryway surrounded by windows upstairs invites me closer, but I grab Ben's arm with my other hand, steadying myself.

Dot gives me a rough back-pat. "Buck up, Buttercup. It's not that bad, is it?"

"It's damn gorgeous." The words sputter out from behind my sobbing. "Mom would've loved it."

"Oh, happy tears. Between you and Cherry, it's hard to tell anymore."

I look at Dot as she bobs beside me. She wears her usual ridiculous oversized overalls—black to match her hair—pink flannel, and boots, but with the addition of a black cap with the words *Boss Bitch* on the front. "How'd you do this?"

"In beast-mode. I padded my original estimates for a buffer. Cherry and I wanted to surprise you. It's not a home without an exterior redo. We called in some favors to make our tight deadline. Your friends helped, too—the Harveys, Aunt Barb's prayer group, Joe's family, social media friends."

"It's beautiful," Ben says.

"It *really* is. And the interior… is *everything* done?"

"Just like you asked. Let's take a look, huh?"

We follow Dot across the yard and up the zigzagged staircase.

Dot attempts to shake the solid railing. "This composite decking is practically indestructible. We're using the same materials at the house. Buying in bulk scored us a deal."

Cresting the second floor, I gasp at the expansive deck surrounding the loft. It doubles the living space.

"There's room for the grill and patio furniture and flower beds and—"

"Proper stargazing," Ben says, softly matching my excitement.

"Cherry outdid herself," Dot says. "Living with that bastard ex of hers, she stockpiled her creative juices, and now they're gushing. The paper wants to do a full-page spread featuring her designs in the home section."

"She deserves it." I lean over the left side for a bird's-eye view of the garden. Turning back to the loft, it's hard to remember what it used to look like, especially standing on a deck that didn't exist before. The sloped, gambrel roof remains the same, but the rolling door once in its center—the cyclops eye—is now a normal front door bookended by long, frosted glass slits and sided by oversized, cross-hatched windows. Cedar boxes hang below them, featuring every conceivable herb. My fingers graze the basil and sage while I breathe in the freshness.

"A gourmet kitchen needs a close garden. No need to walk to the field for some flavor, huh?" Dot says, opening the front door.

Mom's refinished hutch middles the back wall, adorned with her best china and Blue Willow dishes—it's the first thing I see. Mom's urn comes second, sitting between serving pieces.

A glance at Dot forces her hands into the air. "I know. You said not to move her, but she and I talked it over, and she was okay with it. She belongs wherever you are, right?"

She belongs at her tree. Still, I'm glad she's here, in the beautiful place she made possible. She wanted me to dream something better—*this* is it. Or, at least, part of it.

Wonderful imaginings flood me—a movie montage that hasn't been made yet. Ben and me leaning against the granite countertops in our skivvies, practicing sign language while waiting for morning coffee… snuggling on the plush living room couch while watching movies…

warming our hands around the rustic brick fireplace on cold days, not for survival but coziness… sharing romantic dinners or playing board games at the long farmhouse table near Mom's hutch.

These fantasies end in sexy, fun times. *Yes, I know*—we won't always be *this* hot for each other—*will we?*—but it's my fantasy, *damn it*, and going as I please applies to such dreams these days.

The beautifully open space begs for dreaming, anyway. The gourmet kitchen with its twelve-foot island, top appliances, oversized stove, and double ovens calls to me. *Preheat and get baking. What are you waiting for?* My fingers skirt the cool stone circling the kitchen and peeking in the custom white cabinetry. Delighted tears surface when my Kitchen Aid mixer pops out from a hidden shelf in the island, ready to go. *I'll play with you later.*

Around the corner from the TV wall, a short hall leads to a utility room, pantry, and guest bathroom. The original staircase from the barn remains as a second entry, similar to a mudroom. Though more functional than beautiful, I long to stock the pantry and start laundry.

The main space reminds me of Mom's house with its beamed ceiling and fireplace bricks, but it's no cave. The space collects light like fireflies in a jar, thanks to eggshell walls and dramatic windows. Ben and I tour the family photos along the living room wall around the fireplace. Some of my favorites have been blown up and accentuated in black frames. Me, Mom, and Lucas on horses while Dad holds the reins. Mom and Dad at the Saddletree when they first bought the house. Lucas and me laughing in the trailer behind Dad's tractor. Between them, the notes once surrounding Mom's urn are captured in small, rectangular frames, forever secured.

Dream something better. Everything you need is right here.

Things will get better

Ben motions toward the blank spaces. "We'll add to them."

"And incorporate your Ben Wall and pics from our trip, huh?"

Dot leads us through a long hall at the back end of the loft. Two empty bedrooms sit opposite each other before coming to a full bathroom and a linen closet.

Then, there's the master.

It's almost freaky how your own detailed plans still have the power to shock you senseless once realized. *Is it the same for parents first holding their babies or astronauts finally reaching space? Okay, okay…* maybe dream bedrooms aren't quite the same league as babies or planets, but it's breathtaking, anyway.

The master suite celebrates togetherness. Double French doors lead to a two-person settee on the back deck, overlooking the pond and Mom's tree. Tears stream *once again,* with sweet memories replaying at the view. *Lucas and our Loch Ness monster. Mom fishing. Fireworks.*

I turn back to the bedroom, hoping to prevent more baby-like sobbing. The cushy queen bed in grays, light blues, and white stirs many non-tear-worthy ideas, but the art hanging over the bed solicits more waterworks anyway.

"I like the hands." Ben points to the abstract of two hands meeting unevenly at the fingertips.

"Cherry really listened to my chardonnay-induced gushing. She asked me when I first had ideas about us. I said when you rescued me from panicking by taking my hands."

"Mine is when I first visited you here." He smirks. "I win."

"Aw, really?"

"Yes. The house tour, the target practice, the cupcakes… I wanted to prolong the encounter."

He smiles at my bemused look as if reading my mind. *Oh, the things I'm going to do to him later…*

The master bath mimics the togetherness vibe with double-everything, featuring a clawfoot tub and large shower, big enough for two. Ben and I exchange a glance, both wondering how soon we can christen the spaces.

Dot leads us inside the walk-in closet. "We got all your specifications, Lena. Apron hooks. A place for tall boots. Uniform space. Gun safe. Drawers and hooks for Ben's work gear."

He gives me a funny look. "Designated closet spaces? That's a sweet upgrade from our current living situation."

"Oh, that's nothing… I'll show you upgrades." Dragging us to the kitchen, Dot grabs an iPad from the island.

"Get a load of this. You can control your entire house with this thing. Your phones and computers, too, once we get 'em set up. Here's your doorbell."

Chimes fill the room. She taps the iPad again. "With a quick setting adjustment, this could be your doorbell."

Lights blink with the chimes. "A message will also appear on your TV. You can adjust the doorbell's volume, even silence it completely, if, let's say, babies are sleeping or Auntie Dot is napping on the couch. It'll link to any light in the house. Smoke and carbon monoxide detectors, security, oven, laundry, microwave—anything can have an audible and visual alert. Baby monitors, too. If your rugrats even whimper, you'll know, and you'll be able to watch them from any device, from anywhere on the property."

An uneasy glance passes between Ben and me, neither knowing what to say.

Dot gapes, her face suddenly pug-like. "Should you *choose* to have rugrats, of course. Shit. Did I say too much? Someone tells me something, and I'm ready to burst like a kid made to hold it *way* too long. I, um, need a cigarette."

She rushes from the room like it's on fire, and with my anxiety spiking, it's not a bad idea. *Too much. All at once. Can't believe she mentioned kids.* I flick my hands at the wrists, shaking out the nervous energy.

Ben faces me, eyeing my fidgeting. *Is he concerned? Amused? Frightened? I can't tell. This is the worst time for my Ben-senses to fail me.*

Shoving my hands behind my back, I say, "Maybe I mentioned the *possibility* to Dot, but I said many things. I'm not suggesting *anything*. Promise. It's *way* too soon to talk about it, anyway, and whether you want them or not, it's *fine* with me. But be prepared, right? I wanted a home that would change *with* us, *whatever* our reality."

His tough-guy look softens. He tucks my hands around him before running his thumbs along my cheeks. His hesitation makes me want to ramble, but I say nothing else, enjoying his gentle affection.

"I can't believe you did this. It's…" His forehead rests against mine, creating a pocket. "Perfect… and, yes, the follow-you-anywhere rule applies to the maternity ward, too, if that's what you want."

I laugh and tear up together. "Gosh, Ben. I'd go on *any* adventure with you, but I'm happy enjoying this part, for now."

"Me, too. I love this part." His grip on me tightens. He gives me a sweet, lengthy kiss as if it's been too long since the last one. "I love you, Lena. This is a *really* good day."

Good days continue. More transformations quickly follow the barn.

The income from the coins covers both renovations with some leftover —Dot calls it fate. I can't deny the strange beauty in it.

People, too. Teaming up with Dot and Cherry works surprisingly well. Just as I've come to appreciate Dot's kooky brashness, I'm warming to Cherry, too. Her sadness mirrors mine—sacrificing so much for Mark only to feel unlovable and miserable in the end. *But things will get better*—I promise, offering myself as indisputable proof and boosting her hope as Ben's note once did for me. I tell her what I've learned about life and love—that being heartbroken sucks, but it's usually the right thing. And one day, when she's ready to try again, I'll tell her another truth—that falling in love is a risk, but one worth taking.

With the loft finished, Dot, Cherry, and I tackle the house. Mornings begin with coffee and itineraries. Days end with wine, social media, and brainstorming. We pour ourselves into the project, sharing our stories along the way. Our social media accounts grow as our community takes an interest. Whenever something goes viral locally, Dot celebrates with an unflattering but hilarious dance that's a cross between the electric slide and the chicken dance, which also goes viral. It's a vicious cycle.

With help from Will, Max, and Mr. Morris, I sort through every item on the property. Mr. Morris sells the valuables I don't want—*twenty-seven antique canes and fourteen creepy dolls, Mom, really?*—while the boys and I restore what I do. Then Cherry incorporates my treasures into her design—old and new together.

We mow fields and repair fences, reconstructing smaller paddocks on my half of the acreage while Jack works the rest. I restore Mom's saddles and tack while buying my own to fill the tack room with Gloria's help. I even wear breeches and paddock boots, like an equestrian boss. Gloria sells me Shadow, securing his retirement from children's parties. She's helping me acquire more horses, so Shadow won't be alone, though something tells me he appreciates his solitude *and* the lifetime supply of horse treats. My side business with Doc Evie, Gloria, and neighboring horse farms pads my pockets and Shadow's belly.

The garden flourishes into a lush jungle of deliciousness. Construction workers, plumbers, electricians, neighbors, *everyone* goes home with fresh fruits and vegetables—there's no way I can eat it all, anyway. I work and expand my garden, and I cook. *Holy hell, I cook!*

My gorgeous kitchen inspires crazy cooking sprees, sweet and savory alike. I set up bag lunches in the carport every day, so no one needs food from home. Word spreads. People stop by to see the progress and eat a good meal. Mrs. Moore and the church ladies. Gloria, her farmhands, and trainers. The Harveys. The Joneses. As restrictions lift, the kids from Olivia's group home visit. And, for their first field trip in almost a year, the residents of the senior care home. I finally meet Myles's sugar-happy relatives. They eat their weight in cake and have so much fun riding around on the tractors, waving canes at each other, that they force their director to put Saddletree on the schedule for regular visits.

Whenever I want to get away, beyond Sunny's trips, I pack lunches and sweets for Ben and his colleagues. I also make deliveries to the group home and the senior center and visit Shakespeare and his buddies.

Though I do it for free, it's like I have a café long before it opens.

Then, finally, it does. Saddletree Farm and Café opens on a sunny Saturday in October. With its solid customer and social media base already established, people flock to the farm for produce picking, fishing, tractor rides, catered picnics, and, of course, the café. With family entertainment changed because of COVID, people choose the farm over movies, amusement parks, and malls. Yoga groups meet at the pond for morning stretches. Mommy groups bring their kids for picnics. Bike clubs choose my farm as a home base for epic rides. Dot's rowdy chess club meets monthly—yes, it's a real thing. From book clubs to knitting circles, everyone wants to meet here, where it's easy to social distance and lovely, as well. As days go on, the business shows no signs of slowing.

I reach out to support groups—caregivers, disabled veterans, and the hearing impaired. They use our spaces for meetings, parties, and therapies. Sometimes, they show up for getaway moments. We make a walking trail around the perimeter and set up cozy nooks and sitting spots all over the property for people—as Ben so perfectly put it—*to just be*. No demands. No expectations. No busyness. It's a retreat for everyone.

It's our retreat, too—Ben and me.

One night, we talk about his work and recent headlines. The Wilmington Police Department has a new chief; his first order of business was firing three police officers caught having a racist conversation on their dashcams. His action sent a clear message—racism will not be tolerated. With new training programs, policy changes, and more community outreach, Ben's excited about the department's future.

And his own. He becomes a field training officer, an on-the-job teacher for the department's new recruits. And he discusses other instructor roles with his higher-ups for when he's ready to leave patrol —a prospect he no longer dreads.

With the world finally recognizing the need for change, and on the cusp of new leadership and a vaccine, everything feels hopeful.

Especially for *this girl*.

Love, success, plenty of wine money—all the things missing from my life show up and expand, as if Mom's up there, making sure of it.

Forty~Two

EXPECTING A HAPPILY-EVER-AFTER or even looking for one is bound to bring disappointment. It's something you fall into rather than find, and even then, it's never perfect. There's always another battle to fight, crushing sadness to endure, or problem to overcome. What we should hope for is a better-ever-after—when you feel at home with who you are, who you're with, and partner with that perfect someone to fight the battles and share the joys with you. In a better-ever-after, you finally feel like everything's okay, freeing you to be yourself and to make things better for everyone you can.

That's where I am—my better-ever-after.

It's December. The barn, loft, and house are finished. The pandemic still spreads, but with everyone's good precautions, the world has mostly reopened, and travel's resumed.

And now, *finally*, Ben and I drive Lucas, Drew, and Luna up the driveway.

It's a *seriously* big deal for me—finally introducing my family to my dream.

Our backseat passengers let out a synchronized gasp as we pass through the brightly lit Christmas trees lining the lane. It's no longer an old, tired home sinking into the earth—and taking me with it—but the welcoming vision it used to be. Picture windows and French doors bordered in black highlight the freshly painted white bricks and new vertical siding—French country, Cherry says. My favorite part is the deep wraparound porch presently adorned with Christmas trees and lights everywhere—I got a little carried away.

Ben barely parks before everyone pours from the Jeep.

Hands on his hips, Lucas ogles the house. "The pictures don't do it justice. It's the same place, but totally different. How is that possible?"

"Money, a good contractor, and a visionary, although tearful, designer," I say.

Lucas shakes his head. "No. This is *you*. All you. I can't believe you even *thought* to do this, let alone pulled it off."

I squeeze Ben's hand. "I had lots of help…. How about a tour?"

Lucas nods but turns to Drew and Luna. "Is it okay if Lena and I go around together first?"

Drew gives Lucas a knowing look. "Take your time. We're great."

"I want to introduce myself to the horse!" Luna coos, bouncing on her feet.

I smile. "If you feed Shadow peppermints, he'll love you forever."

"I'll show you where we keep the treats in the barn," Ben says.

Once alone, we take in the gorgeous structure, absorbing it like a heart-moving work of art. It's exactly what I wanted but never thought I could have, like Ben in the beginning. Part of me believes *this* is how Mom *always* saw it, even at its worst. A place of beauty and potential, of good times and all the difficulties in between, a refuge, a delight. It's home again.

We ascend the patio, the same concrete slab as before, only extended to connect to the wraparound porch. At twelve feet deep all the way around and trussed with gabled beams and iron fencing, the porch quadruples the living space.

"We used weatherproof decking," I say. "No more worries about tripping over bowed planks or falling through the rotten ones."

"We stubbed many toes that way." He points to the oversized pizza oven. "Can we make pizzas tonight?"

"Absolutely." I slide open the door, and Lucas laughs.

"That's familiar."

"I had to keep the sliding glass doors here. It was too weird not to."

The café resembles the open living room and kitchen it was before. Well, *sort of*. Instead of a long, yellow countertop to the left, there's a glass display case showcasing my Christmas-themed desserts. The end, where I used to keep Mom, holds the iPad register. A professional kitchen stretches across the backside of the house: long stain-less-steel counters, a sixty-inch gas stove with a grill-top and double oven, two more in-wall ovens, a wall of fridges and a stand-up freezer, a farmhouse sink, two dishwashers, multiple mixers, and everything a proper chef could want. The back porch, which once housed Mom's freezers, is a grossly overstocked pantry, as Mom would've insisted.

"Wow," Lucas breathes out. He glances overhead at the original beams and the arched ceiling that've been refinished and painted. Bright white walls and oversized windows ensure that there's nothing cave-like about the space anymore.

He taps at the tiles underfoot and grins.

"I had to get rid of that awful linoleum, but we picked yellow diamond-patterned tiles as a nod to that look," I say.

Lucas points to the right where refinished hutches and sideboards from the barn create a long coffee bar, and a peg wall holds my parents' mugs. "Mom and Dad are everywhere."

"Yes, most things are recycled. The settees are refinished from the barn. Mrs. Moore sewed backings on her old scarves to use as tablecloths."

Lucas moves into the dining area while I explain, "Customers come inside, grab plates, coffee cups, whatever, and then ask for what they want at the counter where we serve it up, home-style. I thought it'd be chaotic, but it works. Plus, it gives the experience a real family vibe."

Lucas stares at a wall of pictures. "What's this?"

"The Buckley Wall. Family pics at the pond, in the garden, riding horses. It's where all my ideas originated. It's our before and after."

"It's beautiful." Lucas leans in to see all the expertly framed pictures.

"There are displays like this all over the house. It's a business now, but I wanted it to always feel like home, too. Dad took tons of pictures."

Lucas steps to the mantel that holds more family pictures. "There's so much space without the wood stove."

"I got rid of both wood stoves and redid the fireplaces—two normal fireplaces, but the house has central heat and air now. Each guest room has its own thermostat. This is the first winter in four years that I haven't had to keep the house warm myself. I still wake up to throw logs on the fire, even put my boots on the other night before Ben asked what I was doing. Isn't that funny?"

Lucas slides his arm around my shoulder and squeezes me close. "Must be a relief when you come to your senses."

"A sad relief, yes. It's jarring, remembering Mom's gone while I'm groggy."

"That must be hard. I bet Ben makes it better, though."

"He makes everything better. Come on. Let me show you outside."

We go out the back French doors to ogle the deck that faces the road. Lucas notices my four Christmas trees right away—one for each of us. Mine is decorated with baking ornaments and snarky wine glasses. His has apples, books, mini-chalkboards, pencils, and notebooks. Dad's is loaded with toy trucks and tractor-trailers, flashing stoplights, and road signs. Mom's ornaments are teacups, fishing poles, vegetables, and horses. Lots of horses.

Lucas tears up. "You've thought of everything, Lena. You've captured everything we're about."

"We'll do trees for Luna and Drew, too. Everyone in the family should have one."

"What about Ben?" Lucas smiles slyly. "Does he get a tree?"

"Yes! I can't believe I didn't ask him already. Worst girlfriend ever."

Lucas peers through his posh, thick-rimmed glasses, scrutinizing me like he would an essay. "Oh, wow. You're so in love with him."

"I better be! I just spent Thanksgiving in Topsail with his entire family."

"Meeting the family, huh? How was that?"

I giggle like a lovesick idiot. "Wonderful. I expected them to be quiet, like Ben, but no. They're all boisterous and larger than life. He could never get a word in edgewise with that crowd. His twin sister Becca's made me her new BFF. They've made me feel like family."

"I'm happy for you, Lena. After Mark and moving home with Mom, well, I thought you'd given up on love altogether."

"I did. Thank God love didn't give up on me."

Back inside, I show him the small front bedroom we transformed into two café bathrooms before taking the short hallway to the stairs, my former makeshift bedroom, and the formal dining room.

"I wanted to keep the dining room. Mom was so proud of it. I thought I'd use it for private dinner parties and support groups."

"I love the updated furniture. Ah, you kept Mom's chandelier. Are these her Christmas decorations?" Lucas points to the fake poinsettias and mistletoe draped over the chandelier's stems and around the doorway.

"Yes. I salvaged what I could. She loved decorating for Christmas."

Another set of French doors, where my couch bed used to be, leads to the porch and funnels light into both spaces—sitting and dining.

Lucas takes a breath before we enter Mom's bedroom as if bracing himself.

Though I kept with Mom's color scheme of pale blue with pastel accents, most things have changed. A fire crackles in the restored fireplace outlined in white marble. Hardwood flooring replaced the blue shag carpets with area rugs to keep the warm feeling. Thick white linens dress the four-poster bed—very hotel-like. The soft white lights on the Christmas tree in the corner complete the cozy look.

"I restored her desk and secretary. They're in my barn office now."

"It's gorgeous," Lucas says. "The bathroom has electricity and everything. It still feels like Mom's room. Are we staying in here?"

"It's your choice. You might like your old room best once you see it."

"Will you rent these rooms out?" Lucas asks.

"Right now, I'm focusing on the café and farm. Ben's family's coming to stay next. Then Jason and his family from Asheville. I'll probably stick to sharing it with family for a while."

We head upstairs, where I show Lucas two other complete suites. His room is now a suite with a small kid's room attached.

Lucas smiles over the barn-style loft bed surrounded by cushy animals in the suite's anteroom. A soft mural of a countryside dotted with horses, tractors, sheep, chickens, and a garden covers the largest wall next to a small Christmas tree with animal ornaments. There's a bookcase with all our favorite books from childhood, along with a chest of toys I salvaged.

"It's perfect. We'll stay up here. It's like you made it for us."

We follow the house tour by walking the property. The garden, now dormant, and Luna keeping Ben and Drew busy with Shadow, we go to the barn and the pond. I show him my posh office, the loft, the chicken coops, and the small pens I hope to populate with pigs and sheep in the spring. Lucas says little beyond small observations.

Does he think I've gone too far, spent too much, gone overboard? I wonder if taking all this in is like scarfing down a big, fatty meal, and he's now overfull and fighting heartburn.

"It's overwhelming," I say as we stare at the icy edges of the pond, standing under Mom's tree.

"You've spent all the coin money. Haven't you?"

"Yes, but the farm's profitable, my pet treats side-business is booming, and leasing land to the Harvey's ensures a steady income regardless. You don't have to worry about me."

"I'm not. It's beautiful, Lena. Truly. You've made it better than I could've imagined. It's so peaceful."

"It won't be so peaceful tomorrow when we're open. But yeah. It's my happy place."

"Yours and everyone else's, I hear. I can't wait to see it all in action."

The tour over, we rejoin the others, make pizzas, and spend the evening eating, drinking, and laughing on the patio around a fire. Though the menu changes, we spend most nights of their visit like this—recovering from full days of tractor rides, picnics, baking, entertaining, and fishing.

Though I expect Lucas, Drew, and Luna to make themselves at home and enjoy the festivities, they pitch in, too. Drew joins Max for tractor-driving duty. Luna sets up a craft table for kids to make homemade popsicle ornaments. Lucas helps Will and me in the kitchen, packing picnic lunches and handing out Mom's old quilts if people haven't brought their own. Despite the chilly temperatures, business booms.

On Christmas morning, we gather around the Saddletree. Lucas recites Mom's favorite verses and plays her favorite song, *Crazy* by Patsy Cline, which makes us tearfully shake our heads, like we used to do whenever she tried, badly, to sing it.

With the sun cresting the trees, shooting gold lights over our makeshift ceremony, we release Mom's ashes around the tree. Her wish finally fulfilled, I picture her, healthy and whole, twirling and shaking her hips in delight like she once did over good report cards or ripe tomatoes or any success, big or small. It's sweet and tearful and perfect.

I understand why I couldn't complete the task before. Then, fulfilling her wish felt like leaving her behind. Now, it's the celebration it should be, of a life well-lived and well-loved. Despite the tears rolling down my cheeks, my joy is complete.

Ben slips his bulky arm around my waist. He's wearing a dark suit, *very handsome*, and hands me a handkerchief from his pocket. *Always so prepared. Mom would've loved him.* Maybe she *does* love him, and she's up there, winking at me and doing another happy dance with Dad next to her, nodding in approval. Leaning against Ben's shoulder, I see us getting married under this tree, playing with children here, more fireworks, all the sappy, Hallmark-esque things I thought would never happen. I used to believe my mistakes rendered me unworthy when actually, I needed my screw-ups to bring me home, make me stronger, and lead me here to my universe where I belong.

Our makeshift ceremony ends with a short silence, capping off this terrible, beautiful year with exactly what it needs: quiet. At the end of the fear and anxiety train, change is good. Necessary. Lovely, even. It breaks you down to build you into something better. It pushes us into our better-ever-afters. Something we're all ready for now.

Luna places a small wreath of pine needles and magnolia leaves at the tree; Ben helped her make it. "Love and miss you, Ma. It's Christmas." She leans down and whispers, "Time for presents."

We chuckle. Luna races toward the house with Lucas and Drew, lagging behind her, arm-in-arm. I linger, watching them.

"Lucas tried so hard to convince me to move to Malibu. You think there's any chance we could convince them to move here?" I'm only half-joking.

Ben contemplates my question. "Yes, actually." He tugs me close. Our breath clouds mingle in the crisp December air. "You convinced me, and I'm fairly happy."

The icy air catches in my throat. "Fairly?"

"One thing's missing." Ben, *always prepared*, pulls a ring from his pocket. It's not even in a box but loose, and he twiddles it between his thumb and forefinger as he gauges my reaction. It's a gorgeous round diamond surrounded by flecks of multi-colored gemstones.

"Fireworks." The word erupts in a whisper as my heartbeat quickens.

"Marry me." He attempts to go down on one knee, but I firmly grab his arm. I don't want him to mess up his suit for the sake of a tradition that implies begging. Ben Wright doesn't need to beg. Though not expecting any proposal *today*, *YES* was in my heart only moments ago when daydreaming about a tree-side wedding.

He doesn't know *that*, though. Part of me wants to play with him a little, keep him guessing. Only I can't pull it off when my face lights up with a sappy grin, and I stick my hand out with a *give-it-to-me* motion, ring finger extended. "Oh, Ben. I love you. I hope you know what you're getting yourself into."

"All in, unapologetic, honest love." I smile at how that describes us completely. "I'm okay with it." He kisses me, his fingers rousing tingles along my back. "I've had that ring since before Asheville."

"Ben!" I gasp again. "What took you so long to ask?"

"I wanted you to have this dream before working on another. Besides, Lucas is here. Your mom is where she should be. The world's returning to normal enough to plan a wedding. And it's Christmas. It's the right time. Finally."

"The perfect time." My hands slide over his chest as I lean into him. "I'm not sure which is better… me getting this ring or seeing your handsome face when I tell you I'm pregnant."

His face alights like fireworks—bursting wide with overjoyed surprise. Gawking, he laughs before grabbing my face in his hands, and —unable to say anything anyway—he gives me a soft, lengthy kiss that makes my heart race and everything inside tingle just like the first time and every touch since.

His hands skip from my face to my belly, as if he's unsure where to put them as he gushes, "Are you okay? How do you feel? Is it weird? Have you been to the doctor? Is there anything you need?"

"Ben, take a breath. Everything is perfect, and there's only one thing I need."

"Tell me."

"This." I give him another long, tongue-laced kiss, pulling him to me by his tie. When we part, I say, a little breathlessly, "Think we have time to make out in the barn?"

I expect Ben to refuse, *for now*, remind me we have guests we shouldn't keep waiting, that it's Christmas morning and there are so many other things to do—*coffee, breakfast, and presents, oh my*—and amazing news to share and celebrate, that we have our whole lives ahead for sexy escapades in the barn and elsewhere. *Blah, blah, blah.*

Only Ben surprises me. He *always* surprises me. With another kiss, he whispers, "Yes."

Lena and Ben's angsty love story continues. Return to Saddletree Farm and Café five years later when Lena has everything she wants... or so it seems. Read Ben's story in *Every Good Thing*.

Access *One Thing Better*'s deleted scenes, Dot's Soulmate Recipe (a short story), and read *Every Good Thing*'s follow-ups in Ben and Lena's BONUS EPILOGUES, free for subscribers!

Scan the QR code below for access to all of my books (including signed paperbacks), bonus content, and more.

bio.site/authorjessicasherry

Thanks, firstly, to every reader who took a chance on this unconventional romance from an unheard-of author set during the pandemic. Geez! Like Lena, her story had many obstacles to overcome before reaching your hands, but I hope you're glad it did. It wasn't written for its sellability. It was simply the story on my heart at the time.

Of all the stories I've written, published or not, *One Thing Better* is my most personal yet. The snarky, foul-mouthed, anxious, and heart-in-everything character, Lena, is me (just younger, cuter, and, well, single). It's inspired by my mom's death in 2018 and caring for my father after his heart bypass surgery the following year. Staying with him in my rundown family home and *making do* with the wood stove for heat, finicky toilets always breaking at the worst times, and the occasional mouse, was not only challenging but terribly sad, remembering how lovely and cozy the house used to be and, of course, missing my mom, who always made it that way. *One Thing Better* is a what-if born from love and sadness, and writing it felt truly like coming home.

Lena's story is decorated with so many small truths from my life. My parents were make-do people who loved country life. Mom was adopted, and they were foster parents. They were Boy Scout leaders and church-goers. Mom loved horses, had massive gardens, and collected coins (though we have yet to score a treasure like Lena's). Dad was a truck driver, supporting four children, and everything we needed was always right there—they made sure of it. Lynne, Louis, Rome, and I learned how to make do, and we're better people for it. (Though all of us have learned to hire professionals for home repairs.)

As Lena learns in the story, the best dreams happen *with* other people. *One Thing Better* didn't happen alone. It underwent several transformations on its way to publication in 2023 and again with its relaunch in 2025. In its earliest stages, a developmental edit by Kaitlyn

Katsoupis from www.strictlytextual.com helped me fine-tune it, and beta readers Julie Ward and Sherrie Sherry, my sweet mother-in-law, brought me to the heart of the story. That story has since reached thousands of readers and earned a starred review from Kirkus Magazine, a rarity for an indie book.

Moved by *One Thing Better*'s reception and longing for Saddletree once more, I published *Every Good Thing* in 2024, a continuation of Lena and Ben's story, this time sharing his point of view. Their intense love through the most difficult times still resonates and makes me wish for home. I hope you feel at home at Saddletree, too.

For this relaunch, I must extend my thanks to Sam Palencia at Ink & Laurel for the revised covers. Gorgeous as ever, it's incredible to finally see Lena, Ben, and Saddletree with all of the sweetness, passion, purples, and blues I hoped for.

Deep thanks go to my friend and professional editor, Jenny Austin. She's one of the coolest people I've met through this roller coaster writing journey. Her knowledge and love of books are surpassed only by her kindness, encouragement, and willingness to cheer me on. I don't know where I'd be without her. Probably still saying hella too much and not writing decent sex scenes, at the very least. Her insightful edits not only make me a better writer but a better person.

Always, my final and forever appreciation goes to Joe. He is the inspiration behind *things will get better*. More than that, in nearly thirty years of marriage, Joe has *never* made me feel bad about my anxiety. Whatever I am, Joe loves me anyway. I'm forever grateful that he's my partner, playmate, and soulmate.

Oh, and he also helps me write better sex scenes. Thanks, babe.

Finally, thanks to all the anxiety sufferers out there for sharing your stories, getting and giving help, and taking each step in the journey. I hope and pray that you have a Joe or Ben or someone in your life who loves and supports you through it. If not, you're not alone, and help is out there. As Lena realizes, *sometimes, we all need a little help*. And if you need a cheering section, reach out to me. The battle against anxiety bitches is real, but winnable if we fight it together.

Making one thing better helps. After finishing the first draft, Joe and I discovered a neat side effect to the story—we started applying Lena's mantra to our work, home, and relationships. Focusing on one thing at a time with a positive attitude means fewer chances of getting overwhelmed and discouraged. The anxiety bitches hate it! Making something better for yourself and others—even the smallest things—leads to greater happiness overall. So, let that be your biggest takeaway from this story. Make *one* thing better. And thank you for letting Lena, Ben, and me be a part of your better-ever-after.

Big Hugs,

Jessica Sherry

www.ingramcontent.com/pod-product-compliance
Lightning Source LLC
Chambersburg PA
CBHW020128310726
48970CB00006B/1780